MW01123541

COMPANIONS

DONALD ARLO JENNINGS

LifeRich Publishing is a registered trademark of The Reader's Digest Association, Inc.

LifeRich Publishing books may be ordered through booksellers or by contacting:

LifeRich Publishing
1663 Liberty Drive
Bloomington, IN 47403
www.liferichpublishing.com
1 (888) 238-8637

ISBN: 978-1-4897-0558-7 (sc)
ISBN: 978-1-4897-0559-4 (hc)
ISBN: 978-1-4897-0560-0 (e)

Library of Congress Control Number: 2015918210

Print information available on the last page.

LifeRich Publishing rev. date: 11/12/2015

This book is dedicated to two exceptional cats, Abby and Annie. To Abby who every morning whether or not I was writing, but especially when I was writing, came to my library door and waited patiently until I gave her the special treats she loves so much. To Annie, who without a doubt and regardless of my attention to work insisted on being picked up and held, cuddled and loved on until she was satisfied. I just had to live with the interruptions. But, this made my efforts more enjoyable.

I express a very special thank you to my wife, Arleen, for her detailed editing of the book. She found many typos and other mistakes that I had made. Correcting these mistakes made the book easier to read.

Preface

The story begins with Ricky Snyder as a young boy growing up with older parents in a town in Tennessee. He is somewhat of a loner and spends time at his private spot by a stream since there are few playmates around. His neighbor down the street has a daughter that is five years older than Ricky and who babysits for him when his parents are busy. Millie Pendergrass is a talented girl, somewhat protective but very fond of Ricky. The two become good friends as well as great companions.

Millie is an excellent pianist, and Ricky wants to learn to play the piano. Millie agrees to teach him how to play. He is a quick study. His mother and father find a used piano and purchase it for Ricky with the insistence he practices routinely. With Millie as his teacher his relationship with her blossoms and they become more than just friends, close companions. As Ricky grows older, his desire is to attend Juilliard and to become a concert pianist. His father insists he must work during the summers and strive to get a scholarship because there is no way to otherwise afford the education.

It is obvious from the beginning of the story that sadness occurs. The story is how opportunities unfold and how two lives become different from youth to adulthood. Understanding what happens and what events occurred during the time is the story. The story goes from the present to the past and eventually the two times blend. Ricky Snyder's career becomes a focus of both the present and the past. Friendships are introduced as well as some of the creative work Ricky does. From a struggling childhood to an incredible success, Ricky struggles with his emotions, time away from those he loves, and memories to never be forgotten.

The story, while a work of fiction, hopefully allows the reader to see how a career can change individuals. The story is about the creativity of the main character, Ricky, so it was important to include some of Ricky's creativity that made his career what it became. Any resemblance, past or present to any character in the book is strictly a work of my imagination. Some of the place and professions mentioned are used fictitiously just to make the story more realistic. I have never met the professionals mentioned, but I have seen some of them perform. I beg indulgence and forgiveness from them and their families for any reference that may seem to be inappropriate.

There are song-lyrics included in the story. These are my original creations given to the main character, Ricky Snyder. I hope you enjoy reading this book as much as I enjoyed writing it.

COMPANIONS
Remembering

"…Don't think of this as a time of sorrow, don't thank of this as the end, don't think about what was, but of reflections of the wonderful times, the friendships, the love, the devotion, and the accomplishments of this wonderful person. Think of this as a new beginning."

I have never seen so many flowers.

Sadness has overcome me with Millie's parting. I know being sad is prevalent, but I know Millie would have been delighted that so many cared and came today. The number of friends and acquaintances truly amaze me. I do remember the beginning as special. I often think about that time. A time for which I never gave one thought that my life would turn out the way it did. In every ending there is always a new beginning.

It wasn't as if I didn't know what was happening because I did, and I liked it more each time. The thrill, the excitement, knowing that no one else knew kept me going back. How could anyone resist? I can't blame anyone, and I surely was not going to share the beauty of the moment with anyone for whom I did not have feelings. Being outside made it more exciting, and each moment alone gave rise to the tides that built up inside me. I can still

1

experience the rush and hear the sounds that you experience when there is nothing else to distract you. The succulents abounded and added aromas that just made your senses smell the sweetness. This is something for which everyone should live. As I grew older, I would still go back and reminisce, thinking back on those days that can never be regained, except through memories. Those are precious memories, memories kids can only enjoy in their own worlds as they embrace the moments that will never be lost in memory, but that can never be relived as age takes over youth.

I am much older now, and I can easily drift back in time to the town of my birth, a small mountain town, sparsely populated with no more than two-thousand people. Most of the people here were fourth and fifth generation families. Small towns do not have the luxuries of bigger towns where industries and shopping malls tend to exist. My home town was a place of family owned businesses, small shops and during leaf season catered to the many tourists who drove through seeking a meal or food and lodging for a few days. This is the area where I grew up to be a young man, before I left for college, before everything seemed to remain the same in my mind over countless years.

As I was growing up, the air was always fresh, and the smell of wood-burning fireplaces still permeates my memory as I remember that smell permeating throughout the area. I remember when I was young, the air had a fresh smell, but maybe that was more me than the air because I was always playing in and around the stream, most of the time by myself. I spent so much time outside that by bath time I really polluted the water. Who is to say that was wrong? I was a kid, an active boy who needed to experience the world first hand. I am glad I did, and I am glad I had the opportunity to do so.

Yes, I am older now, maybe not so much smarter, but wiser. I learned to use the knowledge I gained throughout life. Maybe this was not so much to benefit me as much as to benefit others, or maybe others did not benefit, just a subjective thought. I know I cannot return to the moments of my youth, but I know I can reach out and find those who shared precious moments with me. A few of those close acquaintances still live in my hometown. They elected not to leave and to try to make the town better. It was hard for me to leave, but I knew I must if I were to grow beyond the boundaries of what I learned up to age eighteen. Am I a wiser person?

Yes, imaginably so. Maybe not as wise as I would like to be, but I learned so much from so many over the years. Maybe this did not make me wiser, but I know it made me a better person.

I breathe deeply, and visualize the beauty that was always around me. I want to remember it all, the way it used to be. That probably is not possible. September can take your breath away from just looking at the colors and knowing that in a few days summer will be over and the radiant greens will turn to brilliant reds and yellows. Millie so loved this time of year. It was her favorite. I guess it is mine too. I can still picture her leaning over the side deck of our house just loving every minute of life. She always had something wonderful to say about the colors, and she would decorate the house with many of the woodsy things to bring out the season. She loved autumn, the fall of the year, but, you know, Millie loved every season, but Thanksgiving and Christmas were her favorites.

I drift into a conscience memory and recall a couple of days ago that I drove back to my birth town. Millie was not with me. I remember getting close to the area and I slowed the car because I knew that up ahead is where I am supposed to turn. Things had changed. I was so hoping that my special spot is still there. The rugged rocks have probably prevented anyone from building, and I know that the water has smoothed some of the roughness over time. I hope the small patch of beach is still there. Well, it was not really a beach, but it was my private place, my personal beach. I still want to take off my shoes and feel the sand squish between my toes. I want to feel the rush of the water over my feet. I want to sit and hear the water rush against the rocks, creating that rhythm that can be so relaxing. I want to be alone, as a man, much as I did as a boy. I want that same rush, that same excitement that same thrill to remind me of what I have missed for thirty-two years. It is not that I have not had a wonderful, thrilling thirty-two years; it is just different in a special kind of way. It is special because it brings back the memories of my younger days with Millie.

∾

"…If we could go back in time, and change how we lived, most of us would jump at the opportunity. Many would say they do not want to go back and are glad they are where they are today. But, how many times have we heard

ourselves say 'if I could have known then what I know now things would be so different?' But for those who have had life rewarding experiences, accomplished so much, had a good life, it is time to go home, it is the ending of our experiences in this world but new experiences await us for eternity. It is the ending of an era, but the beginning of a new world..."

∾

I guess the country atmosphere yields a different flavor to those same things we experience in the bigger city, but somehow it is so very different, it is what we grew up experiencing every day. Everything alive seems to be freer, to be more alive, not afraid, and the little wildlife only pauses at the sound of a car. This is so different in the big cities. Now from my car, I see two squirrels jumping from limb to limb on an almost dead tree. They stare at me, but make no attempt to give up their game. A cardinal flies a few feet in front of my car. I instinctually apply the brake thinking it might fly into the grill. We miss each other and I turn a sharp curve knowing that just ahead is my special spot, or so it should be.

One particular day, when as a kid I was at my special spot, I don't know when Millie came or if she followed me, but I can still see her standing above the spot on the narrow road looking down at me. I was so embarrassed, but she paid no attention, after all when nature calls, you have to go and no one was ever around. I was probably eight years old then. Millie was older, I guessed at the time by four or five years. I just thought of her as an older girl. But age didn't matter to either one of us as we grew older. Isn't fate strange?

As I turn the curve, I gawk at what is before me. It is the same. Thirty-two years, it is still the same. Well, not quite the same. There are no buildings, not one house or store, only more growth and everything seems bigger in one way or another, but smaller in other ways. The rocks that I thought were so huge seemed innocently small compared to the way they were when I used to climb over them and slide into the water. There is a pullover by the road close to the spot that I used to claim as my own. Back then the road wasn't paved, and only a few cars traveled along this route. Maybe that was because the road just went from the town up the mountain to old man Higdon's house. He owned all this property,

4

probably still does or his son owns it now. His son was rather weird and about five years older than me, probably Millie's age. The Higdons were a private family, so my bet is that not much has changed. It is strange though that the road is paved.

I steer my little white BMW convertible onto the side of the road and pull into the gravel area, stop the engine, and lean my head back in order to just smell the air. Home, I am really home. From down below on the flat of the rocks, there I used to wade across the stream and make my way through the woods for about a mile or more to the small houses that were nestled along tree-lined lanes. My father and mother lived at number twenty-seven Highland Lane from the time they could afford to buy the house until they both died. It was the only home I knew for eighteen years.

I only returned several times in thirty-two years. I always kept in touch with my parents by phone, and there were many visits over the year with them coming to Nashville, but I definitely came for a few days when dad died and again for a few days to settle the estate when Mom died a few years after Dad. I did return after college from Julliard before I technically moved away from home. I came back several times during my years at Juilliard to be home at Christmas and once for Mom's birthday. Regardless of my age and wherever I resided at the time, if I couldn't make it back, I always sent Mom a dozen yellow roses, her favorite flower. I was there for my marriage to Millie. That is where she wanted to be married so our parents could attend. But otherwise my career kept me away so much. Now to me that seems a long time ago.

I should mention that I was an only child. My mom conceived late in life and Dad was much older than Mom. They were more like grandparents than parents. I never knew my grandparents. They had all passed away by the time I was born. Strange after fifty years I am thinking about these things. Maybe thinking of Millie has something to do with it. I am sitting here smelling the air, clean, fresh, open, no noise, just the rush of the breeze and the sounds of nature. I can really smell the honeysuckles, the aroma is so sweet. I remember as a kid I used to pull the blossom from the vines and suck the sweetness. I guessed if it didn't kill the bees it wouldn't kill me.

I open the car door, step out, and just stand there looking, listening, and enjoying the beauty of it all. I wish Millie were here with me. I push the door shut, and then walk up the road just a little bit. I think there should be a path leading down, but it probably has disappeared over the years. I remember a big tree marked the spot going down. It leaned over the bank and you could climb out on it and almost be over the stream. There it is. I see it. I can't believe it. The tree is much the same, but weathered with age, the bark darker, and the growth spreading more downward than before. It is apparent someone has cut branches off to keep the road clear, but they did not cut the tree. This is magnificent.

I had on my good UGG shoes, I always called them "ugly," but there is no way to resist going down the bank to the stream. I remember this used to be a long way down, but I was young and I always jumped and ran down the path. Now I take it slowly and discover the path is not really long, but steeper than I remember. I hang on to the tree branches as I descend. My age and size does make a difference in my ability to make the same trip I could easily accomplish at eight or ten years old.

"...Don't regret the bad times, there were and always are a few, but don't fret about them. Don't even think about them in a negative way. Millie was such a positive person, so kind, so helpful and yes she had her moments as we all do, and she had bad times, suffering through unpleasant events as has everyone. This is a time of remembrance of good times, good thoughts, a time of rejoicing, and a time to be thankful..."

I had to play alone a great deal of the time because there really were no other boys my age that I liked and wanted to play with most of the time. At school, most of the boys my age that were my best friends were bused from the outlying areas. This remote countryside did not lend itself to seeing close friends on a daily basis. I guess that is why Millie became my closest friend and my companion. Millie and her family lived just a few houses from ours. None of the houses were large, and mainly occupied by older folks who had no children. This made it difficult for me to have a lot of playmates. When my folks were out for an evening, sometimes they would ask Millie to baby-sit with me. Millie was also an only child, something we shared in common. I remember the first time she baby-sit with me when I was about eight, Millie had to be twelve or thirteen, but I really did not know her age at the time and it was not important to a kid my age. Still I complained to my parents that I did not need a baby-sitter.

My folks told me that they would be out for the evening and that Millie would be staying with me until they returned. In those days and time, gosh you could actually trust a twelve or thirteen-year old to baby-sit, and Millie was a very responsible and mature girl for her age. On that occasion I remember telling my folks I did not want a baby-sitter and I really pitched a tantrum, but they gave me no choice. Millie arrived about five o'clock and my folks told her they would be back about ten, to be sure I got a bath about eight o'clock and in bed by nine. Of course I complained for what good that would do.

"…We all know just how wonderful Millie was with kids. Ah, Millie was really a kid in grown up clothes, but she was so intelligent, so fun loving, so easy to be around. The kids just seemed to flock around her, they loved her, loved to hear her stories, to hear her sing, to see her smile, to enjoy her warmth and beauty…"

Millie just smiled at me, ruffled my hair, and said I was a good little boy and she would take care of me. My folks really liked her, and as I grew older I became aware of just how wonderful Millie could be. She fixed me a bowl of ice cream and we sat and watched television until the appointed bath time. Millie told me she would run my bath water and I could take a bath. As soon as I was finished, if I didn't play in the water too long, she would read me a story before I had to go to bed. Of course, I was unhappy about taking a bath and most unhappy she would be in the house while I was naked. I was a little bit shy being seen with no clothes since I had no brothers or sisters or exposure to other kids my age. We didn't take showers at school because for one thing there were none at the school, and two because we didn't start physical education until ninth grade and that is when we were bused to the high school.

Anyway, Millie went into the bathroom, which was off the short hallway to the two bedrooms. This was a small house, but the rooms seemed big to me. I heard the water running and Millie shuffling around. She called to me saying it was time. I reluctantly went to the bathroom where she had the tub full of water and my pajamas laid out across the back of the toilet tank. She didn't leave. I remember asking her if she was going to watch me bathe. She asked me if I wanted her to. I said no. She asked if I needed help getting undressed. I said she could help me pull my shirt off but that was all the help I needed. She did, but she didn't leave. I remember just standing there until she reached down for the front of my shorts to unbuckle them. I jumped back and asked her what she was doing. She told me if I didn't get in the tub she would undress me and put me in it herself. I remember I told her to leave. She asked me why because she had seen my "thing" before when I was peeing at the stream. I told her to please leave. She ruffled my hair again, and then she walked out of the bathroom. She pulled the door partly shut and must have waited just outside because once I was undressed and she heard me splashing in the water the door opened and she came back. The only thing she said was when I was finished if I would call her she would come back and dry my hair. Then she left again.

I remember sitting in the tub thinking if I should ask her to wash my back, but I was a little bit afraid. I didn't know what I was afraid of, but Millie didn't seem much of a threat. After all, she was trying to be nice, and she had almost seen my "thing" before when she watched me at my special place, but she had not seen all of what I had down there. I played in the water for a few minutes, and then called out to her to come help me. Millie must have guessed my intentions because she took her time getting there. When she came into the bathroom, she asked me what I wanted. I asked if she wanted to wash my back and my hair. I remember she came over to the tub and looked at me. The water was soapy so she could not see anything below the water. But when she kneeled down to help me she put her hand in the water looking for the wash cloth. She looked at me and just smiled. I handed her the washcloth and the soap and told her my back was on the other side of me. She laughed and then washed my back and my hair.

After she thought I was clean enough, she drained the tub, stood me up, and started drying me. She paid special attention that I was completely dry and I let her dry my "thing" without complaining or saying anything to her. I didn't know about sex so there was nothing sexual about her drying me, not for me anyway, not at eight years old. She helped me into my pajamas and we went back to the living room where she told me a bedtime story. I think she made it up, but I liked it just the same.

"… All of you know that Millie was a deeply religious woman, even from youth. She was active in the church, and always had her eyes upon God. I am certain God always kept his eye upon Millie…"

When Millie finished the story that she told me, she gently picked me up by placing her hands under my arm pits and stood looking at me. She told me it was bedtime and that she would tuck me in after I said my prayers. I walked in front of her to my bedroom and sat on the edge of the bed. She sat with me and I said my routine prayer, "Now I lay me down to sleep, I pray the Lord my soul to keep, if I should die before I wake, I pray the Lord my soul to take. Amen."

Millie said "Amen" and then she took my hand and said let's ask God for some special things. I asked what she meant. Millie explained to me God would take care of me through the night, but I need to ask Him to take care of others and thank Him for all he does for me. She asked me if my mother and father prayed with me at night. I remember we discussed this for a few minutes because my parents had taught me the nighttime prayer, but we never prayed as a family. We went to church every Sunday, and my father was involved some way in the church, but he never took me with him to any of the meetings, and except for Sunday morning Sunday school, church services, and the class plays I was in, we did not do much with the church as a family. Oh, there was always vacation bible school, and the homecoming events. We always participated in them and Mom would bake a huge cake, make green beans, and a salad to take to the homecoming lunch, but then everyone brought something to eat.

9

I remember that Millie and her family went to the same church. Her dad was always involved in church matters. He spoke almost every Sunday morning during preaching. Millie's mom was active and always ran the luncheon time at homecoming, and for the most part she was responsible for the children's plays and the nursery. As I grew older I learned that Millie's father was the head of the Elders at the church and her mom was the head of all the children activities. This did not mean much to me until I turned twelve or thirteen, then I understood more of what being involved in the church meant. However, by that time, the age difference between Millie and me seemed miles apart. It just isn't right when a boy is thirteen and a girl is eighteen. I stopped thinking about Millie during those growing years and turned my interest to sports and spending quite time at my special spot.

Sports at our school consisted of baseball and football, nothing else, not even basketball because the gym was too small. I loved to swim, but there was not a swim team, nor a community swimming pool. Sometimes a couple of us boys would slip away after school and go to the pond as we called it, strip to our underwear and horse around in the water for an hour or so before going home. My mom would ask why my hair was wet, and I owned up to the fact we went swimming at the pond. Of course, I was chastised for swimming in my underwear, but she would laugh when I told her it was better than swimming without it.

I loved baseball, but did not play football. I played just about every position on the team since there were not a lot of boys at the school. We only played one or two other teams since the other schools were so far away and getting to those other schools or them getting to our school was more of a chore than our coaches wanted to contend. Oh, well, it was a game and we made the most of it. Millie was always there, watching, whether it was me or just the game. Most of the time my parents did not come to the game to see me play, but Millie did. She later told me she wanted to be there so I would have someone to cheer me on during the game.

∾

"...We all know that Millie is with God now. How could she not be? She is walking in Heaven, singing with the Heavenly choir, singing to the

children, and looking down on us today. I hope she is pleased with the songs we are singing and with the choir. I can still hear her melodic voice and wonderful way she lifted up God in song. I can still hear the sounds of the piano and almost see her sitting there today, wow could she ever make those piano keys hum..."

I remember the summer that Millie taught at vacation bible school. I was her star student. She always opened up the class with a prayer and then we sang songs. She would let two or three of us choose a song and she would start singing, then she would make us join in. She had such a beautiful voice. I could have listened to her sing for hours. That may have had a lot to do in influencing me in the career I later was to choose and the course of study I made in college. Because of Millie, I loved music and wanted to learn to play the piano. Millie told me she would help me if my parents would pay for lessons.

My parents were not wealthy, but they worked hard, saved some, and tried to provide me with everything I needed, and some of the things I wanted. When I asked them about taking piano lessons and getting a piano, they didn't blink an eye or even ask me why, but said they would see what they could do. About three days later I came home from vacation bible school, and there in the living room, we called it the front room, was a piano. It was not new, but it surely was a beautiful thing. I rubbed my fingers across the wood, opened the cover over the keys and placed my hands on them as if I knew how to play. My mom said son play something. I remember saying that I didn't know how, but she said feel of the keys and touch them one at a time, then hum a tune and make the keys fit the song. By gosh, I made some noise, and found I could actually pick out a few bars of a song. I guess this is what the old folks called "playing by ear."

"...Can't you, can't you too just see her sitting there at the piano? I know many of you cherished hearing her play and sing each Sunday morning. Millie had that flair with her own style, a rhythm that made you just want to tap

your toes and clap your hands. I remember many times before the actual service listening to her play some of the songs Rick wrote. I know as he sits here today, the loss of Millie cannot weigh heavier on his heart..."

"Rick." I can't ever remember being called "Rick." I have always been "Ricky." I even signed my checks and manuscripts "Ricky." Millie is probably laughing now, but the Pastor knows my name preference. Just a slip of the tongue, trying to be more formal at this very sad event, but I know I will never correct him. This is not something important, nothing I can't survive. What I can't survive is how I can go on without Millie. She taught me so much, gave so much love, and I know her patience with me as a piano student had to teach her strength.

You know I banged on that piano so much my dad told me he would take it out back and break it up unless I started putting some tunes and method to my playing. I asked for the lessons, and by now both Mom and Dad were willing to provide them. Sometimes a kid just has to play his options, no pun intended. I was more than a willing student for two reasons. One, Millie was teaching me, and two, I really wanted to learn how to play and write music. On the first note, well excuse my pun, this afforded me an opportunity to get closer to Millie, who of course, ignored me because she was much older and I was just a kid. I was almost ten and Millie had to be fifteen. She was a teenager and almost grown up. Me, I was a young naïve boy with a dream to play the piano and one day become famous.

My special place by the stream yielded to my desire to become musical. I started practicing more and more until I could play some simple but understandable songs. Dad and Mom were impressed and continued to encourage me. Millie was really surprised by my progress, and I picked up the lessons more quickly. After almost a year, if you were hearing me for the first time you would think I had been playing for a long time. This was not bad for a young boy of almost twelve, well eleven and one-half.

I think I was almost as good as Millie, but far be it from me to ever say that out loud.

∽

"…Ricky, I think wrote his first lyrics for Millie when he was just thirteen as a gift for her teaching him to play the piano. I hope I got that right, Rick. After many years and accomplishments, it always challenges me to remember so far back. I know Millie was always proud of him and stood by him as he always did her. She is watching us today, listening to what we are saying and probably laughing, not at us as much as with us. But we also know the pain she endured in the last few years of her life, so much pain. She has a new body now and is moving around in the wonders of Heaven. I bet she has a grand piano with solid ivory keys and the sound must be marvelous. I really want Ricky to play and sing for us if he is up to it. I think he wrote a special song in remembrance…"

∽

Millie always got upset with me when I would just bang out chop sticks or *"Mary Had a Little Lamb"* on the piano. She would tell me to quit horsing around and either be serious or she would send me home. Well, that was okay once in a while, but other times I was already at home and we would both laugh. Regardless, my progress was so good she couldn't fuss too much. After all, it was either play the piano or go to my special spot and play in the stream. Sometimes I would go there after a lesson and chill out just to keep my head clear. What is a young boy to do?

I loved to play special songs for my parents just to make certain they understood I was good and was definitely learning. They tolerated me, being more like grandparents than parents, but I knew and they knew I was their son, from their genes, and they had no problem warming my behind should they decide my actions merited some type discipline. This didn't happen much, but boy when it did, my dad could swing a mean belt. He always told me it hurt him more than me, but it wasn't his rear end getting belted. Naturally I would cry and be upset and run to my room and hide for a while. Mom would always come in and apologize for dad but she made it perfectly clear I needed to clean up my act to avoid another occurrence of a whipping. She would hug me and tell me they both loved me immensely. I knew that was the truth.

"...Ricky, are you going to play and sing or, or, Ricky?..."

I do remember walking to the piano; gee it was almost as if it were yesterday.

At first I practiced till Mom and Dad couldn't stand the "noise" and asked me to let their ears rest for a while. I only spent two one-hour lessons a week with Millie and, of course, she gave me lots of homework assignments. I spent countless hours writing musical notes, well tried, and putting notes on sheet music, learning the differences between a treble clef staff and a bass clef staff. Millie crammed whole notes, half notes, quarter notes, eighth notes, and sixteenth notes into my head and made me write them again and again. My favorite note after a while was the "rest." I learned "every good boy does fine" and "face" as the way to remember where the notes should be placed. Between this and my regular school homework, I was stressing out. I was also on the baseball team, but that was a distant love to music.

The time came when Millie told me I didn't need more lessons, just to keep practicing and practicing. Millie was getting ready to graduate from high school and maybe move on to college. I still had a few years to go at age thirteen and one-half. My mom and dad by this time enjoyed hearing me play and by golly I was half-way decent on the keys. I was beginning to write some of my own lyrics, just not good enough to put the actual music to them. But I wanted to write something to thank Millie for all she had taught me.

"...While Ricky is getting ready, and please understand this is a difficult time for him, let's think about the words he wrote. I have had the distinct pleasure of reading these before the service. I don't think words can ever express the love Rick and Millie shared during their time together...a special love, a bond that did prove the test of time. It is just so sad her life was shortened by such a debilitating disease..."

I was just thinking as I sat at the piano why Pastor Thomas can't get my name right every time...Rick, Ricky...he knows who I am. Is he that nervous? Shouldn't I be the one confused right now? I began to think about the times Millie and I had with her teaching me to play the piano. We would sit on the same bench and I always made sure I was as close to her as possible. She would take my fingers and place them on the keys. Gee, I told her one time, we are holding hands. She smiled and told me to keep my eyes on the notes. It is hard at first to look at the sheet music and then at where your hands were on the keyboard, eye-eye-hand coordination.

At time passed Millie and I would play different sides of the keyboard to the point it almost sounded good. She was an excellent pianist. I was her star pupil. In fact, I was her only pupil. I remember one time when I was playing Bach's *The Well-Tempered Clavier,* a solo for the keyboard picked out by Millie that I had to play over and over, Millie sat down beside me and looked at me with her beautiful eyes and told me she loved to hear me play. By that time, I was thirteen, well thirteen and one-half, and I was as tall as Millie. She was five-feet four inches and actually I was five-feet five inches. I guess I felt like a real man when she would put her arm around me and hugged me to her. I told her she was the best. What could a young guy tell an older woman who was about to leave for college?

I remember being thirteen and thinking what I could write as a thank you to Millie and as a going away present. I dreamed about her, dreamed what my life might be if we were a team. I didn't think about marriage since she was older, but I knew she influenced me so much I would never forget her. I was riding high on just being with her. At thirteen writing a simple song can be difficult, but I wanted her to know I loved her as any boy can love someone for whom he desperately cares.

15

∾

"...Rick, are you okay? Do you want to tell us about the song before you begin to play? Rick?..."

∾

I remember snapping to attention once the Pastor walked over and stood by the piano. I apologized profusely as tears ran down my face. I looked around at the host of people in the chapel, all friends including Millie's only cousin and his wife. This was the only family members still alive on either side. Millie's father was an only child and her mother had a younger brother, two years younger. He and his wife were killed in an automobile accident going to their son's college graduation. This was a very sad day for everyone.

I stood up and acknowledged the people in the church and then I told them the story behind the song I was about to sing. I said to them that I wrote this song last night, the day after Millie died. Millie was a strong person, never complaining, but the last couple of years she suffered miserably. When she was first diagnosed with cancer she always felt in her heart she could conquer it, but the treatments probably hurt more than they helped. Millie's quality of life suffered and she had many bouts of sickness. Many of the church members, especially those close to her saw the changes every day. Millie would challenge the doctors and tell them she knew she was turning the corner any way to a better tomorrow. I think deep down she thought that better tomorrow was her time in Heaven.

The words were picked with love and I know Millie would probably have recommended some changes, but this is for her and for us, and especially for her from me. I call it, *"Turning Corners"*:

> *Her life was so courageous, so simple so it seemed,*
> *She often danced with angels, but only in her dreams.*
> *The visions of tomorrow outweighed her thoughts today;*
> *But the joys of the moment were the ones to really stay.*
> *She often dreamed of angels and knew they were around;*
> *She often knew the moment for that trumpet sound.*

She often looked to others for the joy of the day;
She often turned a corner facing fears without dismay.
With love she gave so freely, so unbiased in her words,
She gave the live she lived so freely, yielding to her Lord.
Now missing her today is looking for her when
We'll leave this world forever for a better place within
The Heaven's gates to greet her, to sing again and play
The songs we miss so much as we have here today.
When we each turn that corner, the end of all we know,
There we'll greet our loved ones and bow before the Lord.
Let's not regret the moment the beauty and the sounds,
Let's turn the corner willingly and know we're Heaven bound.
I know she's there waiting for me, and I know that I must wait,
But what a pleasant welcoming it will be at Heaven's gate.
I'm not ready to turn the corner, but know I will someday,
And when that time arrives, I know I will be saved.
Her life was so courageous, so simple so it seemed,
Now she dances with angels, not only in her dreams. [1]

The room was deathly silent, the Pastor was in tears. I think my eyes watered over from the words I knew and had written, but they seemed to touch everyone in a very special way. I prayed a silent prayer that Millie had heard me sing.

∾

"...Ricky, thank you for those very, very special words. I know Millie heard them and she is smiling down on us. So beautiful, so meaningful, so touching, thank you, thank you. Let us pray..."

∾

The piano bench always seemed lonely after Millie left for college. I remember the last lesson and the time she said good-bye. We were on

---

[1] Written by Donald Arlo Jennings, December 2012.

17

the piano bench playing *"The Last Date"* trying to be as good as Floyd Crammer, but neither of us at the time could begin to compare. Millie and I played and laughed and then she said she would really miss me and wished I were older. I was surprised at that. She put her hand on my knee and leaned over and kissed me on the cheek and as she did so her hand moved to my thigh, unknown to her to a very excited boy. She squeezed my thigh and told me to always be a good boy. Gee, I guess I was more naive than I realized, but I said I would, not even knowing what she really meant at that time. I was very aware of sex but definitely no experience and at that time I did not have a girlfriend other than Millie as a girl and a friend.

I said to her I had written a song for her, simple as it might be for a budding teenage boy. I told her I wanted her to know I really loved all she did for me and baby-sitting for me, coaching me along in life, teaching me to play the piano, and just being my friend. I told her I loved her. She asked me to play and sing the song. I couldn't write all the musical notes, but I picked out some as I sang the word to a song I called *"A Life of Dreams."* I know I scribbled out the words on a blank piece of paper and then tried to write them appropriately as a musical score for the piano. Talk about rough at the time, but this was a challenge for me. However, I was determined to do something special for Millie.

Millie asked me if I was being shy and told me to go ahead and play and sing, regardless I knew she was going to love it and enjoy me doing it no matter had badly I played and sang. With my breaking puberty male voice I started to sing.

I know this is a Life of Dreams
For life is not what it seems,
It's been so true our life I know
Even you know it's so;
A love that last oh let this be
For you and me.
He's coming high, he's riding low,
He'll be here soon I know it's so;
A love that last, oh let this be
For you and me.
A Life of Dreams for you to see

As soon as you marry me;
And be our love forever true
For I love only you.
He's coming high, he's riding low,
He'll be here soon I know it's so;
A love that last, oh let this be
For you and me. [2]

When I finished singing my face was red as it could be from blushing and afraid she would laugh, but Millie was smiling at me and still had her hand on my knee. She leaned over and kissed me on the cheek again and told me that was the sweetest thing anyone had ever done for her. She told me she was definitely ridding high right then and I was almost ready to burst with pride, needless to say in another way as well. Millie hugged me with both arms and ruffled my hair. Being almost thirteen I was thrilled to have her attention, and I really did love her, probably infatuation but never the less, her affection was wonderful. She was still had her hand on my knee unintentionally almost reaching to the edge of my short pants. She continued to gently rub my knee until I was so excited that I actually exploded. I only hoped she did not notice the wet spot on my shorts. If she did, she did not mention it. I was feeling too good to say anything. She smiled and said I was too young for her now, but to wait for her until she got out of college. By that time I would also be close to heading to college, but I wasn't thinking very good right at the time. Millie left me sitting on the piano bench and I was afraid to stand up just yet. I could feel the wetness in my shorts.

"…If anyone wants to come forth with a testimony regarding Millie, or even Millie and Ricky, please do so. I cannot think of two more deserving individuals than these. Even though Millie is gone, her contributions to this church, to our community, to the children she taught, and to her small family

---

[2] "A Life of Dreams" written by D. Arlo Jennings at age thirteen and published by Nordyke Music Publishing Company in 1960.

will live on forever. Millie and Ricky never had children, but they took care of so many through their contributions and love. Ricky was on the road a lot with his career and his contributions to the music world will long out live anyone in this room. Millie's support of him will always remind Ricky he had a wonderful woman behind all he did..."

∾

I do remember several people coming forth and telling wonderful tales about Millie, how she was always making someone feel good. Her doctor came up and told about the final days with Millie, her suffering, but never shying away from the Lord. Cancer is such a terrible disease. Millie survived so many treatments, but in the end the cure was more devastating than the disease. Her quality of life with chemotherapy treatments made her so sick she would be in bed for days at a time. Lung cancer is something that can last a long time or take you quickly. In the final days it was impossible for her to do more than just lie in bed; she couldn't even sit on the side of the bed. I stayed with her the whole time, canceling all my commitments. Millie was far more important to me than entertaining people.

I never understood why Millie had lung cancer. She did not smoke, and as a young girl living at home, her parents didn't smoke. I didn't smoke. I don't think there was any asbestos in our houses, either from our own homes or where we lived as a couple. I find it strange some people can smoke for most of their life and never get cancer and others, such as Millie, die from the disease. This just doesn't seem fair. But as Millie said, the good Lord had other plans for her and He was calling her home.

∾

"...Thank you everyone, thank you for all the wonderful stories about Millie. Her life was an inspiration to each one of us in a different way. Thank you Ricky for the wonderful song and for those special words. You were always there for Millie and I know your time goes back to the days when you both were children growing up in a small town. This church is your home now and this church holds special memories for you. But the church you grew up in is still a special place for you, then and now. You were baptized in that church

as was Millie. But, you and Millie attended this church most of your lives. You and Millie were weren't married in this church, but by my father who had this pulpit at your home town church. And...now... Millie is back here one last time..."

I couldn't hold back my tears.

COMPANIONS
Changes

"…Let's pause and have a moment of silent prayer for Millie's family and friends, then I will close with the Lord's Prayer and I hope you will recite it with me…"

I sat there quietly as the prayers were silently raised to Heaven, praying my own prayer and knowing Millie was hearing each one. I prayed Millie would be rejoined with her mother and father and that she had joined the heavenly choir, letting all in Heaven enjoy her melodic voice. When the pastor said *"Amen"* the silence that fell on the congregation was still appropriate. The pastor started praying and I joined in with the others as the he recited the Lord's Prayer. My tears were not contained, and my face was wet.

"…Let's join hands and let's sing the first verse of 'How Great Thou Art'…"

I remember the day before Millie left for college. I was deeply saddened as any young teenage boy would be who was infatuated with such a wonderful girl. I knew in my heart that Millie was the one for me, but

I also knew that she may not think the same way, me being so much younger. When I walked over to Millie's house, she was standing on the front porch with her mom and dad and there were two small suitcases and a trunk, probably full of her clothes and things for college. She saw me coming and she smiled as I walked onto the porch. Her mom and dad spoke, saying hello to me, and said they knew we would miss each other, but Millie must finish her education since she wanted to teach school, her first choice being young children. I understood, but by no means was I the happiest kid on the block at that moment. Millie kissed the top of my head. I guess she didn't want her parents to know she had really kissed me on the cheeks before. I started to cry and Millie pulled me to her side and put her arm around me and told me she would write as often as possible. I guess my love for her as the older woman in my life was really getting to me. I knew I would write back if she did and if she didn't I would write to her anyway. I asked if she would be back for Thanksgiving or Christmas and she told me maybe, but it depended on her classes and the amount of work she had to do. She was getting a job to help pay for her tuition and other expenses and that she may have to stay at the school to keep her job. Disappointment is a word that cannot describe how I felt at that moment.

Her father told her it was time to go. I picked up one of Millie's suitcases and as heavy as it was I managed to get it to the car. I wondered what she had in it, but it was not any of my business. I stood there as I watched them drive away wondering if I would ever see Millie again. I knew my life would change and that somehow I would survive.

I continued to practice on the piano and occasionally would venture to my private spot by the stream where I would day dream about life and a world of music and wonder what Millie was doing at college. Sometimes I would think of our times together on the piano bench and relive those moments alone. I would go home and Mom and Dad always asked if I were okay, but of course I said yes. They asked if I missed my piano lessons with Millie and if I wanted them to find another teacher. Of course I said "no, I didn't want or actually need another teacher."

I had grown taller but hadn't put on much weight. I was still a skinny runt but I was really fairly handsome with my brownish-blonde hair and dark brown eyes. The girls at school always eyed me, but I just didn't think of them the same way as I thought of Millie. Yes, Millie was older, but I guess I acted older than my fourteen years. The ninth grade, first year of high school, was a new experience for me. We really didn't have a middle school like the bigger cities. Our entire school population was probably less than most high schools. There were probably less than one-hundred students in the ninth to twelve grades. I remember hearing a discussion regarding bussing us to a larger school, but it was too far away, and in the winter time, it might not be possible to collect all the students and get there by the time classes should start. Regardless, our school stayed open and the teachers were great if not grateful of the opportunity to teach in a smaller school with smaller classes.

"...What a beautiful song, How Great Thou Art, and the words are so meaningful. Yes, our God is a great God. He looks after us every day. We need to be thankful for all He has provided. Each one of us needs to be thankful for our loved ones, especially those still with us, and we need to cherish the good times, well, all the times we have to spend or have spent with those we care for so much. If Millie were standing here, I can assure you she would echo these words.

"We will be closing out this service in a few minutes, but first please take time to stand, join hands, and let's sing the first verse of "Leaning on the Everlasting Arms..."

The ninth grade opened up new horizons for me. I joined the band and was applauded as an excellent pianist, but that did nothing for the marching band. I really couldn't push a piano around and I didn't play a wind instrument or percussion. I basically helped with ensuring the instruments were tuned to the right key and played for some of the dramas or school events. The music teacher taught me more about writing musical notes and how scores should be composed for the various instruments. I did not realize how much that I didn't know until I got that exposure from the teacher. Millie had been a wonderful piano teacher, but she also had not been in the band. She played for church and some other events, but being a piano player does have its limitations.

I hurried home every day to see if Millie had sent a letter. I usually got one from her about every two or three weeks. In a couple of letters she would remind me to continue my piano lessons and missed our time on the bench. Around the middle of November Millie wrote she was coming home for Christmas but couldn't stay except for the weekend, Christmas was on Thursday that year. She asked me if I wanted to come over and see her. She said she changed her hair style, actually cut much of it off to save time getting ready for school and work. She wrote she had accepted a job as a waitress at a small restaurant, and the tips were good helping greatly with buying books and school supplies. The restaurant was within walking distance of the college, so she didn't need a car or didn't need to take a cab or bus. She wrote that lots of students eat there as did many of the professors. The students didn't tip well, but the professors were more than generous. I couldn't wait until December came and for the Christmas holidays.

Thanksgiving Day arrived and my mom and dad invited Millie's mom and dad for lunch since Millie wasn't going to be there this year. Millie called her mom earlier wishing them a "great turkey day" and telling them to enjoy lunch with our family and to give me a great big hug. Millie's dad finally asked me if I missed Millie. Normally he said very little to me. He and my dad retired to the living room, or then we called it the front room, after lunch to chat about old times. My mom and Millie's mom stayed in the kitchen and cleaned up the "mess" as my mom put it. I went to my room for a while but mom called to me to come and play something for them. I hated to play in front of the parents, but I played three songs, but I did not sing. I think they listened, but they were still talking among themselves.

"...I want to thank you all for coming today. Your being here is an indication of how well you thought of Millie and how well you think of Ricky. Ricky will be in the vestibule for you to great him personally, express your condolences, while we prepare to adjourn to the grave site for final interment. We will have a few words at the burial site and afterwards everyone is welcome to join Rick in the main fellowship hall for a meal and for honoring Millie..."

I was so glad when everything got quiet and I could just sit in my room and read and watch some television. I didn't watch a lot of television since my mom and dad didn't care much for the shows on the channels. They would sit and read or when the weather permitted they worked in the yard or would take a walk together. I found I could best enjoy myself in various ways when my parents were busy and were not interested in what I might be doing. They respected my privacy, especially when the door to my room was closed. I guess they suspected what I might be doing and sometimes they were definitely right. Those were the times I thought about Millie.

The Thanksgiving holiday passed and school started back. I embedded myself in my studies and continued to practice piano several hours a day. Now Mom and Dad enjoyed hearing the real music that I played from the keyboard. I received another letter from Millie telling me she was seeing a guy once in a while, nothing serious but that she enjoyed his company and they studied together having several classes in common. She asked me if I was getting bigger. I wasn't sure what she meant, but I figured she must be asking about my height. Well, actually I was getting taller and at fourteen and a half I was five feet ten inches tall. Dad said I might make it to six feet, but he was only five eleven and Mom was five two. I didn't expect to be much taller than five ten. I wrote Millie and told her I was now bigger than she is now that I was getting to be a real teenager.

As I think about all these things, the good times and the disappointments while I gaze at my spot thirty-two years later, I can't help but reflect how I might have turned out if Millie had not been in my early life as my baby-sitter, my companion, and my piano teacher. I wondered if I would have stayed around my home town and worked somewhere instead of going to college and becoming a well-known lyricist and musician.

"...Rick, this is a wonderful turn out. (The Pastor and I were waiting in the vestibule.) *I hope you are holding up mentally as well as you look on the outside. The death of one's spouse is traumatic especially when they are still young, made so many contributions to the community, and still have much for which they could contribute. I know you will miss her every day, but you have to hold on and be strong. God is with you every step of the way. He called Millie home for a reason, and now she has a new body, and is rejoicing with her and your mothers and fathers and walking with Jesus.* (I put my hand on his shoulder and told him I knew Millie was in a far, far better place, but when you love someone from age eight or nine and have shared lives for so long, it is hard to not only lose your spouse, but your best friend and companion.) *You are so right. I know you will survive and I hope you can find solace in keeping busy and continuing your career..."*

I decide to take my shoes off and wade in the stream as I did when I was a young boy. I knew Millie would not be looking down the bank to see me, but I know she will be looking down from Heaven and watching me. The water seems cool. I know now driving here just a short time after the funeral is a good thing. The water is cool to my feet and if I were really brave I would sit down in the water, but alas that is not a good idea for a man my age. Maybe I don't look fifty, but some days I really do feel my age. Millie kept me young, but the last couple of years paid its toll on us both. I see my reflection in the water and can see some tadpoles swimming around. I bet they wonder what creature has invaded their space.

I waded up and down the stream for a few minutes reminiscing of the days I spent here alone thinking about my future. Now I am thinking about my past. I do wish Millie could be here with me.

"...Ricky, let me step away and give you time to fellowship with your friends. I will walk up to the grave site and see how everything is coming along and in a few minutes I will come and get you so we can begin the final rites.

Stay as long as you want to here and if you feel comfortable walking on up before I get back, please walk with someone..."

December was getting closer and the days were getting colder, but I always liked that for celebrating Christmas. I remember being at school one Friday when it began to snow. At first the teachers weren't concerned and the principal announced over the speaker system he didn't think the snow would amount to much, but he would keep an eye on it and watch the temperature. I bet it wasn't thirty minutes later, just after lunch he came back on the speaker system telling the teachers to wrap up their classes, make homework assignments and let the students get to the buses. The snow was coming down hard and some of the roads would be getting slick very soon since the temperature was just right and the ground was frozen so the snow was sticking. I couldn't wait to get home, but I knew there would not be much for me to do but practice the piano and do homework. Anyway, it was the weekend and I had time for whatever I wanted to do.

I wondered if it was snowing at Millie's college. She probably is attending classes and having to walk in the snow between buildings and then walk to work. I wondered if she was studying hard and spending time with that guy she was seeing. I guess I was jealous, but after all I was just in high school, the ninth grade, and she was a college freshman. By all indications she had the right to see whomever she wanted to see and to date whomever she decided to date. I just hoped I wasn't too young for her or that she would forget about me.

When I got home there was a letter in the mailbox for me from Millie. I practically ran into the house to open and read it. I got stopped by my mom because I didn't take off my wet, snowy shoes, and tracked up the floor. Before I could open and read the letter my mom insisted I wipe up the floor and put my shoes on some newspapers to drain and dry.

"...Ricky I am so sorry I was gone so long, but it seems you have been very active in discussions with many friends. It is time to walk up to the grave site.

You know this is the hardest part? I know you have been though this with both yours and Millie's parents, but it is never easy. Losing a spouse is very difficult and saying good bye is even harder. You will be seated on the front row next to the casket, and after I say a few words, have a prayer, you will pick a flower from the family wreath and lay it at the head of the grave. If you want to say a few words you can and if not, I will close and ask people to join you in the fellowship hall for a meal. You do not have to stay for lowering of the casket and closing of the grave unless you want to do so. This is really final and most people prefer not to watch that happen. It is totally your discretion. Let's walk up there now..."

As I think back to those moments at the grave site while wading in the water of this stream, tears come to my eyes. I think it was more the separation knowing Millie would not be home when I got there, that she would not be back, not ever. I remember the kind words from the pastor and his beautiful closing prayer. I think back as I remember him walking to each seated person, taking their hand and thanking them for coming and reminding them that Millie was still with us in our memories, our hearts, and the things she did for the community that will probably outlive everyone there. I was first in line as he made his rounds and as he shook my hand, he didn't say anything except *"God bless you my child."*

People were slow in leaving the grave site, but my closest three friends, Tom, Vic and Darren stayed behind and close by me. Many others came to me just to express condolences. Some told me they regretted not being able to stay for the meal, but if I needed anything just to let them know. Mrs. Lois Anderson, who was one of Millie's closest acquaintances at church, asked me if anyone was going to stay with me for a few days. After all, Millie and I did not have any children, I was an only child, and Millie's family, the ones left, had to get back to their home towns and to work. I remember telling Mrs. Anderson, everyone addressed her that way, that I would be okay and I always had my memories knowing Millie was watching over me. She smiled and told me she would see me at the meal.

I finally sat down on a dry rock with my feet in the water and looked around at the growth. As a kid I don't remember some of the rocks being so small, but then as a kid everything seems bigger. The trees are definitely bigger and at this time of year are really filled out with leaves. The bank up to the road seems less used and probably no one has used it in years. It is difficult to see the road above the bank where my car is parked and where Millie used to look down and "spy" on me. Well, she actually wasn't spying, but I accused her of doing so. Finally I decide my feet are getting bitten by creatures in the stream and pulled them out to dry before putting on my socks and shoes.

"…Ricky, the meal may be comforting to you. You and Millie have so many friends and the church family will definitely be here for you. Have you decided what you are going to do for the next few weeks? You know that is the most difficult time, getting used to the loneliness, the void of not having Millie around. I know if the two of you had children they would be here for you. What about other family members? I know you are an only child…" We continued to walk from the grave site to the fellowship hall and I thought about what the Pastor was saying and knew I needed to have someone around. *"…You seem to be in deep thought. Are you holding up okay?.."*

Sitting here with my feet wet and thinking back to all the good times Millie and I had brings tears to my eyes. I am so glad no one is here to see me so emotional. God only knows how much I miss her. I know as I am putting on my shoes that I should be getting back up the bank to my car and finding some food and a place to stay tonight, but I find myself struggling with all the thoughts about the good times, both here as a small boy and growing up and leaving home. Just remembering the separation when Millie left for college and her coming back and leaving over the four years she was away then me leaving for college and separating from her for four years makes me wonder how we ever got together. Love is very strange and ours was a very special love, we were not only meant to be with one another, but we were best friends for many years. She took good care of me when she was baby-sitting me, and in the end I really think I took good care of her. We were both special loving companions and friends to each other.

I pulled on my socks even though my feet were still slightly damp and I paused a moment before putting on my shoes. I wondered why I didn't wear my older Nikes, but sometimes it is difficult to think clearly when the only thing to think about is the loss of that very special love. Anyway, I finally did get my shoes on and started up the bank. The effort was definitely more now than it was when I was a kid, but I finally made it to the top. Once securely on the top and standing by my car, I made one final look at the scene below, realizing that I may never get here again. So many memories, so much behind me and I seemed to be lost in the past for a moment before I opened my car door to leave.

Starting the motor and slowly creeping up the hill so I could get turned around, I wondered where to stay for the night. I could drive to the bigger city, but that was a long drive and a couple of hours or stay at the bed and breakfast in my old home town. I decided to stay at the bed and breakfast and headed down the road. I was certain the bed and breakfast was still there since there were no major hotels, only a couple of smaller chain facilities. Ten minutes later I arrived in front of the small house that once belonged to one of the more prominent families in town, not that anyone in this town was very rich, but some had more than others. The house once was a pale yellow, but now it was painted white with blue shutters and a neat sign hanging on the front porch that said, "Tammy and Cliff's Bed and Breakfast." I wondered if this was the same Tammy who grew up here and went to school with Millie. I got out of my car and walked to the door, standing on the welcome mat before I turned the doorknob to enter.

Thinking back to the funeral and the meal afterwards reminded me so much of the time Millie came home for Christmas her first year in college. My family was invited over for Christmas dinner that was more of a combination of lunch and dinner than a single evening meal. Mom baked two pies, a pecan and an apple crunch to take. I could have eaten them both. Dad found a bottle of wine he had hidden away for a special occasion and decided to take it to the dinner. I asked him if he was going to let me have a glass. His only response was, I'll see. Anyway, we left the house with the food, wine, and presents and headed to Millie's. I was more excited than ever before.

When we got to Millie's house, I knocked on the door and Millie opened it. She was beautiful and to me very sexy. I found myself becoming very excited and was afraid it would show. I think Millie realized it and put her arm around my neck and hugged me, but of course she hugged my mother and father also. After everyone wished each other Merry Christmas and put our presents near the tree, Mom went into the kitchen to help Millie's mother and dad and Millie's father decided it was alright to open the wine. Millie sat next to me on the couch and was rubbing my leg when no one was watching. I was so hard I was about to explode and knew I couldn't do a thing about it. Millie reach over and took my hand and held it and kissed each of my fingers telling me each one was precious and I should take special care of them for playing the piano. Then she moved her hand a little higher on my leg and I had to move her hand away. I just knew I would have an accident and having the front of my pants wet would not be a good thing. Everyone would notice and I would not be able to explain the situation.

Thank goodness, Millie's mom came in the room and announced dinner was on the table and wanted one of the men, my dad, Millie's dad or me to carve the turkey. Millie's dad said he would. Millie took my hand and led me to the table. After the blessing, dad said I could have a very small glass of wine, but to sip it and not just guzzle it down. Millie sat next to me on one side of the table and Mom and Dad sat across for us while Millie's mom and dad took the captain's chairs at either end of the table. Occasionally Millie would wink at me and once she slipped her hand under the table placing it on my knee. I thought I would die. I couldn't touch her, but I did put my hand under the table to move her hand away. She took my hand and held it for a moment, but we both put our hands back on the table to continue eating. I really don't think our parents paid any attention to us, but the conversation turned to Millie and her first months at college.

∾

When I opened the door to the bed and breakfast, I was surprised to see Tammy behind the registration desk. I did recognize her, but I did not know if she would recognize me. Yes, this had to be the Tammy from high school; well she was in Millie's class not mine. Tammy looked at me and started to say something, then held back. I walked to the desk and asked her if she was Tammy Wild from high school. She responded yes, but she was now Tammy Meadows. She said you are Ricky Snyder aren't you? She said she had followed my career and really liked my latest hits. Then she asked about Millie and I told her Millie just recently passed away from lung cancer. Tammy said I know how you must feel. She had lost Cliff two years before to a heart attack. We both said our condolences and chatted for a minute before I asked if she had any rooms available for the night. I could see more aging in Tammy's face probably due to the stress of managing the bed and breakfast by herself and losing Cliff. She told me she had followed my music career but hadn't heard much about Millie.

After checking in I asked Tammy if there was a restaurant open where I could have a light meal. She said that the Family Diner was still open until eight o'clock that evening. I recall that the Family Diner was probably one of the oldest places in town and one that I worked at as a server during my high school years. I mentioned we should find some time to talk later. She looked at me and said she was always there at the B and B and any time I felt like talking to just drop by. I walked to the diner a block away and enjoyed some home-style cooking of meatloaf, mashed potatoes, gravy, corn bread, and collard greens. The iced tea was sweetened just to the right taste and the service was almost like being at home. I had a second glass of tea, but this time I mixed it half sweetened and half unsweetened. I commented there was no way the food quality and service could be matched in the bigger cities. After eating I walked around for a few minutes and then went back to the B and B.

During the Thanksgiving dinner I did sip my wine and felt a little buzz, but I was still trying to recover from Millie's touch. After dinner, we all pitched in and cleaned up the dining room and the kitchen and that was good, allowing time for me to cool down. It is tough being a fourteen year old boy with a huge crush on a beautiful older girl. In the living room we exchanged presents and enjoyed a lively chit chat. Millie and I were asked to play some Christmas songs and we shared the bench together and played numerous songs, some together and some separately. Millie was still the better piano player at that time. By the time we finished playing and everyone joining in singing the songs, it was getting very dark outside and some snow flurries were beginning to come down. Dad said we better get back home before it really started snowing hard. We all exchanged good-byes and hugs and thanks for the presents. While my parents were in the kitchen putting the shared leftovers in bags to carry back home and Millie's parents were helping, Millie reached for me and this time gently kissed me ever so lightly on the lips. It was not a passionate kiss, but more a "friendly-I-like-you" kiss. I guess this was our first almost real kiss and I became excited. I knew I was going to explode just from her kiss and I did. I did not want Millie to notice and I had to put my coat on quickly to hide the evidence. Millie said she really liked me and would miss me once she got back to school. She also told me she couldn't wait until I was older. I know my face was beet red. I just hoped she wasn't teasing me.

The weekend was fraught with heavy snow and high winds, so it was a white Christmas after all, but it kept everyone inside the house and close to a warm fire in the fireplace. Millie called and said she had to leave Sunday and hoped the roads were clear enough to get out. But the sun came out Sunday morning and the road crews were clearing the roads. I was able to walk over and tell Millie bye and that I wanted her to write me as much as she could. She kissed me again, even more lightly, this time on the cheek, more of just a peck, but I was at ease and prepared and careful in avoiding having another accident. I waved as she and her father drove away, him taking her back to college.

When I got back to the B and B, Tammy was still behind the desk and was checking in a young couple. She pointed to the couch in the lobby room and motioned for me to wait. They seemed so happy and the young lady was standing behind her friend or husband with her arms around his waist. Tammy told them, Mr. and Mrs. Chance, that their room was up

35

the stairs and the third door on the right. I was hoping to have time to talk to anyone after a very emotional time experienced with Millie's death. Even at age fifty, loneliness can be a challenge to overcome. I felt compelled to talk some about my day and wanted to hear more from Tammy about her life since she had remained in our small town. I vaguely recalled Cliff, and I think he was several years older than Tammy and Millie. When Tammy finally came over to where I was sitting, we must have talked for hours.

COMPANIONS
Adjustments

Tammy and I sat in the lobby, she in an armchair and me somewhat reclining on a couch, but not actually slouching. I was right, Cliff was ten years older than Tammy and Tammy was the same age as Millie, but Millie's birthday was two months later than Tammy's. I don't think when you get to be in your fifty's a few years makes a difference, but ten years put Cliff at sixty-three when he died two years ago. Millie was only fifty-five. I found it interesting that Tammy and Cliff only had one son who is thirty-three now and lives in San Francisco. Tammy said she talks to him and his wife a couple of times each month, more around the holidays and birthdays. Her son and his wife do not have any children due to him being sterile. They thought of adopting, but just never followed through. Jason, Tammy's son, thinks he is sterile because of an accident when he was fifteen when he fell while walking on a rail fence and really damaged his family jewels. Tammy said they swelled up to the size of a grapefruit and he couldn't wear pants for two weeks. I smiled and said I hope she didn't make him wear a skirt. She laughed and it was the most embarrassing time of Jason's life especially having his mother see him that way daily.

Tammy changed the subject and asked me about Millie's funeral. I told her that there were so many people in attendance that I did not get around to speaking to each one, but so many expressed their love for Millie. I mentioned the members of my musical troop were all present as well as some of my fans. Millie was a cornerstone for the community, a leader in the church, a super teacher for the children as well as adults, a mentor to everyone around her, and of course a devoted and loving wife.

Marrying her was the best thing that I ever did, and being married to her for twenty-five years were the best years of my life, not including our childhoods together. Just knowing we practically grew up together and later she spent the rest of her life as my wife and me as her husband was so exciting, loved filled, and wonderful. I just couldn't remember a time when Millie wasn't smiling and we had a continuous love affair.

Tammy asked if we had children and I said no we did not. Millie was pregnant twice, but miscarried, and she was finely told by her doctors that she could not have children for health reasons. Because of my career being on the road and travelling the country, and with Millie's community and teaching involvement, it seemed children were just not destined to a part of our personal life. Millie did teach children in the church we attended and in the school where she was a teacher and she would have been a great mother because all the kids at church and school loved her. I can't help but think back to the time when Millie came home from college for the Christmas holiday and after the bountiful dinner when Millie said she wished I were older. That was a special time for me, but nothing was more special than my life with her.

The Pastor was asking me if I was holding up okay since I seemed to be in deep thought, but I was thinking how much I missed Millie. I was thinking I just wish things had turned out better health-wise for her, that there was a cure for cancer, that we could have grown old together, how much better it would have been. As Pastor Thomas and I walked to the fellowship hall, he asked me, *"...Ricky, Ricky, you seem to be drifting somewhere. Are you sure you are holding up okay? The meal will be great. You know how super the women are in preparing dishes. I just can't wait to get some of Martha's broccoli casserole and Pennie's banana pudding. Ricky, you need to eat something and be around people..."*

That much I knew. I did need to be around people. *"...Pastor, really I am okay. It is just difficult for me to know Millie is gone and will not be coming back. I dread going to an empty house with so many memories, but they are all good. I know going home tonight will be hard for me, but I also know I will adjust in time. And, yes, I know it will take a long time..."*

∞

Time with everyone talking and interacting seem to just fly by during the dinner in the fellowship hall. The amount of food was unbelievable, and the Pastor was right, Martha did make the best broccoli casserole and Pennie's banana pudding was to die for...probably a bad choice of words, but true. So many friends came up to me and expressed their condolences while others just hugged my neck and wanted to know what they could do to help. One of Millie's closest lady friends came up to me and told me it was still way too soon, but when I wanted her to help sort out Millie's personal belongings just to let her know and she would be there for me. She said she had to go through that when her husband died and it is a tearful time and it was good she had her sister to lean on. I was deeply moved and told her I would call her as soon as I could bear to start such an effort. Millie was not one to have closets full of clothes, she was very frugal and made a lot of her dresses and skirts herself. She was a great seamstress and it was hard for anyone to tell the difference in what she made and store-bought clothes.

I seemed to wonder aimlessly around the fellowship hall talking briefly with some of the church members, some of my personal acquaintances, members of my musical troop, and my agent and producer. I was surprised when some prominent writers and artists stayed for the meal. I had recorded several songs from one of the writers, but typically I wrote my own lyrics. Several key individuals had come to the service, but due to many scheduled obligations and contractual commitments, it was impossible for many to actually be there in person. I was deeply moved at how many sent flowers and expressed condolences. The number of sympathy cards, I knew, would take me weeks to read. Just responding with thanks would take me weeks. I knew if I had to that I could take the cards with me and respond during the times we were travelling between performances.

The evening slowly came to an end with people coming up to me expressing personal concerns, stating they needed to get home, but if there was anything they could do to just call. I think the group dwindled down to the three ladies cleaning the room, Pastor Thomas and me.

"...Ricky, you have had a trying day, actually a trying week. Why don't you go home and get some rest? Will anyone be there with you? Can I arrange for someone to come and stay for a while? What can I do to help? You know Millie is rejoicing in Heaven with her Lord and Savior and singing in that Heavenly choir. She is looking down and smiling at you, at us, but she is so much better off without all the suffering and pain I know she must have endured. I know how hard this has been on you personally. If you like, I can drop by later or if you wish I can come by tomorrow. This is a new beginning for both you and Millie. What do you want or need right now? How can I help you? Can I pray for you before you leave?..."

I was awed by his thoughts and his prayer. His offer to help was very comforting. I just didn't know what I needed, what I wanted at the moment, but I knew I wanted to get away. I didn't know to where, maybe not even why, only that I felt I needed to be alone. I told Pastor Thomas I might go for a drive. I left the fellowship hall heading home. When I got there, the house seemed so vacant, so void of life. It was so empty without Millie. Her presence was still in the house through all the things she did to make it a home for us. I knew I could not stay the night but I had to eventually face the fact Millie was gone and not coming back. I looked at my watch and realized it was after six o'clock. The funeral services and the meal lasted longer than I thought. I decided to just rest and regain my composure then pack a small overnight bag and take a drive the next morning. I really needed to sleep. I decided mentally I would drive back to our home town. Why? I could not understand, only that it seemed the best place to go. It was about a three-hour drive taking it slowly, but I thought I definitely would go back to our home town, Millie's and my home town.

Even though I needed to sleep, I really didn't sleep well that night at home and got up twice and walked around going into various rooms. I opened the closet in our bedroom and reached for one of Millie's dresses and just held it and I could smell her perfume and sense her presence. I finally went back to bed and drifted in and out of sleep until the sun shone through the windows. It was only then that I realized I had not drawn the drapes. But it didn't make any difference since there were no houses close to ours. Neighbors were close and available, but just not in our faces. This was a great neighborhood and wonderfully caring people. Being on the road travelling from city to city, Millie was home alone many days of the year, and thankfully the wonderful neighbors always checked on her. I lay in the bed just looking at the sun creeping through the windows.

I finally got up and after going to the bathroom, I wandered into the kitchen, fixed a strong cup of coffee, added cream and sugar, had a banana, and sat on the sun porch for a few minutes. I guess I came to the realization I was just in my boxer shorts and should get cleaned up and dressed if I was going to drive to the mountains, driving back to my home town. The coffee was refreshing and the aroma of it brewing permeated the air throughout the house. The shower woke me up completely. I got dressed in some faded blue jeans and a pullover golf shirt. I put on my expensive UGG shoes with ankle socks. My bag was lightly packed and I was ready to leave when the doorbell sounded. By my watch it was just after nine o'clock on a beautiful Monday morning in mid-September. I opened the door to find the Pastor and his wife standing on the porch. Of course I invited them in. Both of them were dressed in their best Sunday attire and I looked as casual as anyone could be. Both looked at me and smiled. I really don't think they cared how I was dressed, but I was a bit more casual than they typically saw me.

I don't think either the Pastor or his wife was completely shocked, but I do think my casualness caught them off guard. At least I wasn't in my boxer underwear. I had shaved and my hair was combed. My packed bag was sitting on a chair making it obvious I was getting ready to go somewhere. Regardless, I offered them coffee or something to drink, but neither accepted. We sat down, and I guess I felt an explanation was in order since it was just the day after Millie's funeral. I told the Pastor and his wife I was getting ready to take a drive and thought I would go back to our home town where Millie and I grew up. I hoped that did not seem strange to them. The Pastor acknowledged my explanation by telling me he thought it would be good to get away for a few days and going back to my home town would probably be refreshing and bring back fond memories of Millie and me growing up in a small town and seeing special friends we shared in the neighborhood. If Pastor Thomas just really knew what some of those fond memories were, he might be shocked.

∾

When Millie got back to college she called her mother to let her know they had arrived safely and that her dad would be driving back and to be sure he called her when he arrived home. Then Millie called me to let me know she was back and wanted to know what I was doing. Here I was a fourteen year old boy with raging hormones in love with a nineteen year old woman who in the past, unknown to her or maybe she knew, had unintentionally, or maybe unknown to me had intentionally stimulated me to the point of almost screaming out loud. I thought about her every day and especially when I was practicing my piano lessons. My school would be starting back on January third and I knew I had to get my thoughts back on my studies and not spend so much time thinking of Millie. Some of the girls in my class wanted me to ask them out or take them to a movie and I always had an excuse related to practicing my piano lessons. Not that I disliked any of them, but they did not mean as much to me as Millie meant. Most of the guys in my class were in some way bonded to a girl, but it just appeared to me to be more infatuation than love. I am certain some of the guys and girls at school eventually did fall in love and got married. I know some did and still live around the neighborhood. Others left for college and married someone from another town, or chose a different path or career keeping them away from their old neighborhood.

To the betterment of my thinking, the school year passed quickly, and I learned so much from the band director about writing scores and musical notes. I routinely played the piano for several school and church plays and special school events including the junior-senior banquet. I also started playing some for the church and even played for one wedding. I hadn't written many lyrics other than the song I wrote for Millie when she left for college the first time, but I was beginning to think of better tunes and actually scribbled some of my first attempts at a good song on paper. I even sent a few lines in a letter to Millie for her comments. Of course she loved them and would have even if they were not the best I could have written.

To my disappointment Millie didn't come home for any other holiday after Christmas until the end of the spring semester. I was getting ready to celebrate my fifteenth birthday and she would be twenty about seven months later. I couldn't wait for her to come home for the summer when she sent a letter saying she would only be home for a long weekend but had to get back to her job and that she was taking a couple of courses during the summer terms. My heart sank to my feet.

∾

It was getting late and it seemed neither Tammy nor I wanted to end the conversation but we both knew we needed to get some rest. She told me as she got up that she always put a sign on the door indicating to potential guests to ring the bell if someone needed to register. She put the sign on the counter at the desk regarding breakfast in the morning and asked me if I was coming down for breakfast. I had to ask if she was doing the cooking. She told me she did some of it but did have help. I then asked if she needed any help in the kitchen. She smiled and told me she would welcome my company. This was a very subtle way of saying "no." I smiled and bid her a good night and went upstairs to my room.

The morning came too quickly and for the first time in a week I slept like a baby. I had forgotten to pack any pajamas since I usually just slept in my boxer shorts, but then I wasn't sharing the room with anyone, so I really didn't care. I knew I had better dress before going down to the kitchen to help Tammy. I looked at my watch and noticed it was almost five o'clock. I quickly showered, shaved, and dressed somewhat better than I was yesterday but was very limited on my wardrobe. I went downstairs and found Tammy and two other women in the kitchen hurriedly preparing various items for breakfast. The aroma was mind boggling, and I hoped the food would taste as great. I could smell the heavenly scent of brewing coffee.

Tammy saw me and smiled, offering a cup of coffee that I graciously accepted and while I offered my help, it was obvious everything was under control and I would only be in the way. Tammy motioned to a stool beside the door and told me to sit and talk to her. I hated to bother her, but I really wanted to be around people at this time. I told her how great the food smelled and she offered to fix me a plate, but I said I would wait for others. She responded that there were only two couples registered and that there was one packing to leave before breakfast. I still insisted on waiting and asked if she would be joining the guests, hoping she would sit with me.

Tammy told me that once she got everything on the tables she would join me and we could continue our chit chatting from last evening. I wandered into the dining room and noticed several tables that were set family style and one table by the window with only two chairs. I drifted to that table with my coffee and sat down appearing to be waiting for someone. I didn't feel badly talking with Tammy since both Cliff and Millie had passed away, but I was acutely aware of how soon it was for me to do more than just talk and be friends. I was not looking for a relationship, only a friendship while I was in town and Tammy was a friend of Millie's from the past. The coffee tasted great. I saw that the coffee pot was on a sideboard, so I took the liberty of refilling my cup. This cup tasted even better than the first. Now I knew that I was awake.

Millie sent me a letter saying she would definitely be home Memorial Day weekend. I became excited reading her letter and got so nervous I was shaking. I rushed down to tell Mom and Dad and they seemed pleased but were calm, in no way as hyper as I was. Anyway, I ran back to my room and looked at the calendar. I had finals at school the next week and school would be out before Memorial Day. That would be great because I could spend as much time with Millie as she would let me. I guess I was also looking forward to her kissing me again not to mention her special touching.

The days seemed to drag and after taking my finals that I passed with very good grades. I only had to wait four days for Millie to be home. I helped around the house as much as possible and once went to my special place by the stream and sat on the rocks. I stripped off my shorts, undershorts, t-shirt and sandals and waded into the deep part of the stream and sat down. I was naked, but no one could see me and the cool water felt good especially around my private parts. I finally laid back with my head on a jutting rock and just day dreamed. I could visualize Millie's face and I thought of all the times we had together when she was teaching me to play the piano. I wondered if she really cared for me or if she was just messing around with me. Almost five years difference in age could be a challenge for her, maybe not thinking I was mature yet. However, I was mature in doing one thing that wet my pants when she touched me or kissed me. I just hope she didn't know what happened when she did touch or kiss me and that she wasn't just teasing me.

The Friday before Memorial Day weekend Millie's father went to pick her up. I wanted to go, but Mom said that was not appropriate and Millie really needed time to be with her family since her time being here would be very short. I pouted but agreed Mom was right. Mom said if Millie called me that I could go over to her house but not to interfere with her family's reunion. I pouted again, but of course that got me nowhere with mom. Dad just frowned and called me a horny teenager infatuated with an older girl. If he knew how she affected me he would have laughed. Mom would have scolded me and probably spoken to Millie informing her to be more careful around me. I was more than infatuated with Millie, I loved her.

Millie got home with her father and obviously enjoyed the rest of the day with her mom and dad and they went out to eat that evening. It was probably around eight o'clock that evening when she called the house and Mom hollered for me to pick up the phone. Millie wanted to know if I wanted to take a walk with her. I almost jumped out of my skin. She said she would come by the house for me and we could walk to the park and sit by the lake if that was okay with my parents. I half way asked and half way told Mom and Dad and they just wrinkled their noses and told me to behave myself and not be gone too long. When Millie came by the house she spoke with my mom and dad and hugged them both and told them if I misbehaved she would spank me. Dad just laughed and told Millie I was too big to spank, but she could try. Millie was beautiful.

Since the weather was nice and warm and there was still a little daylight, I put on my favorite shorts, no underwear, no socks, and my sandals. My favorite shirt was a long t-shirt reaching almost to my knees that had a picture of a piano on the back and across the front it said "I like to play." I wore that one just in case I got really excited while I was with Millie and with the length of the t-shirt could hide my excitement. We walked and I just rattled on about school and playing the piano for church and special events at school and how much I wanted to be as good as her. I continued to rattle on, but Millie was so patient and listened without saying too much. We walked, not touching, but occasionally she would grab me behind the neck with her hand and tell me how cute I was. I felt like I was ten instead of fifteen.

When we reached the park there were still some people there, some walking their dogs, some with children playing on the swings, others just walking around the lake. We sat on a bench that probably was six feet from the edge of the lake and Millie said she really missed me. I asked her about her boyfriend at college and she told me he was a friend and a boy but not a boyfriend in the sense the two of them had something special going on with each other. She asked me if I had a girl friend and I told her no but some of the girls hung around me because they like to hear me play the piano. Then she asked me if I was "getting any." Naïve me, I asked getting what. She scooted closer to me with our legs touching. Then she put her hand on my knee and my thigh and said "sex you foolish boy." I felt her hand move up my thigh, but she stopped short of going under my long shirt. The heat and rubbing of her hand was causing me to get excited, but she obviously didn't notice and didn't move her hand. I told her she was going to cause me to have an accident if she kept that up. She just laughed at me but did not move her hand.

I was looking around to see if anyone was watching and I finally told her to move her hand that I was getting too excited. She stopped and took my hand in hers and kissed each of my finger tips. She reached over and kissed me very lightly on the cheek. That was too much for me. I exploded and it seemed to never stop. I probably shuddered and quickly put my other hand over my mouth. I could feel that the front of my shorts soaked but thankfully the wetness hadn't bled through to my shirt. I was thinking that maybe I should have worn underwear. Millie laughed at me. I think she knew what happened but she did not say anything. I hoped my shorts would dry before I got back home. She said she knew I was only fifteen and that sometimes boys do get excited when they are around girls. She said that she really liked me and she hoped one day when I was older that we could be more than just friends, but I was too young now and that maybe one day we might have a real date. She apologized if she caused me to have an accident, but she was laughing. I wanted to tell her I may only be fifteen but my body is telling me it is ready for more. I guess I should have said it, but I told her I really loved her. She told me I was a special boy and a wonderful companion and she loved me also. She continued to hold my hand and she kissed me on my cheek once more and I felt myself getting excited again.

∾

Tammy did the gracious hostess thing with the young couple across the room from where I was sitting and then came to my table. The two ladies helping her served juice and brought bowls of scrambled eggs and grits for them and for me. They had bacon, fried just right and crispy. The biscuits melted in your mouth. Putting home-made jam with butter on the biscuits just made the meal. Tammy sat across from me, "How is your breakfast? I hope you are enjoying it."

"Everything is absolutely delicious. This is probably the best breakfast I have had in some time. Millie was a great cook, but I was on the road a lot and when I came home we usually just had a quick bowl of cereal, maybe with some fruit, and started a busy day. Do you cook like this every day?"

"No. Sara and Marty do most of the cooking now. I don't think I could do this without their help."

"They seem to be wonderful people. Have they been with you a long time?"

"Sara has, probably five years, before Cliff died. Marty has only been here a short time. She and her husband settled here about the time Cliff died. I didn't know her at the time. Her husband worked in the city. I think he was an insurance broker. Anyway, about eight months ago on his way home some drunken teenage boys were speeding and crossed the center line hitting his car head on. He died at the scene as did the boy driving the other car. Three other boys in the car were severely hurt. The boys in the back seat had some broken bones and really bruised up. The boy on the passenger's side was thrown through the windshield cutting his face and areas all over his body. He obviously landed face down on the hard pavement. He will live, but he will be in rehabilitation for years and will undergo some plastic surgery on his face. He is scarred for life. I don't know what other problems he may have suffered, but none of those three were charged in the death of Tom.

"Since Marty lived fairly close and went to our church, I spent some time with her helping to get things settled. I knew how difficult it is to handle everything when your husband did it all. After that, Marty came over one day and asked if she could help me. I told her I could not afford to pay her much and she said she didn't want any pay. Tom had a great life insurance policy and she was okay financially. She does all she does for me for no pay."

"That is some story. It was great you could help her and she in turn is repaying the kindness. I feel sorry for the boy who died and more so for the boys who have to live with the experience and the death of two people. I just don't understand why the teenagers today think they have to drink and get drunk to prove their manhood."

"What about Sara?"

"Oh Sara is wonderful. She is married and has three grown children. Her husband works at the local hardware store, part time. He retired a few years ago from one of the plants in the city, but they both are active and Sara at one time was a cook in a restaurant somewhere. She just loves to help out and we enjoy each other's company; all three of us, Sara, Marty and me. Do you want more coffee?"

"Thanks. Only if you are having more. I have already had two cups. I must admit this is some of the best coffee I have tasted."

Tammy got up to get us more coffee and stopped to speak to the young couple. I heard the guy asked about fun places to visit so they could spend some time during the morning before he had to meet someone around noon for a job interview in the city. Tammy told them about places they could go but most required driving and would limit the amount of time they would have to enjoy the sites. The couple decided just to take a walk then maybe drive into the city to find the restaurant for his meeting. They sat there a few more minutes then left, I assumed as planned. Tammy got the coffee pot and came back to the table.

"How long are you going to be in town?"

"Initially I was just coming up for the day to get away and for a change of scenery, but it is so nice and quiet if the room is available, I might stay another day or two. Tom, my manager rescheduled or canceled some performances due to the death of Millie, so it would give me some time to adjust. Do you have plans for dinner tonight? Please don't think I am being pushy. It is way too soon for me to think about a relationship, I just want some company. No obligation on your part, just dinner somewhere."

Laughing, Tammy looked at me and said, "And I am not ready for a relationship either, especially after a few hours of talking. But I would love to do dinner with you tonight, no obligation. We can go Dutch if you like. As you may well remember, there is not much around here, but if you are up to it, we could drive to the city and find a nice inexpensive place there."

"You are so funny. Maybe we can find a McDonalds and have a hamburger. Actually I was thinking Italian and a glass of good wine. And, I think I can afford to treat you if you will permit me to do so."

"It's a deal. No strings attached. Maybe leave here around five? That would put us at a good restaurant in time to avoid the rush."

After Pastor Thomas and his wife left, I made sure everything was in order and all the lights were turned off except the two that were on timers. My housekeeper would check on things when she came later in the week. But I did not think I would be gone but one day. I picked up my bag, turned on the security system, and closing the door to the house I entered the garage and decided to drive my white BMW convertible. Millie loved this car and she drove it often. I felt it would make me closer to her. After all the weather was a very nice September day and I might want to put the top down at some point. I put my bag in the trunk and opening the garage door. I got in the car and backed out, closing the garage door and started down the drive way.

I decided to head east knowing at some point I would end up in my home town. As I drove I continued to think more and more about Millie and our times together from me as a small boy and her at the time when I thought she was so much older. Those four-plus years, well almost five years, seemed impossible for me to have her attention, but I know I did in some way. There always seemed to be a special bond between us from the first time she baby-sit for me and even before that when she would spy on me while I was at my special place by the stream. I say spy, but I guess she was curious as to what I was doing, or maybe she was my guardian angel. Regardless, she never came down the bank to join me and I would have run her off if she had done so. This was a special place for me and no girls were allowed.

I made a couple of pit stops along the way. I stopped once for a bio break and once to get a sandwich and something to drink. No one recognized me or if they did, no one said anything. I knew my face was somewhat renowned and in some places I often got bombarded with people wanting autographs. But being out of my normal element, dressed differently, I assumed that people thought I was just a look alike. As I continued to drive, I decided not to linger in other places but to continue to my home town. I arrived and drove directly to my favorite place, surprised to see not much had changed and how much still seemed the same. After spending some quiet time there I left and found the bed and breakfast.

As Tammy had said to me, she was dressed and ready at five o'clock and when I came into the lobby, she looked amazingly different than she had earlier. Her hair had obviously been teased and looked as if she just stepped out of a magazine. Her makeup was perfect. She had on navy slacks and a light blue blouse. She had a scarf tied around her neck and draped to one shoulder. She was carrying a light jacket over her left arm. Me, I must have looked more like a bum because I only brought some nice blue jeans and golf shirts and I still had on my UGG shoes. I apologized for my appearance but she was gracious and said I looked neat and comfortable.

The drive to the city was enjoyable, and on the way we just chit-chatted about numerous things. Tammy said one couple had decided to continue to stay at her B and B and another couple had checked in before she started getting ready for our dinner engagement. She had a reservation for another single individual for eight o'clock, but Tammy said Marty would be there and get him checked in. Small talk seemed to be the source of our conversation without any real focus on any particular topic. I was watching the road and signs for the restaurant when Tammy pointed to a visible sign off to the right thinking it was where we were dinning, but actually our restaurant was on the other side of the street. The red and white checkered sign flashed "A Taste of Italy."

We parked and ventured inside the restaurant where the hostess seated us by a window overlooking the woods at the side of the restaurant. There were a few other people there, but our server told us the rush didn't come for another hour. She asked if we wanted something to drink and I asked

Tammy if she would like a glass of wine. I ordered an Italian Malbec and asked it to be decanted to allow it to breathe. Our server brought out a basket with freshly baked Italian Ciabatta bread, olive oil, and garlic butter and at the same time she brought the bottle of wine and decanted it at the table. We ordered baked ravioli for an appetizer and Alaskan salmon on pasta with broccoli for our main course. I found it both funny and interesting we ordered the same dish.

Tammy looked at me and asked, "What are you going to do when you get back home? I know from experience going into an empty house with so many memories can be depressing. Will anyone be staying with you?"

Pausing to think but having difficulty responding, I said, "I need to leave no later than Wednesday or early Thursday morning. I will barely be home long enough to pack some clothes and get back on the road. I have an engagement gig for Friday through Sunday nights in Branson, so duty calls."

"Did Millie go with you on your tours?"

"No, not usually, maybe once a year, but she had so many commitments with school and church it would have been difficult for her to do so. We always talked every day or night while I was away, even though sometimes when I got to the hotel it would be one or two o'clock in the morning. Millie didn't mind, she just wanted to know I was safe and I loved to hear her voice."

"You must have been very much in love."

"Absolutely! There was never anyone else for either of us. Even though there were times early on with me being younger made me think Millie would find someone more her age, but we both just hung in there. It was definitely God's will that we become a couple."

We had the Tiramisu for dessert and finished off the bottle of wine. I was relaxed but knew it was time to get back to the B and B and get Tammy back for sure since she got up early to fix breakfast. On the drive back, we were both fairly quiet, but she chatted about the meal and how much she enjoyed it and that she enjoyed my company. I did feel a little like I was betraying Millie by the very fact I had dinner with another woman, but definitely there was nothing going on between us except each needing a friend and someone to talk about familiar things. I parked the car and we both walked to the house and I opened the door for her. Once inside, Tammy thanked me again for the dinner and my company and asked if I would be coming down for breakfast. Of course I wouldn't miss that meal for anything. We bid each other good night and without a handshake or hug we went our separate ways.

Millie finally turned loose of my hand as did I hers and we sat on the bench by the lake until it was dark and I had a chance to somewhat dry from the wetness I experienced. Millie laughed at me again and said as I got older I would be in more control of the situation. She kissed me on the cheek again and told me we better start walking home. It was a kiss of friendship. I knew I wanted more, but Millie was cautious and very aware of me being underage.

Her time here would be short before she had to go back to college and her parents wanted to spend some quality time with her. I begged her to please not say anything to hers or my parents about what happened to me on the bench or my dad would scold me. She laughed and said that we really didn't do anything wrong, but regardless she didn't want to go to jail for attempted statutory rape. I frowned and said I only wish it had been rape. She pushed me away and told me to keep my pants zipped until I got older. I pushed her back and said someday I hope we can be more than friends. We continued to push each other until we got close to home and I walked her to her house and then ran to mine. I hoped that neither Mom nor Dad could sense that I had done something for which they would have disapproved. After all I knew if my dad had the faintest idea that Millie and me almost made out, in his eyes it would have been wrong. In my way of thinking, what happened was what teenagers do.

However, my dad just looked at me when I got home and asked what we did. I started to tell him Millie got me excited, but I knew that would not be wise and would be a smart-alecky response that would get me slapped or he would take his belt to my behind. I just told him we sat by the lake and watched people in the park and talked about her college and where I might go and if I still liked playing the piano. He accepted all that and told me I should get ready for bed. I said I think I will take a shower first and read some. He shook his head and said nothing. Upstairs in my room I stripped off my clothes and noticed the crusting on my shorts and a tad had bled on my shirt. I decided I better wash them and let them dry before putting them in the hamper or Mom would definitely want to know what happened. It can be difficult being fifteen and have raging hormones and in love with someone who is older knowing that you can't do anything about it other than taking care of it yourself.

Saturday morning I got up and took care of things before going downstairs for breakfast. I was still in my short pajama bottoms but nothing showed now. Dad had already left for work and Mom told me she had some errands to run and asked if I wanted to go with her. Of course I did not but I just told her I may go back to bed. She frowned and said okay, but I really should practice my piano lessons and get my room cleaned up. She said we may have to start getting the yard in shape from the winter but we can discuss that when she gets back. I fixed a bowl of cereal and had a glass of milk as Mom was preparing to leave. The phone rang and it was a lady friend from church and Mom discussed them doing errands together and that she would pick the lady up in fifteen minutes to head to the city. I knew then Mom would be gone for several hours.

After Mom left and I had finished my breakfast, I went back to my room and took care of things again before going back downstairs and practicing on the piano for thirty minutes. I had to practice at least two hours a day and longer if I could. I then went back upstairs and showered and dressed in knee-length shorts, underwear this time, and a t-shirt that just reached past my waist, no socks and my favorite sandals. After all it was May and the weather was cool, but not cold. I did straighten my room and put all my dirty clothes in the hamper including my other shorts and shirt that were dry from washing them out last night. Mom did expect me to have chores and was encouraging me to become a responsible teenager. I still had growing pains about still being a youth and what was meant to be an adult.

I thought I had better practice some more before Mom got home and after playing for another thirty minutes or so the phone rang. I answered it and it was Millie. She asked me what I doing and I told her I was practicing my piano lessons. She expressed gladness and encouragement and then she said she really enjoyed our time last night by the lake and wanted to know if I had gotten in any trouble because of my pants. I must have turned beet red but told her I washed them and let them dry before putting them in the hamper for Mom to wash. Millie just laughed and said that was a smart move on my part. She said she and her mom were going shopping for a few hours to get some things to take back to college but after they got back she would see if we could take a walk. My heart started beating faster and I felt myself getting aroused. But I stayed calm and told her I would like that. I mentioned Mom and a lady friend were running some errands and dad was at work. She just told me to keep practicing and to behave myself.

I did continue to practice my lessons on the piano and around one o'clock Mom came home. She was pleased my room was clean and I had put my dirty clothes in the hamper to be washed. She told me I could have started the laundry and I was old enough to take some responsibility. I guess if I had been thinking with my head I could have done the laundry and felt a lot safer about my pants. Anyway, Mom wanted to go out and look at the yard and see what need to be done. We decided just getting the sticks and some of the dead flowers out of the yard would be a good start. Some of the jonquils were already blooming as well as the yellow bells, but the grass did not need cutting. I at least had a reprieve there. After about two hours roaming in the yard and doing some clean up, I went back in and to my room where I decided to read about some of the colleges with music degrees. Where I really wanted to attend is Juilliard. I knew I still had three years of high school but I also knew I had to be prepared and I really needed to see about getting a scholarship.

As promised Millie called but it was after super around seven o'clock. She asked me if I wanted to have a quick walk to the lake with her and of course I was beside myself wanting to go. I asked Mom and Dad and they said it was okay but not to pester Millie too much. They even went as far as to tell me I really didn't need a baby-sitter any more. Inside I was screaming wanting to say she is doing more than baby-sitting me, but that would have gotten both Millie and me in trouble. I was smart enough to keep my mouth shut so I asked Dad what he thought of me going to Juilliard and could we discuss it later. He looked at me and said that sounds great if it is affordable.

I went to my room to see what I wanted to wear for my walk with Millie. I was concerned if I got excited again and had another accident that I needed to be careful what I wore. I also thought I should wear underwear. I knew I was jumping the gun and that no touching might happen. Anyway, I chose another pair of long dark navy shorts that were really baggy and another long t-shirt. This one was dark also with only a Nike logo on it. If anything did happen it would not be as obvious. However, I did put on undershorts. I had to calm down before I walked out to meet Millie. I obviously had an arousal problem and Mom and Dad would probably bring it to my attention if my long baggy shorts didn't hide the evidence. However, things did subside and I looked normal as I told Mom and Dad I would be back shortly.

Millie looked beautiful in a loose pair of shorts and a jumper type shirt. I didn't think she was wearing a bra, but I did not say anything. She smiled at me and I was just one big grin. Again we walked and talked about our day but did not touch each other. This time she did not squeeze my neck. When we got to the park she saw a couple of people she knew and stopped to talk to them introducing me as her best friend. We walked around the park some and part way around the lake before finding a bench to sit down.

It was getting darker and many people were leaving when Millie scooted closer to me and put her arm around my shoulders. She looked at me and then kissed me on the top of my head before she touched my lips and kissed me gently as if she cared for me. I was so taken by the kiss I didn't notice she had moved her hand to my knee. I reached over and took her hand in mine and this time I kissed each of her finger tips. I could sense her hand on my knee even though I had it in my hand. I was quickly getting excited in that special way. She pulled her hand from mine and told me that kiss had to last me until she came home again, and if I do get excited to think of only her. I was almost speechless. We gently and friendlily kissed one more time before going back home.

That was one of the best times I had ever had and it gave me a memory to really think about each time I was in the mood. I went to sleep many nights after Millie left for college knowing I would not see her for the entire summer but I had a pleasant vision and a good right hand.

The next couple of years seem to drag out and Millie only came home for Christmas the first year and was deep in studies and working with a company doing some social work that she really loved. We wrote each other and when she was here our time together was short because of my efforts to get into Juilliard and constantly playing the piano. I was even writing more lyrics and trying to put music to them. I had several recitals and once when she was here, I had a recital in the city and a church asked me to provide the piano music for their Christmas play, so I only got to speak to Millie by phone.

I had grown taller, only about an inch and a half, but at least I was a half an inch taller than my dad. My body did fill out some, but I was still slim. I was dressing better and acting more my age, being more responsible and Mom and Dad were really proud of me, or so I thought. I corresponded with Juilliard and had submitted various forms for their review. I knew by the middle of my senior year in high school I had to have everything in order. Juilliard wanted to hear me play and Dad made arrangement for us to go to the school since I wanted also to see the campus. It was a long way to New York so we flew. That was actually my first airplane trip.

COMPANIONS
Separations

I slept well that night in my room at the bed and breakfast. I was thankful that Tammy had consented to have dinner with me. It was a relaxing time for both of us and I really enjoyed her company. I just needed to talk, to be with someone, and to chill just a bit from all that had happened with the funeral and being with the church family. Before getting up, I just stayed in the bed a few minutes, staring at the ceiling, then at the clock knowing I should get up and get moving. I got up reluctantly, but with some remorse, and shaved, showered and dressed in long blue jean from the day before, but a different shirt. I had packed very lightly, so my choices for dressing were few. I went downstairs and as I expected Tammy, Sara, and Marty were fixing a hearty breakfast.

The aroma of the coffee was filling the room. I walked over to where the pots of coffee were and poured a steaming cup, added a sugar cube and a touch of cream. There were more people this morning in the dining room for breakfast than I expected, but I was able to get my usual table by the window. I took my coffee and sat down. Tammy came with her mug of coffee and sat with me for a couple of minutes telling me she would join me after speaking to the other guests. Sara and Marty were busy already serving the guests. I sipped my coffee slowly and read some in the local paper that I picked up in the lobby while I waited for Tammy to join me.

Once she was able to break away from her duties, she came to the table where she and I chatted about our dinner last evening and she wanted to know when I planned on leaving. I was hoping this was not a way to get rid of me versus rather that she enjoyed my company. But, as before, I told her I had to leave no later than Thursday morning. Surprisingly she asked if I would join her for dinner tonight and that if I did, she would cook. How could I pass up such an opportunity? I asked if I could bring a bottle of wine and if so where could I purchase one. She just laughed and told me that would be fine and the grocery store a couple of blocks away carried wine, but the selection was not great. She told me to get a decent wine I would have to drive into the city, but to not do that since she was certain she had some wine in the house. Regardless, I knew I would be going to the city to get a couple bottles of good wine.

The drive to the nearest large airport took a couple of hours and I chatted with Dad the whole way about music, Juilliard and just things in general. When we got there I was impressed with everything. I wasn't too fond of the long line for the security check in, not that I didn't think that was important, but I was excited about going to New York and to Juilliard wanting to get on the plane as quickly as I could. I had a window seat and Dad sat in the aisle seat since the plane just had two seats on either side of the cabin. The airplane ride was scary for me at first, especially when we lifted off and I got butterflies in my stomach, but it was invigorating and I enjoyed the attention from the attendants. I always thought people had good food on airplane trips, but all we got during the flight was a little pack of peanuts and a drink. That part did not impress me.

During the flight, Dad and I did talk about the cost of going to Juilliard and if and how he could manage it if I did not get a scholarship. Just being seventeen, well almost eighteen, and half-way intelligent, I did understand finances, but not really our family's financial situation. Dad said it is over thirty-thousand a year plus other expenses. I had no idea what his salary was, only that he provided for us adequately. He said, "I know you are very good at your studies and have done great in school and are already an accomplished pianist, but it may be a financial struggle to get you enrolled." I listened and then jokingly looked at him and asked, "Aren't you glad you just had one kid?" He gripped my knee and said, "One of you was enough, but without you life would have been dull."

Our flight landed at J. F. Kennedy International Airport and it took a while to disembark and find our way around. We both had packed very lightly since this was just a day and a half trip so we carried our luggage with us so that we did not have to go to the baggage claim area and wait. Dad had reserved a rental car and we found our way to the car rental place. The car Dad rented was an economy model car, but nice, and after leaving the rental area we wanted to drive around and see some of the surrounding community. Since Juilliard is located in the center of New York at the Lincoln Center it was something to see especially when I really hadn't traveled past the big city near my home town. Well, that is not exactly right because Dad did take Mom and me to Disney World in Orlando, Florida when I was ten years old and to DollyWood, a long drive from our home, but at least DollyWood was definitely within driving distance. I became infatuated at the sights of New York and when we found a parking garage close to the Lincoln Center, we walked to the school and it took my breath away. I couldn't help but stare up at the tall buildings and asked Dad if we could go to the Empire State Building and ride to the top. Reluctantly he agreed if we could find our way there after our meeting at Juilliard.

"Dad, I have to come here. I will get a scholarship I promise. I will get a job and work to help pay some of the expenses. Look at this place!" Of course I realized my seventeen year old brain was talking, but Dad was gracious and put his arm around my shoulder and said nothing. I hadn't given thought to the fact how far away I would be from home and away from Millie once she returned from college. After arriving to the Juilliard campus, we found the Administration area and told the receptionist we had an appointment to play the piano for the music instructor. She was extremely helpful and got us to the right person and the right place. The instructor for piano was delightful, and told me where I would be playing for them. He mentioned the Juilliard student to faculty ratio was three to one that ensured smaller classes and student personalization. This sounded so great to me because I was actually used to smaller classes coming from a small town. This impressed my dad also.

After about thirty minutes of discussing how I started playing the piano and where I learned to play and the type music I played, as well as why I wanted to attend Juilliard, the professor sat me down at the piano and told me he wanted me to first play whatever I wanted to play then he would give me some music scores to play. I was sweating bullets but he calmly put his hand on my shoulder and told me to just play as if I were at home. I started out with an easy song and then played some Bach, a little jazz, a religious song, and he finally had to stop me to tell me he was impressed with my talent but he wanted to see how well I read musical notes and how I played particular scores. Since I could easily read notes and played from them often as well as knowing some of the songs he gave me, he was very impressed and looked at my dad telling him he should be proud of my abilities. I was probably beet red and glowing with pride.

Dad wanted to know about scholarships and tuition payments, housing, other expense and just general requirements. I guess I never realized my dad knew to ask such questions and I never really thought about his college education, but I knew he did have a college degree. Dad did mention I still had one more year of high school to complete, but I definitely wanted to major in music and expand my abilities through Juilliard. The professor indicated that the talents of the students here now and those who continually come are amazing. Most are very talented before enrolling and are exceptional after completing their chosen major. He stated very few students dropped out, but some did so because of financial reasons. We talked for another fifteen minutes and the professor showed us around the school, paying special attention to the music area. His career started overseas before coming to Juilliard and becoming the head of the music program with a focus on piano.

After the tour, dad and I expressed out thanks and collected some materials and walked back to the parking garage. I was hungry. On the way we stopped in at a nearby restaurant for a sandwich before finding the way to our hotel near the airport. I was about as excited as any teenager and all I could do was to talk about Juilliard. I could hardly wait to write Millie about my visit. We did find our way to the Empire State Building and after waiting in line for a while, we took the elevator to the top. The view was ecstatic and almost took my breath away. We spent about thirty minutes walking around and I looked through some of the view scopes at various corners of the roof. We rode the elevator down and located the parking garage and our rental car so we could get back to the hotel close to the airport. The hotel was nice, not fancy, but affordable. We had a room with two double beds and a view of airplanes coming into JFK. I knew I had a lot of work to do to get through the next year and prepare for college. And silently I prayed that college would be Juilliard.

∞

I did take time to drive into the city and found the Wine Emporium where the selection of wines was excellent. I chose an Australian Chardonnay and a Chilean Merlot not knowing what type food Tammy would be preparing and whether we needed a white or red wine with the meal. I walked around and went into a couple of stores and considered purchasing some small item for Tammy, but I did not want to be presumptuous or indicate any personal relationship interest. It was far too soon for me and I really did not know Tammy well enough to make such a purchase. I passed on the idea but considered some flowers. The drive back was good and I took time to once again go to that special spot just to enjoy the place another time. I didn't go down the bank, but I did sit on the hood of my car and thought about my days as a young boy and early times with Millie.

After just sitting and listening to the sounds and mentally reminiscing about times when I was a boy with nothing better to do than wade in the stream and pretend I was a superhero, I decided to get back to the B & B and change for dinner. I decided against the flowers and to just take the wine. Being so new at this type relationship, I really just wanted to do the customary attending to dinner appropriateness. After all, I never really dated as a teenager other than attending some parties and my relationship with girls in college were just as friends. I was devoted to Millie and she was the only girl who mattered to me relationship-wise.

The drive back was relaxing and the B & B seemed busier than ever. I understood all the rooms were taken and Tammy was tired, but that meant the no vacancy sign could be turned on and Tammy would not have to stay at the desk for the evening. Usually there were no calls from the rooms after five o'clock in the evening because people were leaving for events or dinner reservations. Tammy only served breakfast, so everyone had to find other places for lunch and dinner. I gave the wine to Tammy in order to chill the Chardonnay if that was appropriate for the meal and asked her what time I should come down. She looked at me and said anytime you are ready, but dinner will probably be around 6:00 this evening. That was good and gave me time to refresh and change into something less casual, but I really did not bring anything dressy. Fortunately my blue jeans were "preppy" and expensive, so I did look half-way decent.

Tammy had prepared a delicious meal with pork chops to die for and served over brown rice, a salad with nuts and fruits and several type lettuces, carrots, cucumbers, tomatoes, and other condiments. I opened the chilled Chardonnay since we were having pork and decided the after meal drink could be the Merlot. Tammy took hot rolls out of the oven, and covering them with a honey butter spread they just melted in your mouth. She had fixed French green beans, seasoned just right, and garlic mashed potatoes. This was almost too much food, but it smelled so good and I know I ate too much.

The following morning, after a small breakfast, we checked out of the hotel and drove to the rental car place to return the car and take the shuttle to the Delta terminal. The security check in line was very long and it took us almost forty-five minutes to get through the process. Once we were at the concourse, we had another almost one-hour wait for the plane and getting boarded. But, the flight back was great, a little bumpy in places, but it was exciting for me. I had a window seat again, so I could see some areas we flew over, but once we were above the clouds that is all I saw until we started our landing approach. I continued to pound dad with questions and my desire to go to Juilliard, and as he always is, he patiently listened and told me I should begin applying for scholarships as soon as possible. I looked through some of the material from the school about different opportunities and told dad I would give priority to finding the best one.

We landed safely, got to our car and drove home. I elaborated on all that happened during the trip to Mom and she told me that I must continue to work hard and to be the best that I can be in order to secure a great scholarship. She also mentioned to me to look for some individuals, teachers, who would endorse me to Juilliard. After we ate, I practically ran to my room to write Millie. This was a long letter detailing everything about the trip, Juilliard, what Mom and Dad told me and my ambitions to make attending the school a reality. I told Millie how much I missed her and wanted to know when she was coming home.

It seemed I waited forever to hear back from Millie, but probably it was only ten days when I received her response. She had kissed the outside of the envelope and I became aroused just looking at her lip prints. I fell in love with her more every day, even not seeing her but a couple of times a year now. I knew she would be graduating from her college before I would be graduating from high school and she would be working and would be a worldly person while I was just beginning college. She included a picture of her with a few of her girlfriends from her sorority and I immediately taped it on my dresser mirror with several other snapshots I had of her. I read the letter three times before Mom told me to come to dinner. The letter and Juilliard again were the main discussion points during our meal.

Both Dad and Mom asked what Millie had said in the letter. As usual I was very evasive and only shared some of the content. I told them that I really liked Millie and that I hoped we could be much closer one day. Mom told me I was barking up the wrong tree with Millie since she was so much older and Dad only shrugged his shoulders and sighed saying it was just infatuation on my part and once I got to college and met some of the beautiful girls I would soon forget Millie and would be a hit with many of my college classmates. He told me that Millie probably had already found someone more her age. I laughed and said maybe, but I doubt that actually happened. Dad just smiled and told me he couldn't wait to tell me "he told me so" in a couple of years. After dinner, I went to my room, did my homework, and wrote Millie another letter. Since I didn't wear lipstick, kissing the envelope would not be noticeable, but on the outside of the envelope I drew a heart with a musical note on it. I also sat down at my computer to see if I could write another song for Millie.

Dessert was to die for as Tammy placed a Cherry Jubilee on the table. I knew with the wine, huge meal, and now dessert I would be sleeping like a baby tonight. I had to ask how she had time to prepare such a delicious and delightful meal while running a full-time bed and breakfast. While we ate the Cherry Jubilee with home-made ice cream, we talked about different things and just enjoyed the moments. Afterwards I helped her clear the table and I insisted helping to clean the dishes. Tammy said okay and while she washed I dried. We continued to chit chat during the clean-up and then adjourned to the sitting room to finish our wine and talk about the full house of guests and from the different places from which they probably came. Guessing what some of them did career-wise by their names was a fun game while we finished the bottle of wine. Tammy wondered if any of them would recognize me and would want my autograph, but being most of them did not see me return, I told her it could or maybe happen at breakfast. I was used to people approaching me when I was out in public, but never in such close quarters. The wine was great and I wasn't getting tipsy, but I did have a buzz.

Since it was getting late, around nine o'clock, and I mentioned I really needed to get to my room and get some rest before possibly leaving the next day to drive home. Tammy and I took our wine glasses to the kitchen and she said she would wash them later. This was a very platonic meeting, nothing serious, just two friendly people having a great time at dinner. I thanked Tammy, and we touch-hugged, but not a serious hug. I went to my room and got ready for bed.

The words were not coming easily to write another song for Millie. I guess being stressed over worrying if I could get accepted to Juilliard was weighing heavily on my mind. It is so tough being a teenager and being in love while trying to decide how the future might unfold for me. I jotted down some words and then wondered if Mom and Dad would be okay if I played the piano some. After all it wasn't really that late as I looked at the clock, almost 8:30 p.m. I had completed my homework and the letter was ready to mail to Millie. I went downstairs and asked if it would bother them if I practiced a while. Dad was watching TV but said "fine" for me to go ahead and practice since the program he was watching was boring. I sat down at the bench, opened the piano and decided to play Brahms Piano Concerto 2. This was very soothing and I think Dad fell asleep. I so hoped it was from my accomplished playing versus just being bored with my music. With dad, it could be either one.

I concluded my piano playing with Beethoven's Piano Concerto 2 and Mom just stood behind me and kissed the top of my head, then told me how wonderfully I played, but it was time to go to bed because tomorrow was a school day. I got up, kissed her on the cheek and kissed the top of Dad's head, then went upstairs. I guess I slept well because once my head hit the pillow I must have drifted to slumber land and only awoke because the alarm clock was buzzing. I must have dreamed about Millie because I was adequately aroused but decided not to take care of business for fear of falling back to sleep. I went through my morning ritual and things went to normal after relieving my bladder and a nice shower. I took my books and went downstairs where Mom had breakfast ready. I ate hardily before leaving for school.

I always did great in my classes and this day was no exception. My mind did wander several times to wondering what Millie was doing, but I was still able to concentrate on my classes and responded to several questions asked by the teachers. I think they expected much from me just because of my good grades. But I had to keep good grades coming to ensure my acceptance to Juilliard and in order to qualify for a scholarship. Practice the piano and study music, make good grades, and just be a good person was my continuous plan. And, I still wanted to complete a new song for Millie. But more than anything I wanted to do well to make Millie both appreciate me and care for me. I knew she liked me, but I wanted her to really love me.

After dinner that evening, I went to my room, completed my homework and pulled out the paper where I earlier had scribbled some words to a song. I tried thinking of a good title and finally came up with one that I thought fit the mood that I lived with daily with Millie so far away, but would be appropriate for both Millie and me without too much mush. I called it "*Separations*." It took me several attempts to get the words right, but when I was finished, I started a letter to Millie and since I could not sing the words to her or play the piano and sing to her, I included the words in the letter and asked her to sing them out loud when she was reading the words.

> *My Dearest Millie,*
>
> *How I miss you and think of you often. I hope college is still going great and that you are not overworking between having a job, studying and trying to keep up a college pace. As I mentioned in my last letter to you, I have been trying hard*

to get into Juilliard, but I definitely must find a scholarship program to help offset some of the expenses. Dad doesn't say he can't afford the tuition, but I know he would hock everything we have to help me.

I know this may seem childish to you, but I miss our times playing the piano together. Do you remember the little song I wrote and sang to you before you left for college? Well, that was a really early attempt at my song writing, so I wanted to write you something that I think is better and of a more mature nature (you can tell me), but don't laugh and please after reading it, sing the words out loud. I call it "Separations", mainly because of our separate lives now, you at college and soon to be a worldly woman, and me, just a teenager still with one more year of high school. Okay, here are the words I wrote. I hope they have a special meaning to you.

I know I was discouraged when you left home that day,
Moving to another place and leaving me to say,
I'll miss you every minute while you're far away,
But I know your heart is here and you will return one day.
Simple as it seems, you were always watching me,
And I loved you as a friend for all that I could be,
But time changes people as time did change me,
And my love for you grew and grew constantly.
The separation distance created lonely times
When we were alone and had our thoughts in mind
About what we would do when you come back home,
And I missed you every day the whole time you were gone.
But as our paths will cross and you come back to stay,
I know I will be leaving and we will have to find a way
To stay in touch forever and agree to never stray
Too far from one another and both come back one day.

Separations challenge the way we're meant to be
Together as companions, friends for eternity;

Life without you diminishes with every passing day,
But together as companions separations fade away.
Let's plan to stay in touch, regardless of the roles
That separations create with our future goals.
Don't let separations change the way we're meant to be
Together as companions, friends for eternity. [3]

I hope you didn't laugh too loud. I really, really hope you
didn't laugh. I guess I am blushing, so I will stop for now.
Please write soon and let me know what you thought about
the words. I am still a novice, but maybe one day I can put the
words and music together and be someone to make you proud.
With love to my special friend,
Ricky

I finished the letter and put it in an envelope, addressed it, put a stamp in the corner, and laid it on my dresser so mom could mail it in the morning. I changed into my pajamas and crawled into bed hoping I would have sweet dreams about Millie. I hoped that maybe, just maybe she was dreaming about me.

∾

The next morning Tammy was in the kitchen as usual as I came downstairs with my bag prepared to check out and to drive back home. I hated to leave, but I knew I couldn't stay any longer. Thursday morning had come so quickly, and I had no choice but to get back to Nashville. Tammy greeted me with a friendly smile and told me I looked like a man with a mission. The table by the window had a steaming cup of coffee already sitting on it, one cube of sugar and a touch of cream added. I was fascinated by how she remembered and it touched me deeply. I couldn't help but think of Millie and how she, too, always had that cup of coffee ready for me when we were together. God, I miss her.

Sara and Marty were busy as two bees serving up the prepared

---

[3] Written by Donald Arlo Jennings, March 2013.

breakfast, and I could smell the various dishes, bacon, eggs, grits, breakfast potatoes, and of course there were other items including various fruits, rolls, pastries, and cereals. If Tammy ever decided to close the bed and breakfast she could open a great breakfast restaurant. I am certain if she asked me, I would become an active investor. However, that was not my intentions, nor was it my intentions to become involved with anyone so close to the time after losing Millie.

Several of the new people recognized me, staring somewhat in my direction until one lady came over and asked me if I was Ricky Snyder. Of course I had to admit it and I thought she was going to faint right there in the dining room, but she motioned to her husband and the other couple and said that this is really the singer Ricky Snyder. After some small talk and how much they loved my songs, I scribbled my autograph for them and they again expressed appreciation for my songs and thanked me.

After watching this eventful interchange, Tammy came and sat down at my table and just looked at me. She said that must be a normal things for me and that she really enjoyed the time I spent here at her bed and breakfast and she not only appreciated the time I spent having dinners with her, but she thoroughly enjoyed the fellowship and friendship. She wanted to know when I would be back, if ever. I had no way to explain when I might return, not knowing what my ever-changing schedule might be. However, I did say we should keep in touch or at least write occasionally about changes in our lives. I asked her to tell her son and daughter-in-law "hello" for me and that I would like to meet them one day.

After breakfast, some last minute good-byes, but not permanent good-byes, Tammy and I touched-hugged and once again bid each other "thank you" before I got in my car and drove away, heading home for a quick stop before hitting the road for several days of gigs. Life changes, but life moves on. I just knew how different my life would be without Millie. I just wasn't prepared for the changes.

∞

I awoke the following morning after dreaming of Millie and what she would think about the words to the song I wrote for her. I think I embarrassed myself knowing when she read the letter and the words to the song she would think I was just an infatuated horny teenage boy. I noticed for the first time in many days that I did not have my usual morning problem, probably from worrying Millie would think badly of me. Regardless, I had to get ready for school. The letter was still on my dresser and I had some last minute doubts as to whether I should have Mom mail it, but after showering and getting dressed, I left the letter there and went down to grab a bite of breakfast before heading to school. I kissed Mom on the cheek, Dad was already gone. I told Mom the letter was on my dresser and asked her to mail it, still with doubts.

The school day passed uneventfully, and over the next several days I waited patiently for the arrival of a response from Millie, but nothing came. I was almost concerned she was thinking I was crazy and did not like the song, but there was nothing I could do but wait. I resigned myself to my studies since the school year was a month away before summer vacation began. Mom and Dad told me I should start looking around for what I would be doing during the summer months, that maybe I should check with the local diner about waiting on tables to earn some spending money and start saving a nest egg for college. Dad made it perfectly clear to me that I needed to continue my research for scholarships if I still intended to go to Juilliard. What pressure for a teenage boy, but I knew they were both right in what they were telling me.

It was probably at least two weeks before I heard from Millie, and to my surprise it was not a letter but a phone call. I almost wet my pants when Mom told me Millie was on the phone. She was excited and immediately started singing the words to the song I sent to her. I had tears in my eyes, mostly because she sang the words so sweetly, but hearing them helped me remember just how meaningful they were for me, and I hoped also for Millie. She just sang so beautifully and my heart sank to my feet. She told me how thoughtful I was and that the song was so wonderful. She had been working overtime, both at the café and for the social worker that with those jobs and with homework, with the end of classes approaching, time had been scarce for any personal time. She apologized for taking so long, and told me she knew it would mean more to me to have her call than to write a letter, and besides that she actually did want to sing the words to me. I was crying, and so proud, both for me and for Millie. I guess I was speechless for the first time in my teenage years. Millie laughed and I could tell she must have been crying also. She told me how much she missed me and that she did plan to come home during the summer for at least a week. I told her I might be working because I had to save some money for Juilliard. I had not received any additional correspondence from them and I was getting concerned regarding whether or not inquires into getting a scholarship were possible.

Millie and I talked for a few more minutes, but I know she was paying for the call and long distance calls were expensive. After we hung up I wondered what Millie would be doing. I know what I would be doing. I spoke to Mom and Dad about going to the café to apply for a job, maybe as a waiter, but I didn't know much about doing that and told them I probably would dump the food on the table or the floor while carrying it to the people. They just laughed and Dad told me that I might dump the food on the customers. He said that maybe I should apply for a busboy or dishwasher position. I frowned at him and he just continued to laugh.

He told me that he was a waiter in his teenage years and had several accidents with both food and drinks. I asked if one of them would take me to the café. At seventeen, I had my driver's license, but we only had one car. I never asked to use it unless I knew neither Mom nor Dad was planning on going somewhere. However, Dad tossed me the key and told me to be careful. I assured him I was a responsible driver, saying it with such intent that I was an adult now. His silence said it all. Parents never trust teenage boys' driving abilities.

I looked in the rear-view mirror as I drove away from the B&B and saw Tammy standing on the porch. If I didn't have other commitments, I might have turned the car around, but I knew that was not possible and I could not get involved in a relationship with anyone, but it was good to know I had created a friendship I could count on if and when I returned. I put in a CD of one of my favorite albums and drove on toward home. I feared the loneliness once I got there and I feared more the emptiness of going on gigs not being able to talk to Millie each night after the performances. It was necessary for me to adjust to the fact for the first time in my life the complete separation from Millie was inevitable, but I knew she was in a far, far better place and not suffering the pain she had to endure for several years.

As I approached the main highway, I noticed the sign indicating "You are leaving Townsend." While not a long drive to the big city, I knew I had several hours in the car and probably another twenty minutes once I reached Nashville before I arrived home, assuming traffic was tolerable. It always seemed strange to me that Mom and Dad really never traveled much and I really don't think we were in Nashville more than a couple of times while I was growing up. But I was aware of all the activities, and thought I would like to live there, never thinking about Millie going to college there or realizing it was closer than I imagined. I also never thought when I graduated from Juilliard I would end up in Nashville.

Home just seemed so distant from everything, but that is the reality of growing up in a small mountain town. Occasionally Dad took Mom and me into the closest larger town where shopping was better, but we had to drive even farther for any big shopping mall or a major hardware store. Our doctor appointments were always with the community family practice and we only had a small clinic for emergencies. It was a long drive to the nearest hospital. Not much had changed regarding that, but I know going back to see Tammy is on my future agenda, not for a romantic encounter, but as old acquaintances and new friends. I knew in my heart Millie would be okay with this friendship.

I arrived home but it did take longer than I expected because of the time of day and the busy traffic, but it was great to see the sites of the city. Part of my delay was that I decided to take a detour and stop by the cemetery to visit Millie's grave and to talk to her a few minutes. I knew she would be listening from Heaven and probably wanted me to get on with my life. After getting to the house, it seemed so void and empty, dark and did not shine with the brilliance of Millie being there. I checked phone messages and had several, several from my agent and one from Pastor Thomas asking me to call when I got home. I knew my agent would be busy anyway, so I decided to call the Pastor after I unpacked and found a bite to eat. I knew he only wanted to make certain that I was okay and what my immediate plans were. I did not know what my personal plans were, but I knew I would be on the road with the troops very soon.

∾

I told Mom and Dad I would be careful with the car and would only be gone as long as to fill out an application at the café hoping I could get some type job. After all, in such a small town there were not a lot of tourists but mostly just locals who gathered in the café more for gossip and fellowship than anything else, other than the very good food. It was always busy there and the people tipped good considering the salary was minimum wage at best. I was there in ten minutes and applied to the owners, a couple who bought the café several years back. Having gotten there as early as I did, no one else had applied, well there weren't than many teenagers in town to apply. I got the job I think mainly because in discussing my reasons, I told them about my plans for Juilliard. I also told them that I would be able to work weekends for breakfast and lunch until the end of the school year, and then I could work breakfast five days or six if I wanted to and could work lunch Thursday through Saturday. The café was closed on Sundays and dinner was not heavily attended because people wanted to be home with their families. I knew I couldn't expect a lot of pay, but anything was far better than I was getting at the time.

I drove back home and told Mom and Dad. They were pleased, but insisted the job could not interfere or replace my required piano practice or my chores at home. Dad told me I was beginning to understand adult ways, but I still had a lot of growing up to do. I just frowned and went to my room.

COMPANIONS
Finishing

The rest of the school year passed quickly and I started enjoying my weekend job at the café. It was good to have some money in my pockets. Because my family had only one car and dad needed it to get to work I rode my bike back and forth to work each day rain or shine I was there and the owners liked me and saw how much attention to detail I had, learning the "ropes" quickly as well as how I interacted with the customers. While this was a new experience for me, it was a great opportunity to get to know people, both from my home town and the tourists who passed through. I was also able to start a savings account at the bank, but not with a lot of money because I received a very small salary and I was mainly dependent upon tips gained from being very attentive and customer friendly. I realized I would never get rich doing this type work.

As promised Millie did come home the week of July Fourth and it was like a homecoming for both of us. I did not see her the first two days she was at home since the Fourth fell on a Friday and I had to work that day as well as the following Saturday, but on Sunday I only had to work breakfast and would be off the rest of the day. Millie called me and told me she would like to see me after church and when I got off from work at the cafe. I could hardly wait and probably did not pay as much attention to my duties as I should, but then I was preoccupied and my thoughts were elsewhere. But I did not neglect my duties to the customers for fear I would not be tipped well.

Traffic for breakfast slowed around ten o'clock, and wasn't too busy because many of the regulars were in church and would be in for lunch.

I left around noon having started at six that morning, went home and decided to take another shower and change my jeans and shirt to some shorts and a long t-shirt. Mom and Dad were still at church and would probably stop by the café or another place for lunch. They figured that with me being seventeen that I could surely find something to eat either at the café or at home. I fixed a tomato and mayonnaise sandwich and had a Coke before I showered and changed. I was so anxious to see Millie I spent extra time grooming myself, combing my hair, brushing my teeth, and making sure certain other attributes were well attended and trimmed since I began experiencing a lot of growth. It was hard to imagine me at seventeen and Millie almost twenty-two, me a rising high school senior and Millie a college senior. Somehow my Mom and Dad still thought of us as just friends who grew up together and thought more of Millie as my baby-sitter and piano teacher. I thought of us as more than just friends and acquaintances, and I hoped Millie thought the same about me.

I was expecting a phone call from Millie, but when I heard the knock on the door, I must have run to answer it knowing it had to be her since Mom and Dad would not have knocked and no one else was expected. I looked fresh and because of my growth spurt, I looked more of a grown-up young man than I had since the last time Millie and I were together. I was shaving my facial beard regularly, but still showed a very light shadow, hopefully it made me look manlier and older. When I opened the door, my jaw dropped to my feet. Millie was gorgeous, dressed in one of those skirts that were also a type of shorts and a t-shirt that had Nashville across the front. Her hair was flowing free and she had on a white visor and sunglasses that just set off her beautiful face. Since I hadn't said a word yet, she looked at me and said, "Well, are you going to invite me in or just stare?"

"You are so beautiful…well; you always were, but wow, you look like a movie star." I stuttered and then hugged her neck and she lightly kissed me on the cheek. "Come in. By all means, come in."

"Ricky, my how you have grown up and are one handsome dude, still a bit skinny, but you look great. I bet you are chased by lots of girls now. Maybe one of those waitresses is hitting on you. By the way, how is the job?"

"Fine, but being a café server is not a very good income source. It does provide for some spending money and I have been saving most of my earnings toward college, hopefully Juilliard. I think if I can continue to work weekends during my senior year and then next summer full time, I will have at least a nest egg for my first year. I am still working on trying to get a full scholarship. Dad said I have a very good chance of getting into Juilliard, but it is expensive and I have to help as much as possible. A scholarship would be a blessing."

"You will get it. When will your mom and dad be home?"

"Who knows? They probably connected with some Sunday school members and went to lunch. I expect they should be home around two, maybe. Why?"

"Do you have to be here when they get back?"

"No."

"Okay, let's go to the park and see what is happening there. You look nice. I like your shorts. You look cute in them, ha ha."

"Why did you laugh?"

"Well, I was just being funny and wondering what you might look like without them now. I remember when I bathed you as a little boy, but you are so grown up and since that time, well, things might have gotten better. Well, I mean better in a good way, not that there were every any problems. I better shut up. I think I am getting too bold."

"Gee, don't make me blush. You are going to get me all hot and excited before we even get to the park."

I probably blushed from the top of my head to the tip of my toes as she put her hand on my face and rubbed the top of my upper lip. I still had a tinge of a mustache even with shaving this morning, but I wasn't letting it grow. She gently kissed me on each eye and lightly on the lips. I sprang to attention hoping it wasn't obvious with the long shirt, but I think she was aware of my mental and physical state. I still could not get over how beautiful she was and how much I admired and loved her. I knew finishing high school and going off to college would mean less time to see her, me being in New York and her probably living in Nashville. I just wished and prayed she would not find someone, some guy she would fall madly in love with and forget me. Millie probably could have any guy she wanted, but I knew one thing for certain, that chosen guy better be a good person and have a strong religious upbringing.

Millie said, "Have you written any more songs? I hope you are still playing the piano and practicing every day. I loved *Separations.* The words still resound in my head. How did you ever come up with the words?"

I blushed again and said, "It is easy to find words when they have meaning for something and someone you care about. I think of you and…." She put a finger to my lips, took my hand and said let's go to the park.

My call to Pastor Thomas was interesting at best. He definitely wanted to know how I was getting along and how my visit back home went. I struggled to tell him about Tammy. I decided to let him know I ran into one of Millie's and my old friends. After all it was strictly platonic and nothing more. He was inquisitive about what I did, from a state-of-mind concern he said, and wanted to know my plans going forward. I really think he was thinking I started an intimate relationship. I did not and could not elaborate to him any more regarding the visit. I did mention to him, changing the subject that I would be leaving in two days for scheduled events that would keep me busy and my mind occupied. I knew most of that was true, but without being able to talk to Millie every night would make it not only difficult for me, but would surely cause some depression. "Pastor Thomas, I will be fine. Don't worry about me. I sincerely appreciate your concern and your prayers. When I get back we will sit down and talk."

"Ricky, you are one stubborn man, but I care for you. Many people here care for you. Please be careful and know that there are many people praying for you every day. If you need to talk anytime while you are gone, please call me, day or night. I will be here for you. God's blessings to you. Remember Millie is watching over you."

After the pastor left, I tried calling my agent, but only got his secretary or voice mail, leaving messages for him to call me. I know he is more concerned about whether I am still writing hits that can make the top ten charts, but he will just have to understand I am doing the best I can given my current situation. Next I called my manager, Tom Reed, and instructed him to get the troops organized and the buses ready so we can leave early morning as we had planned and scheduled. We were heading to Branson, Missouri for three days of shows, with me and my troops being the main attraction.

I do not carry a full piano with me, but keep several electronic keyboards on the bus. There were times I used them and other times when I used the pianos at the theatres. The others usually transported their instruments on the bus or sometimes a limited number of instruments in our manager's van if he elected to follow us for the shows. Sometimes he was staying back to schedule more events and verify arrangements for the next leg of any tour. It takes a lot to put a show together, but much of the routine is repetitive. I will occasionally add a new song I have written, but I found many of the fans still enjoy the earlier ones, and enjoy my renditions of songs recorded by other entertainers.

After making those calls and getting things underway for the trip, finally, I decided to call Tammy.

I closed the door with Millie still holding my hand. We talked about a lot of things as we walked, just chattering like a couple of school kids. We passed a few of my friends from high school and they stared, I am certain, because of Millie being so beautiful. Who wouldn't stare? I was proud of being with not only a beautiful girl but a college girl. Some of my friends knew about Millie and me, not as a couple, but as good friends. I just didn't want it to be only that. I wanted more, and I knew it might happen one day.

When we got to the park it was fairly empty of people. We saw a couple of teenagers, boy and girl maybe fourteen or fifteen years old, obviously necking on one of the benches near the pond. Millie put her arm around my waist and pulled me closer to her and said, "Aren't they cute?" She then easily blew in my ear and ran her tongue across my cheek. At seventeen this was cool to me. This time I was actually hoping someone saw us.

I put my arm around her and we strolled along, still holding hands, but she was careful not to draw attention to us when we passed the young couple sitting on the bench. We found our own bench and sat very close to each other. Millie asked me tell her all about everything I wanted to do after high school and Juilliard. She wanted to know if I thought of my music career as being part of an orchestra, or if I would probably be on the circuit playing classical piano, maybe publishing records. I told her,

"Millie, I am just seventeen. I want to be everything I can be, but at this time my desire really is to be a songwriter and singer. I don't know how things will turn out, but time will tell. I know my thoughts and way of thinking might get changed after attending Juilliard, but I just don't know right now."

I asked Millie what she was going to do after graduating college. She told me that first she would be spending another year at the college to finish up accreditation for her special education teaching certificate. She told me she wanted to work with young people, maybe in some teaching capacity since she would be qualified to be an elementary or special education school teacher. She said she would probably stay in Nashville because there were more opportunities there than in the Townsend area. She liked Nashville because there was so much to do. She told me she thought Juilliard was so far away, but she understood my desires. She said we could continue to write each other and when possible to get together one place or another. This was actually "music" to my ears.

Millie hugged me and kissed me on the lips. We kissed a long time, somewhat of a passionate kiss this time, but I was surprised she did not go farther. I think the other couple being so close would have made any intimacy obvious. I don't know if she was aware of my physical condition, and if she did, she did not go there. I was ready to burst, but knowing I was ready probably was more teasing from her than anything else. I made no move to go farther with her. I think since both of us, well more her, were adults now, pushing farther would have led to something we probably would have enjoyed but would have regretted later. She was careful since I was still under age. Our time by the pond just flew by.

My call to Tammy was good. She seemed excited to hear from me and once again I thanked her for her hospitality. We chatted about the dinners we had shared, how good the wine was, and how many couples were staying at her bed and breakfast. She told me she had one couple who had just gotten married and were on their way to Nashville but wanted to see some of the sites in the area. She said they were coming from Douglas, Michigan, a long way from our little town, but Douglas is not a huge town either.

Tammy wanted to know what my plans were and I told her I was getting ready for a tour in several cities with an initial three-day weekend show in Branson, Missouri. She said she had never been there, but heard there are lots of theatres and musical shows every day. I mentioned the talent there comes from everywhere. Not only the musical talent, but there are other type shows and events. This would be my fifth show there and would be competing for audiences against some top pop stars. As always, I told Tammy, it is the people's choice which shows they attend based on their preferences for music and the celebrity. She told me I would probably sing to sold-out crowds.

Our call was probably no more than fifteen or twenty minutes, but it was very enjoyable and fun to speak with her again. I told her I hoped to be back through the home town one day in the future and if she was still in the bed and breakfast business and had a room available that it would be nice to visit again. She told me the welcome sign was always out, and when I let her know that I will be through that she would reserve a room for me.

After the call with Tammy I called my troop manager again to ensure we were booked in the Grand Palace Theatre and that I would need a piano. Also, I asked him to be sure our room reservations were in order at the Grand View Inn and Suites. We always stayed there when we did a show in Branson primarily because of the convenience and being able to park the buses with no problems. As usual, Tom was on top of things, but he never got annoyed at my questioning about the plans. I felt better for two reasons, one Tammy was pleased that I called and two, Tom had everything under control. I knew I could sleep better tonight.

It seemed the day to leave came sooner than I expected, but there was a lot to do. Getting all my gear ready to go, appropriate clothes packed, well actually most of the show outfits had been cleaned and were in hanging bags, and waiting for Tom coming with the driver to bring the main bus to the house to pick me up. We usually met the entire troop at the storage warehouse where the buses, van, and equipment were housed when we were not on the road. The buses were very nice, fully equipped with dressing rooms, bathrooms, sleeping quarters, sitting areas, and tons of space for minor equipment, food and drinks. It took two buses because of the band and singers traveling with me, but my immediate key members rode on my bus and the singers and the newer members rode on the second bus. Other equipment was transported in one of the vans. Tom usually always stayed on my bus when he was with us so we could continue planning to ensure ever item was in order. He did check with the other bus via cell phone and when we stopped, he always checked both the other bus and the van. The big van followed us with some of the lighting equipment, computers, synthesizers, special microphones mouth pieces, and other things.

We always carried CDs and autographed pictures, T-shirts, buttons, pens, and other items engraved with "Ricky Snyder" on them to sell. Normally, most items across the three-day show event, two shows daily, would be purchased. Tom always had additional items available in the van or on the main bus for the next show, or would have them shipped to the next theatre if we were running low. There was always more at the storage center and our attendant there would take care of getting more of whatever we needed to use. It took a lot of preparation and organization to put a three-hour show on and repeat it daily, then move to the next city and repeat the event.

The buses were something to see and brought attention to the fact some celebrity was on board. They were white with a beautiful black piano painted on the side and in huge blue letter stating "The Ricky Snyder Show." There was no picture of me, thankfully, but there were smaller pictures of guitars and musical notes painted on the sides and back. Across the front of the bus in the same bold blue letter printed in reverse was "*redynS ykciR*" so that people could read it in their rear view mirrors. There was just enough to get the point across that these were show troop buses.

Anyway, getting the buses, the van, all the troops, and equipment loaded was a task and making the eight to ten hour trip from Nashville to Branson, depending on traffic, would be both fun and hectic. This was the case every time we started out, and got noisier as the tour continued. However, after about five cities and a month on the road, the troops got anxious and ready to be back home with families, see their kids, and have some home cooked food. Actually I had the same feelings, but as it is said, "the show must go on." Turnover of members of the band was minimal, so many of us had been together for years. This made it more like a family traveling than a bunch of strangers. I did try to treat my troops as well as I could, and I think they enjoyed being part of my team.

∾

Millie and I sat on the bench for maybe forty-five minutes sharing stories and dreams, but it seemed longer in one way and so short in another. I could never spend enough time with Millie and I knew that our times together would be getting fewer as I completed my last year of high school and she completed her last years of college. I also knew that if I went to Juilliard, it being so far away, that Millie and I could only write one another and call when it was possible. She would be working in the real world while I sweated over getting a college education. Life isn't always fair when there is an age difference and many miles between two people.

I asked Millie if she thought she would find someone when she started working, fall in love, and get married while I was in college. She looked at me and said, "Silly boy, why would that be any different than me asking you if I thought you would find the love of your life at Juilliard and get engaged, maybe even get the girl pregnant and have to marry her?" I said I needed some experience before that could happen, maybe a practice session. She just grabbed my face in her hands and kissed me on the lips and the tip of my nose. "Ricky, you are so special, and what we have is so special. Let's not ruin it by taking chances that could hurt us both in the long run, ruin our chances of finishing college, and having a small problem to handle for many years." She was right, but hormones do get in the way of rational thinking. But, I resigned myself to understanding what she meant and what an "accident" could do to our lives.

We got up from the bench and walked around the park, holding hands, and still talking about "stuff." Topics were from serious music preferences, to complete foolishness. We always had fun together and loved each other in our own special way. I never dreamed at that moment in the park we would spend a lifetime together as a couple. I just thought at that time she was older and cared for me more like a friend than a lover. But, those kisses and some special times were real, not my imagination.

Millie took my hand, "We better be heading back home. Your parents will be back by now and will think someone has kidnapped you. Now wouldn't that be horrible, if they think I kidnapped you and maybe abused you? I could get in serious trouble." I laughed and told her, "First, I would never tell, and if they thought that I would be abused by you they never would have trusted you to baby-sit me years ago." Millie just laughed and ruffled my hair. I shook my head and grabbed her around the waist, pointed and said, "Home."

∾

When the bus arrived at my house, really a simple place compared to the show places of many Nashville stars. Millie did not want an "opulent abode" as she put it because of her teaching career and her church activities. Our house was very nice, and yes big, but not a Nashville mansion. It was gated with a nice circular drive big enough for the bus to make it with no problems. Tom got out of the bus and helped me load my clothes, hanging them up in the closets on the bus. I kept a special keyboard at home that I always took with me, so we loaded that up as well.

Tom pointed out that things really had changed since we started out many years ago. We only had a small van for which I had traded my older car and basically Tom, two guitar players and me were the show. Now, there were close to fifty people making up the show, singers, band members, technical staff, set up staff, and others. But, that was part of being successful, part of being Ricky Snyder.

With everything loaded, we settled in and the driver headed to the storage facility to meet the others and get this convoy on the road to Branson. I always have some repudiation regarding the layout of the stage, the sequence of songs, and mainly about the talent opening the show before we go on stage. I always feared that who was chosen, not always the same group, would not show well or perform well, giving us a disadvantage once on stage. However, Tom informed me the opening group was excellent and would be a super start to the show. The group opened for several other top stars in Branson at the theatre we were scheduled as well as other theatres in the area. This did calm my nerves somewhat, but I trusted Tom and knew things would go well.

Once at the storage facility, everyone was crowded around the areas, some of the band members even had their instruments out strumming away. Lots of chatter going on, but when Tom and I got off the bus, there were shouts from the group that they were ready to go. Everyone started shuffling about putting instruments away, getting on the buses, checking the van to ensure all the equipment was secure, and everyone seemed energized about the tour. This was always the case starting out, but tempers did show occasionally and disagreements did happen. Some of the band members would argue with the music director, and shout to me to get my opinion. This just made for one big happy sibling rivalry family of musically talented people. Even with disagreements, arguments, and hassles, everyone actually got along very well. This was probably why turnover was minimal and the group had been together so long. How could I not smile?

Once underway, the trip was long taking almost eleven hours since we ran into heavy traffic and one accident that held us up for over an hour. We always planned for such incidents. While stopped in the line of traffic, we had people coming to the buses wanting autographs or wanting us to play. We did sign some autographs but declined to put on a show on the road. It would be nice if an Interstate highway ran between Nashville and Branson, but alas we had to deal with the only good way to get there, and that could be slow going.

Arriving at Branson, getting to the motel, parking the buses and van and getting everyone checked in was very well planned, thanks to Tom. Rooms were already assigned, mostly people doubling up or even four in room, some had single rooms such as Tom, a couple of key singers, the music director, and of course me. Vic, my music director wanted to check out the theatre. Vic had been with me a long time and was instrumental in the way our music had a unique sound. I valued his input and recognized him not only as the music director, but as a close friend. There were always one or two rental cars available so Vic took one of them. We had to have a car or two or a small van to make quick trips since it was impossible to take the bus everywhere or even the large equipment van. Daren, the technical manager, decided to go with Vic, but both understood we really could not have access to set up until Thursday evening, after an afternoon performance by another group.

The troops, as usual, broke into their individual peer groups after settling in their rooms and wandered around the area, some going to restaurants while others settled for some quick sandwiches at fast food places. Bars and drinking was off limits before and during any performances. Fortunately, I had a good group who knew the ropes and I never had a situation that I had to handle with anyone being drunk or disorderly. I am certain many groups were not as fortunate. I never drank anything stronger than wine and then only with a meal. I tried to set examples and seemed to have a great following.

Thursday morning came quickly after a good night's rest, at least for most everyone. The troops scattered around for breakfast but by nine o'clock everyone was back checking equipment, preparing to get to the theatre for the initial set up, pre-show performance, ensuring all the props were set up, stage ready, and places established on stage. Vic and Daren were always like two buzzing bees and nervous, but by four o'clock our convoy was headed to the theatre. The fun begins. I checked with the box office and discovered we were playing to completely sold out performances across the three days and six shows. I guess part of that was due to the time of year, and part due to being a known celebrity.

When Millie and I got back to my house, my parents actually were not back from church and lunch. We sat on the front steps and talked some more before Millie told me she should be getting home to check on her parents. She knew that they were there since she went to church and rode back home with them. Before she left I asked when she would be back for another visit. Once again she took my hand, looked me in the eye, and almost whispered that it could be a long time. She needed to spend her last years at college focusing on her studies and making certain she would be employed after graduation. Nashville seemed to be the landing point for her because of job opportunities.

Graduation for both of us would occur in the same year now that Millie was staying at college an additional year for special education. That meant May of the following year because I had one more year of high school. Time flew by and the year just seemed to creep up so quickly. Graduation was imminent. While Millie and I would continue to write to each other about the ceremonies, it did not seem practical that one or the other of us would be at the other's ceremony. However, Millie's commencement would be in mid-May and mine was tentatively scheduled for the last week of May. I mentioned to her that she probably could be

COMPANIONS

there for mine and I would try to convince my dad to bring me to hers. Maybe if my dad couldn't take me, I could ride up with her parents. It really depended on the day of Millie's commencement. There was a possibility if they picked a week day that I would still be in school. Millie told me that she had discussed the time with her parents and the plans were that they wanted to stay for a few days to help her move from her college dorm room and to find a small efficiency apartment. Her plan after college was to maintain her server job at the café as well as continue to help with the social work she was doing. This would be enough to live on until she found permanent employment.

This discussion bothered me in many ways. I knew this meant Millie would probably not be home for the summer and if so, just a limited amount of time. I also knew if I was still working as a server at the local café that we would probably not see each other very much. But what bothered me the most was now I understood Millie would be in Nashville and I would end up in New York. After finishing at Juilliard there would be no telling where I would end up living or what job I might have to take. The life of a musician could be hectic and fraught with many months of unemployment. I did not share my thoughts with Millie, and I kept my tears from coming.

Millie kissed me lightly on the lips and squeezed my thigh. I wished we could do more, but still I understood the age difference for such a temptation. Millie was a beautiful woman now, soon to be an independent person, away from me who cared deeply for her but I did not know how to handle the age difference, the soon to be separation for us. I still had thoughts that she would find someone in Nashville and forget about me. As she walked away, I stood and in louder than a whisper told her to please write me. Her response was that goes both ways. I watched her as she headed down the street to her home before I went in the house to cry.

Before Millie left to return to college she called me and we talked for a while. She assured me she would write and made me promise to do so as well. That was not a problem for me because even if she didn't write me I was definitely going to continue writing her so she would not forget me. Our goodbyes were not permanent goodbyes but more "until next time." After we finished talking I guess I held the phone receiver for at least five minutes. I knew the call had ended but I just hated to hang up.

Millie left for Nashville and I couldn't be there to see her off since I had to work a shift at the cafe. She also had to get back to her job and make certain all was prepared for the coming school year. For me, after that day with Millie, time just flew by. My last year of high school was overly busy. I had to really study hard, communicate additional information to Juilliard, work every weekend, write letters to Millie and respond to ones she sent, even though our letter writing was not as frequent as we told each other in the letters. Millie was cramming for final exams as was I, and she was busy sending resumes to companies in Nashville in order to be fully employed by graduation time.

In November, just before Thanksgiving Day, I got home from school and Mom was standing in the kitchen, nonchalantly holding an envelope. After asking me how my day was and me responding tiredly that it was tough. She handed me the envelope saying nothing. I looked at it and noted it was from Juilliard.

"Aren't you going to open it?"

"It is probably bad news. I probably didn't get accepted. I haven't heard if I got the scholarship or not and Dad can't afford to send me if I don't have some funding."

She laughed, "Open it any way. Maybe it is good news."

Reluctantly I opened the letter, read it and jumped hugging Mom. "Mom! Not only did I get accepted to Juilliard but I got a scholarship that will pay over eighty percent of full tuition. They do state that I have to maintain a B plus average in all subjects. That means I will not have much time to do anything but study, study, study."

"Son, you can do it. Wait till your dad gets home and see what he thinks can be afforded now. You are a smart and talented kid. You will go far in life if you knuckle down and keep your nose to the grindstone."

"Mom, I can do it, will do it. I need to call Millie." She laughed as I bounded to my room, then I remembered that I better ask Mom if I can call Millie since it was long-distance. After getting the okay she said five minutes, no more, or she would hang up for me. I was so excited. I actually got Millie as she was getting ready to go to work at her server job. Working two jobs and taking a heavy course load was tough, but Millie was very smart and handled the situation well. When I told her about the scholarship and acceptance to Juilliard she was as excited as I was. She told me if she were there that she would give me a great big hug and a kiss. I asked if that was all. Her laugh was beautiful as I could see her smiling. Mom knocked on my door and told me my five minutes were up. Millie and I said goodbye and that we would write and tell each other more details. I think I was on my highest peak of excitement.

When Dad got home I rushed to tell him about the letter, the scholarship, and acceptance to Juilliard. He took the letter and read it, and then he actually grabbed me and picked me up. This was something he hadn't done in years. He swung me around and kissed the top of my forehead. "Son, I am so, so proud of you. Very much proud of you. I knew all along you could do this, get accepted and get a scholarship. Even though it only pays eighty percent, the letter indicates you are on probation for the first semester. After that time, if your grades are above average, better than a B plus, the scholarship can be extended to the full tuition amount. You know what that means don't you?"

"Dad, you know me. I will pour everything I have into making my grades the best I can. I have saved most of what I earned working at the café, so I can handle most of the incidental things and will live like a monk if necessary."

"I don't think you have to do that son. Your mom and I have been saving for several years for your college education. While it would not cover the full cost of Juilliard there is enough to cover the balance of the tuition and other requirements, as you call them "incidentals" to keep you out of poverty. We are not rich, but your mom and I do know how to plan."

I hugged them both and kissed Mom on the cheek. Dad just kept his arms around me for a few minutes and I wanted to cry, but at almost eighteen, I wanted to feel like a grown up, not a baby. I was so happy I just didn't know what to say. Mom broke the silence by looking at us and started walking toward the kitchen. "I have to finish fixing dinner. You two can get ready in about twenty minutes. By the way, this is going to be a celebration, Ricky I am fixing your favorite meal."

I went to my room and decided to write Millie a short letter even though we had talked on the phone. I just wished she were here so we could celebrate together, but I knew that was not possible. I also wanted to write something, maybe another song or poem, but I just couldn't find the words at the moment because of my excitement. I had homework to do so

I quickly wrote a brief note to Millie before Mom called from the kitchen and said that dinner was ready. After dinner I focused on my homework and dreamed of going to Juilliard. I also dreamed of Millie and was excited about both college and seeing Millie again.

Setting up the stage area and going through a dry run of the show was a full Thursday evening in preparing for the three-day weekend and six shows. Not having access to the theatre until four o'clock meant we would be there probably past midnight. We also had Friday morning until one o'clock to put the finishing touches on the sound system, lighting, props, and getting everyone placed. While this was a normal routine, having done this hundreds of times over the past years, it still was hectic since every theatre had it own idiosyncrasies. The manager of each theatre always specifies what can be added or changed on the stage. For this particular theatre, no real flames were permitted, but of course that was not a part of our show. No problem there.

At the theatre, unloading the van, getting equipment from the buses, getting the troops to quieten down and pay attention to the music and equipment directors always was a challenge, but eventually everyone settles down and begins to unwind, become serious, and in place. The music fills the hall and practice begins. The introductory group goes on first for thirty minutes before I make an entrance. This time, for the first time, I was a bit shaken knowing that Millie would be watching from above. I planned to dedicate the show to her memory.

Tom and I made a couple of changes in the program for this particular performance. Vic had to make some adjustments with the band to accommodate the changes, and Daren moved equipment around. The initial backdrop, a huge screen to show scenes almost covered the back wall of the stage. This would be showing some special scenes we had developed for several of the songs, especially the opening song. Other scenes always included shots of the area in which we were doing the show, shots of other performances, and some of the band members doing silly things. Also, there were huge monitors on either side of the stage that provided close-ups of the performance for individuals seated farther back in the theatre.

We also had vapor that covered the floor of the stage and that always flowed over the edge of the stage to a couple of the front row seats where people were sitting who may or may not have enjoyed the effect. We did not use the lower band box, but kept everyone on stage. The sound system, coupled with ours, really resonated throughout the entire theatre with no one not being able to hear the music. In fact the sound could be deafening at times. Tom and Vic prepared the lobby for potential sales. This was always good because many of the purchases were before the show. While many people made purchases during intermission, not as many sales were made after the end of the show. We had to focus on getting people to buy CDs, pictures, shirts, jackets, and other memorabilia in competition with food and drinks. Kids always preferred to have candy and soft drinks over our memorabilia.

Thursday evening did run long. We left the theatre around one o'clock Friday morning with plans to be back by ten. That gave most members at least eight hours of sleep, but many would hang out longer and only get four or five hours of sleep. I returned to my room and zonked out after a warm shower. Normally I would call Millie, but that was not possible. I settled in by turning on the TV, not knowing what I was watching, but it did not matter. This was just a sleeping pill for me.

I awoke around seven, again took a nice shower, shaved and dressed in jeans and a "Ricky Snyder" t-shirt, my UGGs, no socks, and headed out to grab some breakfast. Tom, Vic, and Daren were already at a table and had ordered, so I joined them. My show outfits were already in my dressing room at the theatre, so I could at least be comfortable for a few hours before the first show. With all shows being sold out, I had to change several times so having numerous "costumes" was an essential requirement. The four of us discussed some of the changes we made to the performances and Tom thought they were all good and would be improvements for the songs, especially the opening song.

Vic and Daren were elated that everything seemed to be coming together, but the real test was the first performance. We all knew that after the first performance we had to tweak things. This also gave a sense of variety to the shows. The lighting might have to be adjusted, the sound increased or decreased, props moved, and especially placement and movement of the troops. We might even change the placement of songs based on the age of the audiences. Choreography is essential to keep the audience focused on particular areas of the stage, the main singers, and of course me. I did have a tendency to move around on the stage a great deal of the time. I always had a difficult time standing in one place and moving kept me more engaged.

Everyone arrived at the theatre at different times, but everyone was there by ten. We practiced again, not full songs, just what was needed to ensure the props were appropriately aligned with the songs, made sure the opening group was prepared, and everyone understood when to change clothes and be on stage. We had food brought in giving us some nourishment before the first performance and of course snacks at intermission. There was always plenty of water and Gatorade on stage and in the dressing areas. Performers can quickly become dehydrated on stage under the intense lights and heavy sweating. The sweating was another reason to have multiple changes of outfits. Many of mine were the same type to keep continuity while I did change outfits to accompany particular songs. Changing outfits was a chore within itself since very little time was available. Just run back stage, change quickly and run back on stage. Everyone just had to be prepared for this fast-paced life.

COMPANIONS
Intentions

There is no way to describe the events of my final year of high school. I did put my nose to the grindstone and buckled down to make sure my grades were the very best I could do. I made high scores in every subject and knew I would be an honor student at graduation. I continued to work weekends at the café and made very good tips. I saved every penny I could to make certain I could help with the Juilliard expenses. I wrote Millie at least every two weeks and she did the same. She mentioned in one of her letters she had been offered a good teaching position starting in the fall after graduation. She hinted to me she was at the top of her class, but failed to tell me she was graduating summa cum laude. I only found that out when the commencement took place.

Dad could take me to Millie's commencement but Mom was feeling poorly and did not think she could make the trip. After all, Nashville wasn't that far away and we did not have to spend the night. Dad and I took turns driving, he finally admitted I was a good driver, and the trip there was fun. Seeing Millie, even though it was just for a few minutes was exciting. Her parents were going to help her pack the things she had at college, help her find a small apartment, and get things moved in; and then she was coming home for at least a couple of weeks before going back. She was still doing the server job and needed the money since she would not receive a pay check from teaching until mid-August or later.

I knew I had to be prepared to get my act together by the first of August and the beginning of the first semester at Juilliard. I wanted to make certain I could find some type job, server, or something in New

York. I had to be certain I could balance any job with my college workload and my class schedule. I knew there would be competition for any jobs available. I really needed to find something close to the school because I would be walking back and forth. Even having a bicycle would be difficult to handle and have no place to keep it safe. I still needed to make certain my housing arrangements were finalized, and learn about my roommate. After Millie's graduation, mine came next and was still on course for the end of May unless we ended up with more snow days.

Show time. I always loved and hated the two hours before a performance. Emotions ran high and there were always last minute changes because of misplaced costumes, broken strings on guitars, and someone always being last arriving for the opening group. But, somehow everything would come together. Several members inevitably had to get water, go to the restroom; others would leave the back stage area and walk out to the front just to see how the house was filling. And without a doubt, some needed that last minute smoke break. We knew every performance was sold out and that we would be playing to a full house. This was always good, both from being recognized as a major talent and for financial reasons as well.

As can be expected after the opening group performed for thirty minutes and the house filled up to capacity, some tour buses were late, so the opening group's performance provided that buffer to ensure everyone was there before the main performance, that being my group. With the lights dimmed, my band completed getting on stage, music started, the back drop changed to scenes from the surrounding area, some wording flashing indicating certain groups were in attendance, then the introduction from Tom as he bounded onto the stage.

"Hey, wasn't that opening great? Let's give a big hand to Bobby Angel and Mary Tanner and to the Branson Singers." Waiting for the applause to stop, Tom continued, "Welcome to Branson and to the Grand Palace Theatre. How many have been to Branson before?" Many raised their hands and some shouted the number of times. "How many have been to the Grand Place before?" Again many raised their hands. "For how many of you is this your first time here?" Again there were many who raised their hands. "How many of you have been to a Ricky Snyder performance?" Some raised their hands, and some shouted and clapped. "Wow, this is a great crowd. You are in for a super show this afternoon. But before we begin I want to recognize some groups who are here, some coming great distances. Let's see where you are when I call your group name. First, from Newport News, Virginia and a Baptist Church we have the Senior Sunday School Class." The group raised their hands and shouted, but not really loud. Probably thirty people, mostly older women.

"Thank you, welcome and thanks for coming such a long way. Next we have a group from Atlanta, another Baptist Church group." This was a large group, probably sixty middle-age individuals. They stood and shouted and clapped. "Okay, wow! Now that is a large group. Thank you for being here today." Tom went on to recognize several more groups and then made a special announcement. "For those of you who follow Ricky Snyder in the news or on social media, you may have heard that he just recently lost his beautiful and loving wife to lung cancer. This show is dedicated to her and if anyone wishes to make a contribution to cancer research there is a special booth in the lobby. While Ricky is still recovering from his loss, I promise you will receive a great show. Let's welcome Ricky and the troops to the stage. Everyone, RICKY SNYDER!"

The band started playing and the back screen begin to show a bar with a man seated on a barstool, no sound from the scene, but vapor started flowing across the stage and dropping off toward the front row seats. Tom stepped back up introducing Ricky and the first song. "Ladies and gentlemen the first big song that is still a hit today, staying for fourteen consecutive weeks as the number one song on the country charts, again I give you Ricky Snyder!"

The crowd jumped to their feet as the first couple of bars of music from the band started and Ricky came out on stage singing as the audience recognized his first hit song "Shirley." His baritone voice rang out loud as the music resonated and the large screen displayed images associated with the song.

> "This barroom's filled with smoke, Shirley,
> The dim lights make me think;"

This song had words that many could relate to, but mostly the success was because Ricky had composed the music. It was his first major hit that brought him fame as a great country composer and singer. The crowd was screaming, on their feet, clapping younger women and girls almost standing on their seats as Ricky continued walking to center stage toward the piano. Sitting down on the bench, he began playing and continued singing.

The only thing that I can say, is
Bartender, bring a drink.
    Bartender, bring a drink.
The music's playing soft, Shirley,
It fits me through and through;
But all I do is sit and drink
Upon this old bar stool.
    Upon this old bar stool.
From one bar to another,
A different one each night,
And Shirley you're to blame for this,
For ruining all my life.
    For ruining all my life.
Maybe money means a lot,
But if that is all you want,
Maybe I should warn you Shirley,
I ought to, but I don't.
Now let me get this straight, Shirley,
You want nothing that I've got;
    You want his love much more than mine,
Is he something that I'm not?
Is he something that I'm not?
I guess it doesn't matter now
Just what I say and do,
So bartender one more drink
Before I leave this stool.
    Before I leave this stool.
Oh, Shirley, I still love you,
You know that I think,

For when you left you broke my heart
And drove me to the drink.
And now this barroom's empty,
I sit here all alone,
A beer in hand, a tear in eye
Afraid to go home.
Success was once well in hand.
But now I'm near skid row,
Afraid to live, afraid to die
And just nowhere to go.
　　And just nowhere to go.
And now the smoke is clearing, Shirley,
Since everyone has gone;
I beg the bartender, please
One more drink, one more song.
Shirley, I'm afraid to go.
I wish you were back with me;
I can't stay here, the bar is closed
And home's not heavenly.
So, Shirley, that is all I can say,
I'll never make it, so
You're with him and I'm alone
With just no place to go.
(slight pause, slower)
The music's stopped, (pause) the words
No longer whisper in my ear,
The street is dark, the air is cold,
Bartender, one more beer.
　　Bartender, one more beer. [4]

The entire audience was on their feet, the applause and shouting were almost deafening. It was hard to get the noise quieted down. Ricky took a small bow and turned and pointed to the band members for recognition.

[4] Written by Donald Arlo Jennings sometime in 1966. True story of a friend, and the friend died a broken man after his wife Shirley left him for another man.

"Thank you! Thank you! You are a wonderful group. It is so great to be back in Branson at the Grand Palace. This song has such special meaning to me especially as a young and striving, sometimes starving, country artist. In those early days, I wasn't sure if I was headed for success or total failure. Thank you! Thank you!"

As the performance continued, Ricky sang more of his compositions, those of other artists, and as always added a few old hymns.

The end of May seemed to drag on forever. I was pleased when the honor students were named and I was named as the Valedictorian. I had a combined average of ninety-seven point six putting me two points ahead of the Salutatorian, Alice James. Alice was a very unhappy person being number two, but not only did I have a harder curriculum than she did, I had applied myself in every subject because I needed to have the grades to ensure getting a scholarship and maintaining my acceptance by Juilliard. Alice was popular, a cheerleader, queen of fall festival, and also in the honor society with me. She was the President of the honor society, very vocal in her "position in society" and basically, from my point of view, almost a snob. Being second was a major blow to her ego. I had to tell Millie as soon as possible.

I was going to write Millie about being the Valedictorian and about Alice and her bad attitude, but the phone rang and Mom told me Millie was on the line. Wow, was I ever excited. Millie told me she was employed, was enjoying both her job and her small apartment, and figured she could afford to call me, but we had to be brief to cut her long-distance phone expenses. I rushed through telling her about being top of the class, about Alice, and that I was still working at the café. She told me she would be starting her teaching job the first of August, but had to be at the school for several meetings during July. She was going to be teaching first graders and would have an assistant for the first few weeks. She told me that until the teaching job started that she would continue working as a server and helping with some social work. I told her I would be leaving for Juilliard the first week in August. We probably only talked for five minutes, but it was so great to hear her voice.

We said our good-byes and hung up. I rushed to tell Mom and Dad about the call. She listened intently, but finally Mom told me to get ready for dinner. With just a few days left of school, I didn't have a great deal of homework, which I had already finished, so I sat down at the piano and started playing some of dad's favorite songs. I knew he would not only be pleased about my grades and being the valedictorian of my graduating class, but would also be pleased with my piano playing. He came over, ruffled the hair on my head, and just patted my shoulder. Nothing was said between us, it was just understood.

Mom's dinner was excellent as always. There were tears in her eyes and I asked what was wrong. "Ricky, I am so happy for you, for us. I know how very hard you have studied, worked, and have given up a lot of personal time to get to Juilliard. You are a great son, and your dad and I know you will go far in life. I am happy and sad at the same time. Soon you will be leaving for college, and then to start your career. I will miss you so very much. Your dad and I will miss you very much. You know we love you." She got up, came over to me and just hugged me from behind, kissing the top of my head. I cried.

The first performance ended with a standing ovation and shouts for an encore. Ricky had all members and the opening group come to the front of the stage for recognition. The audience's applause continued, but as people left the theatre, some came to the stage for autographs. Ricky always accommodated any requests for signing different things, hats, paper, even one lady wanted him to autograph the back of her hand, but that didn't seem appropriate nor was something the individual could keep. He walked back to the piano, got a piece of sheet music, autographed it and presented it to the lady who was more than pleased. Some of the members moved to the lobby where additional autographs were signed by them while other members joined the booths to help sell CDs, pictures, videos of previous shows, and other memorabilia.

Time was short between performances, so grabbing something to eat meant having it brought in from a local restaurant. The group was always famished and ate heartily to build energy for the evening show. It seemed seven o'clock came quickly. The evening show always lasted longer than expected. Ricky would add a few more hymns since more church groups were usually present, some coming long distances and spending a few days in Branson taking in multiple shows. Ricky always wanted people to remember that his shows were great family entertainment and made an effort to include audiences in a sing-along.

After the evening show, Ricky always presented himself in the lobby to sign autographs and mingle with the audience as they left. He received many congratulations for a great show and also many condolences for the loss of his wife. One older gentleman somewhat cornered Ricky to explain that he came with his Sunday school class as a means of comfort after losing his wife of fifty years to emphysema. Being the gentleman he always was, Ricky stood patiently and listened and tried his best to console the older gentleman. The gentleman asked Ricky what his wife's name was stating his wife's name was Lois. Ricky said that was a beautiful name and he was certain Lois was a wonderful person and definitely in Heaven with her Lord. He told the gentleman that Millie was his wife's name and she had just recently passed away. They parted when, obviously the leader of the class came over and said everyone was on the bus and he needed to go now. Ricky hugged the older gentlemen and wished him well.

This was not unusual as Ricky often spoke with people who just wanted to tell him about events that occurred in their lives. Ricky at times was given papers with lyrics written or typed from people who would tell him to please use the song in a future performance. Ricky was gracious always telling them they should hang on to the lyrics and maybe copywrite them before giving them away. He did not want to accept any unsolicited works that might be considered forgery or if similar to another song could be illegal. He always found it amazing what people would say to him and how many really wanted to get into show business. If they only understood how laborious a music career could be, but at the same time be very rewarding.

Several members of the troop, for the rest of day after the show, including Ricky stayed at the theatre until almost midnight. They had to ensure all the booths' inventories were accounted for and review collected cash, credit and debit card purchases, and Ricky, Tom, and Vic had to discuss any changes required for the Saturday and Sunday performances.

The changes, if any, would have to be presented to the group Saturday morning when everyone was required to be back at the theatre by ten o'clock. Time just seemed to fly by for everyone. Regardless, the shows had to go on in a timely manner with expectations of getting great reviews. Any changes or negative reviews would be addressed before moving on to the next city and other performances. Changes were always made from every performance improving the quality of the shows.

Millie did come for my graduation, but she had to request being off on that particular Friday from her server job to make the lengthy drive from Nashville. Just seeing her made me shake with excitement. She dropped by my house even before going to her parents place. I was in my room trying on my cap and gown and playing around with my gold tassel. Millie came into my room and saw me swinging my tassel from one side of my cap to the other and dancing around. She spoke, and I know I turned red as a beet at my shenanigans. She walked over to me and we hugged while she put the gold tassel on the appropriate graduating side of my cap. Surprisingly, she kissed me on the forehead moving to the tip of my nose and then almost passionately on the lips. I ardently returned the kiss and we just held each other for a few minutes. The door to my room was open, so discreteness was in order, no further touches.

I slipped off the cap and gown and Millie helped me to hang it so as not to get it wrinkled. There was about an hour before we needed to leave to get back to the school for the commencement ceremonies, so Millie wanted to go home and see her parents and told me she would be going with them to the school, but would definitely get with me afterwards, maybe for a celebration late-evening meal, just the two of us. I wondered if more than a meal was part of her plan, but I focused on just loving the fact she was here and thought enough of me to make the trip.

The commencement ceremonies were wonderful. I had to give my valedictorian speech that I had worked on for over a week. I decided to speak on successes of some famous musicians and tie that into life after graduation. I wanted to make the point that it is always important to do the best anyone can do early in life if they wanted to succeed later. My talk was about fourteen minutes and received a huge round of applause. With the other speakers doing their talks and with one of our State Congressman providing the commencement speech, at least an hour passed before handing out awards and diplomas. I received several awards for "Most Likely to Succeed", a music award pin, and recognition for having the highest overall average at the school in over four years of graduating seniors. Ironically, the person who held this honor before me was Millie.

The honor students received first recognition and awarded diplomas first, so I was number one in receiving my high school diploma. This being a small graduating class, the handing out of diplomas only took about twenty minutes including hand-shaking of each student by the Principal and the State Congressman. I got hugs from several teachers before walking off the stage and taking my seat on the front row. After the honor students the other students all rose and marched to the stage in a single line, each receiving their diplomas. After the last student, Mark Zorcroft the third received his diploma, we all shouted and raised our caps, but we did not throw them in the air as some parents expected. The Principal closed the ceremonies, bidding us all farewell and successes in our future endeavors. Sad as it was closing this chapter of my life, I was filled with excitement and a wonderful feeling of accomplishment.

All the students went back stage to disrobe and return our caps and gowns keeping our tassels. I had worn a pull over golf shirt and knee-length shorts under the gown, as most of the students dressed lightly to avoid getting so hot. Millie was talking to some of the teachers she had classes under while I was changing. The evening was warm and I knew Millie and I would be going somewhere to eat. Most of the graduates had dates or were double-dating to celebrate the end of twelve years of school. The majority would be going on to a college of their choice, while some had plans to marry and start a family as soon as possible. I personally knew I had four more years of school far away from home and with Millie even farther away before I could think about marriage. I did want to talk to Millie about our future and in the back of my mind I still wondered if she considered me too young for her and if waiting four more years for me was too much.

After coming back to join Mom, Dad, and Millie, I asked Dad if I could use the car to take Millie somewhere to eat. His only response was to be careful and that I had to take him and Mom home first. Millie had ridden with her mom and dad, so she was going home first to change clothes to something more casual and told me to come and pick her up afterwards. I was actually getting excited and beginning to feel like an adult. Standing beside Millie also made me feel more grown up since now I was at least five inches taller than her.

While driving to Millie's house I pondered where we should go eat. My budget was not very promising to say the least. I could not afford a fancy place which meant driving to a larger town. The local hotel did have a small restaurant and I was betting I might be able to afford for us to eat there. I wanted to be careful in my mentioning this to Millie so she did not think I was taking her there for other purposes or expecting her to pay. However, I knew she would somehow be in control of any forward initiative on my part. I just didn't know how to broach the topic of her waiting for me while I finished at Juilliard. Maybe the topic would be quick with her telling me I should get on with my life and find someone my age or younger during my time in New York. I just had to wait.

The rest of the tour during the weekend went very well. There was light rain falling on Saturday morning, but this did not dampen anyone's willingness to get to the theatre and prepare for two performances. We all had light breakfasts and most everyone was at least wide awake by ten o'clock. By the afternoon performance the rain had stopped and the crowd was filling the theatre. Again, this was a sellout performance as would be the evening performance. I had brought in several changes of costumes for the performances knowing I would sweat a lot under the lights and just moving about on the stage. These performances can be exhausting. Even at my best, I would sometimes forget the words to my own songs and make up words to fill in when I forgot. Usually the audience did not notice, or if they did, just thought it was a version they hadn't heard before. It is interesting what one must to do to keep moving the performance along. When I changed the words, the band had to keep up. Sometimes I was ridiculed afterwards by some of the members. It was all in good fun.

After the performances on Saturday and Sunday, everyone was pleased with the reviews, the sale of albums, memorabilia, signing of autographs, people taking pictures, and just mingling with the people who attended the performances. However, everyone was ready for a couple of days break as we traveled to the next city and more performances. The next stop would be only one day and one performance, but then we were scheduled for another three-day engagement in Kansas City. I knew this would be a great excursion since everyone wanted to get there and enjoy some renowned barbeque. That of course included me.

The road trip with numerous engagements would be at least thirty days unless Tom scheduled more performances during the travelling time. He was constantly on his cellular phone connecting with other agents and facilities. He always attempted to have bookings for at least a year, but sometimes we were booked for several years. This did not mean we were constantly on the road, but typically we could be on the road for forty-five to sixty days before returning home and recuperating before the next series of performances. This interlude always provided me with time to think of new songs, get to the studio and record more albums, which meant the troops also had to be there. After all, everyone wanted to continue getting a pay check. While exhausting, frustrating, and demanding, this was fun, enjoyable, and personally rewarding. We were scheduled later for the Grand Old Opry. Now that would be super fun, challenging, and competitive with other top country singers and groups performing. I asked Tom to see if he could find out when we were scheduled and who else would be on stage.

Arriving to Millie's house and nervously walking to her door, I checked my heart rate and just did not understand why I was not only nervous, but scared. Thinking about the many times I had come to her house over the past eighteen years, both alone and with my parents, I somehow felt this was a new awakening for me. Here I was a high school graduate, Millie a college graduate, with five years of college, with me getting ready to go to college, and Millie starting a teaching career. My knees were knocking as I rang the door bell. Millie answered the door and as always she looked like she had just stepped out of a glamour magazine. I cannot describe my feelings at the moment. If I could have seen my face at that moment I knew my jaw was dropping to my chest. With the warm weather, Millie had on a beautiful flowered sun dress with straps exposing her shoulders and arms. Me, I had on nice slacks and a light blue golf shirt, but she looked like a movie star.

"Well, are you going to come in for a few minutes or just stand there and stare at me?"

"Oh, oh, yeah. Sorry. I just think you look so beautiful. Wow! No, I know you look so beautiful. You are beautiful." Gee, I was gawking and stuttering and my heart was racing. My knees had not stopped shacking. I felt like a blundering idiot. At eighteen I was an adult now and stood at least five inches taller than Millie. I couldn't help but remember when she towered over me. Somehow the years change people. I became lanky and was still skinny, but Millie had become one gorgeous woman. I almost felt as if she was still baby-sitting me. I had to get control of myself.

As I entered the house, Millie's Mom and Dad were sitting in the living room, the television was on, but the sound was turned down. I, of course, went over to both and as her dad stood, he congratulated me on graduating and being accepted to Juilliard. I shook his hand, thanking him. Her mom got up and just hugged my neck and kissed me on the forehead. I hugged her back. She also congratulated me and almost cried.

"Oh, Ricky, now you are leaving. We will miss seeing you. We haven't gotten over missing Millie and it has been five years. Now she is starting a teaching career miles away from home and it…it will not be the same. I love you both, you have been the son we never had, and Millie is our darling girl. She is here for such a short time before going back to Nashville. You are heading to New York. I do hope the two of you will continue to stay in touch with each other and definitely with us and your parents."

"Mrs. Pendergrass, nothing will keep me from staying in touch with you and Mr. Pendergrass and definitely if she will allow it, I will always stay in touch with Millie. I love you all, and my mom and dad would disown me if I did not always stay in touch, one way or another."

Sadness seemed prevalent at that moment, but it wasn't despair but rather a happiness that both Millie and I had reached that point in our lives where we started being independent, Millie now more so than me. But, my time was coming. Millie kissed both her mom and dad and said we were going out to eat somewhere affordable and that we would not be too late getting back. Her dad just smiled waving his hand in the air as if to say go on and have fun, but no words were spoken. Outside I asked Millie what her mom and dad thought about us now that we were, as I put it, going on a date. Millie just laughed, looked up into my eyes, and said nothing.

In the car, I asked Millie where she wanted to eat. First she said this should be her treat as a graduation present, but I was not in favor of that. Dutch treat, no, I had saved and before I left, my dad slipped me a few bucks. Eating at the hotel restaurant was now within reach. I asked Millie if eating there would be okay with her since I had made reservations. She smiled and said, yes if I could afford it. She scooted over next to me. Thankfully, Dad's car had seats that were fairly close but still separated by a small console. Being a conservative individual his entire life, he just did not think trading a good car that still had life in it for, as he put it, the new fangled model with so much to go wrong. Now I was thankful for that while separated by a console, it was not an inhibitor to being fairly close to each other.

We drove in silence for the few miles to the hotel and restaurant. I had made the reservations but would have gone somewhere else if Millie did not want to go there. I realized there would be a lot of other graduating students there with their dates since there were so few places to go in our small town. I assumed some of the couples had plans to stay there that night, but I realized Millie would not consent to such an arrangement, and I was not about to bring up that subject. Millie was careful, but reaching across the console she had her hand on my knee, not really rubbing it, just holding it. I did concentrate on my driving and was careful to stay focused. I did not want an embarrassing situation to happen.

Once I had parked the car, we walked hand in hand to the lobby and I announced to the maitre d regarding our table reservations, we were ushered to a lovely table for two by the window overlooking the swimming pool and center courtyard. As expected, there were numerous other graduates there with their dates, and I spoke to several as Millie and I went to our table, hand in hand. Many of my classmates were jealously gawking at Millie as we walked together. The table had a reserved tent on it with my name. That was impressive. I guess for the first time I felt like a grown up. I did the mannerly thing and helped Millie by pulling the chair out for her and scooting her forward to the table. I was seated across from her, able to look into her eyes. If crying would have helped me, I think I could have shed a million tears of joy. I, however kept myself composed and reached across the table and took one of Millie's hands in mine. I said nothing, but she seemed to understand just how happy I was at this moment.

Kansas City, Missouri can be beautiful in the spring time. Our entourage, convoy as it appeared, approached the city after a four plus hour drive from Branson. Everyone was hungry and wanted to find a great barbecue restaurant in order to "pig out", pun intended. A quick Internet search by Tom had us heading to the Freight House District and to the Jack Stack BBQ place. I am certain the manager there was both delighted and overcome when he saw our buses and vans arrive. Even though they are accustomed to handling large groups, ours was not exactly a quiet group and it brought attention to the fact we were celebrities, obvious from the name on the side of the buses. We received a lot of stares and a few people ventured to our tables for autographs. As always we obliged.

While just a one-day, two-show event, we were performing at the Arvest Bank Theatre at the Midland. This was a first time at this theatre, but being on Main Street provided us great accommodations at the Crown Plaza only a block away from the Theatre. I only wished we had more time in Kansas City, but the road show had to move on to other places. These quick two to three day engagements, that being arriving one day, doing the performances the second day, and packing up to get back on the road the third day is utterly exhausting for everyone. However, the next performances would mean we would be in one place for almost a week. This time allowed everyone some personal time to scout the area, make purchases for family as memorabilia and to a degree rest a while. Not that rest came easily, but it at least one day provided down time.

The time and performance in Kansas City at the Arvest was good and another sell-out. We were bringing in the crowds and giving great shows, shows that obviously people liked. Tom continued to make the introduction regarding the loss of Millie and the impact on me, but never the less, everyone would have a great show. I opened Kansas City as I did in Branson with "Shirley" and as in Branson, received a tremendous reception. Recording sales were booming. These performances did help ease the pain of thinking about Millie, but in no way erased the memory or the love we shared. I missed her every day.

From Kansas City we had eight other cities for performances before heading back home to Nashville and other places. The members weren't all in Nashville, but most were within driving distances. Leaving Kansas City we headed to Lincoln, Nebraska then to Denver, Colorado. From there the next stop took us to Salt Lake City, Utah. We had to move quickly from Salt Lake City to get to a three-day performance in Las Vegas, Nevada. We were originally scheduled for five days including a weekend, but Tom had negotiated a lesser tour but more performances. This stop was always a treat for everyone, but money was lost to gambling and some of the members did get a bit tipsy with the environment. Leaving Las Vegas we traveled to San Diego, California and enjoyed the wonderful temperature and view of the Pacific Ocean. Here we added an opening Hispanic group that went over very well with the audiences.

It was hard to leave San Diego, but Phoenix, Arizona was waiting on us for another three-day performance. The dry heat of the desert got to some members, but everyone survived. I was getting tired and actually needed some time to rest my voice. These are hard tours to make and can really test one's endurance. Phoenix was great. We had been playing to capacity crowds at every location. The weather was getting hot and we ran into some heavy rains as we headed east to Santa Fe, New Mexico. This was unusual but the desert can be mean at times. Santa Fe was sold out and our time there was short, only one performance in the evening, but a great audience. We had one more stop in Oklahoma City, Oklahoma before heading back to Nashville. Oklahoma City gave us a great reception, again to sold-out performances. Needless to say, once on the bus heading home, I just collapsed and wanted to sleep for hours.

∞

Millie put her other hand on top of mine and we just looked at each other. Finally she looked up and our server was at the table. He was a young guy, probably my age at eighteen. I did not know him from our school, but I asked him if he was local. His response was that he actually was older than he looked and graduated three years ago. He was saving to go to a technical college to study computers, but he needed to work to help his mother who had been in the hospital and was recovering from cancer surgery. Millie and I both expressed our sympathies. Turning away, he gave us a few more minutes to look at the menu. Millie asked me again if I could afford the meal and I frowned as if she had insulted me. "Don't worry, I have it covered. Order what you want. This one is on me and I want to do it."

She smiled. We ordered, but both of us picked items that were not especially expensive, no wine or drinks other than sweet tea. We shared a dessert. I actually would have money left over, even after a generous tip considering the situation of our server. During the meal, I constantly looked at Millie until she finally reached over, touching my face saying, "Ricky, what is it? You seem to be in deep thought. Tell me what you are thinking."

At least she opened the door to what I wanted to say. I guess I stuttered at first, but her eyes never left mine. As we shared the dessert, I probably blundered, but said, "Millie, I want you to know how much I care for you. I know there is an age difference, but it is not as important now that we are adults as it was when I was thirteen and you were eighteen. I haven't cared for anyone as much as I care for you. I hope that is not too presumptuous on my part." She was smiling. "I know you will be in Nashville and me in New York for at least four years until I graduate from Juilliard that is assuming I pass and don't get kicked out. I just don't want you to forget me and run off and marry some wealthy entertainer you meet in Nashville. You are so beautiful you will definitely be sought out and approached by a lot of men, men more your age than I am."

She put her fingers to my mouth, hushing me, looked into my eyes saying, "Ricky, oh Ricky. You are still my favorite guy. I don't care about the age difference that I am older than you. As adults five years is nothing. As kids, it is worlds apart. Who I care about is you. We have in our own way been a couple since you were a little boy and me a bigger girl. Now you are grown up, as I am, and must I say, one handsome young man. My fear is much the same as yours. You will be at Juilliard with lots of pretty girls who will want to get to know you better and you will probably date one who will win your heart. Do you not think that I worry you will be swept off your feet by that beauty and forget me? I do not have anyone in my life at this time, and should I date, as you might also, doesn't mean we are not special to each other. If it concerns you, let's wait and see what happens. We can talk on the phone, write letters, and when you are at a break between years or whenever, let's plan on seeing each other, somewhere, at home or maybe you can come to Nashville."

I was speechless.

∾

I did probably sleep for hours before Tom woke me just on the boarder of Tennessee. Everyone was famished and wanted to stop and eat before disembarking and going separate ways. We found a great Perkins restaurant in Cordova, and enjoyed "pigging out" before hitting I-40 continuing on to Nashville. We still had almost two hundred miles to go and probably close to three hours of driving, pending any traffic slowdowns. Everyone was anxious.

Tom and I worked on plans for the next tour. After all, almost forty-five days on the road was a bit long, but the next tour would take us east hitting several major cities in various States. The southern tours were always fun because we would pass through or have shows in some of the members' home towns. This always brought out a lot of families and friends and we received a huge welcome every time. We would pass close to my home town, but no stop there.

We finally arrived in Nashville. Everyone was hugging, saying their farewells, and heading to parked cars at the storage facility. Tom would arrange for the buses to be serviced before the next road trip. Instruments would be stored or taken with members, or at least those instruments that were easy enough to take. A number of members car-pooled coming from the same areas. Tom told everyone to enjoy their time away, but he expected to leave in ten days to meet performance obligations. First stop, Knoxville, and then hitting I-40 again to Charlotte, North Carolina. I just wanted to get to my car and head home. However, I knew it would be an empty house without Millie. I had to turn from Tom or he would have seen tears in my eyes.

∾

COMPANIONS
Understandings

Plans never work out as anyone thinks they will, but Millie and I talked for a long time after the dinner. We sat at our table while watching other couples leave, some going to rooms to spend the night embracing one another in either true love or total infatuation, regardless enjoying the fact graduation was emanate and high school was behind them. I looked at Millie and she took my hand saying, "Ricky, don't you even think about what you are thinking about. The answer is no. We'll not go any farther right now. You have to be patient and understand we are not lovers, but we love one another. Time will tell about us, and then we can enjoy the luxury of a physical relationship. But you are not ready for that now. You think you are because you and I had some special moments for which I do regret and I should not have been encouraging you or teasing you in that way. That is not a cop-out, not an older woman telling you, but it is me because I care. I care about you and I care about our relationship."

"Can't we just try?"

"No! Let's enjoy our time together and not spoil it by having a physical relationship that is a one-night stand, then moving on with our lives. Ricky, we would always regret that. I would regret that. When I look at you I see a person, now a man I really love and I hope you see when you look at me as a woman you love and care for more than you care just for sex. Please, let's not go there."

I could have cried. But I knew in my heart she was right and that if we went all the way now, it would never be the same for us later in life. I wanted more, but I had to wait. I had to respect Millie's wishes and control my urges.

There were other ways to handle my situation later. So much for a first time and what most of the guys I knew were doing tonight and probably had done many times before. I just hoped that I would not end up a hermit and a virgin forever.

Millie and I left the restaurant, walked to my dad's car and I opened the door for her. She scooted in and as far to the console as possible. I closed the door and walked around to the driver's side, got in, and looked at Millie. She reached over and took my hands in hers. She kissed the ends of each of my fingers and held my right hand to her lips. She leaned over taking also my left hand and kissed me, almost taking my breath away. I breathed deeply, returning the kiss. She turned loose of my left hand, keeping my right hand in her left hand. She ever so gently rubbed the inside of my right thigh from my knee to my crotch. She could tell I was excited. Gently she moved her hand farther up until she was aware of my hardness, softly rubbing, but stopped saying, "Ricky, let's not do this. I am sorry. I shouldn't be teasing you. I want to be with you as much as you want to be with me. But this isn't the time and it isn't right."

"No, don't be. It is alright and I only wish we could, but I do understand. I love you Millie. I want our relationship to be founded on what is right, not on what we feel at the moment."

She moved her hand from my thigh and turned my right hand loose. I started the engine but not before kissing her again. I knew then and there that Millie was the love of my life and being away from her for four year or longer would be difficult to endure. We drove to her house in silence with her touching my shoulder and in as much as possible, leaning her head against my shoulder. I was crying inside, but smiling so big. I am certain Millie was also.

When we got to Millie's house, I parked in the driveway, turned the engine off, and looked at Millie. "You know I love you. I always will. I will be away for four years, but as we talked about it, we will keep in touch. Please don't go off and fall head over hill for some guy. I know with your beauty and intelligence you are a real winner for any man. I still have an education ahead of me, but after that..."

She shushed me, kissed me, and said, "Silly boy. You worry too much. Trust me and I will trust you." She patted my crotch saying, "Keep that in your pants and don't go wild in New York. Study hard, stay soft, and know that I love you."

The rest of the summer passed uneventfully. I worked a notice at the café and the other employees gave me a great send off. The other servers obviously had saved some of their tip money and the owner, his wife, and the cooks chipped in giving me one hundred dollars as a going to Juilliard present. This was so gracious of them. I promised to come back during the summers if possible and to drop in and visit when I came home for the holidays. Some cried, but I got a lot of hugs and kisses on my cheeks from the ladies, and the owner looked at me and told me to be good, make great grades, and that he knew I would be successful in life.

I was completely packed and Dad and Mom were going to make the trip to Juilliard with me because Mom wanted to see where I would be staying. This would be a lot of expense for them, but they wanted to do it. I did have a good scholarship, but I needed to make super grades to keep it and to turn it into a full tuition scholarship. Dad and Mom were encouraging with the fact they both knew I could make that happen.

After putting all my things in Dad's car, I wanted to walk over and tell Millie's mom and dad that I was leaving.

Home at last, but to an empty house. I can almost hear Millie's voice resonate off the walls as I stand in the house she and I shared for many years. We bought this house in a gated community after I had gained some success as a musician, singer songwriter. It was close to the school where Millie taught, one of the better communities in Nashville, but Millie did not want anything too pompous, as she put it. While still a fairly large place for two people, we had planned on a family, kids to share our home, but unfortunately that never happened.

I was lost for the moment and tears came to my eyes. It would be sad to be here alone tonight, but I knew I had to become accustomed to the emptiness. I was in no way ready to share my life with anyone else, and would probably never do so again. But, as the old saying goes "never say never." I sauntered into the kitchen where I once would have had a nice meal prepared and waiting for me only to find emptiness again. Reluctantly, I decided to call Pastor Thomas just to let him know I was back in town, doing okay for the moment, and to once again thank him for his kindness.

Before I could make the call, my cell phone vibrated. I looked at it and saw a text message from Darren, my technical manager, saying all equipment was accounted for, safely stored and he was heading home. I texted him back with a thank you and to get some rest. I looked through my contacts on my cell for Pastor Thomas' home phone number, assuming he would be there at this time. I called and his wife answered the phone. It was really good to hear her voice and we chatted a few minutes before she handed the phone to her husband. Pastor Thomas is a super delightful and caring person, and the first words out of his mouth were, "Ricky, are you okay?"

"Pastor, I am fine, but coming to an empty house has gotten to me. I did not think it would be this hard. I was only here a few days after Millie died before hitting the road for almost two months. Being busy and with people helped to ease the pain of losing her, but now…now, it is hitting me that she is really gone and will not be here again."

"Ricky do you want Sue and me to come over? We can be there in thirty minutes."

"No. I will be okay. I need to get some rest and think about how I need to go about adjusting. I am only here for ten days before we hit the road for another tour. I will be gone again for almost two months. I just don't know how to cope with the emptiness."

We continued to talk for a few more minutes. Pastor Thomas always had a soothing voice and a way just to make you feel good, not only about yourself but about life in general. I felt better after talking with him and as he recommended, I found something to eat that wasn't spoiled with no one here to look after things. My housekeeper did keep everything clean, but there was no way she could stock a refrigerator without knowing what I wanted to eat. I went to our bedroom, well my bedroom now, and just flopped down on the bed. After lying there for a few minutes, I got up, undressed, and took a long shower. While showering I thought about calling Tammy if it wasn't too late. I just wanted to hear a familiar voice, nothing more, no commitment, and definitely not trying to start a relationship.

∞

At Millie's house, her mom and dad hugged me and told me how great it has been to see me grow from a kid to a very handsome young man, and that they knew I would do great at Juilliard and would be a success in life. They told me Millie had written them several times, the last letter telling them she had started her job as a teacher and had prepared for the kids and the classroom. I mentioned to them she had also written me, but I did not share the content of her letter with them. I gave Millie's mom and dad my Juilliard address insisting they write me and that I would also write them about my experiences in New York and at Juilliard. They made me promise to do so, hugged me again, and I left to go with my Mom and Dad for the drive to the airport and our trip to Juilliard to, as Mom put it, "to get me settled in."

The trip was great, the airplane ride was smooth and fortunately we had a plane with three seats on one side so we were seated together and chatted about a lot of things. Mom especially was talkative expressing to me how I needed to pay attention to my studies, stay clean, eat well, and not become "one of those New Yorkers." I promised all points to her, reminding her I was grown up and could take care of myself. She admonished me for such a comment, saying she had cleaned my diapers and took care of me for eighteen years. I laughed. Dad just grinned and told me to behave myself.

Arriving at Juilliard, we found Meredith Wilson Residence Hall located in the Samuel B and David Rose buildings. That was the place I would be staying because it was required for first-time students. Timing was critical to be on campus ready to move in on August twenty-fifth between nine in the morning and noon. We arrived right at eleven o'clock. I was assigned a room on the tenth floor. My roommate had already arrived and was unpacking when Mom, Dad, and I carried my things to the room. My room overlooked the Hudson River. This was spectacular. I am certain I was gawking. Finally I introduced myself and Mom and Dad to my roommate. I knew his name from the correspondence I had received, Joshua Collins. He introduced himself as Josh Collins from Cave City, Kentucky. As he put it, Cave City is the home of Mammoth Cave National Park not far from Lexington. Not being familiar with Cave City, Mammoth Cave National Park or Lexington, never having being there, I just nodded my head and said "great."

Mom and Dad wanted to get something to eat after I got settled in and before they found their hotel for the night to rest before flying back the next morning. I quickly put some things away, but knew I had time to get organized before classes started in a few days. Dad asked Josh if he wanted to join us, but he declined saying he had arranged for meals and would eat later. I also had taken the meal plan option, but tonight was special and the last time I would see my parents before the Christmas break. The residence hall closes just before Christmas and reopens after the New Year holidays, so I either had to go home then or find some place to stay in New York. My parents did not approve of me staying and had insisted I come home for the holidays. But, that was a few months away. I needed to get my act together and get settled in to a life at Juilliard.

After eating, getting back to the Hall, bidding Mom and Dad goodbye, I settled in to finishing unpacking and organizing my half of the room. Josh was a very shy boy, and while he didn't talk a lot, I thought we could be not only roommates but friends. He opened up more the next day and we walked over to the campus and looked around, finding some of the places we would be having classes. I told him I was studying piano and he told me he was into the arts and acting, a drama student. He had acted in some school plays, community plays, some church plays, and really wanted to be a stage actor one day. His dream was to be on stage on Broadway. I told him I wanted to be a concert pianist. At least that is what I thought about at the time.

Walking back to our room, I asked Josh if he had a girl friend. He told me that there was one special person he had been seeing fairly steadily. I didn't question who, but told him I had a very special girl who was in Nashville and hoped more would develop between us after I graduated. Later in the room, Josh was writing a letter to someone, so I decided to write to Millie and tell her about my trip up, my roommate, and give her my address so she could also write me. The day dragged somewhat, but Josh and I walked around some more. We mailed our letters and I noticed his was addressed to Michael Jones in Cave City. I know I am somewhat naive about a few things, but I am astute enough to realize that Josh's special someone was another guy. That didn't matter to me. He and I had separate courses of study and regardless of his preferences; he is a very nice guy.

∞

I got out of the shower, dried my hair vigorously, toweled off the rest of me, put on a bath robe, and settled in my favorite chair in our, well now my bedroom. I had Tammy's phone number for the Bed and Breakfast in my cell phone, so after hesitating for a couple of minutes I decided to make the call. She answered after the fourth ring, just before I almost disconnected, "Good Evening, Tammy's and Cliff's Bed and Breakfast, Tammy speaking. How may I help you?"

"Hey, Tammy. This is Ricky Snyder. How are you?"

There was silence for a moment and then I thought she was going to hang up. "Oh my gosh! Ricky Snyder. I thought you had fallen off the face of the earth. It is so funny but I was thinking of you the other day when a couple registered who had just come from a bus tour in Branson and attended your show. I told them I knew you and you had stayed here. They wanted to know if the room you stayed in was available and it would amaze their friends when they got back home knowing they had stayed in the same room as a famous person."

"I am honored. Thank you for telling me. I hope the room was available for them."

"Fortunately it was because it was a slow week. How are you? Are you adjusting okay? Where have you been, I mean doing shows?"

I proceeded to tell Tammy about the tour, almost two months, and that the time at home was short, ten days roughly, before we started again. I mentioned we would be traveling very close to the home town as we moved to Knoxville and Charlotte. She wanted to know if I could stop, but that would not be possible this time. We talked for probably thirty minutes with a couple of interruptions with one couple registering and another couple seeking information. I decided while I was talking to go to the kitchen for something to drink. Maybe a green tea, I would look and see what was in the refrigerator.

Tammy wanted to know how I was adjusting without Millie. I told her coming home to an empty house was very hard for me. She related her experience with the loss of Cliff. "It gets easier, but sometimes the initial impact can be very difficult and hard to take. I know how you feel especially when everything that Millie had is still in the house, in the same place, and the thought of moving it just eats at you. It took me almost a year before I gave Cliff's clothes away to the Salvation Army. I kept a lot of his personal items, but over time now, I have sent some to my son, and placed other items in some of the guest rooms. People enjoy seeing them, but they have no idea what is behind them being there. Sometimes I have a guest make a comment about one of the special items in the room, or in the lobby, but that is rare."

"Well, I had a lady at church asked me at the funeral if I wanted her to come over and go through Millie's clothes and some other personal items. At the time, I was hesitant, but you know, I think that will be a good idea. I probably will cry my heart out with each item, but it is something that I must do, as you had to. I just never thought about these things since Millie handled the issues when her mom and dad passed away and again when my mom and dad passed away. I was on the road, and thankfully I did not have to make a lot of decisions. Neither of our parents had a lot, and both had scaled down to just the necessities of life as they got older and needed less. Hey, I have talked your ears off so I better let you go and get some sleep. I probably will crash and sleep for days."

"You are so funny. Thank you for calling. Let's do keep in touch and when you are back this way, please, please come to visit. Oh, if you are free for Thanksgiving, I do a real feast here."

"I will keep in touch, and definitely let you know about Thanksgiving. Take care, sleep well, and we'll talk later. Have a good night."

That call was great for me just hearing a nice friendly voice and not having to plan another tour. I was not trying to start a relationship, just needed to talk to someone. I thought about what Tammy had said bout Thanksgiving, but I had no idea what if any tours were planned around the Thanksgiving holidays, and even more so, I had no idea what I was going to do tomorrow. I finished my green tea, retired to the bedroom, slipped into some pajamas, and just crashed knowing I would probably sleep for hours. I think I fell asleep before my head hit the pillow.

Things started happening at college, orientation, signing up for classes, having some auditions as part of the piano classes, meeting a lot of great people, guys and girls who had talent flowing from every bone in their bodies. I remained awed almost every way I turned. I checked a bulletin board where a lot of items were posted checking for any weekend job opportunities. I also checked with student affairs about working part-time. The only real experience I had was being a server at the local café back home and of course playing the piano for church and other charitable occasions. I knew if I could work some, with the buses and subways and just places within walking distance of Lincoln Center that I did not need worry about transportation.

I found that there were a lot of restaurants within walking distance of Juilliard and took some time to put in a few applications. I only wanted to work on weekends, preferably breakfast or lunch and no more than maybe sixteen hours. After four interviews at different places I was offered a job as a server. I accepted just for the breakfast time two days a week and on weekends. The two week days were okay because I did not have classes starting until ten o'clock on those days. I had to get up early to be on the job, but that gave me plenty of time to rest each night and definitely time to study and do any class work required. I scheduled time to practice piano and spend time in the library. The extra money from the job, as I promised Dad, would help offset my personal needs. While the salary was not great, I knew if I did a good job that the tips would be good. However, typically tips at breakfast are not as big as at other meals.

I had to write Millie and let her know what was happening with my first few days at Juilliard and to find out how her teaching job was going. I hadn't received a response from her for the letter I mailed earlier, but she probably hadn't received it yet or had not had the time to respond. Regardless, I would write another letter.

The first few weeks were very busy for me, Not only did I have to adjust my time for my classes, get a routine for studying, allow time for cajoling with other students, especially those in my classes, time for fun, and time for work. I was beginning to understand what college life was all about.

I finally received a letter from Millie. She apologized for not writing sooner, but was adjusting to a routine of the new job, learning student names, preparing classes, and just learning her way around Nashville, now as a resident versus as a student. I really did understand where she was coming from based on what I was going through establishing routines. She asked me if I had written any more songs lately. I had to think about that because I had been so wrapped up in the first few weeks of college and with the new server job, that I hadn't given thought to any creative writing.

I would find time to focus on something to send her. I did respond to her letter telling her I would send something soon.

Time just flew by, and soon it was nearing Thanksgiving Day. Some of the students did go home but it was just too costly for me to do so and I was not about to call Dad and asked for money. Mom and Dad wrote routinely asking how I was doing and if I was studying hard and not working too much. They wanted to know what I was going to do for Thanksgiving and I told them the cafeteria at Juilliard was having a good meal for day and that there were no classes the Friday after Thanksgiving, but I would be working an extra shift at the restaurant, so I would have plenty to eat.

I was meeting so many nice people, lots of friendly students and professors at the college and some great contacts with individuals being a server. I had a couple of great invitations to share Thanksgiving dinner with several of my customers, but I respectively declined each invitation stating I either had to work or study. However, I was very appreciative of the invitations.

Josh invited me to join him and some friends for Thanksgiving dinner, but I told him I would be working. He went with some of the students from his drama class to a favorite restaurant for Thanksgiving dinner and told me he was staying over with a friend. I wanted to ask him who, but he finally confessed that Michael Jones from Cove City had moved to New York. Michael was four years older than Josh and they had been very close friends growing up in the same neighborhood. Josh being away was okay with me since that would give me time to think about the words to the song I promised Millie. I had an idea of what I wanted to write. I just needed to make certain I could put it into decent lyrics.

The next morning after having a couple of cups of coffee, I thought about what Tammy has said about Thanksgiving. I called Tom and chatted about what our plans were for a tour during the holidays. He told me that he had scheduled a Christmas performance for the following weekend after Thanksgiving, but he had not scheduled any performance for Thanksgiving weekend to give the troop a chance to get to their homes and have family time. That meant I could drive back to Tammy's and have Thanksgiving dinner with her and the folks at the Bed and Breakfast.

After asking Tom what city we would be in for the last performance before Thanksgiving, he said he thought we would end that leg of the tour in Charleston, South Carolina since several of the members families lived in South Carolina, North Carolina, Florida, or Tennessee. I liked what I heard. But what that did mean was the members had to get back to Charleston to continue the tour. From that point we were heading to Savannah, Georgia and then to Jacksonville, Florida and to Orlando, Florida for Christmas performances. I made the call to Tammy.

The days at home passed quickly but I did take time to called Pastor Thomas and scheduled a couple of the church ladies, including the Pastor's wife, to come to the house and see what could be done with Millie's clothes. This was going to be emotional for me and I really needed a support group. No one could be better than the Christian ladies who are very caring people. When they came over, Sue, the Pastor's wife took charge and everyone was so considerate. I had no family to give Millie's clothes and jewelry to, so Sue suggested having a memorial rummage sale at the church with monies received going to supporting the youth programs. I know some of the jewelry was very expensive, but what was I going to do with it if I had to keep it. I did keep certain pieces of special items Millie loved, and the rest I agreed could be in the memorial sale. This made the task very easy with the ladies taking everything away. It goes beyond saying how saddened I was, but Millie would have wanted it this way. She didn't have a will, neither of us did, but it made me think about getting with my attorney and having one drawn up. This was another task for another day.

The day finally came when I had to get it together for the, as Tom called it, "the southeast tour." The usual occurred getting the buses and vans loaded, the troop organized and everyone on board. Finally our convoy was ready and we headed to our first engagement in Knoxville. This was not a long drive; Interstate all the way, plans in place for the opening group, and a three-day weekend performance at the Tennessee Theatre. There I opened the same as before with the hit song "Shirley." We performed to an almost capacity audience due to a very heavy rain storm preventing some ticket holders from attending.

From Knoxville we headed east on I-40 through western North Carolina to Charlotte where we had another three-day weekend performance at the Belk Theatre. Charlotte for us is always an interesting city to visit and do performances. Audiences come from all over because of the easy access to the city via Interstates as well as an international airport. Three of the band members were from Charlotte giving them time to visit family and reacquaint themselves with friends. We had much better weather here, but it was getting colder and only three weeks from Thanksgiving Day. We had to finish our tour here, head to Charleston, South Carolina for a full week of performances before the tour would take a break for the holiday. Everyone had plans for Thanksgiving and most had made travel arrangements to go home either by driving or flying.

I made a quick call to Tammy to make certain she was still doing the Thanksgiving dinner and most of all to make certain I had a room there for a few days. I would probably not go back to Nashville, but stay close to Townsend. From there it is at least a three-hour drive to Nashville. Dad and I made the trip several times when I was growing up, but then it seemed it took forever. Now, even though it is not a bad drive, I wanted to enjoy some of the familiar places that always amaze me now about small towns. I loved growing up there and now to see the surrounding areas as a blooming tourist attraction gives me goose bumps. I can understand why Tammy never left, well somewhat because of Cliff.

The call to Tammy yielded exactly what I expected. She had reserved the same room for me that I had stayed in previously. She told me this was for two reasons. First, she wanted to put up a plaque stating *"Ricky Snyder stays in this room when he visits his home town of Townsend,"* and secondly, to make me feel as if I have a home away from Nashville. I was thrilled, but a bit taken back by the plaque, but definitely felt honored. I wasn't sure everyone who stayed there would know who Ricky Snyder was. I told Tammy that I hoped this didn't make people want to change rooms especially if they were not a fan of mine or hated my songs. She just laughed and said that she would see me when I arrived. Laughing, she told me the turkey would be ready. I got the pun.

∾

I worked Thanksgiving Day at the restaurant, the breakfast and lunch shifts, and after my shifts, the manager boxed me a very hearty turkey dinner that I took with me back to my room. It was almost more than

I could eat, but somehow I managed. While I was "pigging out" on the meal, I was jotting down the words to the song that I planned on sending to Millie. My thoughts were centered on the months I had been in New York, Juilliard and all the people I met at the restaurant. I wanted to focus somewhat on the area with all the talented people, and at this time of year, the weather was very cold and breezy. I didn't have immediate access to a piano, so no possibility of creating a musical score. That could come later. I just wanted to capture what I not only saw, but what I personally felt being so far from those I loved, especially Millie. My letter to Millie, I think, definitely made the point I thought of her every day.

> *My dearest Millie,*
>
> *I hope you are staying warm. It is cold here, very cold, but I am surviving. It is Thanksgiving Day and I just finished a delicious meal that the manager of the restaurant gave me for working the extra lunch shift. A lot of the servers wanted off, but some needed to work and since I had nothing better to do, I volunteered. The tips were good and added some additional pocket change to my diminishing bank account. I walk back and forth to the restaurant and for that matter just about everywhere I go.*
>
> *I hope you are having, I guess by the time you receive this letter, had a great Thanksgiving Day. I wondered if you went home to have dinner with your parents. My mom called and told me that a lot of the families would be doing a big dinner at the church. I hate that I am not there, but New York is a long way from home.*
>
> *You asked me if I had written any songs lately. I gave a lot of thought to that, and over the last couple of weeks I mentally made some notes about some lyrics. Josh is away staying overnight with his friend, I guess they are more than just friends, but that is none of my business. However, this gave me time in the room to put my thoughts together. Let me know if you like it. I call it "**Beautiful People.**" I hope this reflects the way I see people here, how they move about and seem to be enjoying life, brazing the wind, but doing what they want to do. I know there is no*

way I can capture the essence of life here with millions of people,
but anyway I hope the words have meaning.

Beautiful People
I've got a feeling I want to be free,
Be one of those people with fresh air to breathe;
Making believe, a chance to be free,
Giving what love was meant to be.
Going all over, meeting with friends,
Knowing what it's like to live again.
Giving myself a chance to be me,
Seeing the world the way it should be.

Beautiful people, that's who I shall meet,
Beautiful people, how softly they speak.
Knowing that I am just what I am,
Listening forever to that soul searching sound.

God grant me freedom; God grant me life;
Show me the world through my own eyes.
Beautiful people, their hair blowing free;
Beautiful people, being who they should be.

I've got a feeling down deep in my heart
That my life's just now about to start.
God grant me long life, God grant me will;
Keep me forever I hope until
Tomorrow won't come and today is gone;
And I have the feeling that I've sung my song.

Beautiful people, that's who I shall meet;
Beautiful people, how softly they speak.
God grant me freedom, God grant me life,
Show me the world but keep me from strife. [5]

---

[5] "Beautiful People" written by Donald Arlo Jennings July 29th, 1973.

*I guess if you could see me right now I would be blushing.
I will close now. Write me and let me know if you like the
song.*

My love always,
Ricky

I had to build up courage to send the letter to Millie. I just didn't
know if she would like the words or if she would laugh. Now that she was
a teacher, I almost thought she would grade the lyrics and return them
to me with red marks. Carefully I folded the letter, put it in an envelope,
addressed it to Millie, put a stamp on it and laid it on my small student
desk to mail Friday.

Charleston was great, the audiences had been wonderful, and we put
on a very special performance each time. Now that it was time to take our
break, my choices in leaving Charleston to go to Townsend were to either
take one of the buses or rent a car. As many of the members who actually
planned ahead and reserved rental cars or had airline tickets probably were
better off than I was. Several members rented cars and shared driving to
their destinations. I had originally planned to stay in Charleston until we
continued the tour, but after speaking to Tammy, I elected to rent a car if
one was available and drive. Tom wanted to know if I wanted to ride with
him since he was actually taking one of the vans home, but that would
only take me part of the way. Obviously, I chose to rent a car and make
the trip knowing it would take me about six hours. That would give me
some time to think, maybe despair about losing Millie, but think about
the wonderful years we had together.

The group departed going separate ways with instructions from Tom
as when to be back in Charleston, no excuses, so we could head on to
Savannah as the start of our Christmas southeast tour. I called Enterprise
and they brought me a nice Toyota Corolla, not exactly a BMW, but would
be good should I run into any snow, not that any was presently predicted.
Gas mileage would be good and the price was very reasonable. I figured I
would probably drive close to eight-hundred miles going and coming plus

any local driving. I thought this was a small price to pay for what I knew would be a fantastic Thanksgiving feast.

Arriving at Tammy's bed and breakfast was exciting. The place was packed with guests. Tammy had the place decorated with harvest and fall memorabilia items making the place look festive and inviting. Tammy welcomed me with a slight hug, not a passionate hug, but more as friends would hug. She mentioned many of the locals would be there for dinner on Thanksgiving Day. She had been working like crazy to get everything prepared. Two days away from the big day and for the first time since losing Millie, I felt happy. I checked in, went to my room, and the first thing on my agenda was a long, hot shower. After that, I wondered if Tammy had time to just talk and maybe have a glass of wine. I had stopped along the way and bought several bottles, some of which I would give to Tammy for those guests who wanted wine with their meal. A special bottle I kept separate to share with Tammy.

Probably as quickly as I had ever received a letter from Millie, I got a response to the one I sent to her. She had not returned the lyrics, grading them with red marks as I might have expected, but she was raving about them. She told me in so many words that I had captured the essence of not only being with people, but understanding how wonderful it is to enjoy freedom. She did not mean freedom from parents, but freedom of enjoying life. She included in her letter how wonderful it was to be home with family for a few days but missed me being there. She said it was different sitting at the table not having me next to her. I was beginning to get tears in my eyes.

She wanted to know if I would be coming home for Christmas. With the residence hall being closed during the Christmas holidays, my choices were to stay somewhere in New York, but where was questionable. I didn't have the funds to rent a hotel room and I didn't want to lose my server job. I had some money saved, but very little. I knew I had to call Dad, collect, and see if he would cover bus fare for me to come home, and I had to speak to my boss at the restaurant to ensure he would save my job when I got back after the first of the New Year. If I could get those two things accomplished, then I could write Millie and let her know that I would be there.

The days passed quickly, and I got an offer from Josh to stay with him and Michael during the holidays, but I would have felt so out of place with them. I know they wanted their personal time and having me intruding would probably spoil it for them. Dad did send bus fare and I got a ticket after arranging with my boss about my job. He was really very supportive and told me I was one of his very best servers and that he definitely would hold my job. Everything was coming together and I would be home for Christmas. I wrote Millie to let her know of my plans. She wrote back as quickly letting me know she would be there at the bus station to pick me up. I was getting excited just thinking of actually seeing her again. Only one more week before school closed for the holidays and I would be on the bus home.

Thanksgiving was wonderful with Tammy and her guests. Her son, Jason and his wife Alice had made the trip from California. I was happy to meet them and they were somewhat in awe with Tammy knowing *Ricky Snyder*. They wanted me to sing, but I thought that would not be appropriate, so I respectively declined. Tammy and I did not have a lot of time to just sit and talk, but after the big dinner, I help her, Sara and Marty clean up and get everything back to some orderly manner. Jason and Alice had to leave to get back to work, so their visit was very short.

Tammy and I discussed the Christmas holidays and as I mentioned to her, unfortunately I will be on the road a lot during the holidays doing the normal Christmas performances. I told her my last stop before Christmas would be in Franklin, North Carolina at the Smoky Mountain Center there, and I might be able to pass through quickly telling her I needed to be back in Nashville to help with the Christmas play at church. While disappointed, she understood. I was beginning to think this could develop into something more than just friendship, and I wasn't ready for a deeper relationship. I didn't make excuses, only knew I needed to keep some distance between us at this time.

As promised, Millie was waiting for me at the bus station. She hugged my neck so hard I was certain I would suffocate, but I returned the hug and we kissed, this time passionately. "Gosh, Ricky, how I have missed you. I didn't really know how much you meant to me until now. I love your letters, and the song you wrote, wow! That really touched my heart. You really know how to put your feelings into words."

"Millie, oh Millie, you make me feel so great. I really do love you. I want us to be a couple. Is that something you want? I know our age difference is not as meaningful as it was when we were kids, and the distance between us now, you in Nashville and me in New York, is going to make it difficult to see each other very often. I have three and half years of college left. Will you wait for me?"

Millie smiled, took my hands in hers, on tip toes she kissed me. For the first time in my life I really felt like a real grown-up, felt as if I really had a girl friend, and even though dating in person would be out of the question, I knew we were now a couple and that the age difference was not an issue. The holidays passed with us being together most of the time and we both cried when the time came for us to go our separate ways, for now. We shared a special love, platonic as it might be now, but I knew our love would develop when we could be together later, at least after I graduated. We both vowed to wait.

COMPANIONS
Togetherness

The day after New Year's Day Millie left driving back to Nashville. Our parting moments were special. We kissed, this time passionately, and hugged each other and promised to write every week. I could not travel back to New York and Juilliard until the residence hall opened for the spring semester. Any earlier arrival meant nowhere to stay and I could not afford a hotel for several days. I knew I could contact Josh and stay with him at Michael's, but I really did not want to get involved personally with them. I had no problem with their relationship or their lifestyle. My concern was that I had promised the restaurant owner I would be back on the job as soon as I could get access to my room. He fully understood the rules at Juilliard and was gracious with his acknowledgement of my situation. I hated to leave Millie, hated to leave Mom and Dad, but I was anxious to get back to my studies knowing the sooner I finished college, the sooner Millie and I would be together.

I stayed with Mom and Dad and enjoyed some family time just reminiscing about growing up, hearing stories from them about their teenage years. I didn't realize that Dad was such a hunk in his younger years, but Mom assured me she did everything she could to win him over. I probably blushed thinking about them as teenage lovers, but then again, they were older when they got married and I came along much later. I valued their relationship, and hoped that one day my life with Millie would be as wonderful as Mom and Dad always seemed to be.

Two days before the residence hall would open, Dad drove me to the bus station, and Mom, of course, went with us. I wished I could have flown, but there just weren't the funds to pay for a plane ticket when a bus ticket was a fraction of the cost. Our parting was tearful, but Mom always cried when I left. Dad tried to be a stoic about me leaving, but he actually hugged me and that brought tears to my eyes. Here I was, approaching my last months at my first year at Juilliard, planning what to do in the spring, to either just work with no place to stay or continue with summer classes. I decided this was a no-brainer unless I went back home for the summer and worked in the café there. I know Mom and Dad would like for me to be home, but staying here during summer might be the best option. However, after checking, I discovered there are no summer classes, just some specialty workshops. I knew I could not afford to do that, so my choice was to go home and risk not getting my job back here and running this risk of not getting one at the café back home. I was beginning to think life hands out a lot of challenges, but I knew in time I would succeed, especially if Millie was going to be with me.

With the Christmas and New Year's holidays behind me I knew I had to get with Tom and Vic regarding the next tours. We typically planned several events around Valentine's Day, St. Patrick's Day, and of course the beginning of spring. I was struggling with new songs, attempting to write some lyrics that could be used for each event, and needed to sit down with Vic about the music and also get with Tom regarding any new talent as openers to the new shows. I knew Tom was booking a first tour in the south-central part of the country to avoid some of the harsher weather in the northeast. Having been to school in New York, I feared getting stranded in some of those wonderful cities with snow storms and inclement weather. I cannot say I miss that part of my living arrangement while in New York, but fully appreciated having the opportunity for a Juilliard education.

Being at home in Nashville for me now can be both exciting and lonely without Millie. I think of her often, miss her every day, and her mark is left everywhere in our house for me to appreciate her talents. I moved a beautiful picture of her from the hallway to the foyer where I can see her face every time I come and go from the house. My love for her as my wonderful wife and constant companion lives in my heart and mind every minute of each day. I will long remember the great times we had together. I know she is playing the piano and singing in the heavenly choir, teaching the children and loving every minute of the day. She was so special on this earth and I know she has gained recognition as a wonderful and beautiful person in Heaven.

After getting settled in at home, unpacking, and raiding the refrigerator, finding nothing of any sustenance to eat, I decided to order a pizza. That would be quick, no dishes for me to clean up. The lady who looks after the house always mentioned to me to let her know when I would be home and she would have the refrigerator stocked, but with the holidays, I did not want to take her away from her family. I know that two of her children travelled from other cities to spend time at home. I changed into some comfortable clothes, slippers, and found a bottle of wine in the pantry. I figured one glass was very deserving after the drive home. The pizza delivery would be in a few minutes, and chasing it with a good Malbec would just hit the spot.

When the pizza arrived, I settled in at the breakfast table, opened the pizza, grabbed the telephone, had my glass of wine, and called Tom. We had a lot to discuss, and before I realized it, I had eaten all but two slices of the pizza and was on a second glass of wine. Millie would have had something to say about that, but I guess I was famished. Tom and I agreed to get with Vic and lay out the schedule, get the troop together, and in as much as we both somewhat dreaded a long tour, we were also excited about this one.

A south central US tour would take us southwest from Nashville with a first stop in Little Rock, Arkansas the last weekend in January. From there we were heading to Fort Smith, then to Oklahoma City, south to Dallas, ending our tour in Fort Worth, Texas. By that time I knew everyone would be exhausted, but the tour had more stops. We would head east to Shreve Port, Louisiana. From there we planned to travel to Baton Rouge finally ending our tour in New Orleans with Mardi Gras. This would serve two purposes. First, we would be there entertaining during the entire days of Mardi Gras, and second this would provide the troop some time to enjoy the event before ending the almost two months on the road. This was a very long time for everyone to be away from family, but Tom and I knew this was an important tour with major bookings. No way to turn back now.

∞

I arrived at the bus station in New York and had to take a cab to Juilliard. I longed for the time when I might have a car, but again too much expense while I am struggling with meeting financial ends now. I found the residence hall open and available and my new roommate, no longer Josh since he had moved in with Michael, was a super guy named Victor Kilman, Vic as he preferred to be called. We talked and he seemed to be very talented, played several instruments and desired to be a music director after graduating. He came from Georgia and this was his first time as well in New York. We actually hit it off and were friends immediately. He had a girl friend back home, ironically two years older than he is, and he was surprised that my girl friend was five years older. However, I claimed she was just a little over four years older.

The rest of the year went well. My classes were super and I was learning so much about the piano, writing scores, and just making friends with other students. I wrote Millie every week as I promised and she was diligent in her writing. I thoroughly enjoyed hearing about her teaching and what some of those kids could say, the things that came to their minds, and how they would just erupt with information that probably their parents did not want shared. Of course, Millie, being the type person she is, listened carefully, laughed a lot, but had to be serious with the kids. Her letters always made me smile.

Millie seemed to have a sense of caring for me in other ways. When I received one of her letters and in opening it, unfolding the paper, a money order for one-hundred dollars fell out. Her note to me said: "This money is for you to save so you can get home for the summer vacation. It is for you to purchase a bus ticket, not to spend on anything else, especially dates with girls."

When I wrote her and expressed my sincere gratitude for the bus fare and told her I would be home for the summer vacation, she was excited and told me we must spend some special time together. She never mentioned the money. She wanted to know how my classes were and if I was keeping my zipper shut. I had to smile, but wrote back telling her if I did that all the time I would not be able to go to the bathroom. I knew what she was saying, and without a doubt I knew she understood that there were no other girls, or even another girl. I vowed to be only with her in time and she was definitely reciprocating.

Tom, Darren and Vic were waiting at the buses and most of the band members had arrived. We had the usual chatter and everyone greeting each other after a long holiday, exchanging stories about children, grandchildren, some funny but all exciting. As expected there were individuals who dreaded being away from family for this particular tour. Tom tried to keep everyone happy, but the true excitement would not happen until we were underway and at our first performance. I wanted to introduce a new song I had been working on, but Tom wanted me to open with "Shirley" since there seemed to be an expectation from the audience to hear that one. I consented knowing Vic would have the best musical arrangement for the opening.

Tom scheduled a new male singer, Alvin Singer, for the pre-performance. I had to comment on the last name, not that it was unusual, just ironic. Tom told me that really was Alvin's last name. Alvin was young, probably twenty-one, no hit records, but trying to break into the business. Tom told me Alvin would be traveling with us and opening at each performance. I only stated that if he bombed, that would not happen. Tom laughed and told me to keep an open mind that Alvin would be great. Some of my band would be backing Alvin up with instruments and voice. I figured Millie would definitely approve of this approach, giving a young man the opportunity to be on stage in front of what we learned were sell-out performances for all events. I figured Millie was up there having a hand in making a lot of this to happen.

The buses were loaded, vans and other vehicles aligned our convoy and with some of the members' tempers flying and others seemed elated, we got underway heading for Little Rock. We would be performing in the Barton Coliseum, one evening show on Friday, two shows on Saturday, and an evening show on Sunday. We would stay through Monday and pull out heading to Fort Smith. Weather permitting this would be great first and second stops before heading farther west.

Arriving in Little Rock and getting everyone settled in at a hotel takes time. We actually arrived Wednesday evening as planned. Thursday would be the time to get to Barton, set up the equipment, practice, and I definitely wanted to hear Alvin sing. He joined up Wednesday at the hotel and I was pleasantly surprised. Alvin was a very clean cut, slim, very good looking young man with obvious manners. I immediately felt like his father. At dinner, he told us about his desire to be a good performer, a desire he'd had since he was a little boy. What made me feel old was he had been following my career and knew most of my songs from memory. I had to admit I liked him more but warned him he better not sing and perform my songs better than me.

As always the evening was long and Vic insisted the members plan a short night and be available Thursday morning after breakfast of their choosing, and at the buses no later than ten o'clock. Ahs and disappointments were expressed, but everyone understood not being on time was not an option. It was always good for me to sit back and watch Vic work his wonders on this group of disparate and highly talented individuals. Alvin seemed surprised at the reactions having little exposure to such a diverse group and in watching my reactions, seemed to relax. I told Alvin tomorrow he would see a different group of people, same individuals, but attitudes become very professional and the dedication to their music would be impeccable.

What goes on behind the scenes to make a full performance production would surprise most people. Arguments abound, shouting, tempers flying, instruments being tested, guitar strings breaking, piano out of tune, someone forgot finger picks, sending runners to stores for forgotten items, a lot of hassle and chaos, but it all comes together and the performance seems flawless. If the audience only knew how difficult it is to orchestrate each performance, they would probably either be surprised or shocked. This was Alvin's first real exposure to seeing a performance come together. He would be first on stage and I think he was so scared he mentioned to Tom he was afraid he would wet his pants.

The practice sessions went well Thursday. These are not "dress rehearsals" as you might expect, but more getting organized and prepared for what songs would be performed and in what order. Vic always has this part under complete control. Alvin blundered a couple of times during his practice, but he has a marvelous voice, his youth coming through with enthusiasm. He was prepared to sing several older songs by some well-known performers and several newer songs that had been on the hit parade charts. Tom and Vic endorsed this approach and I approved. I knew Alvin would be a great opening performer and the audience would accept him.

I have to admit the weekend went very well, all shows were completely sold out and Alvin was well-received getting a lot of kudos and a lot of the younger girls approached him at the intermission and again at the end of the show for autographs. I think they just wanted to get close to him. After all he is a young stud. I wanted to tell him his blue jeans were too tight, but I guess he knew what he was wearing would impress the ladies. Millie would have made me change pants if I had worn anything that tight on stage. Regardless, everyone was thrilled with the performances, got a good night's sleep after a very hearty meal and probably more "cheers" than needed. I had a couple of glasses of wine with Tom and Vic. Darren only drinks beer and stayed mostly with some of the troops who helped him set up and break down the equipment. That is a tough job getting it up and down, packed back into the trailers securely and safely only to repeat the process many times during a tour. Thankfully, Darren is paid well.

I put the money away safely as Millie instructed, saving it for a bus ticket back home as soon as classes ended and the residence hall closed. The rest of the year, while it was going very well, was actually dragging for me personally because I thought often of being with Millie in the summer as much as possible. I know she would be in Nashville, miles away from home, but somehow I was betting we would get together several times. My classes required studying a lot, consuming much of my time, and soon final exams meant cramming, cramming, and more cramming. I was becoming more accomplished on the piano, and Vic started teaching me how to play the guitar. I probably could have learned quicker, but classes demanded much of my free time, that along with still working at the restaurant. My boss was preparing for me to be away for the summer, but promised me my job when I returned. This alone took a lot of pressure off me.

If miracles happen, one did as the end of the year approached and my final exam scores were posted with me receiving "A's" in all subjects. I was so elated and relieved, I actually shouted. Vic had very good grades as well and his mom and dad sent airfare for him to fly home. I envied that, but I was fortunate to have the funds for a bus ride home. I vowed one day I would fly from place to place. Little did I know what the future would bring. Vic and I said our goodbyes and vowed to be roomies again in the fall. He said he would be working some with the music director at his church during the summer and probably would find some part-time work at a fast food restaurant. He said he worked at McDonalds during high school and while the money is not great, he enjoyed meeting a lot of people and made some great friends at work. I told him about the café I would be working at during the summer and that the only saving grace was tips, the salary was pitiful.

I worked my last day at the café, returned to the residence hall to pack what I needed to take home, not that I had much to take, and said my good-byes to several close classmates, called for a cab and headed to the bus station. I can't say that after riding the bus several times made the trip any easier or enjoyable. My saving grace was knowing I would soon be seeing Millie again and hopefully would have a great summer vacation. The café job would yield some spending money but not sufficient for really having the funds to treat Millie to a decent dinner when she came over from Nashville. I would have liked to be able to travel there and get a summer job that would be more in line with my planned music career, but I would have no place to stay, and while I was certain I could bunk out in Millie's apartment, that would be frowned on by our parents. I had to resign myself to staying at home and making the best of the situation.

As usual, the long ride home from New York to Tennessee was laborious. I settled in a window seat, read a magazine article about the New York Philharmonic Orchestra and dreamed that one day I might be a part of that great symphony as one of their finest pianists that was if I could not find a job in Nashville close to Millie. I vowed to myself to check into possibilities when I returned to Juilliard in the fall. In the back of my mind, I was wondering if they would take an intern, even for no pay, to gain experience and exposure. Well, I could dream. I also had time to think about how I would spend some time with Millie. She would be out of school for the summer vacation, but knowing her she would be working somewhere with children.

Being older now, almost twenty very soon, I wanted to have a more serious relationship with Millie. I just didn't want to upset her in any way by being too serious, but I had to admit to myself that I wanted to hold her, kiss her passionately and feel her touch as we did in the past. Knowing Millie would not go for any very serious relationship outside of marriage, I had to accept the fact we would have fun and enjoy any time together, but I knew a sexual relationship would not happen, well other than intimate touching. Regrettably I could accept that.

I must have dosed off for some time and was awakened by people shuffling around. We had made an intermediate stop for which some people got off the bus and others boarded. There had been no one in the seat beside me for the ride so far, but a young man sat down next to me and introduced himself as Darren Toffler. He was on his way to Nashville, the final stop for this bus. He said he attending a technical college and hoped one day to enter the music business. We talked for the rest of the time until my stop about my music and time at Juilliard, and exchanged mailing addresses vowing to keep in touch. He seemed to be a great guy and we hit it off immediately. I told him the love of my life was in Nashville and that our plan was to marry after I graduated. The love of his life was attending college in North Carolina and they were engaged. No wedding plans since he needed to finish college also and get a job. They had been going together since junior high school. I told him Millie and I were friends since childhood.

It is a small world. When I got to my destination, Darren and I shook hands and both of us wondered if our paths would ever cross again. Little did I know at that time what the future would bring. Mom and Dad were at the bus station and I got hugged so tightly I almost stopped breathing. I was as glad to see them as they were me. During the drive home, talk was un-stoppable; so many questions about my first year, my grades, friends I had made and the restaurant server job, and were Millie and me still in touch. I hardly had time to answer one question before another one landed. I was thinking "did they not read my letters?" I knew Mom and Dad just wanted to know all about everything. When Dad asked if I had met any girls that I was serious with, I told him only one, Millie. He laughed and told me he really never thought that Millie and I would be a pair, but admitted he had resigned himself to the fact we were serious with each other and that she is really a very wonderful person. He didn't think I was making a bad choice.

∾

The trip from Little Rock to Fort Smith was uneventful. The troops finally settled in adjusting to the tour. It usually takes at least one or two stops and half a dozen performances to get everyone wound tightly and working together without killing each other. Vic and Darren were incredible in their approach with the group, but did not tolerate any major outbreaks. It is inevitable that a couple of the guys will always argue about something, but for the most part they controlled themselves and behaved as adults.

Fort Smith was great, another complete sell-out and Alvin was spectacular this time, no blunders. I did convince him to buy some blue jeans that did not display his personal physical attributes so obviously. He admitted the tight ones caused him some pain moving about on stage. He decided on a pair with some pocket designs, looser in the crotch, and as he put it definitely more comfortable when he danced around on the stage. I am certain the young ladies in the audience were just as impressed with him because of his good looks, great voice, and probably the new attire made them wonder as to other non-obvious bodily features.

I wanted to open, once again, with my new hit, but Tom and Vic still insisted I open with "Shirley" and save the new song for New Orleans. I resorted to the fact the boss doesn't always get his way. I did dedicate the performances in Fort Smith to the memory of Millie. I still missed getting back to the hotel room and calling her to tell her about the shows and hear about her day. I thought a couple of times about calling Tammy just to check in with her and see how things were going, but I felt it might be presumptuous on my part and that she might misinterpret my intentions as more serious than they were. It does get lonely on these trips, but I can truthfully admit I had never stepped out of line, and I had no intentions of starting now.

Oklahoma City and Dallas were invigorating for everyone. Alvin wanted to do one of my songs during the opening at Dallas. I finally consented and Tom was beside himself not wanting Alvin to sing my song. Tom expressed this openly to me, but not in front of Alvin. Alvin continued to wow the young ladies and he always had so many gathering around him at intermission and after the performances just wanting to touch him and get his autograph. Sales of his recordings and memorabilia were very good. I was beginning to think this might be Alvin's show instead of mine, but the audiences gave me standing ovations and wanted encore songs. Every show lasted longer than planned, especially the second performances of each day. Weekend attendances were always to capacity, and I came to the realization that while I was the main attraction, word had spread quickly about Alvin and there was definitely an increase in the younger audiences.

On the way to Fort Worth, we experienced a flat tire on my bus. Obviously we picked up something that punctured an inside back tire. This caused a major delay of several hours finding a resource to come to us to make the repair, actually bringing a new tire. Seeing our convoy on the side of the road brought about a great deal of slowing traffic, even with a couple of people stopping seeking autographs. One car of young girls went wild when they saw Alvin and he enjoyed the recognition and "fellowship" with them for a while before they had to leave. I bet there were at least five State Highway Troopers' cars mingled in our convoy. I am certain this was to make sure we got back on the road and did not create any more turmoil by slowing traffic and people stopping. This is just another day in the life of a travelling musical group.

Fort Smith was great, and the tour on to Shreveport proved uneventful. The audience was great. We had super motel accommodations and probably pigged out at some of the local restaurants. Shreveport is the largest city in Louisiana and offers not only a great place to entertain, but the casinos offered a time for some of the troops to relax and lose some earned income while others did well. I thought some of the troops got a little tipsy too quickly, but everyone was completely sober for the performances. While I did not overindulge, I did enjoy some great sea food and wonderful wine. Tom kept a close eye on everyone and I guess that was one of the few times he let his hair down and seemed to really enjoy being himself.

Baton Rouge just about killed me with all the oysters and crawfish. It seemed the more they boiled those little creatures, the hotter they got. I wasn't sure I could perform after indulging myself and feeling so stuffed.

Many of the troops had beer and wine, no hard stuff, but enough to raise the loudness temperature. With so many of us, the restaurant management had to turn away a number of customers. We probably stayed longer than needed, or even appreciated by the manager, but a lot of money was spent and the tip was huge. They couldn't complain.

Alvin opened in Baton Rouge, but Vic would not let him use another of my songs fearing Tom's disapproval. He did a couple of Jim Reeves' songs and some from his latest recording. Overall, he was getting better and I discussed with Tom and Vic about having him on our next tour. After all, the money he was receiving was probably more than he had ever earned in his lifetime and his billing with Ricky Snyder was a great promotion for him.

I opened in Baton Rouge, not with "Shirley," but with "Beautiful People" the song I wrote to Millie about my adventure in seeing people in New York. We were there for four days of performances at the end of April and things were heating up everywhere in preparation for Mardi Gras in New Orleans. Hotels there were quickly filling rooms so thankfully Tom had booked our accommodations almost a year in advance. With the number of troops, we pretty much filled a lot of any hotel. Baton Rouge was a wonderful audience and we left there with good humor and high energy. We would need all the help we could muster up for New Orleans and Mardi Gras.

Alvin came to me and was concerned about what would happen after Mardi Gras, our last stop of this tour. I assured him we would take a couple of weeks break to allow everyone to re-connect with their families and relax for a while. He wanted to join our next tour, asking where it would take us. I called Tom and Vic in and we all emphasized what a great job Alvin was doing and appreciated the fact he was drawing a youthful audience. I joked with him about his blue jeans and he insisted his privates were more comfortable now.

We arrived in New Orleans four days before the opening of Mardi Gras and had one nightly performance the day before. Spirits were high, the crowd outside was enthusiastic, louder than any group we had previously performed to, and some were unrecognizable because of their pre-Mardi Gras attire. The management of the coliseum did not allow face masks to be worn during attendance as a matter of security. Security was at an all time high, and we had difficulty getting back and forth to our hotel because of the crowded streets. It was almost impossible to travel by vehicle, and Darren was grateful the buses could be parked inside the coliseum. He was also concerned about all the equipment and was assured it would be safe.

Alvin, of course opened wearing a new pair of blue jeans with sequins and very obvious no-covered zipper fly. The jeans did not show any outstanding character features, but I am certain the girls wanted to see what lay behind that golden ring pull. I said nothing to him since the young girls were jumping out of their seats when he started moving around. He left his shirt unbuttoned almost to his belly button displaying a very smooth and hairless chest. I thought of my younger days in the business when most of us wore suits and ties on stage or more elaborate sequined outfits. Times had certainly changed. Millie would have made Alvin button his shirt.

When I was introduced, the applause was thunderous. I was not Alvin, but still good looking for a fiftyish old guy. I opened with my latest hit and the audience was on their feet. While not as popular as "Shirley" this song was very appropriate for Mardi Gras. As usual, Vic was right on. The first few bars raised the temperature in the coliseum as I started with my baritone voice:

> *The lava light's a pretty sight,*
> *But it makes it dim in here;*
> *I smoke another cigarette*
> *(And) I drink another beer.*

"Ladies and gentleman, my latest hit, ***Bartender, Call Heaven.***" [6] I hope you enjoy this one. Welcome to our Mardi Gras performance!" I continued singing:

> *I can't help it if I'm lonely,*
> *This bar has been my home;*
> *I've been here almost every night*
> *Since I have been alone.*

---

[6] Written by Donald Arlo Jennings April 22, 1984.

Bartender, bartender,
Please serve me a beer,
Bartender, bartender,
I can't get away from here.

I've slept in muddy ditches,
(Lord) I've walked in freezing rains,
I've hitched-hiked semis, stolen rides
And even hoboed the trains.

But now I sit here at this bar
And shake my dizzy head,
And pray that when I wake up,
I hope that I'll be dead.

Bartender, bartender,
How long has it been?
Bartender, bartender,
I need me a friend.

This beer is getting hot
From the holding of my hand,
And the cigarette smoke
Is now more than I can stand.

So I'm thinking as I'm walking
Out the door, one more time,
Bartender, call heaven,
I've reached the end of my line.

I've gone through the stages,
Of forgetting about her;
I've gone through the motion,
But it is all now a blur.

Bartender, bartender,
Call Heaven for me,
Bartender, bartender,
She's set my soul free.
  Bartender, bartender....

The audience went wild, hollering and screaming. I am certain many there could relate to the words. The rest of the performance was just as eventful and we actually went over almost thirty minutes past the scheduled end time. I brought Alvin out one more time and we sorta kinda did a duet. That was fun mainly because it was not rehearsed. We blundered some but it was well-received.

We had three more days of performances, two per day for which I ended each performance by sitting at my piano playing and singing "Piano Man" with a unique performance by Vic playing his harmonica. He seldom got any billing, but this was great for him. At the end, the audience was on their feet, a standing ovation with thunderous applause. These are the times it is hard to wipe a smile from my face. A tear came to my eyes knowing Millie was watching from above and would approve. The troops all came to the front of the stage for a final bow.

After all performances the troops would have some time to enjoy what was left of Mardi Gras and enjoy New Orleans before we returned to Nashville. Many of the individuals were anxious to get to their various home cities, see wives and kids, and just relax. I was actually anxious to get back home and to Nashville, but dreaded the empty house.

We hadn't been home but a few hours with Mom insisting she feed my skinny body, wanting to know why I wasn't eating properly working at restaurant. I loved her cooking and probably stuffed myself. I just did not want to gain a lot of weight or my skimpy wardrobe would have to be replaced and I did not have the money to do that. I did not want Mom and Dad to take on that expense either. Sometimes one must adjust to being on the poor side of existence.

We had adjourned to the living room when the doorbell sounded. I figured it was for Mom or Dad, someone from the church, maybe even checking to see if I got home okay. Mom answered the door and was very quiet. She looked back at me and said, "Ricky, there is someone to see you." I reluctantly got out of my comfortable position and sauntered to the door. I almost jumped out of my skin when I saw Millie standing there. I am certain that Mom and Dad for the first time saw Millie and me really kiss and cling to each other. My excitement brought tears to my face. Millie simply said, "Well, are you going to invite me in?"

There were more hugs from Millie with Mom and Dad and quickly talking about when Millie had gotten home, how was her teaching job, was her apartment nice, what was the school like, and on and on. I finally told Mom and Dad they were questioning Millie to death. Millie only smiled and said, "No problem. It is really good to catch up and know everyone is okay. Ricky, it is so good to see you. You must have grown several inches since Christmas." We chatted for a couple more minutes and then Millie asked me if I wanted to walk to the park. I was thinking what a foolish question, but I smiled and acknowledged that I would love that. I had on my blue jeans, sneakers with no socks, and a pull over t-shirt. I really wanted to change into something less confining, but thought better at the time. Millie had on a beautiful pair of knee-high yellow shorts, and a cream-colored sun top. I was already getting excited.

As we walked to the park, hand-in-hand, touching heads together in as much as possible now that I was at least a head taller than Millie. We chatted about everything and nothing in particular. I put my arm around her waist and pulled her closer to me. She acknowledged that by doing the same. Fortunately when we found our favorite bench by the pond it was available and we sat down, just staring into each other's eyes. We kissed again, more passionately. Several couples walked by, hand-in-hand, and we smiled. Millie reached over and rubbed my cheek telling me how handsome I was. I kissed her again and responded that her beauty made the sun look dim. She is beautiful, such clear radiant skin, her hair is like silk, and just flows around her face, highlighting her features even more. Her eyes just take my breath away, especially when she looks directly into my eyes and smiles showing those gorgeous brilliant white teeth. Oh, I melt at the very sight of her, just wanting to hold her and love her.

We sat there touching each other and it was very obvious that I was excited. Very discretely she rubbed me and I had to move her hand. I told her that was dangerous for both of us, me because accidents do happen to me when I am with her especially when it has been a while with no relief, and her because my excitement just wants to be closer to her. She laughed and said that we had agreed to wait. I said I am waiting, but parts of me aren't. We cuddled closer and unfortunately she did keep her hands away, much to my chagrin. I knew, however, one more touch and we both would have seen the results bleed through my jeans.

I guess we sat and kissed and hugged, talking and joking with one another until it was almost time for dinner. She asked me if I wanted to come to her house for dinner, that she had mentioned the possibility to her parents. I readily accepted without any notion that my parents would be expecting me to have my first dinner at home with them. I knew they would be okay with my decision. I was so in love at the moment, I probably would have agreed to eat with Millie anywhere. We walked back, first to my house to explain to my parents, then to her house for dinner and an enjoyable evening together. I knew at that time, regardless of not being intimate, my life was changing and all I wanted was to spend the rest of my life with Millie. I decided during dinner, as I listened to her parents, that sometime that evening, I would ask Millie if she would wait for me. After all, I had three more years at Juilliard, no major source of income, no car, no house, and my future looked bleak with no more than a waiter's job. Millie was already on her way of being successful.

After dinner and helping to clear the table and do the dishes, Millie and I exited to the front porch and sat in the swing. We cuddled and in a somewhat bashful way I said, "Millie, I want you to know that I care more for you than anything on this earth. I love you, really love you and you have been the only girl I really cared for. There really have been no others. I have not been intimate or had sex with any girl or anyone. I crave that intimacy with you, but we agreed to wait. What I am really asking is if you can wait three or four more years for me to finish college and get out in the world? I know you have a great job, one you enjoy and will be so successful. Here I am a struggling college student with no real plans for a decent career. I worry if we will become a true couple later and if I will be able to support you."

Millie shushed me by putting two fingers to my lips. She laughed and kissed me on the cheek, then said, "You always amaze me. You worry about tomorrow when you can enjoy the day. First, I want you to know that while I did date a couple of guys in college, they were friends. No, we did not go all the way, but I admit I did kiss them. Regardless, neither was you and was not special like you. Ricky, I loved you when I baby-sit for you, but that was more a kid liking a kid as a friend. I grew even fonder of you when I was teaching you piano lessons. I grew much fonder of you when you started writing songs and when I left for college, your letters kept me going. I watched you grow into the fine young man you are today and I admire you and love you more each day. Ricky, I would wait ten years for you, and if I had to hold down two jobs to support us, I would gladly do so. But, you know, I think you will be a huge success and I swear I will be by your side pushing you every inch of the way. I promise, and excuse my English, but I will personally kick your ass if you don't hang in there and be what I know you can be."

I was speechless. All I could do was to hold her face in my hands and to kiss her until we both couldn't breathe. "I love you so much. You not only told me what I wanted to hear from your lips, but now I know you feel the same way I do. Oh, I love you!"

We sat in the swing, not speaking for a few minutes, just holding each other and it seemed involuntarily kissing. I had my left arm around her waist pulling her close to me and my right arm under her breast holding her tightly. She was gently rubbing the inner side of my left thigh, occasionally going higher. I was already excited and the intimacy reduced me to a very excited boy resulting in a sudden emotional release of ecstasy for which I immediately knew Millie could tell by the way I squeezed her more tightly and was breathing hard. Neither of us said anything.

In a few minutes, I looked her deep in those beautiful eyes and asked her to marry me. She responded, "Ricky, I said I would wait for you and I will marry you, but not now, not until you finish college. You don't need more distractions than you can handle. Besides, I would be in Nashville and you in New York. What kind of relationship would that be for three years? And then, what would you do job-wise? No, no, we must wait. I know you will survive and you will only be twenty-two years old. I will be twenty-seven and that is still young for us both and plenty of time to have a great relationship. We will want children and we cannot risk me getting pregnant while you are still in school. Okay?"

What could I say? Millie was always the more reasonable and logical one, especially with me and she dealt so perfectly with my raging hormones, not letting me do something both of us would regret. I guess that is why I loved her so much. After a few more minutes, we kissed and she went inside and I walked home, needing a cold shower.

March weather in Nashville can be interesting, either very cold with snow, or maybe very nice and sunny. When I we arrived from New Orleans at the end of the long road tour, it was raining, cold with the temperature in the low thirties. My housekeeper knew when I would be back and had the house warm and lights turned on in several rooms as well as the outside area lights. That was welcoming, but still for me it was sad knowing I would enter an empty house.

I didn't unpack, but went straight to the kitchen and found a bottle of wine, opening it, pouring a glass, getting a chunk of cheese, and retiring to my favorite chair in the den. I turned on the gas logs, and just chilled for a few minutes. I thought of Tammy and decided to call her. Again, I told myself, this was nothing serious, just someone to talk with and share our events of the past couple of months.

Tammy answered on the third ring and seemed excited to hear from me. I sipped my wine and we just chatted away for almost an hour, endlessly taking turns about the crazy people she had staying with her at various days and some unusual expectations, especially for food. She was interrupted a couple of times by guests asking question, but we picked back up on our conversation as soon as she came back to the telephone. I relayed information on the various performances and some of the people we encountered wanting autographs. She laughed some and told me that she expected me to sign many autographs.

I told her about Alvin and his tight jeans, but how much the younger generation, particularly girls, loved him and just swooned when he walked onto the stage. We talked about when we were younger, and how we presented ourselves versus the young folks today. We laughed and had a great time talking. She had a customer come in, so we said our goodbyes and agreed to keep in touch. Nothing serious, I told myself.

COMPANIONS
Partings

Time seemed to fly by for me at home in Townsend. I worked daily at the local café and received several good tips on how to spend my time at Juilliard. I was advised by several of the locals that I would do well, but I should return home and take a job at the church playing the piano and become the music director because Doug Tyson would be retiring by the time I graduated. I acknowledged each marvelous opportunity and assured each one that their idea was one for me to think about. I also received good monetary tips from some of the people who knew me best. Mom and Dad dropped in several times for breakfast or lunch, primarily to brag about me and really, I think, to see what type server I was for the café. They knew this would probably be my last year working here and maybe my last year coming home for the summers.

I thought of Millie often, calling her once or twice, but she mainly called me at least once a week. I wrote her almost daily, but only mailed the letters once a week, not separately, but I put them in one envelope to save postage. Millie and I talked about her job, what she was going to do during the summer to stay employed until school reconvened in August. We spoke softly about our future and as would be expected, I got mushy a few times, but Millie brought me back to the real world. I knew in my heart she would be good for me and I would be good for her.

She continued to encourage me regarding my studies at Juilliard, insisting that I continue making good grades and to start looking at finding some type internship that could help promote my music career. Of course she insisted I continue to write lyrics and music and to send some to her even if I personally did not think they were my best work. She said she would be the judge of what was great, or just good. I half-way promised to do the best I could, but told her that studying and working left little time for being creative.

The summer days seemed long and lonely. I guess because it was partly my attitude and partly because the café owners had me working almost every shift. While the pay was not great, the tips were generous in allowing me to at least bank some spending money for the coming school year. The long days also prevented me from sulking about not being with Millie. I was so tired at the end of each day that I just wanted to go home and go to bed and sleep. Mom insisted I still practice my piano so I would not forget how to play. I personally thought that was impossible, but I did so to please her. This was actually relaxing for me and calmed my stress.

With the end of summer soon approaching, I started preparing myself to move back to New York and take up my fast pace and routine at Juilliard. I knew the second year would be tougher in one way and easier in others because I now knew my way around both the campus and the immediate vicinity. I also knew my server job at the restaurant was waiting for me. Thinking about what Millie has suggested, I vowed to start looking around at some opportunities to improve my future career in music. I also thought about my time on the bus home dreaming about being a part of the New York Philharmonic Orchestra and if they would take an intern. I definitely would check in to any and all opportunities. Well, a guy can dream. What else can you do on a long bus ride?

The summer seemed to drag during my time in Nashville. I continued to walk about in the empty house thinking about how my life with Millie had been so great and now just seemed so empty. My phone call to Tammy was good, but I knew in my heart no one could ever take the place of Millie regardless of how much we could care for one another. Besides I was not ready for a relationship but I wanted and needed companionship and just someone to talk to about theirs and my daily events, the good and the bad times or just whatever came to mind. Emptiness can bring back so many memories, and with Millie the memories were all good. I guess to relieve my sadness, but in making me sadder, I retreated to my music room, opened my grand Steinway and started playing Piano Man. This was both a happy and a sad song. I sang the lyrics with no audience, but I felt the effects of being in a bar. I had a glass of wine sitting on the top of the piano, and watched it vibrate as I pounded the keys with true enthusiasm. Millie always would enter the room and stand next to the piano whenever I played that song. Sometimes she would join me in singing the lyrics. How I miss her and those moments.

I had just finished playing and picked up my glass of wine when the telephone rang. I had to step out of the music room to the hall to answer it since I would never allow a telephone in my music room in order to not be disturbed when I was either just playing or in the mood to write a new song. Millie would always catch the call and if it was critical she would gently approach me, but otherwise she would not disturb me. I also respected her the same way if she was in the music room playing the piano and singing. Oh, how I loved to hear her sing. I always wanted her to come on a tour with me and to sing with the group, but she constantly refused telling me that was my career and she had hers. I reminded her that if she hadn't taught me to play that I would never have had the opportunity to be what I am. She always smiled and touched my shoulder. No words were spoken.

The phone call was from Tom, as I expected. He wanted to know when I wanted to get together to plan the next tour. I knew he already had most of it planned out and booking in place, reserved theatres and motels or hotels. This was Tom. He wanted to start soon. He told me this next tour would take us to the northeast, starting at the civic center in Portland, Maine then moving south to Vermont, New Hampshire, Boston, Massachusetts, Connecticut, and the last stops in Rhode Island. He estimated approximately, though not all scheduled yet, some ten to twelve cities, mostly just weekend performances and a few with four days across a weekend. He anticipated another three months on the road including travel to New England and back to Nashville. I almost gasped at being on the road three more months. Tom reminded me that I chose my career and his job was to ensure I filled it to maximum. You just had to love Tom.

I had finished the call and hung up the telephone from Tom when it rang again. This time it was Darren. He wanted to know if I wanted to go to dinner with him and Tracy. I told him I did not want to intrude on his time at home with his wife and family, but he insisted, even consenting to come by and pick me up. Being somewhat lonely at the time and needing some human companionship, I consented and asked where we were going, and he told me he had picked out a nice restaurant, nothing fancy, but away from the maddening crowds where, even though I would be recognized, we could enjoy an outing without being mauled. I agreed, and after hanging up I went upstairs to change into something presentable, but comfortable.

The dinner and company of Tracy and Darren was good for me. Just getting out, having a good meal and enjoying being out and not having to perform was absolutely fantastic. I insisted on paying the bill and after Darren and I discussed it, he relented and for me this was a benefit to have time with special people for whom I really cared. I knew going back to an empty house would not be enjoyable, but the inevitable had to happen. I guess, thinking about being in an empty house, that being on the road with people I enjoyed, and doing what I really enjoyed, performing, was definitely better than the alternative.

I called Tom the next day and asked him to come over so we could finalize the plans for the New England tour and when we would have to get the troops together to get on the road. As always, Tom was well organized and had plans outlined for cities for which he still needed to book the events. He had names and numbers, and trip routes, theatres selected if not performing in the main coliseum of that area, and of course he wanted to get Vic involved to make certain the music was appropriate. He wanted to know which songs I wanted to open and close with, and if I wanted Alvin to join us again as the opening entertainer. I really liked Alvin and the way he brought in the younger crowds, especially the teenage girls. My vote was that Alvin is a keeper. Tom would make the arrangements with Alvin.

We called Vic and kept him on the telephone for more than two hours going over some of the details regarding the tour. Vic is first class in arranging the music to "fit the city" ensuring some of the songs are popular with all age groups. He wanted to know if I had any new songs and I mentioned I was working on one, but that it was not finished. I had not had the time at home, or alone, to complete the lyrics and the music.

As usual, Vic was very understanding knowing how intense creativity can be. Tom, Vic and I completed our lengthy conversation and Tom and I concluded with a nice full glass of wine. We talked about Millie for a while, reminiscing some of the times we had all been together, having fun, and enjoying each other's companionship.

Tom left, and I retreated to the kitchen in discovery of what the contents of my refrigerator might be. I settled on fixing a ham and cheese sandwich and eating by standing at the kitchen island. The day was beautiful, and I really wanted to be outside. I had a lawn service and they were there working in every corner of the yard, mowing, trimming bushes, edging, and all the things that should be done to keep the yard looking as if someone really lives there. I decided it was probably time to go back to the music room to complete the new song. I rather doubted we would use it on tour especially since it would not be recorded in time, but we had introduced songs before in order to get the audience's reaction. I played the music, changed the notes several times, changed the words several times, and finally decided that I was brain dead and needed to rest before making any more changes. I really needed to decide how to cope with my present state of mind and the changes now so prevalent in my life.

The bus trip back to New York and to Juilliard seemed to take forever. Even though I had made this trip on the bus several times, both between Townsend and New York and New York to Townsend, it just seemed to get longer rather than shorter. This trip an older gentleman sat down next to me, smiled, but was quiet for a while before asking me where I was going. When I told him I was on my way back to Juilliard for the school year. He smiled again and I became somewhat curious as to why. "Did you go to Juilliard?" I asked.

His reply was interesting. "No, not really. You see, I retired many years ago after thirty years of teaching at various schools. I actually taught for a couple of years at Juilliard, more in a substitute position. I was just not talented enough for that school, but I admired everyone who taught there and especially the students who were so talented and dedicated to a fine arts career."

"Where did you go after Juilliard?"

"Oh, that is a long story. You see I was not from New York, but grew up in Boston. I moved about for a while then married the love of my life. We moved to Philly where we raised two sons. My wife passed away three years ago, and I am returning to Boston after stopping in New York to visit my older son. My younger son lives in Nashville with his wife and daughter. My older son, funny as it may seem, is a professor at Juilliard. I guess that is why I smiled when you told me you were headed back to school there."

"Do you live in Boston now?"

"Oh, no. I still live in Philly. I am going back to a class reunion in Boston. Fifty-five years. I know many of my classmates have passed on, but there are still a few of us old fogies still hanging in there. I think it will be good to see some of them and see if we recognize each other after all these years. This will be the second reunion I have attended. The first was my ten year reunion. Time and commitments just did not allow for me to attend the others."

We talked about a lot of things, mostly just him reminiscing about old times, his sons, grandchildren, and what I wanted to do with my life. He wanted to know how I ended up at Juilliard and if I had someone who was the love of my life. I took pride in telling him about Millie. He was surprised she was five years older, but confessed his wife was a few months older. He wanted to know what I was going to do after graduating from Juilliard. At that time, I guess it was difficult for me to explain my ambitions, but I mentioned to him that I really wanted to play with the New York Philharmonic Orchestra and if possible to see if I could get an internship with them. Ironic as it might have been, he said his son played with them occasionally when one of their cellists was under the weather for some reason. He said he would speak to his son about helping me with getting to the right person. I was awed. Sometimes just being in the right place at the right time is amazing.

The rest of the trip was as interesting and after sharing names and me giving him information on how to reach me in case his son could help, we parted and I took a cab to the school. Upon arriving I found Vic had already checked in and was happy to see me knowing we would be roommates again. His enthusiasm was inspiring. I told him about my trip up and about the gentlemen on the bus and the possibility that his son, a professor at the school, could help me get an internship with the Philharmonic. I still had to keep my server job at the restaurant since I doubted I would get paid as an intern.

Vic had a wonderful summer. He told me he actually did go back and work at McDonalds and worked at the church helping with the music direction. The music director wanted him to come back after graduation and be his assistant. I told Vic several of the customers at the café in Townsend recommend that I return home after graduation and take the music director's job at our church. Vic laughed and told me he could never see me being so isolated in that type routine.

Vic never ceased to amaze me with his energy and willingness to help others. I mentioned to him about meeting Darren on the bus trip to Nashville and that we had exchanged contact information. Vic did not know Darren, but was interested in knowing more about our conversation. He was not just being nice, but was truly interested. I felt very relaxed around him. We talked about some possibilities after Juilliard, but neither of us had definite plans. Vic, however, did want to become a music director at some point in the future.

Several days later, I received a message in my mailbox to contact Professor Hansen in the music department. Even as a student of piano and in the music department every day, I had not encountered Professor Hansen, but after meeting him, I discovered he was the son of the gentleman I met on the bus. Professor Hansen talked to me about my goals and desires and actually wanted to hear me play the piano. He provided me with a contact, and recommended that I should attend a concert with him and his wife if my schedule permitted. I had to be honest in telling him I could not afford a ticket to the concert. He laughed and told me I would be his guest and not to worry about the ticket. I graciously accepted.

Back in my room, I told Vic all about the visit and he actually told me he would go with me to apply for the internship or whatever opportunity would arise out of my seeking to work with them. He wondered if he could somehow benefit from the visit by volunteering to help the music director. I was pleased he was interested and welcomed him going with me. We decided to go after class one day in the following week. After all, getting started in all our classes was our first priority and for me getting back to the routine of being a server at the restaurant working around my class schedule was my second priority. I definitely needed the job and could not pass up either opportunity.

I had not given Tammy my home phone number since I was on the road more than I was at home, but when the phone rang, I was surprised that it was her calling. I guess I acted shocked, but after hearing that she got the phone number from the check in registry, it made sense to me. I had forgotten I wrote my home phone number when I initially registered. She apologized for calling and asked if I was busy and just wanted to know how I was doing. I must have brightened up quickly telling her I was so glad to hear from her. I continued to eat my sandwich and rattled on about my day. I asked her how her days had been and if the house was full of customers. She told me there was only one vacancy and if I hurried I could have the room. We both laughed.

She gathered that I was somewhat depressed being alone without Millie and mentioned it would take some time. It took her over a year to get over the fact Cliff was not lingering around somewhere in the house. She said the worst part was going to bed at night knowing the other side was empty. She wanted to know when my next tour started and where we would be going and how long it would be before I returned. I told her about what Tom, Vic and I had discussed and about our plans for the New England, northeast tour. I promised to call her a few times while we were on the road to give her an update. After about forty minutes we hung up and I realized I really missed Millie more than ever.

With plans finalized, Tom had reservations in every city at various hotels and motels, confirmations with the coliseums and theatres for which we would be performing. I realized that many of these commitments had been in place for many months. I knew Tom planned so much in advance in order to secure spots at various theatres since most booked events many months ahead of time. Tom had scouted out desirable food places and gas stations along the route and ensured that bus parking was available. He also had inventoried all our memorabilia for selling and arranged for all the vehicles to be serviced prior to the long journey. I asked him if he was having the tires checked to make certain we didn't have another flat.

He smiled and told me the tires were great, the roads may be the most hazardous with pot holes, and motel parking lots were always a challenge with nails and broken glass. This is just part of the fun of being on the road. With rising gas prices now, especially diesel fuel, expenses were definitely increasing and multiple credit cards were in order.

We had two more weeks at home before "hitting the trail" as we often referred to our trips. Tom told me Alvin was anxious to get started again and had been performing two or three nights a week at a local night spot. Without any doubt, I knew those spots were filled with young ladies swooning over him. I was surprised he was still hanging out in Nashville, but was definitely glad Alvin had not decided to go solo. I suggested to Tom that he, Vic and I attend one night and see Alvin's performance. Tom agreed and we decided the coming Friday evening would be good for everyone. We expected Alvin to be surprised.   Friday came sooner than I realized and even though Vic could not join us because of plans with his family, Tom, his wife, and I showed up at the night spot and secured a table close to the stage where Alvin could look right down on us. When he came on stage, with a thunderous applause from the younger folks, especially the young ladies in the place, I noticed he once again had on some very tight jeans displaying attributes that I would probably not want to show. His shirt was unbuttoned down to his navel and he obviously had shaved his chest. His appearance was definitely to woo the women and be a sexy hunk as well as to ensure he earned his pay. He saw us and immediately nodded as he opened with one of my songs. Afterwards, he told the audience that the author and original recording artist, Ricky Snyder, was sitting at the front table. I stood and took a bow, raising my hand to acknowledge the applause. Alvin joined us at our table after he sang two more songs. I remained impressed with his performance style and as he expected, I admonished him for his attire. He laughed and told me I was getting old. I had to remind myself that, yes, I was old enough to be his father. Tom and his wife just bent over double laughing at both Alvin and me. We enjoyed the performance, the fellowship, and hated to see the evening come to a close.

The two weeks just flew past before I had a chance to get everything completed that I had told myself I would do. I still had not finished the new song, but vowed I would work on it some while we were travelling. It seemed words did not come to me as easily now as they did when I started out so many years ago, and of course I had the inspiration of Millie, her encouragement, and sometimes her criticism when I was being more of a fool than an artist. If I had kept all the songs that I trashed, I probably could fill a three-ring binder. I also scribbled many lines on napkins, once on a piece of toilet paper when a thought came to me while nature was calling. I was finding it more difficult to create as age becomes the resident manager of one's brain. But I am so thankful for the talent God gave me and for the years of success that are still with me today.

I ran into Josh on campus one day. He looked tired and almost washed out, his skin was pale and his eyes almost blood shot. He told me he was leaving school and would probably not return. I asked if he was still living with Michael and he said yes, but the relationship was not good. While he and Michael had thought they were playing it safe, Michael had a one night stand after he and Josh argued over some of the bills. Michael rushed out of the house and did not return till after noon the next day. A few weeks later he became sick and because the two of them had made up, Josh said he also got sick. Michael discovered his one night stand had AIDS and did not share that fact with him. Some time afterwards Michael became very sick and was hospitalized with a severe case of AIDS and not expected to live. Josh discovered he was HIV positive and Josh said he was being treated, but the outcome was poor. Now they both are suffering from a foolish fight that will probably end in one or both of them dying. I was speechless, offering to help in any way I could. I knew nothing about AIDS, only what I heard or read, but I knew the alternative life style that Josh and Michael lived could be dangerous. Josh was in tears as he walked away. I knew I would never see him again.

I went to my classes and afterwards Vic and I grabbed a bite to eat and I told him about Josh and Michael. Vic was more aware of AIDS than I was having had a high school classmate die from AIDS last year. I did not work that evening due to a late scheduled class. In our room, while Vic studied for an exam, I took the time to write Millie a long letter. It seemed my second year had a lot of excitement. My server job was going well, the tips here were much better than back home at the café. Vic and I had an appointment at the Philharmonic office on Thursday, my grades were good, very much above average, and I was thoroughly enjoying my classes. Professor Hansen reached out a couple of times to let me know he thought my chances were good to land some type internship or back up for the piano with the orchestra. He also thought I was a very accomplished pianist. Through all of this I somehow managed to get into a letter to Millie.

Several weeks later I asked a classmate of Josh's if she had heard from him. She told me that Michael had died and she went to the funeral. Josh was not there and she understood that his parents had come up and he had gone back home with them for further treatment. She said it was just a matter of time with Josh. What a shame. He was a very talented actor and would have made a great name for himself. I thought how thankful I am to only have Millie, and of course our sexual experiences were nonexistent. I expressed my sadness and asked if she had Josh's address so I could write him a letter or send a card.

The school year just flew by much faster than I expected. The interview with the Philharmonic resulted in both Vic and me getting opportunities to work with them. Vic was more of a volunteer, but was getting valuable experience working with the music director, and even helped plan some of the events. I was given an opportunity as an understudy with one of the finest pianists I had ever heard. He was so impressed with my playing that he gave me the opportunity to play a couple of times with the orchestra. When and if he had to be out, I was allowed to take his place and practice with the group, but due to my class schedule and work, those opportunities were very few. Being part of the practice sessions did not mean I had the opportunity to play at actual events.

I wrote Millie routinely and received such sweet letters from her. Teaching was great for her and her class this year was a mix of raw talent, as she wrote me. The kids were special, and she was obviously engaged with each one on a unique basis. The school principal was excited about Millie's teaching habits and how the kids just loved her and wanted to be the best for her. I could imagine what our kids would be like with Millie as both their mother and their teacher. I could hardly wait to see her again. With only two more months of the school year, I was anxiously awaiting being able to go home and spend some time with Millie, either with her coming home or maybe me going to Nashville.

As things usually go, my plans did not unfold as I expected. However, this was not bad. Vic and I both had the opportunity to continue working with the orchestra for the summer and to participate in some of their events. Vic and I both were able to keep our jobs, but we were faced with a place to stay since the residence halls would be closed for the summer. We agreed to share a small efficiency apartment that had one bedroom, a combination kitchen and living room and a small bath. We agreed to take turns sleeping on the sofa bed and the only bed in the apartment. Both the sofa bed and the main bed were comfortable and I told Vic I had no problem using the sofa bed all the time. He insisted we take turns. I agreed. Between us we could afford to make this work for the summer and the landlord was grateful because the place would be vacant until the fall when other students would rent it for the school year. Vic and I also agreed that after the residence hall opened again, we would go back to Juilliard and give up the apartment.

I wrote Millie that I would not be coming home for the summer and that I would miss her so much. She was anxious to see me and hinted that she might make a trip to New York for a visit. My heart must have jumped out of my body when I read that she might be coming. Just the thought of her being here was music to my ears. I told Vic she might come and then I called my parents collect and let them know of my plans. They were sorely disappointed, but completely understood. I was surprised when they told me they might also come up and see some of the New York sites. I laughed and told Mom that I thought they would never come to see me. Time just seemed to slip away and the school year ended. I could hardly wait to start my third year knowing that soon I would be working and would be able to be with Millie all the time.

It was hard to realize how quickly time flies as you get older. I guess in one way I was happy to be back on the road with my troop and ready to be back on stage performing as I had been doing for many years. But, I was still grieving from losing Millie and missed her so much. I knew that once I was on the road and involved in all the planning required to make any tour successful, that I would have less time to think about personal issues and spend time thinking about each city and each performance. Sometimes I actually dreaded all the travel and being stuck in hotels, motels, on the bus, and eating out every day. I had to control myself so that I would not gain a lot of weight or as the case could be, lose weight because of bad eating habits. I knew that starting the tour in Portland, Maine would be at least a three-day trek, probably over twelve-hundred miles from Nashville. This meant staying in several hotels or motels along the way, but Tom had it all arranged. The excitement, not necessarily the travel, was what kept me going and being on stage performing under a lot of lights, sweating until I was soaked to the bone, actually helped to keep my weight down. Laborious as it was, it was my life, my livelihood and a career I had chosen.

This tour would also be a strain on most of the band members because of short or weekend performances, packing and unpacking and keeping instruments tuned with little time to practice. Road trips of this magnitude may provide opportunities to see parts of the country we normally would not visit or go for vacations, but are interesting places and meeting the people makes it worthwhile. Well, I must admit that some of the people we meet may not make the grade. For the most part it is fun and enjoyable, but stressful to say the least.

After being on the road for many hours, heading to Portland, I slipped back to my private quarters on the bus and pulled out the song I had been working on to see if I had enough brain power to finish it. I really wanted a new song, but also wanted to have time to put the music to it and make at least a preliminary recording before using it on stage during a key performance. I thought I might talk to Vic about it and get his input. Somehow during this creative period I must have fallen asleep. I heard pounding on the door and Tom was bellowing that we were stopping for the evening. Time was flying by faster than I could keep up with it.

I asked where we were and Tom told me we were stopping in Wytherville, Virginia after six hours on the bus. That is rather typical of driving time since the convoy is fairly large and drivers do not switch off during the trips. I knew we did not have a performance in Wytherville, in fact I have never heard of the town, but it was quaint and quiet and had good accommodations for the troops and places to part the buses and other vehicles. Tom told me we would stay just for the night then move on to Hartford, Connecticut, at least a ten hour drive the next day. From Hartford it would the last leg of the trip and another long day of almost ten hours of travel to Portland, Maine. I was already getting tired from just listening to Tom explain the trip. I actually asked him why he didn't schedule events along the way to fill in some of the gaps. He looked at me and said nothing. I dropped the discussion.

Vic explained that in Portland we would have great performances, and Alvin was already getting excited. I told him to be a bit more "clothed" for these performances, and he laughed telling me he thought he would just come out on stage in his tighty-whities. I told him if he did that I would throw a bucket of water on him and the audience would have a wonderful view of his personal attributes. Actually, I thought of Alvin more as a son than as one of my troop. He actually performed well and the audiences liked him to the point I was getting concerned they were coming to see him instead of me. I told Vic and Tom we really needed to give Alvin more time on stage and bring him back after intermission. I also wanted to do a real duet with him at some point.

Wytherville had some great food and the people were very accommodating. We were asked to perform but time did not permit. The lady at the hotel desk insisted we return and "put on a show" as she succinctly stated. I promised that one day we just might do that. Alvin, Tom, Vic and Darren were all with me at that point, and as I imagined, some young girls came from out of nowhere and wanted Alvin's autograph. After that, they did ask for mine. I just knew Millie was up there looking down and smiling and enjoying watching me play second fiddle to a young hunk. She would have really liked Alvin and I know he would have treated her like his mom.

Vic and I got settled in our summer-time apartment; fortunately for us it was furnished. We bought some basic food supplies, things we could fix in a hurry: TV dinners, frozen things that were microwaveable, milk and juice, and the basic hot dogs and buns, bread and, of course, peanut butter. Even working in a restaurant neither of us would have ever made a chef. We worked almost every day, sometimes gone at the same time and other days we had different shifts. Our work with the Philharmonic was time-consuming for the amount of time we had to do so. My shifts at the restaurant yielded some good tips, thankfully, since the salary was still pathetic. Vic actually made more money than I did, but we were okay in sharing the expenses. It seemed we got along very well.

We were about three weeks into the summer vacation when I received a call from Millie that she, Mom and Dad were coming up for the weekend and maybe staying a few days. She wanted to know my schedule and if I could get some time off from either the restaurant or the orchestra. I was so excited I just told her "yes" not knowing if I could get off or not. Just seeing her and being with her would make my summer work worthwhile. I wanted her to meet Vic and wanted approval from Mom and Dad for what I was doing. When I hung up, I told Vic they were coming and he seemed excited, but wanted to know if he needed to find another place to stay for the time so Millie and I could be together. I laughed and told him that Millie would flatly refuse to stay here and that regardless of how much we loved each other, sharing a bed was out of the question until we were married. He wanted to know if she would be willing to have the bedroom and stay here in the apartment with me sleeping on the sofa bed. I told him that Mom and Dad would die if either of his suggestions happened. We both laughed.

Millie, Mom and Dad arrived and fortunately I was able to arrange my working schedule so that I could spend some quality time with them, especially with Millie. I just wanted to hold her and kiss her and just talk until we could not speak anymore. I met them at the airport and Dad suggested renting a car so they would have some transportation and I highly recommended he use public transportation since driving and parking in New York was nothing like driving and parking at home. He consented and we took the hotel shuttle back. They were actually staying at the hotel where Mom, Dad and I first stayed when I was enrolling at Juilliard. Millie had her own room at the same hotel. She looked so beautiful, and it was all I could do to contain my emotions as well as other anatomical attributes. My excitement was pretty obvious to me, but well concealed from others with my appropriate attire of a long shirt outside my blue jeans.

Mom asked about the Philharmonic job and was I actually playing the piano for them. I laughed and told her I was a novice compared to the talented individuals who are "real" members of the orchestra. I just fill in when the actual members cannot make some of the evening sessions preparing for a performance, and then it may be just a few minutes. However, I have had the opportunity to play duet on stage during a performance and introduced as a Juilliard student. Actually, I was told I played as well as any of the actual orchestra members, but I would not tell Mom that. I did not want to sound pompous or to have her convince me that being with the orchestra should be my chosen career. I did want to keep my options open and I knew in my heart and mind that New York was not my chosen place to live with Millie in Nashville.

Vic knew for certain after several weeks with the orchestra that he really wanted to be a director for a musical company, not any specific one, but he wanted to keep his options open as well. Neither of us gave the slightest thought that we would one day be working together with our own group. Fate has a way of making dreams a reality.

Millie and I spent a lot of time together, both separately and with my parents. We did things that tourist do. We went to the top of the Empire State Building, took a ferry to the Statue of Liberty, attended a concert at Radio City Music Hall, and even saw a play on Broadway. Millie and I shared some time just being close and I wanted so much to be very close to her, and she seemed ready, but we stopped as we got very close to being intimate due to our Christian upbringing. At one point, when we were alone in my apartment, she took that special liberty of arousing me to complete expulsion and I had to change clothes before we could meet my parents for dinner. I also aroused her to the point she made me stop, but I couldn't control my urges before it happened. We kissed and vowed to a long relationship once I was out of school and we could get married. Fortunately for both of us, Vic arrived at the apartment right after I had changed clothes and Millie and I were just sitting side by side holding hands and talking. It would have been embarrassing, especially to me, if Vic had arrived while part of my anatomy was visible.

The evening went well and the time flew quickly with Millie and my parents having to return home. I hated to see them leave, but I had to get back to work and get my act together with the realization that the sooner

I could graduate and become self sufficient that Millie and I would get married and be together for the rest of our lives. Her job in Nashville was very important to her, and we discussed how things would work if I took a job in New York and she was in Nashville. I had to really think about that and how our lives would be if we were married and a thousand miles apart most of the time. She really did not want to live in New York, and frankly, neither did I.

I continued to struggle with finishing the new song, and after tossing away numerous renditions that did not tell the story I wanted to convey with the words, I stretched out in my private area on the bus, and just stared at the ceiling while the bus rolled along. I plucked away at the keyboard since it was impossible to have a full piano on the bus and tried to put basic music to the lyrics. Vic asked me several times if I had finished and I hated to admit that every version I wrote wasn't what I wanted. He justified it by me being preoccupied with losing Millie and reminded me that she was probably the most encouraging person regarding my ability to come up with great lyrics. Darren came in and wanted to know how I wanted to open the performance, not the Alvin intro, but my first opening song. After pausing for a few minutes, I said let's do something different and open with just playing *Music Box Dancer* instead one of the hit songs. Then we moved to *"Bartender Call Heaven"* before jumping into the full night's performance of songs. I also wanted to know what Alvin would be singing.

Having struggled with the new song for several reasons, I finally came up with a version and the lyrics that satisfied me, but did not ring true with me personally. Millie and I had a wonderful relationship from our early years until her untimely departure from this earth. The words of the new song did not apply to us in any way, and we were both very faithful to each other always, even when I was touring on the road for months at a time. It was trust, trust between us, knowing our love was strong. So for me to write lyrics that actually went against the grain of a great love affair was strange, but I knew the words would be true to so many people. Relationships can be strained; people alone without companionship will tend to seek out someone to fill the void. For Millie and me, that was never an issue, never a problem, and that void was filled with a strong love between us, and even with her passing, I still have those feelings.

I got with Vic and showed him the lyrics. At first, after reading them several times, he asked me to play the score as I would want the song to be set to music. We were alone, as I wanted it to be so no others could hear the new song. I sat at the keyboard and played and sang the song as I thought it should sound. It was slow, sung softly, as if two people were actually talking. The final verse I sang after some soft music, paused, and added with emphasis as if to visualize to the audience that there were two lovers holding each other, looking in each others' eyes, her crying, and him trying to explain the situation. Vic took his guitar and added a rhythm while I played and sung the song again, more softly and with focus. Afterwards, Vic said. "I like it. Let's use it about the middle of the next performance. Even though it isn't published yet, we can get a feel from the reaction of the audience regarding how well it may do." I agreed.

The next performance as always started with Alvin and his gyrations that wowed the ladies, especially the younger girls in the audience. He is awesome and such a hunk that sometimes I think the people just come to see him. I was not jealous, but pleased that he attracted the younger audiences. After Alvin, I came out and started with a medley of Jim Reeves songs that always brought the older audiences back into the show. I had to do this sometimes to remedy the results of Alvin's performances since my gyrations just did not compare to his hip movements, and of course at my age now, those tight jeans just did not add a thing to my older body and I definitely was not a Willie Nelson. After the medley of songs, I brought the entire audience to attention with the hit "Shirley" that is always a winner. The audience responded well with a thunderous applause, even those younger people who obviously loved Alvin.

A few more songs and introduction of the band, then I paused and said, "This next song is one I struggled with for some time, and I want to do it for you, but it is not recorded so you are the first audience to hear it. It is not about anything in my life. I was very happily married for many years to my childhood sweetheart. Millie passed away less than a year ago after a terrible bout with cancer. I miss her dearly. This song may ring a bell with some of you, but it is not about anyone in particular. I hope you enjoy it."

The audience was quiet, as Vic came to the stage with his guitar and I moved to the piano. The band would add a compliment as we had practiced and the music started with first a few cords from Vic and then with me on the piano. I had debated whether to use the electronic keyboard, but I thought the rhythm and slower sounds from the piano would be more effective. The song emphasized each word in more of a soft approach to allow the sadness of the meaning to be completely understood. After a couple of bars, I said to the audience, "I call this song *Our Secret's Out.*"

> If you cry again tonight I'll understand dear,
> I'll understand the reason because she knows,
> Your teardrops fall, but I'm leaving,
> Because our secret's out, I've have to go.
>
> We can't keep on coming out at night, not this way, dear,
> I can't keep on seeing you because she knows;
> Just remember that I love you,
> And because our secret's out, I have to go.
>
> Just kiss me one last time before I leave dear,
> Let me hold you in my arms so tight.
> Remember just because that I'm leaving
> Really means that this will be our last night.
>
> My kids don't understand why I'm not home dear,
> And excuses to my wife don't seem to work,
> And I know it's hard for me to keep on saying,
> Things that aren't the truth that really, really hurt.
>
> I know I've said this time and time again dear,
> And your tears have always seemed to bring me back,
> And I know you're crying now, I understand dear,
> But darling turn me loose and let me go on back.

I know my wife's waiting up at home dear,
And the kids are up waiting for me to show,
So let the tears drops stop, and dry your eyes dear,
For because our secret's out, I've got to go.

Just kiss me one last time before I leave dear,
Let me hold you in my arms so tight.
Please remember just because that I'm leaving
Really means that this will be our last night.

And I know you're crying now, I understand dear,
But darling turn me loose and let me go on back.[7]

The audience was quiet for a moment after I finished, but then they were on their feet with wonderful applause. I stood from the piano, bowed slightly, and provided several "thank yous" and pointed to Vic and the band. I was definitely pleased with the reaction and knowing how much I had struggled with the words, I had a sense of relief understanding when it was published and available on CD that it just might become another hit. But, I also understood that I had a captive audience with the performance and in real life, songs could either be big or just flop.

The performance continued and we did our best to keep the audience happy and entertained. At intermission I had many compliments on both the performance and many questions regarding when *Our Secret's Out* would be released. My response was that I hoped that would be soon. As expected, many CDs and other memorabilia were purchased and lots of autographs were requested even during intermission. Normally we did not come out during intermission, but because of the new song, I wanted to get comments and reactions from people. I couldn't have been more pleased.

After Millie and my parents left, all flying back home to Tennessee, I went back to the apartment and just thought about how life would be

---

[7] Written by Donald Arlo Jennings in the early 1980's and revised April 2014

with just Millie and me and where we would live and what I would do for a living. Millie's career was well under way, but mine was still up in the air. I knew I wanted to have a music career, but staying in New York with Millie in Nashville would not be conducive to a good marriage. I wanted to be close to her where we could have a nice home, at least two children, a boy and a girl, and still have the good life. I knew it was much too soon now with three more years of school, but it was critical that I plan my life for the future.

Getting through three more years of school at this moment sounded like an eternity, but I knew it would probably go faster than I realized once I got back into a steady routine, classes, studying, the restaurant, and the Philharmonic internship. I would be busy. I did need to decide how Millie and I would stay in touch and see each other now and then. This would be a challenge for us. She literally had a life in Nashville, and in as much as I hated to admit it, I was still a college student. My life was encased in an academic student mode while Millie's was definitely an academic teaching mode. How far apart we actually were was an understatement at the moment, but I was hopeful we would fine a common ground and balance to unique lives.

When Vic got to the room, we compared notes on my time with Millie and my family and his days of working, classes, and hanging out. I envied him, his more carefree approach to things, but he was very serious and had his life somewhat more planned as to where he wanted to be and to do after Juilliard. We talked a long time and then went to grab a bite to eat.

COMPANIONS
Opportunities

The next years continued to pass quickly as I dealt with routine classes, my jobs, both at the restaurant and the Philharmonic. I had become extremely professional on the piano, much to my surprise and was doing very well on the guitar with Vic's constant teaching. Vic seemed to be so talented with music, but his passion was still to be a music director and he was learning so much from working with the Philharmonic in the office and with stage initiatives. I had numerous opportunities to play both duets and some "first seat" performances with classical music with several at home events. However, I seemed to lean more and more toward wanting to write and sing. My songs became more on the country music approach and less directed toward classical piano. I did not receive that type opportunity with the Philharmonic who did not lean in the direction of country music.

I had been writing Millie as often as possible keeping her up to date on my studies and my work with the restaurant and orchestra. She did the same with me regarding her teaching talented students, most of whom could be a challenge. She told me fifth graders were both creative and attention deficit. Our letter-writing-dates actually brought us closer and closer than I ever imagined. Summers for those years brought us together either with me making some brief visits home to Townsend or to Nashville. Millie made sure she came to New York every summer for at least a week. At least one of her visits included her mom and dad. I enjoyed seeing them and re-doing the sites that Millie and I shared with my parents when they visited a couple of years ago.

During her stay in New York we had quality time together growing even closer, sharing a love that only the two of us could imagine. The discussions that we often had were about my career and if I would be staying in New York travelling with the Philharmonic, or if my plans would center around writing and singing. I was challenged with that and with knowing Millie and I planned to get married as soon as I landed a decent job. For me the question was what a decent job might be. Vic was already looking around for opportunities and had definitely decided not to stay with the Philharmonic past graduating from Juilliard. My music writing was getting better, or at least I thought so, but the music director of the Philharmonic wasn't interested in the type songs I was creating. That meant seeking some other type opportunities besides being a bar-room entertainer or a career as a café server.

Graduation time arrived and for me this was the most exciting event of my lifetime, at least up to that point in my twenty-two years. Millie was turning twenty-seven and was well established in Nashville in her job and had become a very strong leader in a local church with the children's program. I knew this was so important to her and my thoughts continued as to how I could manage a New York career and have a wife and family in Nashville. I struggled every day with this. My mom, my dad and Millie, along with Vic and his family celebrated graduation together with a super dinner, and as I thought would never happen, champagne. I actually got almost high since any alcohol was not something I was used to having. Vic actually got giddy and laughed at almost anything that was said. Our parents and Millie just smiled and told us our limit had been reached, so no more champagne for us. Millie took my hand and told me I should stick to music and not celebrating with champagne. She kissed my cheek and said how much she loved me.

I guess I was somewhat beside myself the day after graduation because I actually did not know what to do. The routine for which I had become so accustomed to for four years no longer existed. Millie and my parents helped me to get my personal belongings from my dorm room. That was when I came to the realization I had no place to live and the jobs that I had would not suffice in supporting the rental of some type living quarters. It is funny how things will turn out. I had no more classes, was supposed to be at practice with the Philharmonic at ten o'clock that morning and be at my job at the restaurant at three o'clock for my shift. Millie told me that I needed to come to some understanding with myself as to where I wanted to work and if music was to be my chosen career, that I needed to give up the restaurant job and get focused on a real job. The problem was that the Philharmonic had only mentioned a part time position requiring many hours of practice as well as being on the road whenever they needed me. This was, to me, so restraining and would not pay the bills since I was now on my own and could no longer live at Juilliard. I needed a more substantial job.

Vic told me he was going back home and that he was not staying in New York. He was promised part-time jobs at two local churches and was planning to teach guitar lessons. However, he told me this was definitely temporary and that he would only do this until he found a full-time job. This meant I had no one to help share the expenses if I stayed in New York. My best bet was to find a very economical place to live, see if the Philharmonic would hire me full time, but even with that, the income would not be sufficient to support even having an efficiency apartment. In New York even a very small efficiency can be very expensive and basically I could not afford to stay here. My choices were few and I was definitely getting nervous. I could not ask Dad and Mom for support. Dad was getting close to retirement and I probably needed to get my act together soon if I had any plans in the very near future of marrying Millie. Life changes definitely were making me grow up faster than I ever imagined.

The immediate problem was what to do. My personal things were in the rental car that Dad has secured for the visit. We scouted around and discovered that a room was available that I could afford until something better came available. That is available and affordable. Dad helped with the first month's rent, but Mom was concerned whether I should even stay in New York regardless of the two jobs I had. I could return home to Townsend, but then I would be without a job and living at home did not seem to be to be the best option. Bewildered was evident in my thoughts. There was much for me to think about and many decisions to make. I was quickly coming to the conclusion that staying in New York for the time being was my best option, but not what I really wanted to do.

"Our Secret's Out" seemed to be a good hit with the audience. Daren and Vic definitely thought it could be an opening song at the next show, but Tom was concerned that since we had not recorded the song we should be careful how we used it on the road trips. Because of the audiences' reaction to it, our immediate plan, once we were back in Nashville, was to get the song recorded as soon as possible. Tom emphasized not using it again until that time. Reluctantly, we all agreed. Vic did suggest finding a local recording company and make a cutting of the song, send it to our Nashville studio and have it released. I didn't think that was the best idea, but we did not trash the thought immediately.

As we expected the rest of the tour was the usual eventful performances, issues to handle at every place, equipment failures, and previous performances leaving debris that Tom had to get the center managers to clean up before we could get to the stage, motel or hotel rooms not ready or in the process of being cleaned. Incorrectly booked rooms or not enough rooms at the motels that meant for some of our members Tom had to find other accommodations. This was not unusual, but in spite of all the headaches, we managed to spend the three months on the road without killing each other and even with tempers flying at times, everyone eventually cooled down and our performances were done with the quality audiences expected. Fortunately we had "sell-out" performances at every place except one because of a mix up with the event manager; they had us booked as a religious quartet under the name David Kempt, whoever that was. Still, the performance, once the house corrected the information, was more than ninety percent attended.

I made it a point to call Tammy at least once a week to check on her and to let her know how the road trip was going and to ask her how the B and B was doing. As I always expected, she told me there was a room waiting once I found the time to get back to Townsend. Our conversations did not open any doors in discussing a relationship, personal or otherwise. We both understood we needed a shoulder to lean on occasionally. Tammy knew Millie, and with each of us losing our spouse, it was good for each of us to have someone to console and share special moments of the relationships with our spouses. However, my thoughts were always focused on Millie and personally, I just wanted to get back to Nashville and crash at my own house, in my own bed, and cool my jets with a nice glass of wine and enjoy the comforts of not having to climb on and off a bus every day. I knew Millie would not be there, but I knew she was in a far better place. Time flies, but how so slowly it seems to pass.

Being in New York alone can be a staggering experience. The rooming house was okay, but I was getting cabin fever when I was there. It is hard to move around in one room. I hated that I had to wait my turn to use the bathroom down the hall, but affording a better place at the time was not within my reach. Here I was at twenty-two years old, struggling to survive, working at the restaurant every day, waiting tables with a degree from Juilliard. I can tell you right now that did get some attention from some of my customers, especially the professors and staff from Juilliard who ate at the restaurant and whom I served. They wanted to know why I was a waiter when my talent was for being a musician. I did inform them that I was still doing some work with the Philharmonic and was talking to them about being a full-time member of the orchestra.

Three months of bouncing back and forth with these two jobs, I discovered an advertisement for a piano player and singer at a local night spot. I interviewed, played a couple of songs, and was offered the position. The pay was much better than I expected, but the job was only three evenings a week. I accepted knowing I had to some way to juggle my other two jobs. I scaled back on the waiter position much to the disappointment of the manager. My explanation was that I was trying to use some of my education in the field of music. I dared not tell him I was playing piano and singing at a night club.

I received a call from Vic one evening and we literally cried on each other's shoulder about not landing the jobs we knew we would with wonderful musical degrees from Juilliard. Vic was still doing the part-time music director at two local churches and had seven guitar students he was teaching. His parents were happy for him to be home, but he was not being fulfilled with any promise of great things to come. I said to him, "Vic, if you could see me in my shabby one-room efficiency apartment, struggling to stay alive, wondering when I will or if I ever will be able to marry Millie and support her, bouncing and juggling three jobs, you would think you had gone to Heaven. I am beginning to hate getting up every day wondering if there is something better for me. Be thankful you can stay with your parents and at least have some semblance of using part of your Juilliard training. For me, singing in a night club and playing piano at times with the orchestra just doesn't cut it."

Vic laughed, "Ricky, you made me feel better. Hey, whenever you decide to get out on your own and start a real career, keep me in mind. I still need a job that pays decently and will be a long-time career. I am having a hard time thinking what I will be doing in five years. I definitely do not plan to continue teaching guitar lessons to snooty wet-nosed kids who have a hard time understanding the difference between a C note and a G note."

I guess we made each other feel better, but I was a long way from feeling great. I had to get ready to head out to the night club for my performances there. Some of the songs I played and sang were chosen by the manager, some were just fill in as I tried to keep the music going. Mostly the songs were requested from the customers, some who left generous tips if I could play and sing their requests. Actually the tips plus the penitence salary for the three days was more than I was making on the other two jobs. All in all, I was able to save a few dollars, pay the bills, and have some spending change for the first time since I came to New York.

One evening I was playing and decided to toss in a couple of Jim Reeves songs that I played and tried to imitate his style. The crowd seemed attentive and the tips were good since I got several requests for other Jim Reeves songs. I kept several song books of different artists on the piano due to the fact I could not and did not know the words to many songs requested. I especially needed the music scores to keep pace with the demands. While I was pausing and looking for what I would play and sing next, a gentleman came up to me and asked if I knew *Piano Man.* Fortunately I had the words and music among the litany of songs on the piano. I said, "There is no way I can do justice to the song since I do not have and cannot play a harmonica, and I am definitely no Billy Joel but I will attempt it. Forgive me if I don't do a great job."

I played and sang the song, trying to do the best I could without the compliment of the harmonica. Afterward, the crowd astonished me with a blast of applause. As I started another song, something that seemed to weather the attention from many, a gentleman approached me, introduced himself as Tom Bixler. He complimented me on both my ability to play and sing, as well as to keep an audience's attention. I thanked him and started to play something else, when he looked at me and asked if I ever considered going professional. I obviously stared at him before realizing I was doing so.

He looked at me, somewhat as I was looking at him then, he said, "I manage a couple of singers, not anyone you would know, and no one on the charts, but one is doing well with his CD sales. I have some contacts that might help you get started." He continued, "I spend a lot of time in Nashville and have some contacts there that might be interested in hearing you play and sing."

I replied, "That sounds great, but I can't afford to get to Nashville on the money I am making here. If I could, my fiancé is in Nashville, and if I could find work there, I would jump at the opportunity."

He laughed, handed me a business card and told me to call him if I found out I might want to try my hand in Nashville. I slipped his card in my shirt pocket and said, "You can't be much older than me. How can I trust that you can do what you say you can do?"

He laughed again, "Age isn't a factor if you have contacts." He walked away and joined some people at his table. They all looked at him, and then looked at me and I decided at that time I would call him the next day.

Three months on the road, even as fruitful and promising as that can be, it takes so much out of me now, not as it was when I first started. I had energy back then and lots of enthusiasm about each new venture. I think about the road trips as I remember them, having long telephone calls with Millie almost every night, knowing she was still up waiting for my call even though sometimes it was way after midnight. Now, while I enjoy the audiences and singing, I find it more of a struggle to be creative, to relax, and in looking forward to the next performance. Maybe with Millie's passing I lost something that was so important to me. When she was with me, even though she wasn't travelling with the troops, I always called her and we would have those long talks. That kept me going. My return home was always exciting, knowing she was there and greeting me with hugs and kisses. We had that special love that lasted. We wanted to grow old together, and we talked about sitting on the front porch sipping a glass of wine and enjoying our friends when they visited. At one time we even talked about spending time at the local orphanage or having some college students stay at our house. Those times are gone and when I arrive home now, facing the emptiness and loneliness of a large house, some of me just melts away.

Regardless, the trip back to Nashville from our northeast tour was uneventful. We did have a marvelous time, met some great people, and best of all Alvin became one of the troop family. It seemed that Alvin, Vic, Darren, Tom and me bonded more at each point along the way. Alvin had that boyish way about him and at the same time was quickly becoming a headliner. His youthfulness wooed the younger generation and actually Tom and I started billing him as part of the show. We arranged for him to meet our publisher in Nashville and as most of the performances were recorded live, we would publish CDs with covers of both him and me indicating the live show in a particular city. This was great news to Alvin and he definitely got better and better. However, I still had a difficult time with his attire. So much for my input, ignored, and admonished by Tom ensuring me that if Alvin's way of dressing brought in the younger audiences that I should be happy and not complain. I yielded to this.

I still remember the old poem about "home again, home again" and as we approached the storage facility where we kept the buses and other vehicles, we unloaded all the equipment, headed for respective cars, and as usual having been picked up, I had to get a ride with Tom to my house. We spoke of many things on the way, mostly about what the future might bring. Now in my fifties, with almost thirty years in the music field behind me, many top billings, gold and platinum records, numerous hit songs, and reminiscing how it all came about almost brought tears to my eyes. Tom sensing my emotions changed the subject and wanted to know if I wanted to join him in a celebration drink before he left to join his family. I declined, saying that I just wanted to chill out and hit the sack, to be in my own bed for a change. After all, three months on the road makes one very happy to be back home. Tom understood, felt the same way, and after dropping me off, headed to probably do the same at his house. The difference being his wife would still be there.

∾

The next day, after meeting this Tom Bixler guy, I looked again at his business card and considering that I had no real desire to remain in New York, I decided to give him a call. If things could work out with him, that might mean I would be going to Nashville and that would mean being closer to Millie. I had to wonder if this Tom Bixler was serious or just another scam on some poor soul such as me who would love to break into the Nashville music scene and become a star. I looked at myself in the mirror. I saw a nice looking guy looking back at me, not a shabby fellow to say the least. I knew I could play the piano very well and the guitar somewhat, thanks to Vic. However, I had to wonder if my singing voice was good enough to woo an audience. I wondered what a Nashville career would mean. My thoughts centered on whether or not Tom Bixler could make anything happen. I had to call him.

I had no money, at least not enough to travel to Nashville if he told me to meet him there. I pondered whether to call Millie and ask if I could stay with her if this worked out with Tom Bixler. I decided two things; first I would call Tom Bixler and find out if he was serious. He seemed young but sincere and if he could introduce me to the right people, maybe, just maybe I might get an opportunity in Nashville. Secondly, I had to arrange with my bosses at the restaurant, the night club, and the orchestra for some time off should the Nashville trip actually happen. First things first, I called Tom Bixler. The phone rang four times before being answered, "Hello, Tom Bixler speaking."

"Mr. Bixler, this is Ricky Snyder. We met last night at the club and you gave me your business card telling me if I ever wanted to become a professional to give you a call."

"Definitely I remember. You did a number of songs, but I remember mostly your rendition of *Piano Man*. You have a strong talent with the piano and not a bad singing voice."

"Can we meet and talk about what you are proposing?"

"Most certainly. When and where?"

"Where are you now?"

"I am staying at the Days Inn on 94th Street. There is a café on the corner just down from the hotel. Can you be there in an hour?"

"I think so. I will have to take a cab, so depending on traffic this time of day I could be a little later, but definitely I will be there."

We said our good-byes on the telephone and I almost jumped out of my skin knowing that a possibility could exist that would get me back to Tennessee, closer to home and in Nashville closer to Millie. I had to decide what to wear to make the best impression. I opted for my blue jeans and a nice light blue golf shirt. My wardrobe was not very impressive, so the selection was extremely limited. I had no intentions of wearing the suit I had for the Philharmonic events. I thought that would be too much and if we were going to talk about country music, then my blue jeans seemed most appropriate.

I actually arrived at the corner café before Tom Bixler arrived. It was a neat place and offered a good menu. I found a table close to the front window so I could easily be spotted. Tom Bixler arrived just on time and immediately saw me and came to the table. He said, "Do you want to get something to eat and talk, or just talk? I definitely need some coffee."

I stuttered but said coffee would be nice. He jumped up asking me if I took it black or with condiments. I told him that I usually have some sugar and cream, but I can drink it any way. He came back with two coffees and assorted creams and sugars. I thanked him, offering to pay for mine but he insisted that he could cover the cost. While we drank our coffee he asked me, "Do you mind if I call you Ricky or do you prefer Richard or Rich?"

"My name is actually Ricky and that is my preference. May I call you Tom or be more formal with Mr. Bixler?"

"Oh, gee. Mr. Bixler was my father. I prefer Tom. My given name is Tomlinson, an old family name. I went by Tommy as a boy, but I think Tom is more adult. Tell me something about yourself. What are your ambitions, your goals, desires, what drove you to the music business?"

"I hope you have plenty of time. I learned to play the piano at an early age from the girl who was my sitter at the time. She later became my best friend, and now she is my fiancée. We grew up in a small town not too far from Nashville. My desire was to go to Juilliard and to become a concert pianist. I started writing some lyrics early, but these were mostly more ballads or maybe more in line with country music. Now my hope and desire is to break into the music industry as a country singer, perform by playing the piano and singing on stage, cutting some records, and maybe become part of the Grand Old Opry. Do you think I am being overly ambitious?"

"Ricky, how old are you?"

"I feel like an old man sometimes, but other times I think I am thirteen again. Really, I am twenty-three, well almost twenty-four. Why do you ask?"

"As I told you before, I really enjoyed your style on the piano and you really do have a great voice. I manage a couple of other artists, singers, but not with the talent you show. I want to introduce you to a couple of people that may help get you started. Do you have any demo tapes of your playing and singing?"

"No. I really haven't given any thought to doing so."

"Well, that is going to change."

We finished our coffee with him expressing that he would get back with me very soon. My heart skipped a beat, but my emotions were mixed. At this time there was not much I could do. I couldn't quit my jobs or get time away until I knew for certain that Tom would come through with something. He promised me he would get back to me, but he never said when. I had my restaurant server job that afternoon and I was so afraid my mind would be preoccupied wondering if some opportunity might exist that would break me into the music industry, take me away from New York, and take me closer to Millie. I really needed a good job, a career, and I wanted to marry Millie.

My days continued with my routine of the restaurant and the Philharmonic, but my mind was telling me that Tom would never call back and that my dream to be closer to Millie was not working out the way I wanted it to. Just when I thought my world was going to be New York, a place many people want to be, I received a message from Tom asking if we could meet at the same corner café the next day. He left a phone number and I immediately called him with a positive response. I was hoping this was not bad news and that he wouldn't be telling me that things just couldn't come together for me. How wrong I was.

I was so anxious that I arrived at the café thirty minutes before our appointed time to meet. I was so hyped up that I was actually sweating. I tried to look calm, but I feared the worst. When Tom arrived, he walked to the table, looked at me and his first words were, "Can you get time off to go to Nashville with me?"

I nearly jumped out of my skin. "Of course, of course. When do we need to leave?" Then I realized my anxiousness was very prevalent. Tom smiled and told me he wanted to leave Friday morning, two days away. I felt I needed to offer more explanation to my bosses what with needed time off on such a short notice. However, I replied I would make it happen. Tom told me to pack for at least a week, but pack lightly. He would make travel arrangements and let me know. I looked at him with some uncertainty knowing I did not have the money to pay the expenses. He somewhat comprehended my anxiety, and then told me that all the expenses were being paid. I gave a sigh of relief but failed to ask who was paying. For the most part I didn't really care who paid as long as I did not have to and that I could get to Nashville and maybe see Millie. My next thought was to make the arrangements with my bosses, call Millie, and my parents. I really wanted to call Vic, but maybe later.

The next two days just seemed to drag, but as promised, Tom picked me up in a rental car, telling me we would drive to Nashville so he could make a stop in the Shenandoah Valley to hear one of his clients perform at a local theatre. We would stay there overnight and then drive on to Nashville. Tom told me that I would be meeting several people at the record company to introduce me into the world of recording. He mentioned that I would audition for them, playing and singing. He mentioned I should think about the songs I would perform. I was getting more nervous, anxious, and at the same time happy.

My earlier call to Millie actually had me shaking while we talked. As usual she was her calm self and told me all would be okay and that I would do well. I told her I would call as soon as I could and keep her informed about what was coming down. I told her Tom was delightful and I knew she would approve of the way he was conducting business. I wanted to have time with her depending on how long we would be in Nashville. Both of us wanted this time together and prayed everything would work to our benefit. I think I was shaking more about seeing Millie than I was about being scared about the audition.

The trip was good, and I became more relaxed in time. Our arrival in Nashville was more than I expected. We had rooms at the Opry House Hotel, probably more luxury than I had ever had in my lifetime to this point. We had dinner that evening and Tom insisted I invite Millie. True to my statement, Millie liked Tom and they seemed to hit it off quickly. He later told me that if I every changed my mind about marrying her, that he would personally stomp my butt. Tom left us alone after dinner and Millie and I had some time together to just roam around the hotel looking at all the wonderful scenery in the atriums, but we had to say out good-byes through tearful eyes, promising to get together again before I had to go back to New York. She assured me, again, that I would be great and that she would pray for me.

Tom and I had breakfast in one of the many restaurants before leaving for my audition with several of the members of the recording studio. I had discussed and decided I would perform a couple of Jim Reeves' songs since these were smooth and I could easily play them and sing with my baritone voice. Tom agreed, but also wanted me to indicate to the group that I did write lyrics and was working on a song but that it wasn't finished. Not quite true, but almost, so not to tell an untruth, I hummed the tune that I wrote for Millie a few years ago. I knew for certain this song would never make the charts, but at least I could truly say I had written some lyrics.

We arrived at the RCA studios and this was a complete shock to me. As we entered, I saw Chet Akins and recognized a couple of other famous singers. I felt so out of place and such an amateur compared to these artists. I asked Tom if he was sure that I was in the right place. He just laughed.

The room for my audition was complete with a piano, a table and several chairs. I was astounded when six people entered the room, all introducing themselves and stating that Tom had told them a lot about me. I became more nervous, but one of the most senior gentlemen told me to relax and to just play and sing as if I were at the club in New York. I played and sang four songs before they stopped me and asked Tom to step out of the room with them. Now I was more nervous than ever.

When they came back, Tom was all smiles. They all looked at me and said that Tom would get with me regarding a recording contract if I was interested. I thought I would die, and I am uncertain how I responded. Later Tom and I had a long discussion. He wanted to be my agent and arrange the contractual agreement. The catch was that I needed to stay in Nashville for a while, but the good news was if I signed quickly, a sign on bonus would be provided to help me get started. Tom would arrange some engagements.

∽

Three months on the road can be challenging, exciting, and exhilarating, but it can drain a man while stifling creativity to a degree. I really wanted to come up with some new lyrics that would be good for our next road trip. I wanted something that maybe Alvin and I could use for a duet, this time a real duet not like the one we did on the spur of the moment. However, now was not the best time for me to be creative. I just wanted to rest for a couple of days, get to church and see some good friends. I knew Pastor Thomas had a continuous worry-spot in his brain about me and how I was continually handling the loss of Millie while continuing to perform. I owed him an opportunity to ask. Surely I could find time tomorrow to reach out to him. I also needed to reach out to Tammy and let her know I arrived home safely.

Tom would probably rest for a day, and then start planning the next road trip that I knew was already booked. Alvin would probably do some performing at the local club that he was doing before we took off for the northeast trip. Vic never stopped planning, working on best musical directions, and Darren just worked to ensure all the equipment was in top-notch condition. I realized how fortunate I was in teaming up with these three amazing people. Besides Millie, these three and their families were my family. Now all I have is them, and to some degree, a platonic relationship, though remote, with Tammy.

The first two days did fly by with me meeting with Pastor Thomas, having lunch with him and of course, as always, his quizzical approach and his continued teasing and probing me about cooling my jets some and maybe not being on the road so much. The call to Tammy was definitely different with her consistency of telling me my room at the bed and breakfast was always ready, just whenever I took the time to relax and get away. In the back of my mind, I really wanted to go to Townsend and visit with her, but I was always cautious that my loneliness missing Millie would not make me jump to some involvement that was not in either Tammy's or my best interest at this time. I just wanted to be friends and have a companion to whom I could reach out and who understood losing a loved one.

As usual and expected, Tom, Vic, and Darren came by after a couple weeks of having time with families and just chilling out with feet on known grounds. Tom wanted to start discussing the next road trip. Vic wanted to know if I was making progress with another song. Darren wanted to review how Alvin would be staged since he was now going to get some top billing with me. Frankly, I had no responses to any of the questions and actually was wondering why we had to get on the road so quickly. I had not totally adjusted to being single again, and I had no idea where my life was heading at this time. I shook my head and decided we should do a Tennessee tour. I was stared down by six eyes wondering if I had lost my mind.

I really think Tom was more excited than I was with the contract signing. I think I was scared and bewildered as to what would be expected from me. Tom told me he would start reaching out for engagements, but that I needed to think about leaving New York. He told me I should start thinking about a song I could record for my debut. He had some thoughts, but first things first in my mind were to resolve issues in New York with the restaurant, the club, and the Philharmonic. Plus I needed to close out my room arrangement and I wasn't certain I had the funds to travel there and get everything done. To my surprise, Tom informed me all that would be taken care of by him and his staff and I needed to concentrate on pulling together some music for performances.

True to his word, Tom handled everything in New York having my few personal things from the apartment shipped to me. He helped me find an efficiency apartment in Nashville, nothing elaborate, but close to where Millie was living. The nice thing about this efficiency was it was more than one room and actually had its own bathroom. I felt like I had reached the big time. I called Millie and we talked for a long time, and then met for dinner. I was so nervous, so excited, and I am still uncertain as to what I told her. We just held each other and I kissed her passionately. It was then we vowed to really date and see each other at every opportunity we had. While somewhat with an estranged engagement, her in Nashville and me in New York, now we could really be together. Tom had promised me that for the first few months I would be in Nashville since he wanted me to get introduced to a number of people and whenever conceivable, to be on some local country shows.

Millie helped me to get my apartment set up, with both of us wondering when we could scale down to one place after marriage. I wanted to set a date, but Millie wanted to wait until I really had some time to think through all the changes I was experiencing. I wanted more than ever to skip all the issues and just get married. After all, I wanted to really share that part of our love we had agreed to wait for marriage. Millie, as she is always the great comforter, hugged me, kissed me all over my face, and said the best is yet to come.

COMPANIONS
Careers

I made up my mind to call Vic and let him know I was in Nashville and had a contract. I also wanted to find out what he was doing. As I was rummaging through things while unpacking the boxes from New York, I found a business card from Darren Toffler. That had to be more than just a coincidence since I had forgotten about him and the discussion we had on the bus. I laid his card on the kitchen counter by the phone and decided that I would reach out to him soon and find out what he was up to. I doubted he would remember me.

While I was unpacking, Tom called and asked if I was getting my music together and that he wanted to go over any lyrics and music I had written. I had been working on a ballad, but it was not completed, and it was somewhat sad. I guess at the time I started writing it, I must have been in a depressed state of mind being away from Millie. I started writing it in New York, but really needed to rethink my words and maybe change it to be a little less "sad." Tom told me he would be over in a couple of days, hopefully with my first engagement. Already the demo records we cut had been circulated and Tom had several shows that expressed interest, but they wanted to meet me and to actually have me audition. I had to meet almost every day with someone at the recording studio and Tom wasn't always there. I just hoped that I was doing and saying the right things. I soon realized the value of having an agent and manager.

I worked on the lyrics of my ballad and couldn't set it to music since I did not have a piano in the apartment. The studio definitely offered an opportunity to be there and had areas where musicians could have some peace and quiet to be creative and compose, but I needed peace and quiet and no one around to be creative. Tom called every day inquiring about my progress and in his last call he informed me that there was someone he wanted me to meet. He wanted me to think about a song, maybe one of Jim Reeves' that I could do for this individual. He failed, on purpose, to let me know who we were meeting. I could only assume that he had someone who was well known and willing to meet with raw talent.

Tom came by on a Wednesday to pick me up. We traveled to a studio in Nashville, parked and entered a building that was really neat. I found myself heading to Studio B at RCA where many great artists had made recordings. We entered a room and waited a few minutes when the door opened and Porter Wagoner entered. I was beside myself, but Mr. Wagoner was so gracious and shook my hand with both his and his smile just eased all the tension and stress I was experiencing. After talking for a few minutes, he insisted I call him Porter and asked me to play and sing something for him. After a couple of false starts, blunders on my part, with Porter laughing, I think he was impressed both with my piano skills and my voice. He invited me to be a guest on his TV show. Of course Tom negotiated the deal.

Tom, Vic and Darren continued to stare at me when I mentioned just doing a Tennessee tour, but I explained there was a reason. I really wanted to start in Townsend and hit some of the smaller cities versus huge performances in major cities across the State. I realized this did not mean the revenue that Tom would normally expect, definitely not the large audiences we normally performed for, but I wanted this to be more of a memorial tour. After listening to me, there was still some major reluctance from Tom, but I wanted to do this for Millie. She loved Tennessee, loved her home town of Townsend, and she loved Nashville and the people. She never desired fame or even recognition for all she did, but she deserved more than I could ever do for her. This tour would be for her, her memory and our life together.

I told Vic that I was working on a song that I wanted to open with at Townsend, regardless of the audience. We would record it first, and make certain it would not be released until after the performance. I asked Tom to begin preparing for what would be probably a several month tour across Tennessee with booking in theatres and available auditoriums, probably some high school auditoriums in some towns. He frowned, patted me on the back, and told me I was about hard-headed as a rock, but he loved me just the same. Vic insisted that as soon as I had the lyrics finished that he wanted to hear them in order to ensure the appropriate musical arrangement accompanied me. What a troop. I often wondered why they put up with me.

After they left, I called Tammy and told her of my plans and that I hoped she would have most of the rooms available at the B&B so a lot of the members could stay there. There were limited rooms, but then the hotel could possibly handle the others. Tammy was amazed and told me she thought my plans were great, regardless of what Tom thought. I realized then that Tammy was much like Millie with her support. I also realized that having a friend like Tammy was good, just a platonic relationship, someone to talk with much as I did every night I was on the road and called Millie.

I decided to resign myself to my music room and finish the lyrics and set the words to music. I wanted this to be something that would be good, a remembrance of Millie, and a tribute to our love that lasted from childhood. I sat at my piano, lit a candle, and watched its light flicker casting shadows across the memorabilia in the room. I thought about Liberace and his candelabra as I sat here with my candle. What a difference.

Three weeks later, Tom, Vic, Darren and I met again and Alvin joined us to discuss the tour outlined by Tom. I shared the lyrics and the song I had finished with them, and I was uncertain of the silence of their response when Vic looked at me and said, "Gee whiz, Ricky, how do you come up with these words? I think Millie would have loved this song, and it is truly a tribute to her. I think about her playing the piano, and the lovely soft angelic voice she had, and I can hear her singing this with you. You did good."

All I could say was, "Thanks."

I called Millie and told her about Porter Wagoner wanting me to be a guest on his television show. She said we should celebrate. We went to dinner that evening and for the first time we both had a glass of wine. There were some very famous people dining there and I felt as if maybe one day some of them might recognize me. Millie and I walked around after dinner just enjoying each other's company when we stopped to window shop at a jewelry store. There was a beautiful diamond ring on display and I told Millie I want to get that for her as an engagement ring. She laughed and told me she preferred something less flashy and definitely less expensive. Always the conservative and humble person, Millie just made my heart flutter. I would do anything for her. I wanted to get married that night, but she told me my hormones were talking and not my head. We sat on a bench across from the jewelry store and kissed before I walked her home to her apartment and then I headed to mine.

At my sparsely furnished efficiency apartment, with no piano, I looked at the ballad that I had written and wondered if it would be a good song to sing as my opening debut for the Porter Wagoner Show. I would share it with Tom tomorrow, but first I decided to call Vic and asked if he wanted to accompany me on the show backing me up on the guitar. After all, I owed much to him from our days at Juilliard. On top of that, he was just a good friend and a great guy who believed that one day I might be famous. If that would ever be the case, then I wanted him to share that spot light. I knew he would like Millie and I knew he would be straight with me regarding anything I wrote.

Tom called the next day and informed me of the time I was scheduled for the show and that he had booked me for a recording session. This was going too fast for me and I was having a hard time keeping pace with all the changes in my life. From a restaurant server to a pianist for the Philharmonic to a club singer to a recording artist and ending up as a guest on television show with a very famous person, to whatever might come next. My head was spinning. My career was beginning to take off and I think it was flying ahead of me and dragging me along. Tom asked about the ballad I was writing and wanted to hear it and see if this one could be the primary song on the recording, probably a cassette tape, but that I would need at least nine other songs for the recording. I knew I could do some that other artists had recorded, but Tom would have to approve the songs and obtain the appropriate authorization to record them. This was definitely not as easy as sitting at the club in New York playing the piano and singing whatever came to mind. I was thankful that Tom had come into my life and that he knew what he was doing.

Vic agreed to join me and accompany me with his guitar on the show. I introduced him to Millie at a dinner and they hit it off marvelously. Vic wanted us to meet his fiancé and told us he was getting married in two months, a small wedding, but he wanted us to be there. He even asked me if I would be his best man. My response was only if he would reciprocate as my best man when Millie and I married.

The show must go on, and I was back stage with Vic and we both were as nervous as we could possibly be. Even though I had played and sung in front of a lot of people, being on television was a new experience for me, and Vic had beads of sweat on his forehead even before we stepped out when Porter introduced me as a new talent with a fresh recording being accompanied by Victor Kelman on the guitar. Porter stated this was my debut and that I had the promise of becoming a great performer. My problem was that I was following Dolly Parton and there was no way I could match such talent.

I slowly came out and Porter greeted me with his arm around my shoulders, and led me to the piano with Vic following. Porter told the audience that this was a song I had written. I thanked him, and responded, "This is a ballad that I wrote and it does convey sadness as many ballads do." I began to play the opening bars and Vic blended his guitar music with the piano. I said, "This song is called, *Stay By My Side Tonight*." I opened with the words of the song, sang softly, almost speaking and to a degree sadly.

She stood at his side, by her son
As he lay on his death bed,
She hid her eyes and hung her head
As he said through tear strained eyes,
Now Mother dear, don't stray from here,
Stay by my side tonight;
It's not that I'm afraid of death,
I'm not afraid to die.

It's just that it's so lonely here,
So lonely here in life;
So Mother dear, don't stray from here,
Stay by my side tonight.
These words came tearfully from her child
As he lay on his death bed;
The words were choked and hard to come,
The sweat rolled off his head.
His lips were dry, his eyes half closed,
He almost wore a smile;
She looked at him in agony,
She stayed there by his side.
But there was nothing she could do
To lease his terrible pain;
She stood and cried, she tried to smile,
She brought him his play things.
He only looked, he did not take them
Like he would have done;
She looked at him and said dear Lord
Why must you take my son?
And then her son reached for her hand,
And gripped it oh so tight;
He looked at her and tried to say,
Stay by my side tonight.
Now Mother dear, don't stray from here,
Stay by my side tonight;
It's not that I'm afraid of death,
I'm not afraid to die.
It's just that it's so lonely here,
So lonely here in life;
So Mother dear, don't stray from here,
Stay by my side tonight.
And then his eyes were closed in peace
To never see the light.
His hand on hers it fell so loose,
She knew her son had died.

Oh Lord, oh Lord, why was he chosen
Now to be the one?
Oh Lord she loved him for ten years,
Oh Lord she loved her son.
But now in your hands he's safe,
You now have his life.
And she remembered his last words,
Stay by my side tonight.
Now Mother dear, don't stray from here,
Stay by my side tonight.
It's not that I'm afraid of death,
I'm not afraid to die.
It's just that it's so lonely here,
So lonely here in life.
So Mother dear, don't stray from here,
Stay by my side tonight. [8]

The audience that was in the studio was silent before any applause occurred. Porter, who had heard the song previously, walked over to me and again put his arms around my shoulders praising me and thanking me for such a wonderful song, sad, but thought provoking words. I left the stage with Vic retreating with me, both of us wondering what was next. I had no idea after that performance if my singing career had just ended or had just started.

The planned Tennessee tour was being debated heavily among the four of us with Tom expressing the most disagreement as well as some dissatisfaction. He said that he could somewhat agree if we included a Branson, Missouri performance. He was certain he could get us booked for at least a week there, maybe start in Branson and work our way across Tennessee to Knoxville, or even to Townsend, probably Townsend with the last performance being there. He also wanted at least two weekends

---

[8] Written By Donald Arlo Jennings sometime in the 1990's and revised August 2014

at the Grand Old Opry, and maybe a four-day performance in Memphis with some focus on special Elvis songs. Alvin was champing at the bit to perform some of Elvis's hits. I laughed and told Alvin he definitely had the gyrations and hip motions to wow the audience, as usual the younger female generation. He just wiggled his hips in response imitating Elvis.

After a lot of dynamic exchange among us, I consented to Tom's plan, but with his total recap of the tour, it was decided that a month would never work. The tour would probably take at least two months if we hit Branson first and ended in Townsend. The tour included time in Sevierville and Pigeon Forge. With connections with Dolly Parton, I knew we could get at least a weekend booking at one of her theatres there, but Tom needed to get on that early. Having met Dolly early in my career on the Porter Wagoner show, we had the opportunity to cross paths many times over the years.

I really wanted to start in Townsend and open with my latest song, but Tom was insistent that we save that for the last since it would have more meaning in Townsend to those who remembered Millie. Branson as the opening engagement would mean many of the older songs, repeat of songs by other country artists, and Alvin doing his thing. I decided that Branson, with some reluctance on the part of both Vic and Tom, that we would do a tribute to Johnny Cash and do a number of his songs as well as my major hits. As is always the case, Darren had his work cut out for him to ensure the technical side of everything and to make certain he worked with Vic on the right sounds for background music. I didn't want this to turn into a difficult engagement, but I knew, regardless, the difficulty of making it all come together was never simple.

Time creeps up so quickly and preparations, even though Tom was so efficient, took a month to get everything planned out. Because the tour was so soon and not planned out a year in advance, booking some of the theatres was really tough. Tom even worked out sharing the stage during one weekend with a local group performing during the day and with us performing during the evening. This type engagement means extra work for Darren and his team, and put Vic and the musical group hustling to set up and then tear down before and after each performance. Moving equipment and putting the stage back for the local group's performance was exhausting.

Over the next two months, the tour went well, even though we encountered some heavy rains, and virtually went on stage in one city just in time for the first performance, having to apologize to the audience for being a tad wet, but we made it. There are always hazards and bumps for which compromises must be made. For the most part, we had sold-out performances, but as expected in some cases the short notice of our appearance provided smaller audiences. I was wondering just how our performance in Townsend would be, if more of the locals would be attending, or if the draw would be more from the surrounding areas. I was surprised when we arrived to find banners on many of the store fronts, one even spanned across the road, and as I might have expected, Tammy had a full blown cut-out of me and banners all over the Bed and Breakfast. Of course I stayed there, as did Vic. Tom, Darren, and Alvin. Tammy just loved Alvin, telling me he reminded her of her son.

Townsend was great in every aspect of the end of this tour. I took the troupes to the café that I worked at more for my sake more than anyone's. The family management had changed and the café was now operated by the oldest son and his family, but still reminiscent of past times. A picture of me waiting on tables hung on the wall beside pictures of me during my career. The theme was that Ricky Snyder worked here. Tammy was with us at the café and enjoyed the attention that was focused on not only me, but the entire team. People tried to crowd into the café, but there wasn't room. Outside many waited to get in or for us to come out so that they could get autographs and snap pictures. Of course there were so many cameras busy inside the café I thought I might be blinded by the constant lights. This was not what I expected since I had been in Townsend several times with little or no publicity. Regardless, it was great.

We opened the engagement with Alvin's performance that got woos and wows from everyone. I know he put on his best show here, and with his good looks and young body, the crowd went wild. However, when I came on stage, I thought the building would fall with the thunderous applause and an immediate standing ovation before I even opened my mouth. In some way I actually felt at home even though the number of people I knew was limited. But I did see several of my old classmates. Some looked the worst for wear, while others seem to have never changed. I guess the years pay toll on each of us. I know they have on me. This was far from a class reunion, but reminiscent of my younger days at home.

After the audience quieted down and settled back in to their seats, I said, "Thank you, thank you! It is so great to be back home, in Townsend. You may not know, but I do come through here every once in a while and stay at the Bed and Breakfast, but I usually slip in and out as quietly as I can. I usually try to stop by the cemetery and place flowers on my parents' graves. Once I even visited the place by the stream where I spent a lot of time as a young boy. You know, I grew up here and was married here to my boyhood sweetheart, Millie Pendergrass. I lost her to cancer, but I have many fond memories of times here with her before we both moved on to our careers. I wrote a song that is reflective of a wonderful life, saddened by her loss, but has strong meanings to me. I have not performed this song before, because I wanted to do it here first. I hope you enjoy it, and for those who knew and remember Millie, I hope it has a special meaning to you also. I call it *Candle Light and Silver.*"

Slowly Vic led with opening cords on his guitar as I moved to the piano and the band began playing. The words came out of my mouth with strength and love.

> *Make-believe is only what man just hopes to be,*
> *And dreams are but an image that seldom we do see;*
> *When love is lost what can we gain, things never are the same,*
> *And here I sit alone tonight with nothing but a flame.*
> *A flame that glows so honestly it knows not of a fear,*
> *And the silver reflects a saddened face, the shadow of a tear.*
>
> *Candlelight and silver, golden moon and stars,*
> *Shines just right, reflects the light*
> *When placed the way they are;*
> *Dreams reflect the image of things that cannot be,*
> *And hope remembers love's bright center*
> *That glows so endlessly.*
> *Candlelight and silver, linen snow-white lace,*
> *A chance to dream of never things*
> *With a saddened tear-stained face.*

Give me all your promises or give me none at all,
Show me that I can stand up, catch me if I fall.
Let me live by your side don't let me go away.
And if I wrong then teach me right, never let me stray.
For now I sit here by myself, my eyes reflect the flame,
And I am left with memories, a picture and your name.

Candlelight and silver, golden moon and stars,
Shines just right, reflects the light
When placed the way they are;
Dreams reflect the image of things that cannot be,
And hope remembers love's bright center
That glows so endlessly.
Candlelight and silver, linen snow-white lace,
A chance to dream of never things
With a saddened tear-stained face. [9]

I was personally almost crying as I finished the song. The audience stood and with thunderous applause once again almost shook the building. The band continued to play the background music as I acknowledged them and Vic walked over to the piano and touched my shoulder. I sat back down at the piano and sang the closing verse again. It took a few minutes for the audience to settle down and into their seats before the show could continue. I said, "That one is for Millie."

That evening, after my performance on the Porter Wagoner show, feeling as if I probably just completely bombed out, Vic and I discussed what each other thought. He was more upbeat about the performance than I was. I was deeply concerned about the song and the fact that it was somewhat of a "tear jerker." Vic and I parted for the day, and I called Millie to cry on her shoulder. Her comfort was refreshing and I seemed to chill

---

[9] Written by Donald Arlo Jennings May 29, 1970

out a little bit by her telling me that first impressions can be deceiving. I accepted that and retired for the night.

Seven o'clock came quickly and I was awakened by the phone's continuous ringing. Struggling out of bed, I found the phone and sheepishly said "Hello."

"Wake up! Get up! Meet me at the studio in an hour." It was Tom.

"Why?"

"You were a smash on the show. My phone has been ringing off the hook wanting you to appear on other shows and the studio wants to record the song on record and get it out to radio stations as quickly as possible. No time to waste. Get moving. An hour. Be there." Tom hung up.

I was dumbfounded. I quickly got ready and dressed, called Vic and told him to meet me at the studio by eight o'clock. Vic was still half asleep, but woke up quickly. I wanted to call Millie, but she was probably already at school. As I thought about Vic and my discussion the night before, after the show, he was right, and I probably panicked too soon. Maybe this was the beginning of a good career. Regardless, one appearance, one good performance, doesn't mean success. What it means is that now I had to get my act together and live up to expectations.

COMPANIONS
Happenings

Time can do so much. After the Townsend performance, we did our normal routine of signing autographs and selling as much memorabilia as we could to the audience as they were leaving. I encountered several people that I knew from my high school days. Some looked very mature and had aged well while several others looked the worst for wear. Many individuals commented on my career and some expressed condolences for Millie's passing. Regardless, we all shared a few minutes of old times remembered but long forgotten.

I glanced from the corner of my eye and saw Tammy lingering in the midst of a throng of people. I was certain that she was waiting on me. I was pleased she had attended the performance, but I wished that she had told me she was coming and I would have arranged for her to have a front-row seat. However, knowing her, she would not have wanted any special attention.

After the crowd thinned out, I walked over to Tammy and met some of the people with whom she was standing. A couple of older people remembered me as that kid who played a lot by himself and spent time at the stream. I was surprised that they remembered the stream was my favorite place. I tried to place them, but out of respect, I finally asked how they knew me. I discovered they lived two houses down from my parents' house. Finally I came to the realization that time can do so much to change everything. We parted with them praising me for a good performance, telling me that they knew that one day I would be great. They also expressed their condolences regarding the loss of Millie.

Tammy, being always so gracious, told me she was going back to the house and that she would see me once the members that were staying there returned. She wanted to know if I would join her in a nightcap drink on the veranda. How could I refuse? I told her if she would wait a few more minutes I would tell Tom and Vic to close everything up and I would ride back with her. She told me that was not necessary, but I really wanted to get away from the bustle of all the activity and just chill out for a while. "The troops will understand Tom will handle everything. Sometimes I just get in their way. They know what is needed to be done." I told her, "They will want to go celebrate a little and have some time to themselves. After all, what is there to do in this town? Tom will get everything arranged for the next performance, one more here, then back to Nashville. This has been a long but a great tour. I feel honored you came tonight and more honored you saved all the rooms in your Bed and Breakfast for us. The least I can do is to spend a few minutes with you." We both laughed.

Tammy and I talked for a while sitting on the veranda that overlooked a small but lovely flower garden. She told me the garden was her only "green thumb" capabilities, along she said, with good dirt and much fertilizer. She laughed as she told me for the most part she had more promise with weeds than with flowers. My response was very close telling her I was not certain I could get weeds to grow.

The members staying at the bed and breakfast returned from their outings and adjourned to their individual rooms. Stepping back into the main lobby, Tammy and I bid each other a pleasant good night. In my room I took a shower and just fell onto the bed. I must have fallen asleep immediately because the next thing I remember was Tom beating on my door. These trips can be hectic and much sleep is lost to the routine of getting every detail together quickly. I quickly dressed and joined the troops and Tammy for breakfast. Famished as I seemed to be, I ate heartily and probably way too much. We had to get packed and everything ready for the last performance, back on the road afterwards and home to Nashville. I just wished that I could have called Millie and told her I was on my way back.

Time can do so much to heal wounds, but the emptiness experienced by a lost love is sometimes hard to digest, much less make a full recovery. Millie was my encouragement, my reason to be creative, my reason to go on, but now while somewhat depressed, I somehow have the strength to keep on keeping on with my career. It is important for me to do this for Millie. If she had lived, I know she would have made some comments about Alvin, and she would have been pleased that Tammy was still around and doing well.

∞

Vic was waiting in the lobby of the studio. He had brought his guitar even though we had not discussed what was coming down and in reality, even I didn't know. Tom found us and pushed us over to a corner. "Gee, I had no idea the show would be that good for you. Everyone seemed to love the song and the words just seem to grab the right people. They want you to record it as a single and we have to pick a song for the flip side."

"Tom, I actually walked off that stage thinking I had failed miserably. I really thought this was the end of my Nashville experience and that you would be putting me on the next plane back to New York. I had no idea what to expect and was somewhat startled just as you said that you didn't know the show would be that good for me. I immediately thought the worse for a moment. I remain somewhat dumbfounded. Where do we go from here?"

"We will meet with several people, find some background singers, and while Vic will definitely being playing his guitar you will be on the piano and singing. There will be a full back-up band. If this goes as well as I expect, we will need to get our own band together and probably need some technical support. There is a lot at stake here and we, well you, Ricky, better not flub it up. Understand?"

"Completely."

"Let's get upstairs and get this started. I am as nervous as a lady of the evening in church. How can you two be so calm?"

Vic said, "Calm? I am totally speechless. My knees are knocking. And if I don't get relaxed soon, I think I might pee in my pants."

We all laughed. We needed a light moment before everything changed our lives forever. If the record was good and booking came quickly, we knew days ahead for each of us would be hectic. I needed to tell Millie. I wanted to let her know that something good could be happening. However, that call had to wait since we had much work to do to get the record made.

I had no idea the stress involved in making the recording. I had to work with the assigned band to get the music for the song aligned and this took hours with many replays. We did probably a dozen retakes before we were informed it sounded good. I probably drank two gallon of water to keep my throat from totally drying up. Vic had a couple of bouts requiring him to go to the restroom. He told me that he threw up one time from just nerves. I don't know how we pulled it off, but after working most of the day, the producer was pleased with the final recording. The flip song was easy since everyone had a music score and could be together with the music. The words were easier for me, and I was less nervous. However, the song on the flip side was not the song scheduled to be released.

Stay By My Side Tonight was now going to be released as a single and Tom was already on the phone trying to book engagements. Vic needed to make some contacts to get a band started. I knew a technical guy that I had met on the bus some time back as I was going home to Townsend from Juilliard. I decided to contact him to see if he had any interesting in joining a rookie singer with a newly released recording, a non-existent band and an unplanned degree of engagements.

I still had Darren Toffler's business card in my wallet. I wanted to call him as soon as possible, but first I wanted to call Millie and let her know what was happening. This was all coming down too quickly for me to absorb. Vic was so excited about the possibility of being a music director for a band and Tom was definitely beside himself with enthusiasm about the song and getting engagements scheduled. If Darren could join us and Vic can create some semblance of a band, with booking engagements, we might just have a start toward a career.

I needed to get my creative hat on and maybe come up with some more songs and work with Vic and Tom to lay out what we will do on our first engagement. I was pondering this when Tom approached me telling me that Porter Wagoner wanted me back on his show in three weeks. I think my deodorant just left me. I wasn't certain I was ready for all this so quickly.

I called Millie and told her what was happening. She insisted we celebrate that evening. I wanted more than ever to be with her right now. We both were in tears, tears of joy. I told her if ever I would leave you it would be only while I am away and I would always be back at your side.

"Millie, I want to marry you. I want to be your husband and you my wife. I want to have a family with you and to grow old with you. Millie, I know it is early and I need to get settled in some way with this new career, but Millie, will you marry me soon?"

Her one-word answer was, "Yes."

I called Darren and got his voice mail. In broken sentences, I left him a message that we had met on the bus some time back and that we discussed him being a technical manager for a music group. I mentioned I was in Nashville and just released a new single record, was getting a band together, and would be doing engagements. We needed a good technical manager who could tie everything together. I asked that he call me as soon as possible if he would be interested in joining me in this new venture.

Townsend is my home, but Nashville is where I live. Every time I open the door to our house, Millie's and mine, I still feel that sensation that she is still here. It still seems so unreal to me. Being as tired as I did from the tour, I just dropped my luggage in the foyer knowing I would retrieve it later to unpack. Walking into the den I paused at the bar to pour myself a glass of wine. I felt that I deserved a small drink to just chill out to be alone for a while without the company of Vic, Tom, and Darren, each one who had been with me from the beginning, and for which the four of us were more like brothers than some real brothers. We do care for each other and look after each other.

I sat down, more like I flopped down in my recliner, and remembered the old song that Jim Croce sang, *Time In A Bottle*. He was right, there never seems to be enough time to really do everything that you want to do. I knew Millie was the one that I wanted to go through time with, but sometimes life doesn't turn out the way one expects. If I really could have made the days last forever and my wish had come true, Millie and I would be sitting here together talking about her time while I was away and my time on the road. Even though we talked on the phone every night I was away, just reminiscing was part of our routine. We always shared those moments as if we had been with one another. Yes, time can do so much, but you can't save it in a bottle. My eyes were wet.

I must have fallen asleep. The wine glass was still sitting on the side table by my chair and obviously I had not drunk but a small amount. Looking at the glass, knowing I was getting hungry, I picked up the glass and sauntered into the kitchen. I could sometimes expect to find some great food that my house keeper had prepared for me and left in the refrigerator. She always knew my schedule and whenever possible she prepared some delicious dish the day of my arrival, putting it in the refrigerator with a note to either eat it cold or instructions for heating. This was good, but not as wonderful as when I would come home and Millie greeted me with hugs and kisses and we sat down together with a super meal she prepared ahead of my arrival or soon afterwards. How I so miss that, and miss her wonderful smile.

After eating the great and delicious meal that had been left for me by my housekeeper, I finished my wine in the den, at the same time looking over some of the mail that had accumulated while I was gone. There was lots of fan mail, some sent directly to my home but much that had been forwarded or brought to my house from the studio. I loved reading some of the letters, some a tad strange, but most were wonderful thoughts regarding performances that fans had attended, some even followed the group from one place to another. One of the neatest comments someone wrote was thanking me for adding Alvin to the performances. Having fans follow the tours always surprised me, but fans are great and they are the people who keep you going and keep your career on top. There was no way I could respond to every letter or to every fan, but I always chose a couple of very special letters and wrote personal notes to the individuals.

After a couple of hours of going through the mail, I decided to call it a night. I really needed the down time and some peaceful rest and sleep. I knew that tomorrow Tom would be calling or coming by with news about the Tennessee tour, reactions, and tabloid comments. I thought about my first recordings, that first song *"Stay By My Side Tonight"* that I thought might end my career. I thought about my very early first hit song, *"Shirley"* that put me on the charts. The platinum record is hanging in my music room and has more meaning to me than all the other gold records and albums that I achieved over the years. It is so good to know fans hang in there with you. I am pleased that *Shirley* is still a hit with audiences. This was enough of me reminiscing about old times. Tom would be calling tomorrow and will want to begin planning stage events for the next tour. Really, I think I am getting too old for this all this jumping around the country.

Darren returned my call, but I missed him. When I called him back he said he remembered me, but had lost my contact information. He seemed excited and wanted to hear about what I was proposing. He told me he was between jobs at the present time and just doing some ad hoc work as a music technical advisory. He was still in Nashville and definitely wanted to meet and have lunch. I picked out a coffee spot not far from the studio and we agreed on a time. I asked Vic to come with me. Tom wanted to come also, so here I was with my music team going to meet Darren in hope that Tom and Vic would like him and he would want to join our group. Vic was still working on putting a band together and making great progress. Tom was urging me to be creative and come up with at least one more song for another single release, or maybe an album.

Tom and Vic liked Darren immediately and Darren was excited to become part of our group, even though at this time it was a bit risky not knowing if I would be successful or not. This is the way the music industry goes. It is difficult to be on top one day and struggling to keep a career going the next day. I really wanted the band together before we did a repeat performance on the Porter Wagoner show. I also wanted to at least work with Vic for a special sound. Darren had numerous thoughts on that aspect. We all wanted a unique sound, but one that would be catchy and up-beat.

Several days later, after much discussion, the single was being played on most country radio stations around the country; it was getting both great reviews and some that were discouraging. Ballads can be both heart-wrenching with the story and accepted highly or not accepted openly. I was concerned that the song was not going to make the top ten, partly because no one knew Ricky Snyder and because I had not at the time made a lot of personal appearances. Tom was working on improving that initiative.

Tom approached me after the song had been out for a couple of weeks, and after the second performance with Porter Wagoner, telling me that we had made the top fifty list and the song was number thirty-nine. I could accept that. However, thirty-nine was a long way from the top ten. I knew I had a lot of work to do. I did not want my new group to become discouraged or worried.

Millie continued to provide great encouragement to me. We were dating regularly, well between times when Tom did not have me in some performance. Millie would come and listen to the band now that Vic had found some great instrumentalists, all looking for a chance to be with a successful artist. With Darren's help and technical advice, Vic developed a unique sound. We re-recorded *Stay By My Side Tonight* with our own band, giving it a new sound. While this did not change the rating, just getting it out to the radio stations helped to get it to number thirty-three. I guess that was the best that could happen. I had to find a song that would do better and not be such a tear-jerker.

Scratching my head while sitting in my small apartment, I started writing the lyrics to a beer-drinking country song. I guess this was because I was somewhat depressed, but at the same time so excited about what could be a promising career. With Vic and Darren on board, and Vic having put together a band, I knew it was up to me to create a basis for moving forward, or at least create some lyrics that would either send us to the charts or send us back to the trenches.

It seemed hours that I sat there and was coming up with words for the song that I wanted to be my next release, if Tom liked it and if it was accepted by the producers. Too many "ifs." I did not have a piano in this small apartment. After I finished, seemingly satisfied, I called Millie and asked if I could come over and use the piano in her apartment. After I finished playing and singing the song, Millie and I had some quality time together, and she gave me some pointers on the song, I created a score for the words. Millie loved it and said everyone would love it. I called the song "*Shirley.*"

The following day I got with Vic and Darren and played the song for them, expecting some criticism, but they jumped all over the possibilities and wanted to get to the band and practice what could be a unique sound. I had not shared this with Tom yet, and did not want to until we had what was probably a good version. However, Tom arrived while we were practicing, and the look on his face was astounding. He was beside himself wanting to get to the studio and make a demo run of the song. He truly thought this could be a hit.

Knowing that in a week I was scheduled to have another appearance on the Porter Wagoner show, Tom thought this could be a great introduction of the song while at the same time getting it released as a single. In as much as I was excited, I was also petrified of failure. Tom wasn't, and his energy was almost too much for everyone. However, regardless of my inhibited approach, we did record the song and scheduled it to be released following my appearance with Porter. Vic and the band had created great music for the song and Tom worked to ensure everyone would be appearing for the initial presentation. Of course, Porter wanted to hear the song before the show, and he seemed almost speechless afterwards. He was pleased and told me he believed I had a hit. He also mentioned that this would be the second time I had appeared on his show followed by the release of a great song. I felt encouraged.

After appearing on his show, and introducing the song, the single was released and immediately started climbing the charts. It only took two weeks for the song to rise to the number one spot on the country hit parade. I was getting more engagements than we could realistically handle. Tom was picking crucial shows and performances, the band was elated, and Vic and Darren told me that while they thought coming with me was risky, it was a great move for them.

Millie was so pleased, and as we sat one evening dining out for a small celebration, I looked at her, took her hand, and said, "Millie, I love you so much. I want to marry you. I have told you this several times, but it always seemed that I was so uncertain as to what my career would be and if I could actually be a good provider for you. I think, maybe, with *Shirley* doing as well as it is, it may be the time for us to really plan our life together." I had no idea how *Shirley* would be received, and no idea that the demand for the song would follow me throughout my career.

Sometimes silence is golden. Millie looked at me after a long pause. I thought here comes rejection. But she said, "Ricky, I always knew you would do well, become somebody everyone would look up to. I have dreamed of the day we would become married, but I knew it had to be with your timing. I want us to be married. I want a family with you. I want to be part of your life, but I don't want our companionship to interfere with your career. I love you. I love you more each day, and more than you probably realize."

Millie and I tried to see each other as much as possible. Tom was booking engagements that put the troops and me out of town for many days at a time. This was definitely necessary to keep my career going, but while it did help my career being away continuously could have put a strain on my relationship with Millie. Thankfully this did not happen. Tom had the group appearing in Branson as a guest on two or three top performer shows. We cut several more single records of older songs, none that really made a great deal of success. Nothing we did unfolded as well as *Shirley,* but I started to become a household name and in high demand. Finally I wrote several songs that really jumped high on the charts, and by then Tom decided it was time to book our own show. Looking back, it seemed time was flying. A year had passed since I arrived in Nashville with Tom to try and start a career. I guess if Tom had not been in the club that night, and if I had not been playing the piano and singing, none of this would have happened. The old cliché of being in the right place at the right time is true.

Tom was struggling with what our next tour should be, where we should perform, and how long we should be on the road. Essentially we had traveled to all parts of the lower forty-eight States, had one booking in Juneau, Alaska and one in Waikiki on the Hawaiian Islands. Early in my career we did a tour in England, but no real European tours. What Tom was considering was an island tour on several of the Hawaiian Islands, but wanted to ensure the expense of making such a tour would be openly received and net full audiences. Traveling with the full complement of the group meant airfares, hotel rooms, food, and everything else required for transporting equipment. This requires a great deal of work. However, I thought not only would this be fun, it would almost be a vacation. I suggested Tom put it before the troops for their reaction. I could only imagine their reaction. After all, this would put many of the members away from their families for at least ten weeks and in a vacation spot most of the families would like to visit. I liked the idea, but was skeptical of being gone too long and trying to cover so many island places.

As expected the troops had mixed emotions. Tom decided to focus on just Oahu and Maui, spend no more than twenty days including travel, and return to the west coast and spend no more than twenty days in California, probably San Diego and Palm Springs. While this was still two months away, it seemed to be okay with everyone. I had no new songs for this tour, so Vic wanted to open with some of the past hits, and do more of a trip down memory lane. He was working on a plan that would start with my first recorded song and work toward the last few recorded. Alvin was chomping at the bit for this tour. He had never been to Hawaii and decided he might choose attire conducive to the climate and culture. I gasped at the thought of him coming on stage in tight shorts and a Hilo Hattie shirt. If it would bring in the younger crowd, so be it. I could always shake my head after his performance when I came on stage.

Time is always of the essence when preparing for a tour, doing the tour and coming back home. As usual the Island Tour as Tom called it was very successful, but everyone was ready to be back to more common grounds and spend time with families. I really wanted to discuss with Tom, Vic and Darren how we could maybe just do some television appearances, settle into a routine in Nashville at clubs, do recordings, and maybe become a regular on the Grand Ole Opry. Actually I was very tired of traveling. While nothing serious was happening between Tammy and me, and I hadn't even spoken with her in weeks, I wanted to spend some more time in Townsend and just enjoy her company.

It was hard to believe that it had been over a year since Millie had passed on to be with her Lord and Savior. My loneliness had been somewhat succumbed to new lady friendships even though opportunities had arisen. I just wasn't ready to jump into a new relationship, respecting the memory of Millie. I still sit at our home and think about the times we dated once I arrived in Nashville and started recording. Those were special times. I remember when I invited her out to dinner at Morton's and was recognized by several people dining there. I requested a table with some privacy and ordered champagne. Millie smiled, and slowly sipped hers. I reached across the table, I remember it well, and took her hand in mine.

∞

That first year in Nashville was tough on everyone. Tom was finding it easier and easier to book engagements. This provided less and less time for me to spend with Millie. She did understand. Vic and Darren hit it off well and seemed more like brothers than one would guess. They worked together well. The band that Vic and Darren put together had great talent. Darren's technical abilities were way beyond my expectations. The sound that Darren and Vic established for the group made the songs just jump out with a statement of success. I was ecstatic and very happy not to be in New York waiting tables, playing at a club and being so far away from Millie. Nashville was becoming home to me. Mom and Dad stayed in contact with me, and were so encouraging. I owe so much to them for standing by me. I knew that my success would definitely benefit them and I would take care of them in as much as they would permit me to do so.

Between performances, some out-of-town engagements, and studio recordings, I found time to spend with Millie. We became closer and closer and just enjoyed each other immensely. I called her every day after a performance. If she were not there to answer the phone, I left a message. We talked as much as possible. When I was back in Nashville for some R & R and to record more albums, I called Millie and wanted to take her to dinner at a very posh and expensive restaurant. What I really wanted to do was to give her a ring I had purchased and propose we set a date to get married. I thought it was time, and now with me being twenty-five and her at thirty years old, starting a family was at the right time. However, I knew being on the road and away a great amount of time would be difficult in raising a family. We, Millie and me, could work through that issue.

I booked reservations for two at Morton's. I could actually afford to eat there now instead of wishing I could. Millie looked adorable, and as always she is beautiful. She got a lot of "looks" when we entered Morton's and some people recognized me. I had a fairly private table, and had ordered champagne that was cooling by the table. We had a delightful meal as Millie sipped her glass of champagne and we just stared eye to eye with each other. I reached and took her left hand in mine, and then I kissed each of her fingers, pulling the ring I had purchased and slowly sliding it on her finger, asked her if she would marry me and become my wife. Even though we had planned this to happen, I wanted it to be more romantic. Her eyes answered my question as her lips said "yes."

COMPANIONS
Happiness

In reminiscing about the time Millie and I had our first dinner at a fine restaurant and I was now able to afford it was both happy and sad for me. Definitely happy because that was the time I proposed to Millie and we decided to get married. It was at that dinner that I gave her an engagement ring. It was sad reminiscing that time because Millie was not here with me for both of us to enjoy the beginning and to laugh about how poor I was, a struggling student, waiting tables, singing and playing piano in a night club, and just trying to make ends meet. This brought to my mind as we sat there staring into each others' eyes the line from Shakespeare, *"Beauty is bought by judgment of the eye."* How true that is. As I looked into Millie's eyes, saw her beautiful face, I knew her beauty was not only outward, but her internal beauty, her heart and soul was the essence of her wonderfulness.

I think back as Millie and I were dining that first time at Morton's, both of us younger, and as I held Millie's hand in mine, we were sipping champagne, and as I slipped a ring on to her finger, I wonder now if I thought about what our lives would be like tomorrow and the tomorrows following our marriage. I know my career was just starting at that time, and I know now it has been a good career, but will my time performing on stage and my songs be forgotten? Yes, it is true; as I think now that Millie's and my yesterdays were the paths we followed. My sadness peaks each time I think of losing her to cancer. I just hated watching her suffer during that time. I found it hard to comfort her, but more so in that I had trouble being comfortable with the situation. I wanted to be there with her every minute of the day and night, but I had to continue on with my career. This is what Millie would expect. Remembering those times that Millie and I shared are for me everlasting memories. Memories I will never forget.

While now it has only been a year since Millie passed away, it seems like forever. The emptiness I experience now is not only depressing, but leaves a void I can never fill and I think about whether I ever want to do so. I guess after the Island Tour and being at home in Nashville, the home Millie and I shared for so many years, I had settled to reminiscing old times. The ringing of the telephone disturbed my thoughts and brought me back to reality. I knew it had to be Tom or Vic calling, but I was surprised that it was Tammy. I am so glad I didn't answer by saying, "what do you want now?" I guess my answering sounding depressing with a solemn "Hello."

Tammy's sweet voice responded, "Well, hello yourself. What is going on? You seem so sad. How was the last tour?"

"I am so sorry. I was thinking back to the time when I proposed properly to Millie and how much I miss her. Thanks for bringing me back to reality. How are you?"

"I am fine. Just making it through each day. Ricky, please know that I understand how you feel. I still miss Cliff and think of him often. You are not alone in sitting and reminiscing about good times with the one you loved. It takes time to really recover from the loss, but you never get over the love and happiness shared, the good time, and yes, those awful arguments that are just part of marriage, two people trying to live together. But enough of that. Tell me about the tour and how you are really doing."

"Actually the tour was great. Hawaii is wonderful, any time of the year. We had great weather, wonderful audiences. Alvin was a hit with the younger generation, well, and definitely spiked some eyes from the older ladies. He is the son I never had. But sometimes I just want to turn him over my knees and spank him. He will go far in his career and he has really made our tours, should I say, more interesting and entertaining. I still admonish him for the tight jeans, but in Hawaii his choice of dress was more island wear. Or should I openly admit, eye-land wear?"

"Don't be jealous. You were young once."

"Oh, it is not jealousy. I think it is pride. I am really proud of him and he is so liked by the entire group. His personality just shines through. I really can see some of me in him back in my early days. I struggled so much to find myself. Without Millie's encouragement, I don't think I would be where I am today. I probably would still be waiting tables at the café there in Townsend. Who knows?"

"I doubt that. You are way too ambitious and too talented. You are where you are supposed to be, and helping Alvin with his career is a good thing. What is next for you? When is your next tour, and when are you coming back to spend some restful quality time here?"

"Tom hasn't book the next tour, but I want to spend more time locally, more time with the Opry and maybe have my own show. I have thought about just doing a routine in a theatre in Branson, but I don't know. What do you think?"

"I think you need some R&R, away from the maddening crowd. Why not come here for a few days. No obligations, no commitments, no nothing. Just to enjoy some freedom and have good meals and great conversation. Selfishly, when you stay here you are good for business. But that is not the reason you should come. And, I should not be the reason you come. You should be the reason you come. Does that make sense?"

"Yes. That makes very good sense. You are a wise person. I really appreciate you." There seemed to be a lull in the conversation as we both were probably silently thinking.

How could I begin to deny what Tammy was advocating? We both knew any relationship was purely platonic, no commitments, just friendship and good companions. We can cry on each other's shoulder, not literally, figuratively speaking, and can enjoy a dinner together without expecting anything in return. I said to Tammy, "Okay, give me a couple of days to square things away here and I will call you before I come. I have to get with Tom. He expects me to check in routinely, definitely before I decide to escape to somewhere for some private time."

The call ended without either of us saying "good-bye", but both understanding that we would probably be seeing each other soon, just friends, good companionship, a few laughs, a few smiles, and some great food and probably some great wine.

My happiness at Millie's response accepting my proposal of marriage just brightened my day. She was, is, and will always be the love of my life, my inspiration. Her love constantly touched my heart and soul. As she accepted my ring she looked at me and said, "Are you sure you want to marry an older woman?"

"Oh, am I ever sure. I love you so much."

"And, Ricky, I love you more." Her smile said it all as she kissed me and as I returned her kiss.

"Well, I guess I am committed now and better make certain my career is on track at least well enough to support a family."

"First things first. We will need to start planning a wedding, set a date, decide where we should get married, who to invite, the reception…oh so much to do. And I need to decide on a wedding gown." She paused, looked at me and said, "Ricky, if you are in agreement, let's plan our wedding back home in Townsend where our parents can be a part of the plan, be involved, and have real enjoyment in this very special time. After all, we are both only children of our parents, and they need to share this moment with pride. I will call my mother tonight."

"Absolutely no problem on my part. When should we tell them we are getting married? Will you tell your mother when you call her? I think we should go there this weekend and share the news in person. But, if you call your mother and tell her tonight, it will not be a surprise to them and your mom will tell my mom and, and…. What do you think?"

"That is so sweet, and so like you. Yes, let's do it."

That night I sat in my little apartment and thought about the times Millie and I shared growing up. She was not only my baby-sitter, but she was my best friend, my constant companion, my piano teacher, and she became the love of my life. I cherish special moments that only she and I shared, some that bring tears to my eyes as I remember times we were apart, but still constantly thought of one another. We grew young together, now we will grow old together.

I slept well. I hoped Millie did. I know in my heart that I want the time to come when Millie and I share a life and do not have to part after a date and go to our separate homes. We share a love that meant we would wait for each other, not expose ourselves to a relationship that was more than just pure love. While others live together and cohabit before marriage, we agreed that would not be the relationship we would embrace, but share ourselves with each other after marriage.

I called Millie after I got up just to say "good morning, and to tell her that I love her more each day. We agreed to go to Townsend the following Friday evening once she was free and after I found out if Tom had committed me to some engagement. My time seemed to be more and more tied up with commitments, but this commitment with Millie definitely was going to take precedence.

Tom told me the weekend in question was free for Friday, but I needed to be back by Saturday evening to meet and have dinner with a television show host that wanted to interview me as a rising country music star. There was no way to pass this up, and I was certain that Millie would understand. The point of our visit to Townsend was just to inform our parents about our up and coming marriage and that we wanted to be married in our family church with the reception following. We also wanted our parents to be involved in the planning and to share in our special occasion. This would be more difficult if we had decided to be married in Nashville. Our parents were elated at our decision.

The next few days were busy with Tom, Vic and Darren planning our next steps, Tom briefing me on questions that might be asked by the television show host, and practicing with our newly formed band so that Vic and Darren could continue developing our special sound. I was beginning to realize how complex this career was going to be. But, this was what I wanted, and having three great guys with me to help pave the way was both exciting and scary. While nothing was ever said by them, I am certain that this "adventure" was just as scary for each one in their own way. I don't think they doubted that I could be successful, but feared more if they could help me with success.

When Tammy and I finished our call with no good-byes, I pondered if I should really go for a visit. I realized things were just moving with us as friends and that I definitely was not going to get serious about a relationship. I knew, well believed, that Tammy felt the same way. My career had blossomed to the point that with almost thirty years on the road, performing, recording, staying in one hotel after another, being on one stage after another, experiencing many long nights without Millie, I could almost see myself settling down to a more relaxed and calm environment, but I also knew that this would not happen soon. Frankly, I knew that I did not want this to happen soon.

Tom, Vic, and Darren as well as Alvin and the troop had been with me for a long time, and I had to not only protect them from me wanting to suddenly quit, but I had to ensure their livelihoods and their families were taken care of. Alvin was just starting, so his career will take off and he would be great. The four of us, Tom, Vic, Darren and me were close in age, over fifty and knew that many of the new, younger country singers and groups were to some degree leading the way with the X-generation. Music was changing, styles were changing, but older songs still seemed to be in demand. Satellite radio stations were beginning to win over conventional stations. Eight-track tapes, cassette tapes, and CDs seemed to be being pushed aside for more modern mobile technologies, songs downloaded from the Internet. I think about all the change and realize I am getting older.

I still think about all the good times with Millie and as I walk through the house, our house, I remember when we moved into it. Millie had to do most of the work herself because I was always gone, on the road, at the recording studio, practicing, and all my energies consumed by my career beginnings. She had to do all of this plus manage her teaching job. I remember buying the piano that still sits in our music room. Millie's old upright piano is in the den. Millie and I both would sit in the music room at the new piano and play, sometimes together sharing the keyboard. These were great times. We would miss certain notes and just laugh and then mess up on purpose. Then we would cuddle, make love, and just enjoy the time before I had to leave again.

Millie wanted children. I did too. We tried. Millie had at least two miscarriages before the doctors told her she could not carry a baby to full term. We were so disappointed and talked about adoption. Millie cried and I cried, but we both knew it would not be the same for us. We both were only children. While adoption was possible, we decided that with my career and with me being gone so much of the time and her commitment to teaching and church activities that it would be best to not adopt. We were saddened by our decision, but realized this would be the best for any child that would somehow be a part of our lives. Millie would have been a great mother. I doubted how much of a father I could be not being home most of the time.

The phone rang and brought be back to reality. I thought it might be Tom, but it was actually Alvin. "What a surprise, Alvin. What's on your mind?"

"Can I come over and let's talk?"

"Of course. When do you want to come?"

"Is now too soon?"

"No. Come on over. What's on your mind?"

"I want to do a mind drain. I think I am in love and just need to understand how you and Millie coped with being apart so much."

"I look forward to the talk. Sometimes absence makes the heart grow fonder. Millie and I were together for many years, before we were married. We grew up together and shared a lasting relationship, more than love, we were constant companions. That is what it takes to keep it together."

Alvin arrived and we talked for over two hours. He shared with me things about his special girl, five years younger than him. He is so young himself, but I had to realize that I was young once and had strong desires to get married. "Alvin, my advice to you is to wait a while longer. Don't rush into a marriage especially to someone you have only known six months. I would worry that you are more infatuated than in real love. Give it time. If she is still as anxious and available in six months, then get engaged for a while, don't just marry her and then stay on road trips with our group for the better part of a year."

"Gee, I knew you were going to say that. I know you are right, but she is so beautiful and so sweet and we seem to jive with one another. She likes my singing."

"Alvin, that is not a reason to marry someone. You can sing to her anytime and she can listen to recording. This is definitely not a reason to marry at all. She may be beautiful and sweet and if she really loves you, she will wait for you. You need to think this through."

With much remorse he conceded that I was probably right and would stall. He agreed that if she was the one for him that she would wait. I told him that Millie and I stood the test of not only time but distance. Our marriage was one made in Heaven and lasted as our vows stated, until death do us part. I let him know that we never had children, but we had each other and our love kept us together. That is what I wanted for him.

Well, with that behind me, I decided to throw a few things in a duffle bag and call Tammy back to let her know I was heading her way. I called Tom and told him my plans. Of course he had mixed feelings, needing for us to get together and plan our next tours and engagements. I told him to do whatever he felt best for the group and to let me know. I would be in Townsend at Tammy and Cliff's bed and breakfast. I could hear him snigger as he hung up the phone.

Millie and I drove to Townsend on Friday. I could tell she was more than anxious and I was so nervous my knees were shaking. Millie teased me that I was getting wet feet and I told her that more than feet would be wet if I couldn't calm down. She leaned over and kissed me on the cheek and told me everything will be all right. Our parents, hers and mine, probably expected that one day Millie and I would marry, but they could never understand how two young people could grow up together and be so keen on each other. They could never remember a time when Millie and I got into arguments. This was probably because Millie was older and she kind of kept me in tow. After all, she had been my baby-sitter.

We stopped at Millie's house first and her mom almost squeezed us to death. I was quietly praying that this was a happy hug and that she wasn't really trying to squeeze me to death. Her dad was more calm, but very happy and almost shook my hand off while at the same time hugging Millie. They were happy with our announcement and told us that my mom and dad were anxiously awaiting us to come over there. Millie's dad, as I would expect, insisted that after the six of us have dinner, that Millie would be spending the night in her own bed. Millie assured him that was the plan and that I would also be spending the night at my parents house, in my own bed. You would think that we were teenagers instead of me being twenty-five and Millie thirty. Oh well. Que sera sera.

Friday seemed to just fly by and our parents wished us the very best and definitely looked forward to the wedding in our home church. We had to get back to Nashville by Saturday evening, so there was not much time Saturday to spend with our parents. Millie and I now just had to get plans in place, pick a date, and also decide where we would live. We would no longer need two small apartments, and besides that, mine was so small it would not accommodate two people. Millie's place was nice, but again it was not large and we really wanted the American dream of a house and a white picket fence, a dog, a cat, and two children, a boy and a girl. What more could one ask for other than that to make certain we all loved the place. Millie told me she would work on some plans, get with our moms and put some events together. My chore was to decide on a date and to make certain my schedule was clear for a honeymoon. I teased that I had the hardest job.

Back in Nashville, I hooked up with Tom who was waiting patiently for my return and anxious to get the interview completed on Saturday with the show host. He assured me this was a right step for my career and re-briefed me on what I should say with neither of us knowing what type questions might be asked. I was a tad anxious and more than a little bit concerned that I could respond. I asked Tom if I would actually be live on the show or was this just a casting. He again assured me that this was just preliminary and that if the show host, for whom Tom did not disclose a name, liked me and my responses that I had a very good chance of actually being selected as a guest on the show. This would provide a great deal of publicity for me and the group. Tom told me he would not be part of the discussion, but that he would be on the side line in the same room. He, of course, had been instructed not to be involved during the interview. Expectations? I could not even begin to guess.

Fortunately for both Tom and me the interview went very well and I think I impressed the show host. I quickly learned once at the studio that the show host was Ralph Emery, host of Nashville Now. I had to think that because Ralph was impressed with me and that is the reason he invited me to be on his show. Knowing that over the past years he had interviewed many very talented and top performers who had major recording hits and some with their own television programs, actually made me feel good about myself and thankful for a great career start.

What a weekend. First with Millie and me going to Townsend and telling our parents we planned to get married, and then to be invited on

Nashville Now. After telling Vic and Darren about the interview and the soon-to-be appearance on the show, they were elated. When I told them that I wanted them and the group to be part of my wedding it brought happy smiles and a need to celebrate. Happiness just seemed to be bountiful at the moment. I had to call Millie and let her know about the interview, Ralph Emery, and Nashville Now.

Tammy always is such a wonderful hostess. As I arrived she greeted me as if I was a celebrity, being as such that I was instead of an old friend. I quickly found out that she had some special guests who wanted to meet me since they were avid fans. Of course I played the part that evening, but afterwards as Tammy and I sat on the patio having a glass of wine, we laughed at her "fan-raising" shenanigans knowing this was important for business. We talked about what had happened in her life since my last visit and she wanted to know how my tours had been and what my plans were moving forward. Unfortunately, I did not really know.

At breakfast the next morning, the couple who were avid fans insisted that I sit at their table, wanted pictures of them with me and definitely wanted me to autograph a couple of CDs they brought with them. I asked where they were from and found out they were traveling back from a vacation in Williamsburg, Virginia to their home in Naples, Florida. I told them that several years ago I did a concert in Naples and they assured me they were in attendance. Asking when they were heading back, their smiles dropped and told me that unfortunately they were leaving after breakfast, but wanted me to know that their visit here and seeing me was the highlight of their vacation.

Tammy and I talked again after breakfast and after several guests checked out. I asked her about dinner and she readily accepted. One condition was that we viewed this as friends and not as a date. I assured her I wasn't ready to date even though it had been over a year since losing Millie. We both knew we could be friends and be friendly without romance or any obligations. I just wanted to be away for a while, rest and relax, while at the same time enjoying the company of a great lady friend.

I stayed the weekend, but had calls from Tom several times. He was insistent that when I returned to Nashville that the four of us, him, me, Vic and Darren, sit down and discuss what I really wanted to do. I mentioned this to Tammy and she asked me why I didn't stay off the road for a while and maybe just perform routinely in a theatre. I actually had given much thought to that idea before, but hearing it from someone who had no vested interest in my career really provided a more open point of view. I knew at that time what I would be saying to Tom. I also knew the troops would probably be elated to be closer to home more of the time. After all, most of us had been together a long time and we were growing older together. The sadness of it all was that Millie was gone and would not be there with me to enjoy us being together more frequently.

I drove back to Nashville and arrived home as Tom was pulling in my driveway. We had talked several times while I was driving and his timing at my arrival was impeccable. I think he was tuned in to my brain more so than I realized. He took my bag as I unlocked the door and told me he had found a theatre that wanted a daily performer who could be committed to a good contract for several years. I would be the main-tent performer and I could choose who other guest performers would be, also I could choose how often I would do performances. I wanted to get the troops together and hear their thoughts since they had a lot invested in my career.

"Tom, this sounds like exactly what I would like to do, but you haven't told me where or which theatre. Are you holding back for some reason?"

"It is not in Nashville that I can definitely tell you. I know you wanted to be closer to home, but the theatre is in Pigeon Forge. That is about a four hour drive, but the good thing is that you only need to be there Thursday through Sunday each week. There are other shows in the theatre the rest of the week, but the crowds and high attendances are on the four-day weekends. What are your thoughts on this type arrangement? Your real thoughts?"

I looked at Tom, knowing he was serious and had done a great job in finding the possibility, but I just didn't know about that type engagement. "Let discuss it with the troops. I know some will like that, especially not having to travel for months at a time. However, I am concerned that the four days will actually turn into six days getting there and back. This can be as bad as being gone for extended periods of time. Did you check on just a routine spot on the Opry? I don't want to just totally drop out of sight on the circuit, but frankly I am tired. I know you, Vic, and Darren are also tired. Tom, we have been doing this for thirty years. I am not quitting, not giving up, but let's slow down. Please. What if we checked into a television show one day a week that could introduce new talent and promote some of our own work?"

"Well, that is not a bad idea if we can find a network that will carry us."

"Check around. You have lots of contacts."

Tom and I changed the subject and settled down with a glass of wine, much needed on my part. Probably much more needed on his part with me being evasive and non-committal to Pigeon Forge. He assured me that he would check with several of the networks, but he would focus on those local to Nashville, primarily the CMT network. If they could find an open spot and if we could get some promotions and sponsors, this might work. We wanted to lay the options on the table with the group. I was concerned about Alvin who probably still wanted to be on the circuit around the country versus confined to a television show. Ironically he could do both now that he had recordings on the market and while he did not have a major hit song, he did bring in the younger generation. This could be a great selling point for our show. Tom had a lot of work to do. I had a lot of thinking to do.

Millie and I got together as much as possible in the planning of our wedding, but she was handling the majority of the details, well actually the majority of everything. Her mother came to Nashville for a few days to help Millie with the plans, to help her pick out a wedding dress, and to help decide who the bridesmaids should be and what they would wear. Since the wedding would be in Townsend, this meant travel for a lot of people, including the band members. Tom would be my best man and Vic and Darren agreed to be groomsmen and help usher. We had discussed who would be the ring bearer and flower girl since neither of us knew a lot of children in Townsend, but Millie had that covered. As a teacher, she had lots of friends with children, and her maid of honor had two children, fortunately a boy who is eight and a girl who is ten that could provide this need. We had to pick a day when school was not in session and people were available. This meant during the summer. We decided on a June date. My biggest concern was that with my career just beginning, that I did not encounter a conflict. Regardless, marrying Millie was the biggest event of my life and Tom would just have to arrange my schedule around it, plus give me some time for a honeymoon.

The words to the song *"Impossible Dream"* just kept racing through my mind, *"To dream the impossible dream."* To me being able to marry Millie at one time seemed to be an impossible dream, but a dream I'd had since we both were children. Well not when I was just eight or ten, but when I reached age thirteen and began to understand what love was. I wanted to reach that unreachable star, to make real that impossible dream, and now it is coming true. My quest was soon to be completed and my love for Millie would continue to be my life-long dream fulfilled. What more could I ask now that my career was happening and I was getting married. I really felt alive and so happy.

My thoughts were interrupted by the phone ringing. It was Millie. "Hello my love. Are you okay? Mom and I are having fun picking out a wedding dress and colors for the bride's maids. Mom is so happy, and so am I. I hope you are making preparations for a tux. What are doing?"

"My love, my Millie. I was just thinking that I love you so much and I wonder if I really deserve you. I have picked out my best man and Vic and Darren will be groomsmen. I have a tux on reserve. I am not as organized as you are, but I am getting some things together. You know you are my dream come true?"

"You are being silly. I think it is the other way around. Do I really deserve you? Ricky, this is a moment I, too, have dreamed about. I am so anxious, but at the same time I am concerned that you will regret marrying an older woman…"

"Now who is being silly? You are the love of my life. There has never been anyone else for me and there will never be anyone else. I can't wait until we are married and can be together for the rest of our lives. I just regret that I may be on the road much of the time if my career unfolds as Tom tells me it will. I can't wait for June to get here. I have to admit though that I am a bit nervous. I told Tom that I did not care what he did but not to book me anywhere from early June through the end of the month. I want us to have a honeymoon and we need to decide where to go."

"Ricky, your career will be fabulous. You are so talented and I will always be there supporting you. I may not get to travel with you much because of my teaching, and I do want to continue teaching. You know how I love kids and I want us to have one or two."

At that time I was so excited and as we disconnected, the phone rang again. This time it was Tom telling me we had to get over to the recording studio. Unbeknown to me Tom had scheduled a week long engagement in Branson to continue making certain I was visible on the circuit, an appearance on the Grand Ole Opry, and two sessions to record more singles. He wanted more singles, some of my work as well as others before we recorded our first album. We had done numerous tapes and CDs, and had begun to think about recording live some of our engagements. Tom mentioned that Vic and Darren were already at the studio setting up. The band members were excited and, of course, skeptical at the same time since I was a "newbie" with only one hit song, *"Shirley"*, to my credit. However that was a big hit and was still on the charts.

Early June came quickly. I was getting nervous about the wedding, but Millie and her mom, along with my mom, seemed to have everything under control. That is they had everything under control except me. Tom had held booking the troops with the understanding everyone would be in Townsend for my wedding and then everyone would have some R&R until the end of June when Millie and I would be back from our honeymoon. We decided to spend some time on the west coast, touring California from San Francisco down to San Diego, places neither of us had been but both wanted to visit. Millie's mom helped her pick out some places and since I was on the road just about every day with engagements, Millie booked hotels, got rental cars reserved, even booked reservations at several restaurants, and scheduled some special events, for which she did not tell me about everything. She wanted some to be a surprise. We did spend some time picking out wedding bands when I was back in Nashville. We also had time for some "alone time" just enjoying each other and having special dinners. I was recognized in a couple of places when Millie and I were together, but other than asking for autographs, we were not really bothered.

A week before the wedding Millie went to Townsend. I arrived two days before the appointed date with Tom accompanying me. Vic and

Darren were traveling together and were followed by the band members. We had to get set up in the church hall for the reception. We had the rehearsal the Friday evening before the wedding on Saturday and, of course, the rehearsal dinner with everyone in attendance. For me this was the biggest event of my life, including the start of my music career.

Millie seemed so calm, but both our parents were on edge as could be expected wanting everything to be perfect. My dad had to make a speech at the rehearsal dinner telling everyone about me as a little boy. I should have been embarrassed but at least he didn't tell anything bad that I did. Millie's dad had to tell the story of Millie baby-sitting me and teased us both that she would still be doing that for the next many years. That brought laughter from everyone. I just hung my head and tried to disappear.

The CMT network of Nashville was excited that I wanted to have a weekly show with special guests. They wanted it to be both fun and entertaining. Tom had to find at least one major sponsor for the show. He was amazed at how easily he got sponsors, more than we really needed, but funding the show was very important. We needed a premier show to test the market for potential viewers who would tune us in on a regular basis. Tom and Vic worked with the network to get a time slot for the premier and worked with the sponsors to ensure we were covered. I had so much to do planning what would be on the first show, how we could make a success of it, and with Darren we worked diligently with the troop for the appropriate set and staging of where I would be and how we would introduce guests. Of course, it was Tom's job to see who he could get on the show, both initially and continuing, to ensure we would have people tune us in. Our producers were actively engaged and excited about the opportunity with a premier show.

I never knew how much effort this would take until we undertook the opportunity. We all calmed down somewhat after the stress of getting time slots, sponsors, guests, sets, appropriate songs, and all the other million points of light, not being funny, but lighting was essential as well as sound. The premier was in six weeks, so getting advertising on the network ahead of time and getting some advertising in special bulletins was critical. We all pitched in with this effort. One week to go, several practice sessions, aligning with our special guests, we did a high-five that we were ready. I was somewhat used to being in front of a camera, but this was a live show being broadcast across the country, so mistakes would be obvious and uncorrectable. This was a tad scary for me, but Tom just brushed it off. Sometimes I think he hides his fears.

The premier went well and the results from viewers indicated a high rating. CMT decided, based on the ratings received, that this would be a good show to broadcast. We would be on Thursday night prime time, and if the rating continued to climb, CMT stated that they might find a slot on Saturday or Sunday evening that would be a time more viewers would tune in. First, though, we had to prove that we could continue a show with acceptable ratings. While I usually brought in good audience attendance for performances, with Alvin bringing in the younger group, we needed to make certain that our guests did the same. Choosing weekly guests and getting them booked meant that they had to be available and not on the road with their tours. Frankly, for some of the stars we needed to give them a year's notice. I told Tom I just hoped we were still on the air in a year.

Everyone was excited about doing the show and being closer to home. This was such a relief for me. I was beginning to feel the stress of constant travel and somewhat loneliness without Millie. Being closer would be more restful in one sense of the word, but being home more mean being there without Millie. There was no comfort in all the travel and yet there was a steady loneliness at home. Pastor Thomas dropped by a couple of times and, to some degree, was encouraging me to sell the house and maybe consider something smaller. However, Millie never wanted a huge house and ours was not small, but definitely not a Nashville mansion. I told Pastor Thomas that this was home, the home that Millie and I shared for many years, and while she was not here, there were so many memories in every room that I just could not give it up. He understood.

After the premier television show and getting everything and everyone scheduled for the first real weekly show, I decided to call Tammy and let her know what was going on. She is a great listener and will tell me objectively what she thinks, but with constructive criticism. We can talk and be friends without obligations. That is what I want and I know she feels the same way. We talked for over an hour with her wanting to know all about the show, which performers would be on it, and what day and time it would be on the air. She definitely wanted to see it and would make certain she posted the time at the bed and breakfast and had the television turned on to the station in the lobby. I am eternally grateful for all she does to encourage me, she is a good friend.

Saturday came too quickly but not quickly enough. I did not think I would be nervous, but my knees were actually knocking. The church was packed with not only many of the locals from Townsend, but a lot of my comrades from Nashville that were available were present. I know some of the people showed up because my musical troop was there and would be performing at the reception. Getting a free show, even though it was very limited, was considered a good thing by many in attendance at the wedding.

Millie looked gorgeous in a beautiful white gown with a flowing train behind her. The children who Millie recruited to be the ring bearer and flower girl were brother and sister. They were both dressed so cutely and their smiles just made me laugh. Millie's dad was escorting her down the aisle and giving her away. Both our moms were dressed beautifully and all the attendants were dressed to compliment both Millie's colors and my black tux. I was waiting at the altar with my best man, Tom, and the others as the music started and we watched Millie proceed down the aisle. My heart was thumping so loud that I could hear it.

The wedding ceremony was wonderful as we took our vows and exchanged rings. I kissed the bride and she kissed me and we just clung to each other for a moment before the preacher announced, "I give you Mr. and Mrs. Ricky Snyder." Millie and I loped up the aisle and waited at the back of the church as people greeted us. The reception almost seemed to have more people than were at the actual ceremony, but maybe my eyes were deceiving me. Millie and I had a ton of pictures taken before and after the ceremony and many taken before the reception.

During the reception there were so many coming to us with congratulations and well-wishes. We could hardly get away to be seated so some of the "roasting" could be done about Millie or me and then the two of us. My dad shared some of what he called "precious moments" and my mom just cried. Millie's dad had a prepared speech, but actually tossed it away when he got up. He just spoke from his heart. Neither of our moms spoke. Some of our friends made great comments, some cute, and some told a few things they remembered as special moments of our lives. Tom started to get up and I was afraid of what he might say, but then he held up his wine glass and proposed a toast.

After everyone did their thing with the toasting and while my band was slowly playing some of my songs in the background, I stood up, first with a toast to honor Millie's dad and her mom and thanking them for having such a wonderful daughter as Millie. Then I turned to my mom and dad, I thanked them for believing in me, for loving me in spite of all my childhood misgivings, and thanked them for sacrificing so much for me. I gave a great toast to them. As I spoke I kissed Millie on the cheek, kissed my mom on the cheek, shook Millie's dad's hand and hugged my dad as I walked behind him. I walked over to my band and took the mike. I said, "Mom, Dad, how can I ever be as thankful as I should be for all you did to get me to this point? Your encouragement, your personal sacrifices, your commitment to me has been overwhelming. I want to sing from my heart the song I think says what I mean." The band hit a few notes and I started singing Josh Groban's *"He Raised Me Up."* Afterwards, my mom, Millie's mom and both our dads stood and I said, "That one is for you. I love you more than you know. Thank you!"

Needless to say the reception went well and Millie and I had our dance, pushed cake in each other's face, drank some champagne, changed clothes and left through a barrage of tossed rice and Rose petals. My car looked as if it had been sprayed painted with "just married" and other innuendoes that revealed a happily married couple. Millie and I headed to the airport for our honeymoon. I couldn't wait to just be with her and start our lives together. Neither Millie nor I had been to the west coast, so we really wanted to enjoy the sites as well as have a special honeymoon. We had waited long enough for each other, both of us very faithful, and both not experienced with lovemaking. This would be a new experience for us but one that would come naturally. I was so excited and loved Millie so much. We enjoyed the plane ride and welcomed landing in San Diego to begin a life together.

COMPANIONS
Conceptions

I could only have imagined how wonderful it felt to be with Millie, just the two of us. We took in all the sites in San Diego, traveled up to see the Red Wood Forest, drove to Mexico's boarder but did not go into Mexico. We spent special time in our hotel room, breakfast in bed, and just bathed in the wonders of being a newly married couple. We talked about having children. She wanted at least a boy and a girl, with the boy being the oldest so he could protect his sister much as she watched over me. We both laughed about that. We talked about the times we sat together on the piano bench and she paid special attention to certain anatomical parts of me. Gosh, I was so naïve at that age, but those were the times that I fell madly in love with Millie, and, she with me. We probably did not know at that age, neither of us, that one day we would be here in San Diego as husband and wife. Millie and I laughed about those times and she said she always felt guilty afterwards. I told her that I did not feel guilty at all.

Millie and I discussed her teaching career, my music career, where we should live and what type house we should buy. She wanted at least a house big enough for the family we discussed, but she didn't want any place that would be so capricious to the life styles we were accustomed. Millie was not a flamboyant person, and did not want to be a "show-off" as she so emphatically stated. I listened and was definitely okay with her reasoning. After all, I grew up in a two-bedroom home with a small room to myself and shared a room during college with a roommate and then had a small one-bedroom type efficiency apartment. Any place bigger than either of those accommodations would seem like a mansion to me. What we wanted was a four-bedroom house, one bedroom for each of our children and a guest room for either of our parents when they elected to visit. This made very good sense to me.

We both knew our honeymoon would not last forever and that we had to get back to Nashville and find a place to live, knowing that we could combine our simple lives into her apartment for a while. We agreed to stay at her place and close mine out until we could find the right place. We would look for a house, or she would while I had to get back on the circuit. Tom had already called several times during Millie's and my honeymoon time to alert me to planned engagements that were scheduled and committed. My latest song had become a hit and record sales were going great. I couldn't stay away much longer, regardless of how much I just wanted to be with Millie. The onus would be on her to find us a place to live and I realized that I would be away more than at home. It didn't matter. Millie and I were married and I knew we would be together forever.

Our first CMT show was a great success. We had planned and planned and invited great guests, major country stars who welcomed being a part of our first program. The Neilson rating was superb and landed us a stronger contract with the CMT network. Tom, Vic, and Darren were ecstatic as was I. As promised, Tammy had watched both the premier and first show and called to offer her congratulations and expressed how wonderful the programs had been. As also promised she had posted the time and station for our shows at her bed and breakfast and ensured that the television in the lobby was turned on at the appropriate time. She told me that guests were not only impressed that Rick Snyder had the show, but that he was a regular guest at the bed and breakfast. Naturally Tammy gleamed with pride and a sense of telling everyone that she knew Ricky Snyder when he was a boy in Townsend.

Tom, being the efficient person that he is had numerous shows lined up with top stars, some just not singers, but he had some well known song writers and musical score composers scheduled. He had religious groups, some hit parade groups, and thought that maybe adding some comedy relief would be good. Tom also wanted to plan a huge Christmas show with family members of the band being introduced. He also wanted to include a tribute to Millie. I was actually enjoying being the master of ceremonies by introducing guests and adding my time singing. Vic and Darren worked endlessly to ensure the music was great and the background props complimented each show. If I lived to be very old, I could not have appreciated more the team that had been with me from the beginning. I was thankful every day for each one.

The line-up for the Christmas show was unbelievably wonderful. In addition to each of the band members, Vic, Darren, and Tom bringing their wives, significant others, and children, the guest stars also brought some family members. The set was dressed for the Christmas season, and of course it was dressed to remember the real reason for Christmas. We had one of the band members to dress up like Santa Claus and present the kids with small gifts. This was exciting to watch the expressions on the children's faces. This was definitely a highlight of the show. Vic had groups of family members singing carols as well as some of the children from various band members singing songs accompanied by respective band fathers. CMT expanded our time slot to provide for the entire show. The ratings were extremely high.

I did feel a little annoyance, not left out since I was the host, but somewhat sad that I had no family members to introduce, no children, and of course no Millie. Millie and I both was the only child of our respective parents, and we had no children. Since Millie had passed away, I thought of inviting Tammy, but that just did not seem appropriate and I thought that it would send a message that there was more to our relationship than truly existed. Instead, I contacted the school where Millie taught for many years, and asked the principal if she would arrange for a group of children to participate and sing a carol or two in remembrance of Millie. They were more than agreeable and made the necessary arrangements. This was at least a group I could relate to and introduce as part of Millie's life even though I actually did not know the children personally.

I did notify Tammy about the show and, of course, she was watching with the television in the main lobby tuned in to the performance. Her guest list was slim because of the holidays, but those present, according to Millie, enjoyed the show. She said that it was snowing in Townsend and that added a touch of realism to the Christmas show. She told me she served eggnog, some spiked with a bit of rum, but offered plain to those who did not partake of alcohol. However, Tammy said, only the spiked was consumed. I told her that I wished I could have been there in person, but the show was live and there was no way I could make the trip. I promised Tammy I would come sometime around Christmas for a day or two just to spend some time there for the holidays. I made her promise not to go overboard and definitely no gifts. I think I only wanted to be with her since both of our spouses had passed away and Christmas just isn't the same unless you are with someone for whom you care.

Millie and I, well mostly Millie since I was on the road most of the time, must have looked at almost a hundred houses before she found the one she liked the best. The house was in Brentwood, a very nice neighborhood with some younger couples, but mixed with some famous individuals. The house was not large, but met Millie's requirements with four bedrooms and a nice, but compact lot. This was just what she wanted for a family. Once I got back in town for a few days, and since Millie had put a small deposit on the house to hold it, we got with the realtors and the banks and closed the deal. I was afraid it was more than I could afford, but I was doing well with record sales and performances.

We moved in just before Thanksgiving. Between my sparse furnishings that we had put in storage from my apartment and her limited furnishings from her apartment, we figured we could adequately furnish one bedroom, part of the den, and have a half-way decent kitchen. Millie did have a table that we put in the dining room, but it was lost within the size of the room and she only had two chairs. We laughed and decided some more furniture had to be on our priority list. I was actually away for Thanksgiving on tour so Millie drove home to Townsend to have Thanksgiving with her parents. My parents also joined them for the dinner. I called and talked to everyone, apologizing that I could not be there in person. I told Millie to eat some pecan pie for me.

With the Christmas holidays approaching, Millie and I decided if our parents were coming, we needed to decorate and at least purchase two more beds. We were both continually laughing since the sum total of our decorations was a small tree that Millie had used in her apartment and a small wreath she hung on her door. I had nothing to contribute. We had a lot to do before having a party at our new house. But the fun part was before us. Millie's piano was placed in the living room that we referred to as our first music room. At least we could gather around it and sing Christmas carols. The table Millie had in her apartment was nice, and as we knew it was lost in the dining room and just accommodating two people. Even so when her parents came to visit at her apartment she had to pull up the piano bench. Now with six of us for a Christmas meal we did not have a table large enough. I was getting concerned if we had enough table place settings for six people. If we combined my dinnerware with hers, we had such a mismatch that it would be embarrassing.

We were just beginning to understand the complexities of setting up a house versus simple apartment living. I was so thankful Millie had most of this under control. She decided we must buy a dining room suite. As long as she liked it, I was okay with whatever she picked out. We both realized that neither of us had been exposed to any great wealth and simple living was okay with us. Millie wanted a simple life with a family and was quickly coming to the realization that with my career she may have more exposure than either of us wanted for our family that is once we had a family. We decided while sitting at the table for two in our large dining room that regardless of where my career took us that we would keep our family protected from unnecessary exposure to the public.

I was back in the studio for much of each day, on the road with performances, interviews by some of the music industry magazines, made some appearances on both television shows and on stage; all of this while Millie picked out furniture and prepared for the Christmas gathering with our families and inviting Vic, Darren, and Tom to join us for our very first planned meal in our new home. We were so excited. Millie and I thought we were on top of the world. The only drawback was that I was away from home more and more.

Christmas Eve seemed to creep upon us, but somehow Millie and I found time to buy presents for everyone who would be at the house on Christmas Day. Our parents were pleased with the way Millie had decorated the house and was pleasantly surprised with the house and furnishing. When the door bell rang, Millie opened the door and her mother just stared at her for a moment and then they hugged. Her mother said, "Millie, Love, you have done so much to decorate the outside, how did you have time? The wreath on the door is beautiful." It was not the wreath that Millie had hung on the door of her apartment, but one she recently purchased. It was beautiful.

"Mother, Dad, just don't stand there. Come in, come in. Ricky is in the den. You must see the tree he and I decorated."

"Millie," her dad said, "this is one beautiful home. I can't wait to have a tour."

"Dad, Ricky and I had to scrounge around to at least furnish enough rooms to make it livable, but you will have a bed to sleep in. Ricky's parents called and they are not too far behind you. I expect them in abut thirty minutes."

As always, Ricky was the consummate host and offered eggnog to everyone and setting out two cups for his parents, preparing for their arrival. Millie's dad wanted to know who picked out the house, and Ricky had to openly admit that Millie did all the hard work in choosing the neighborhood and house. Ricky told him that Millie and he both agreed on this one and both loved, not only the area, but the floor plan suited them as well as one day accommodating a family.

Ricky's parents arrived and after hugs and kisses, everyone enjoyed some spiked eggnog while both Millie and Ricky entertained a grand tour of the home. The bedrooms for their parents were very comfortably furnished and after a light dinner that Millie had prepared earlier, they gathered in the den and just talked for a couple of hours. Both Ricky's and Millie's parents wanted to hear about Ricky's career and what was going on with him regarding his music group. Ricky's Mom said, "You know, Ricky, if Millie hadn't forced you to keep practicing the piano you might still be working at the café."

"Oh, Mom! You and Dad as well as Millie made me what I am today. You both sacrificed to buy me a piano and Dad keep telling me to play something meaningful or he was going to sell the piano. What choice did I have?" We all laughed. I looked at Millie and we just sniggered remembering some of the times we sat together on the piano bench as she taught me about other things beside the keyboard.

The night was getting long and as everyone nestled in for the night,

Millie and I enjoyed christening our bedroom as we elected to try starting a family. I could have gone all night, but Millie thought twice was enough, but we cuddled and both slept like babies hoping that a real baby might come into our lives as a result of our love-making.

Before ten o'clock Christmas morning as a family, everyone had finished a light breakfast, had all the inside and outside decorations turned on with the tree being the center of attention. Each one shared some Christmas past stories and opened our family gifts. I think Millie went a tad over board for everyone, and when I opened a gift that she had somehow hidden from me, I discovered a beautiful Martin guitar with my name inscribed on the neck. While I only played the guitar sometimes, Vic had taught me enough to be okay. Knowing he would be here later, I knew he would take a shine to the new instrument. I kissed Millie openly and thanked her for being so thoughtful and wonderful.

Around eleven o'clock, Vic, Tom and his wife and Darren and his significant other arrived bringing more gifts and more food. After another round of spiked eggnog, we opened more gifts for which even our parents surprised us by having small gifts for my group. Millie had chosen beautiful gifts for each of them. We settled back until Millie said, inviting the other women there to help, "Mom, Mother shall we all venture to the kitchen and see if we can get the meal on the table while all these hungry men talk about what men talk about?"

Our Christmas lunch was delightful. Millie, my mother, and her mother prepared a super meal and we all definitely ate too much. I felt like a stuffed lobster afterwards, but no holding back for the amazing deserts. Tom's wife fixed a pecan pie to die for and while Vic and Darren weren't married, each had brought a bottle of wine. Vic wanted to bring his girlfriend, but she was spending time with her family and while was excited about coming, respectfully had to decline the invitation. Regardless, Vic had a great time as did we all.

With Christmas behind us, and with me being a part of three holiday performances, Tom, as the insistent manager, advised me we had numerous shows for New Year's Eve and a special performance on New Year's Day. He also had scheduled another recording session and kept insisting that I get creative and come up with a new song. I felt pressured, but knew that Tom's best interest was in my success. After all, this was what I really wanted instead of being a waiter in New York and subbing as a piano player for the Philharmonic.

∾

I arrived at Tammy's bed and breakfast very late on Christmas Eve. I had taken time to purchase a small but impersonal gift for Tammy and a couple bottles of extra special wine. Fortunately or unfortunately Tammy advised me that no one was booked at the bed and breakfast for Christmas Eve, but that several couples had made reservations for Christmas brunch. This was the only time all year that Tammy opened the dining room for just a meal. She told me it was great to have, as she referred to it, an extended family for a meal. We sat up and talked until a little after midnight, sipping wine and munching on some light hors o'devors she had put out. I decided before either of us drank too much that I needed to turn in for the night. She gave me a big hug and told me how wonderful it was to have me back, as she put it, as her special guest.

I slept like a baby and woke early Christmas Day. After my routine of shaving, showering and refreshing myself, I ventured downstairs and found Tammy in the kitchen working away preparing food for the brunch. I said, "Here's wishing you a Merry Christmas." I hugged her neck. "Thank you so much for letting me be here. What can I do to help get the brunch prepared? Do you think the light snow will deter any one coming today?"

Gladly accepting, Tammy said, "The snow won't last, but just makes it feel more like Christmas. It is so thoughtful of you to offer to help. Yes, I have a turkey in the oven that I hope I have not cremated and that you can carve once it is done. For now I have a ham that is ready to slice, if you want to do that."

"Of course. I probably will not do as good a job as you would, being the gourmet chef that you are, but I will do my best."

"I am certain any attempt will be wonderful on your part. People here will eat the ham and turkey regardless of how it is carved. You can also help with opening some of the condiments."

That became my job. I did a fairly decent job in slicing the ham and placed the slices on the platter Tammy selected for just the occasion. I opened cans of cranberry sauce, pineapple slices, and after the turkey was ready, my job was to carve it. I had a virtual mess with turkey bits all over the counter top, but the results presented nicely and my carving actually wasn't bad.

Everything had to be set up and ready for the guests who would start arriving before noon. Tammy told me that she started the buffet exactly at noon and ironically the news of my being there had precipitated three more couples to call and see if they could come for the brunch. This meant more food than planned, but Tammy was prepared. I had so much fun helping her. For me, this was a special Christmas Day. The only missing part was not having Millie there with me.

Tammy was right; the snow added a touch of both Christmas spirit and beauty to the day. Everyone that had booked a reservation did show up. The brunch was a real success, and I was convinced to sing some Christmas carols joined in by everyone who came for the brunch. It was almost three o'clock before the crowd left and Tammy and I started clearing tables and cleaning up. There was so very little food was left that made it easier to put stuff away. Several couples took doggy bags and Tammy added more to each container than was left on the plates. We put dishes in the dishwasher as well as washed and dried numerous special plates and containers used on the buffet and individual tables. Actually I was having a lot of fun, so much different from being on stage or eating at restaurants where I had grown accustomed to taking daily meals.

When we finally sat down, rather flopped down, sipping on our unfinished glasses of wine. I told Tammy about Millie's and my first Christmas dinner in our new home. She recalled hers with Cliff and I think we both experienced similar situations. She told me that at the time she had never baked a turkey and forgot to take out the bag of goodies placed inside the turkey breast for use in making stuffing. The plastic melted from the heat, and for the most part the turkey was over cooked, but eatable. She told me she forgot to take the bread out of the oven and it was so hard that Cliff wanted to save one and use it as a hammer. They shared that for many Christmases and had continued to laugh about it. Their parents were there that first Christmas, and the saving grace was that each had brought dishes that made the meal, not a monumental success, but one to remember.

Tammy wanted to know if I was staying for New Year's, but I told her I had obligations and Tom had booked me for some special events. We also had the CMT New Year's show to do. It just seemed that the more I wanted to relax and not be overbooked, the more I seemed to get involved. However, the best part was that I was staying in Nashville and not travelling around the globe. I promised Tammy I would be back but couldn't say when. My last night there was filled with memories of my first New Year's Eve with Millie.

With Christmas behind us, and with Tom booking events, I wanted to at least be home with Millie for our first New Year's Eve celebration. Little did I know until Tom had advised me that we had numerous New Year Eve and New Year Day performances. I really couldn't do anything but be there since I was the main tent attraction. Explaining this to Millie was regrettable. As always she understood, but we took a few minutes to just be together and talk about the coming New Year and what our plans would be. She was so hoping that she would be pregnant from our many times of trying while I was actually home. I promised to call her every day while I was away, and I did. I, too, wanted to hear those three words from Millie, "We are pregnant." I just had to wait. Maybe we tried enough while I was there, and maybe not enough.

Millie scheduled a visit with her OB-GYN physician and when we spoke, she told me that the results were negative. She wasn't pregnant. I wondered if it was because of me and I was sterile. I promised to get a check up and a sperm count when I got back to Nashville. That occurred and I was pronounced healthy and fertile with a high sperm count. The doctors told us that we may be trying too hard, to just relax and not to be nervous. I guess with me running around the country with my music team, spending time in the recording studio, and when on the road and at home, trying to come up with new lyrics was really stressing me out. Millie told me to "cool it" as she put it to me.

We tried to get pregnant at every opportunity. The days that followed were as stressful for Millie as they were for me. As promised, I continued to call every day. I remember that on my call to her around Valentine's Day, she told me she had a surprise for me. "Ricky, I went to the doctor today.

He said I was gaining weight. I know I have been eating a lot, but the last few mornings I have been a little nauseous. I did not tell you when you called earlier, but now I can tell you for certain, we are pregnant."

My heart skipped a beat. "Millie, my love, this is wonderful. I can't wait to be back home so we can celebrate. Do we know if it is a boy or a girl? I know you wanted a boy first to watch over our girl."

"Ricky, not yet. Let's wait. It is more important to have a healthy baby regardless of its gender. I don't care if it is a boy or a girl, just that we have our baby and we can love him or her."

"Oh, Millie. I agree. But, let's start thinking of names for both a boy and a girl. That is at least something we can talk about. I would really like to name a boy after me, but not call him Junior. I hate that tag."

"Ricky, I think any son of ours would be honored to carry on your name. I would like to name our daughter after both our mothers. What do you think?"

"That would be special, a real tribute to both of them, and I know our moms would be thrilled."

I called every day, sometime more than once even if I just left a message on the machine to check up on Millie and make certain she was doing okay and taking care of her and the baby. I was home for a few days and there definitely was no indication Millie was pregnant. She laughed and told me it had only been a couple of weeks. The baby was probably no bigger than a dime. We laughed and I wanted to know if it would hurt the baby if we made love. She told me that at this stage the baby had nothing to worry about and it would be okay.

Back on the road, at the close of every performance, I called Millie. She was right at four weeks when I called one night. Her mom answered the phone and I could tell she was shaking. I asked what was wrong. Millie came to the phone, crying, she told me she had a miscarriage and lost the baby. We both cried and I tried to comfort her, but to no avail. My main concern was that Millie was okay. She told me she was fine, but it had happened during the night and she called her mom who drove over to be with her. Millie told me that she had hesitated telling me while I was away, but her mom insisted that I would want to know. I asked if I should cancel some performances and come home immediately, but Millie told me she would be fine and for me not to cancel. We both agreed to try again as soon as she healed physically from the loss. When we hung up, I just sat down and cried.

∞

Our New Year's Eve program on CMT went well. Out biggest competition was against Dick Clark's New York performance of the ball dropping. While in New York studying at Juilliard, I attended this wild and voracious celebrating with many of my classmates. I was asked to perform twice during my career on stage there. I relented and did so, but promised myself twice was enough. Now that continuing celebration became my main competitor for audiences. A couple of the performers we wanted on our show had previously committed to being in New York or Los Angeles for the celebration. That was okay. We had a super group of performers and CMT advised us that regardless of Dick Clark, we had good ratings.

The weather was predicted to get very bad with rain turning to snow and high winds. The temperature was in the low twenty's and New Year's Day was not about to get me out of bed. However, when I reached over to Millie's side of the bed, knowing she wasn't there, and this had been over two years since her death, I didn't have the nerve just to lie there and waste a way the day. Later I had to meet the group for practice and a performance at a local theatre. I finally roused myself and just in my boxer shorts went to the kitchen and fixed a cup of coffee with a little sweetener and a tad of cream. I turned off the security system and opened the door to the screen porch. Walking out there was chilling to the bone and I shivered standing there in my boxer shorts. After a few minutes I was wide awake and frozen to the bone. The wind was harsh and cutting. I hurried back inside and closed the door. Leaning against it, I sipped my coffee and wondered what I could fix for breakfast.

I checked messages on the machine and only one was there. Tammy had called probably after midnight to wish me Happy New Year. I knew I had to call her sometime today, but I needed to get my act together first. I shucked my boxers, tossing them on the bed, and walked to the bathroom. Looking in the full-length mirror, I saw a fifty-two year old man with a body that lacked exercise. I made a resolution to myself that I would start some type routine soon. The equipment we had at the house was used a lot when Millie was alive and we would both exercise, but for the past two years, my heart just wasn't in to doing that now. I toileted, shaved, showered, and dressed in my regular outfit of blue jeans, a tank top with a pull over sweater, and of course my country boots. This made the mirror reflect a better image than it did of a naked old man. I could only stand there and laugh at myself.

Looking outside, the wind had died down somewhat, and the rain had changed to heavy snow flakes. If this kept up, getting anywhere would be difficult. I called Tom and asked if he had heard from the troops. "With this weather, Tom, do you think the theatre will be open tonight? It is New Year's Day and many places will be closed normally, not just because of the snow."

"Ricky, I'll check with the theatre manager but he probably will not be around until around ten if he makes it at all. I have his cell number, so if I don't reach him at the theatre, I will call and see what the plans are. I know this is a big show for him and probably already a sellout. I guess we better be prepared to be there. I will get with Vic and Darren and contact everyone. After a late night and our New Year's Eve performance, I know the troops would not be disappointed if the show tonight got canceled. I will get back to you."

I decided on a bowl of cereal and toast for breakfast. After eating I adjourned to my music room, sat at the piano, but did not open it to play but instead returned to the den and called Tammy to wish her a great day and a Happy New Year. We must have talked for over an hour before Tom called to tell me he had reached the theatre manager and the show was still on for the evening. He, Vic, and Darren were in the process of contacting the troops and since he had a great four-wheel drive vehicle he would come by and pick me up around two o'clock. I was ready, but not prepared to brave half of the audience attendance that I expected. Tom called back later and advised everyone could be there except one of the guitar players. He told me Vic consented to play in his place for the performance. Vic was a great guitarist so no complaints on my part.

I was pleasantly surprised by the turnout for the performance. The house was almost filled with only a few seats empty because of the weather. I was happy that our special guests showed as promised and the theater manager advised us the attendance was better than expected, obviously the inclement weather did not dampen people's spirits to get out for the day. The snow continued to come down heavily. I hesitated but finally asked the audience if they wanted the show to end a little sooner to allow for safer travel and got a responding "yes." I was more concerned about their safety than doing a long show. The theatre manager expressed his satisfaction by me doing so.

Tom took me back home and stayed a few minutes to have a drink and to discuss the next show. I encouraged him to go before the roads got impassible. He called his wife to let her know he was on his way. We would talk tomorrow by phone for any items that needed closure. I decided to relax, taking a nice warm shower and just putting on a robe. Sitting in the den, I flipped the remote for the television and then the remote for the gas logs in the fireplace, settled in with a nice glass of wine and some munchies that I found in the kitchen. I knew the housekeeper would not be there for a couple of days having given her time off for the holidays. While it was lonely without Millie or someone to talk to, I found solace in just being by myself after a harrowing day.

When I finished crying about our loss and being so concerned about Millie's condition after the miscarriage, I picked up the telephone in the hotel and called Vic's room. I wanted to tell him first since we had become great friends from out days sharing a room at Juilliard. He immediately came to my room and, in as much as possible, tried to console me. We decided to go to the lobby and have a glass of wine. Unbeknownst to either of us we found Tom and Darren in the lobby and was stupefied by the fact it had begun snowing at some point and the accumulation was frightful. We decided that being in Wichita, Kansas in January was not an ideal place to perform. However, our obligations were set and as the old cliché states, "the show must go on." We would settle in for the night and see what the weather would be tomorrow.

The weather got no better the next day, but we did make it to the theatre and had a great audience, even though it wasn't packed, obviously because people were skeptical of venturing out that evening with six to eight inches of snow and somewhat hazardous driving conditions. This show wasn't broadcast but was tape recorded, so those who missed it could later purchase the video recording and sound track if they so desired. After the performance, we had to travel again heading farther west to Las Vegas for a performance. I was actually getting concerned for the welfare of our team. Our bus and vans made slow progress but finally we arrived at the hotel in Las Vegas and I hurriedly got to my room to call Millie.

Her mother once again answered the telephone and told me Millie was sleeping but that she was doing okay. She wanted to know when I would be home, that she was afraid to leave Millie by herself until some of her strength returned and she felt much better. Millie had called the school principal and a substitute teacher was handling her class. Millie's doctor advised at least a full week of being off her feet and bed rest before attempting to get back to work. I told her mom that we had several more performances to do and probably would not be back in Nashville for another three weeks. I was almost paranoid knowing Millie could possibly be by herself for a couple of weeks. I was not really concerned about her health so much as her state of mind after losing the baby. Her mother told me that Millie is a strong-willed person, not that I didn't already know that, and that she would be okay once she had more rest.

The three weeks seemed like an eternity before I got back to Nashville. It was late around eight o'clock in the evening, almost close to Valentine's Day when I arrived. I had Tom stop so I could purchase some flowers and a box of candy for Millie. I think our reunion once I arrived was more than I expected. The flowers and candy were a thoughtful touch, but our holding each other was such a blessing. I think it was still too soon for more intimacy, but the comfort of being together was wonderful. Millie wanted to make me happy with special touching, but I felt if I could not return the feeling for her that we could wait until she was better both mentally and physically. Our love for each other made it possible that holding was immediately sufficient.

Time was flying by, so much faster than I was realizing. It was hard to believe that it was approaching one year of marriage in June and that I would not be home for our first anniversary. In fact, it had been about six weeks since I had been back to Nashville, but with two more hit songs on the charts, many engagements with sold-out performances, my troop was nationally known. Tom advised that we were getting requests from England, Australia, and Canada for tours. This would mean leaving the country and Millie behind for even longer periods of time. However, as she and I discussed these opportunities over the telephone with our nightly calls, she encouraged me to take advantage of possible tours to continue facilitating my career. She promised me she would be okay and that she would always be there when I returned.

In late July I returned for at least a two-week rest and recuperation and to just spend quality time with Millie. We again made many attempts at conceiving an offspring, hoping that she would get pregnant and be able to carry the baby full term. Back on the road in August, after a long day of performances in San Diego, I called Millie and could tell she was excited. She calmly said, "Ricky, don't get to wound up, but we are pregnant again."

Wow, was I elated. "Millie, my love, my only love, this is such great news. Are you okay? Are you taking it easy? School is about to begin for you, can you handle it? Should you take time off now?"

"So many questions, be calm. I actually started school to get my classroom set up yesterday. That is not stressful, but refreshing for me. You know how I love the children. No, I don't think I need to take time off now, but if I start getting morning sickness this time, I may ask my substitute to handle the class. I will be careful. Neither of us wants to lose this baby. Now, what is new with you?"

"Millie, Tom has booked us for a month-long tour in Canada, more the western part of Canada and then wants to get to Juneau, Alaska for an engagement. This means that I could be gone almost two months with the travel before ever getting back home. I worry that you are being alone so much and that I am not there to be with you."

"Don't be foolish. We both knew that with your career that you would be on the road and away much of the time. I cherish the times you are here and our talking every day helps me to stay close to you. Just don't find some other beauty out there to replace me. I know the girls would like to have a good-looking country singer who is so successful."

"Millie, don't ever think about that. I loved you from the time I was a small boy, and I will love you forever. There is and will not be anyone else."

∾

Tom and Vic kept encouraging me to come up with a new song that we could introduce on the show and record. I had been somewhat dry with ideas and I guess much because that Millie wasn't there to gently push me. Many times I sat at my piano and tried to think of some words that would or could express my feelings and at the same time would be acceptable to record. I looked at my walls and saw the many gold and platinum records, singles and albums that during my long career show the strength of my successes. Instead of being creative, I always ended up playing some of the songs I loved the best. This calmed my mind, but did nothing to comfort my loss of Millie. I knew that I would never get over her, but that now more than two years later it was time to at least move on with my life. I knew Millie would want that. I just didn't know how to do that. Music was my life, and now being more at home with most performances being local, I feared withdrawing more into a shell.

Finally, after many hours at the piano, many thoughts running through my head, I jotted the words to what I thought would be a great opening song at one of our performances. I called Vic and he came. I went over the lyrics with him and he made a couple of suggestions. We agreed on the changes and both thought Tom would like it. I would think of a title later. When Vic and I shared it with Tom and Darren, they were pleased. Tom arranged a time in the studio for recording it, and we released it as a single.

We hadn't been in Canada more than a few days when Millie's mother called me to let me know that Millie was having major cramps and that her doctor wanted her to have plenty of bed rest. Millie's mom told me she was going to Nashville to be with Millie and would call me when she got there. I was beside myself and immediately called Millie. She sounded so weak, but as the type person she was, told me she would be okay and for me not to worry. I told her I would cancel the tour and come home. She refused to let me do that.

I called Millie every opportunity I had between performances, at night, early morning, whenever. I wanted to make sure she and the baby were okay. However, two days later, her mom called to let me know that

Millie was admitted to the hospital because the cramps were more than she could tolerate. I was afraid of what was happening, and as she and I talked, she paused for a moment to speak to the doctor, then crying, she told me Millie had miscarriage again. We both cried and I told her to let Millie know I would call as soon as she was able to talk on the telephone. I found it difficult to get through the performance that evening, but somehow I drew strength knowing at least that Millie was okay.

We opened the Canada tour with the new song. I introduced it as my latest work. The audience was receptive and I could not have been more pleased as I opened saying, "Ladies and Gentlemen, thank you for coming. I hope you enjoy my latest creation. I call it *Shaded By Memories. Thank you, thank you.*" I began to sing.

> Shaded by memories
> Taunted by dreams,
> Searching for reasons
> For love still unseen.
> Broken by stillness
> Tattered by life,
> Giving the most
> But all just in strife.
> Broken by promises,
> Broken in heart,
> Asking for reasons
> For drifting apart.
> Reasons without answers,
> Questions still unknown,
> Shaken by everything
> From living alone.
> But why do I worry
> When crying is no help,
> Reaching for freedom,
> But not finding out
> Why life can be hard
> And taken away;
> Why keep on living

Just day after day.
Shaded by memories
Awaken from dreams,
Shaded by memories
Unsure what they mean.
Broken by stillness,
Hearts broken by chance,
Tattered by living,
Dreams just a rare glance.
Shaded by memories,
Shaded by life
Taken away
Alone in the night.
Shaded by stillness,
The silence of dark,
Shaded by memories
The path I embark....
    Shaded by memories.....
    The path I embark... [10]

It was hard to keep my mind on singing thinking about Millie and worrying about her. Time, while there is no way to stop it or slow it down, seems to be the biggest hindrance for me to be with Millie as much as I desired. After the Canada tour and performances in Juneau, I was home for couple of weeks before Tom got us back on the road again. This time we were travelling to England for a month-long tour. Millie and I had as much quality time as possible, but she told me her doctors advised her that she probably would never carry a baby to full term. We both cried. She was advised to have a hysterectomy or to continue on the pill to prevent another pregnancy. She wanted to wait until I got back from England before we made a decision one way or the other. Her doctors told her that staying on the pill could also be damaging to her system. It was way too dangerous for her to try to carry a baby. We came to the realization that we would never have our own offspring.

---

[10] Written by Donald Arlo Jennings December 2014

Millie and I discussed adoption possibilities, but while she loved children and worked with them daily, her desire was not to adopt, but to birth her own. While this now was impossible, we both felt that with me on the road most of the time, away from home, that taking on an adopted child would place too much burden on her, even if we hired help. We really wanted a son or daughter, but decided we could be happy with each other. I know and she knew that both sets of parents wanted grandchildren, someone to carry on family names, but this would have to be done by a distant cousin and his family.

I walked into the studio one afternoon and was greeted by Tom, Vic and Darren. As had become our usual conversation, Tom wanted to know if, as he put it, "the spirit had moved me to be creative?" I could finally smile and told him I was working on a new song and hoped that I could finish it soon. I got the lifted eyebrow look as if he was saying he would believe it when he heard it. Vic smiled because he, having known me the longest, realized that if I said I had an idea coming that I really meant it. Tom badgered me some more informing me that my fans expected something new occasionally. My response was easy and as I smiled at Tom, I said, "Tom, you are so right. I have been negligent but please understand, even with almost three years behind me, I still struggle when I sit at the piano knowing Millie is not there. Someday you may understand, but I beg your patience and understanding. I am hoping that you will like the words I am working on and I pray that Vic and Darren can build the best music to accompany the song. I will tell you that it does have a touch of sad."

Vic laughed and Tom just shook his head. After many top hits, some written by other writers and of course some not so great, Tom realized that many of my songs had made it to the top. We never bragged about that fact, nor flaunted it in any way, we just knew if we did our best, the best for us would be realized. Tom was the oldest, and now with me approaching my mid-fifties, Tom was hitting his sixties, and he wanted sometime, as much as I did, to slow down. We had made great progress with the local programs and just being on television with our weekly show helped immensely, but Tom still expected me to have some original ideas. What he did not realize was that I also wanted me to have some original ideas coming out of the long dry spell that I had just gone through.

COMPANIONS
Challenges

Regardless of how much we grieved about losing two babies, we knew that we loved each other and cared for each other very much. Millie and I, while never resigning the fact that having children would have been joyous, we realized we had beautiful people around us, and Millie worked almost every day with children. I saw so many people, including children of all ages, during my tours, and many who approached me for autographs. Our happiness was with what we had, not what we didn't have.

Tom continued to press me for new song ideas and came over to the house one evening when I was in the middle of being creative. Millie would sit in the music room with me while I pounded, literally, on the piano and wrote notes, literally, for new songs. Tom, sitting there, was occasionally critical and suggested some word changes. We would argue, not being mean with each other, but I had to insist that it was my song. Millie was an inspiration to me just being there. Occasionally she would walk over to me, putting her arms around my neck, and while not saying anything about my work, she would playfully hit my chest telling me to cool it and calm down and tell Tom that he needed to cool it also. She insisted that I take a break to rest my mind before continuing. Sometimes she just left the room returning with a cool glass of juice, coffee, or at times brought wine for us, pulling me away from the piano into a comfortable chair. Her reason was to rejuvenate me. It always worked. Tom just frowned.

When I returned from England, Millie and I met with her doctors and listened intently to what they had to say regarding her physical condition. Her OB-GYN doctor advised us that she would have a better quality of life if she decided to have the hysterectomy. Since we all agreed that getting pregnant again could be life-threatening. Millie reluctantly agreed to the surgery. We scheduled it at a time I knew I would be home for several weeks spending time at the studio doing recordings. Vic and Darren continued to work with the lyrics and piano scores that I had written to develop the sound that became the "logo" for our music. Tom stayed with me at the hospital while Millie was in surgery. I was probably more nervous than I ever had been in my life, but when the surgeon came out and told me that Millie came through with flying colors, I was greatly relieved. However, he told me that we were fortunate to have done the surgery now because he had discovered a developing tumor on one of her ovaries. He had to remove them as well.

When I arrived at the studio the next day I had a little grin on my face that was immediately noticed by Vic. He looked at me and said, "I know that grin. You wrote something, didn't you?"

"You know me too well Vic. Yes, I had been working on some lyrics, but tossed most of them in the trash because the words just didn't go where I wanted to go. But now I think I have something you can work with and what I really want is some great music that emphasizes our logo. I probably wrote the lyrics three or four times as I pounded suitable music on the piano. Now it needs your touch and a great sound."

"Let me see the lyrics and hear what you did on the piano."

As I handed Vic the lyrics, Tom came into the studio. He looked at Vic and me, "Something is brewing here. I can tell it. What have you two done?"

Vic laughed as he always was doing and said, "Ricky finally wrote something and just reading the words, I love it. He is about to play his version and I want to see what we can do to put a great sound to it."

"Well, get on with it. It is about time something new is on our plate." Tom was half way kidding and half way serious. I realized he was as anxious as anyone to have a new song to record.

I started playing then sang the song as I felt it in my heart. Vic picked up his guitar and began adding an accompaniment as I played. Tom just sat down and I really think tears came to his eyes. I don't think it was that I had finally written a new song, but I think the words of the song got to him. When I finished he smiled, looked at both Vic and me and said, "By golly, guys, I think we have a new hit. Let's get Darren and get this one recorded as soon as possible. I want to introduce it as the opening song on our next program. Wonderful!"

This reminded me of the last time I wrote a new song while Millie was still with me and Tom came to the house to hear it. I always thought that if Millie liked the songs I had written, oh well, created, that she was subjective, but Tom on the other hand was very objective and sometimes critical. This time he opened up immediately with liking the song and had nothing critical to say. Not only was I surprised, but I was very pleased and happy with him. Usually we could get into an argument that some words needed changed, but this time he offered no suggestions, only to get it recorded immediately. Our arguments only lasted a minute or two and they were never mean-spirited. We could banter back and forth and still be great friends.

Vic worked with Darren and with a recording of just me playing the piano and singing the song, they developed an accompaniment with our music logo that was just simply great. The music emphasized the words more than I could have imagined. We practiced it at least a dozen times before starting the recording. This would be a single to start, but Tom wanted to use the title for a new album. When we finally finished, hours later, I think we were all exhausted. The entire troop was thrilled with the results as well as being through for the evening. I did not realize that we had been at the studio all day. It was nearing dinner time and we hadn't stopped for lunch. I insisted we order something and have it brought in. We all needed some food.

Tom and our producer scheduled the release of the song to be the day after our television show on CMT. As he wanted, the show was planned with incredible guest stars and as Tom also wanted, Vic and I planned to open the show with the new song. I was struggling how to introduce it, but finally decided to just be simple with my words expressing my feelings from my heart.

As the program began, Tom did his usual introduction of me and I did my usual acknowledgement of the troop. With just some light instrumental music from the band playing, I opened with, "Thank you for tuning us in this evening. It is always great to be here. We have a great show planned for you and I think you will enjoy our special guest stars. I want to open with a new song we recorded that will be released tomorrow. I struggled with this one, but I think the words say it all. This one is for Millie, my beloved wife who passed away over three years ago. Millie, I still love you and miss you! Ladies and gentlemen, *When Life Passes On*." The band started playing, and the music was beautiful. I started singing…

For love doesn't end when life passes on,
The feelings still linger even though you are gone.
The memories still fresh always in my mind,
Are blessings to remember for me for all time.
I cherish the moments that we had in your life,
I cherish the good times and even the strife.
I awake to each day with you fresh in my mind,
I've forgotten no promises I made any time,
I cherish the love you gave with your heart,
I cherish just knowing how each day will start,
I long for the moments I reached out and touched
Your face with your smile that meant so much
To me as I watched your wonderful smiles,
I cherish the gleam in your beautiful eyes.
But when life passes on, the memories are there,
And I remember the good times that we both shared.
I'll never forget you, but miss you each day,
And I cherish the moments we had just to play
And hold each other in our special way,
And cherish the words that we would both say.
For love doesn't end when life passes on,
The feelings still linger even though you are gone.
My memories of you are fresh in my mind,
And I long for the moments and will for all times.
I will never forget you and love you, you know,
But life passes on like the melting of snow.
The beauty of living is to be in time

When life passes on and one left behind
Will bring us together and smile when we see
Each other to love for eternity.
For love doesn't end when life passes on. [11]

After the show, our producers told us that the telephones were ringing off the hooks with people calling in wanting to know where they could purchase the song and if a recording of the show was available. I think we had a hit. And as Tom predicted, after the release, the song hit the top ten in just a few days and soared to number one in less than two weeks. I think much of this was due to the fact that Vic and Darren put great emphasis on the music and the sound that was our signature, our logo recognizable to our fans. I was both pleased and proud that while it took a long time for me to get the words created, I knew in my heart that Millie was up there clapping her hands and cheering me on. That thought alone just made the day worth everything to me.

The next few days seemed to just soar by with me working with Tom regarding how we could promote the new song without having to get back on the road again. I seriously did not want to spend countless days and weeks traveling across the world any longer. However, Tom and Darren, along with some reservations from Vic, recommended, well that is saying it way too loose, advised me that a good thing would be to have a road show in several major cities, broadcasting live from the theatres. I reluctantly agreed.

Millie recovered well from the surgery and I was more than elated. She returned to work after the appropriate healing time and was welcomed back in the classroom by her students and the faculty of the school. I was back on the road and in the studio most of the time. Millie and I continued to talk every night after one of my performances, regardless of the time of day or night. I really tried to not call after midnight, so some times my call to her was at intermission. I would skip being in the lobby at intermission

---

[11] Written by Donald Arlo Jennings January 22, 2015

allowing the guest musicians or groups to have that time. My troop and I would always be available after the show for autographs and just mingling with the audience as they left. Sometimes there were so many wanting autographs that Tom would have to come over and steal me away just to allow the crowd to leave. There were disappointments, but Tom always had a reasonable explanation.

The England tour prompted Tom to schedule an Australian tour that would mean being away for at least two months or longer, hitting New Zealand and touching on the Cape of South Africa. I argued that this would be too much for the troops, but they were all excited. I talked to Millie about the trip and was concerned since she would be alone and begged her to take time away from school and go with me. Her face brightened, but she put her hands on either side of my face and told me that it was not practical for her to be away that long. She expressed that she definitely would like to see Australia, but maybe another time when just the two of us could enjoy the scenery and each other without having a cast of thousands following us around. I loved the way she thought.

Being on the road and away so much of the time I came to realize just how much I missed being home and with Millie. Tom was married, but Vic and Darren were still single and several of the band members were still single. This made it easier for them to be away, but those of us, including Tom who was married, had to deal with fact that our careers were what paid the bills. As always during the tours, regardless of the country, I called Millie every evening and early on Saturdays and Sundays. I found it difficult to keep track of the days, weeks, months, and even years, but time in one instant was slow but it seemed in other ways it was moving so fast.

As impractical as I thought it was, time seems to always get ahead of me and as Millie and I continued doing our thing, me being on the road for months at a time and Millie teaching school and her activities at church, I suddenly realized that five more years had passed and Millie and I were quickly approaching our tenth anniversary. I definitely wanted to be home for that one since I had missed being there for our five-year celebration. But I always remember and sent Millie beautiful flowers and brought her the appropriate anniversary year's type gift. For each anniversary, we would dine out at a great restaurant when I got back home even though it did not always fall on our actual date. We would dine out and then enjoy each other long into the evening. Millie always had a wonderful surprise for me; sometimes it would bring tears to my eyes.

For Millie and my tenth anniversary, I told Tom not to schedule any engagements for at least a month. Wanting to know why since it was approaching June, I told him Millie and I were going on a vacation, just the two of us. He laughed and told me that if that was the case, he and his wife would take some time for a vacation. I laughed and told Tom that he needed to take some time because if he stayed around he would book us to death and when I got back, I would not be able to breathe for months trying to meet his planned schedule. He only smiled.

When I got home one evening in late May, Millie and I decided to have dinner at a fine restaurant. After enjoying a great meal and catching up on the day, I looked at Millie and handed her an envelope. Reluctantly she gazed at me and carefully opened the envelope taking out two first class airplane tickets to Australia. I told her we were going there for our tenth anniversary. She got up from the table and walked over to my side and kissed me while everyone around us at other tables just stared. When she held up the tickets and said we are going to Australia, people applauded. I was totally embarrassed. But this was Millie. She just had a way with my heart and I could only smile and got up and kissed her openly to another round of applause.

As I expected, the entire troop was elated with having some time during the summer to spend with family and friends. Tom definitely was taking time off to be with his family. Darren decided to join with his family, and Vic with his significant other, to take advantage of just being home. They both confessed that all the travelling exhausted their desire to have an "away vacation." Personally, I agreed, but it was unfair to Millie for me to see half the world and have her miss out on many adventures. This trip, to Australia, for us would seem like a second honeymoon. After all, ten years of marriage probably meant me being home no more than a combined total of five years. But, that is life on the road.

Millie was elated with the opportunity to see Australia, New Zealand, and to make the trip, just the two of us. She spend countless hours mapping out places to see, trips in the outback areas, shows, and just time to be together. She discovered some of the best hotels, restaurants, and planned site-seeing adventures. For me, I was happy she was doing this and I agreed to every place and every event she planned. It was a time for me to be what I wanted most in life and that was to be with Millie, period. She insisted that I not think about work, not call Tom every day, and made me promise to, as she put it, "just relax and hang loose." Oh, how I love the way she was always had things under control.

We left the first weekend in June with our return being the first weekend in July. This gave us plenty of time for our vacation, and allowed me to return to a busy schedule in early July, missing of course the Fourth since Millie and I would be flying back that weekend. Our flights were great, both going and coming home. We had dinner cruises around both Australia and New Zealand. We spent time on the beaches, walked in many parks, enjoyed fine meals, and enjoyed hanging out in some of the local night spots. I was recognized many times, but avoided any fanfare primarily because if the opportunity arose, Millie would grab me by the arm and lead me away. She told several people who wanted autographs that I was on vacation and if they would leave their names and addresses at the hotel desk, that Rick would send an autographed picture when we got back to the States. I was beginning to think she was a great manager as well as a great wife.

Home again meant back on the road, many engagements, more studio time and much to catch up on with Tom. Being away for over a month gave me new insights into being creative and I did come up with some new songs. The troops were ready to get back to being musicians, but everyone stated they enjoyed the time off. Our producer was beside himself because we were so out of pocket and he could not reach Tom or me. I told him he should take a vacation. Regardless, the grindstone was running and we had to put our noses to it and do what we knew we had to do, perform our best. I had two songs on the hit parade, one at the top of the charts. This meant that we had to be visible and available.

Tom worked hard on developing an agenda and securing spots on both stage and television to promote the new song. As I had requested, he did not extend the promotional road trip all over the country, but stayed within what I thought was a respectable distance. He did schedule Branson, St.

Louis, Memphis, Charlotte, and Kansas City. The way he worked this with both our CMT producer and our promotional media was that we would either broadcast our show each week from the city in which we were performing or tape it for broadcasting. This provided an avenue to keep the show on schedule with our television audience and at the same time performing live in numerous cities. But, this meant more equipment and probably even having to record a performance or even several and put them together for a weekly broadcast.

With the Fourth of July approaching, we knew we also had to put together a "firecracker" show to compete with competitive channels ensuring our ratings remained appropriate. I was hesitant to some degree realizing that almost three years to the Fourth of July that Millie and I were flying back from Australia for our tenth-anniversary vacation. Knowing that I lost Millie so long ago still brings tears to my eyes. Even with some encouragement from Tom, Vic, and Darren to find someone as a companion, I just knew in my heart that I was not ready. My communications with Tammy and being with her as just friends gave me some solace, but I found it difficult to share the love I had for Millie.

Tom, as always, had every detail planned to the finite degree. I expected no less because this was Tom. I never interfered with arrangements, but I always questioned "why?" or "do we have to be gone so long?" Eventually I yielded to the plans and everything worked liked a fine-tuned clock. We would be on the road performing as planned for about eight weeks. Since this was now the exception versus the norm, I was actually looking forward to the venture. This was probably because I fully understood, and emphasized to Tom, that I was getting too old to spend countless hours in a hotel or motel room and eating unhealthy foods that we just crammed down our throats between performances.

Finally, before the start of the trip, I called Tammy and told her our plans. She really wanted me to relax and enjoy the road trip, but insisted that once we returned that I promised to take time and come to Townsend and really relax at the bed and breakfast. While hesitant, she insisted and I relented and promised to come as soon as it was feasible. While that was not the commitment she wanted to hear, it was the best I was willing to consent to. We always enjoyed our telephone conversations, there were never any words expressing any feeling between us. I guess that is what made being around her, in person and on the telephone, so easy for me. She had lost Cliff and I had lost Millie, and we could console each other through words. After all, words seemed to be my livelihood.

I really hadn't given much thought to the cities that Tom scheduled for our performances, but Vic and I were talking one evening and he said, "You know, Ricky, this reminds me of the road trip Tom scheduled after you and Millie returned from Australia. I think we hit the same cities. Do you remember that or am I just thinking we did?"

"You know, Vic, I think you are right. Wow! That was a long time ago. I guess I had forgotten, but then how many cities have we been in over the past eighteen years? That was Millie's and my tenth anniversary. It is hard to think that we were married twenty-five years and she had been gone for three."

"You had a great marriage to a super wonderful woman. I just hope that my wife and I can both live to an old age together. She, probably much like Millie sometimes regrets me being gone so much, but she is so understanding and we share a great love now."

The road show was great. We all enjoyed our time, but everyone was anxious to get back to Nashville and to a less hectic routine. As promised, I worked around a schedule in order to get back to Townsend and spend some quality time relaxing and enjoying the friendly atmosphere of Tammy's bed and breakfast. To make that happen, we prerecorded two weeks of shows that would be broadcasted by CMT. It was hectic doing this, but at the same time with fall approaching, it would be great to drive through the mountains and enjoy the beautiful colors of the leaves. Millie and I always enjoyed the fall of the year as much as we enjoyed every spring. I still miss her, and knew that with Thanksgiving coming up soon, that I needed to be with friends.

Millie was very active in church. She not only taught Sunday school for the children but she played the piano during church services and was active in both the women's and young adult ministries. She helped with all the celebrative plays at Easter and Christmas as well as directed the children's special service and their annual play to the congregation. I was on the road much of the time and not at home for many of the Sunday services. However, Pastor Thomas always treated me as if I were there every week. Everyone respected Millie so much and I guess because of their respect for her that I was known more as "Millie's husband" versus Ricky Snyder the famous country music star.

Everyone in church remembered the times that Millie would play and sing, especially the old gospel songs. At one of the services that I was fortunate to be at, Pastor Thomas approached Millie and me after the service and wanted to know when we might consider doing a duet with one of my songs. I definitely liked Christian music and the band and I had recorded several religious albums of various older gospel songs and of course several Christmas albums with both traditional and religious seasonal songs. Pastor Thomas thought it would be good to have the two of us, Millie and me, sing together for a service.

"Ricky, haven't you written something that would be great to share with the congregation and that would be a great duet for you and Millie?"

"Seriously, Pastor Thomas, I haven't written a truly religious song, but let me and Millie ponder over what we can do."

Millie looked at me, grabbed my arm and entwined it with hers, "Oh, Ricky, I think Pastor Thomas' idea is wonderful. Maybe you can come up with some new thoughts that would be great for us to do together. We can talk more about it. Pastor, give us a few weeks and when Ricky has engaged his brain for some words and when he is back in town able to attend church again, I promise we will entertain everyone with something good."

"Millie," said the Pastor, "I don't doubt that at all."

In the car on the way home, Millie and I laughed and talked about what we could do. There are songs, many great songs already and for me to come up with something unique would be difficult. We talked about numerous possibilities, but Millie continued to insist that I could create a song that would be meaningful as well as a great duet rendition. I think Millie had more faith in my ability than I did. I only promised to try.

With fall of the year approaching and Thanksgiving coming up soon, I wondered what I could do to think in terms of the normal harvest while at the same time reflect on something unique, different than just a typical religious rendition of an older gospel song. I also knew that this would keep me awake at night and stretch my brain trying to come up with lyrics. Without my band and with only a piano accompaniment I needed something different. I had some time to think about this since Tom had us booked on the road again for over two months.

There were days that we were on the road and not performing, so I decided to try and be creative to some degree. I always found solace in working on songs while the bus was in route and usually just with Tom, Vic and Darren on the bus, well and the driver, with me. Many times the three of them were napping or planning the engagements while I stayed in my private quarters on the bus either being somewhat creative or sleeping. I started jotting down some thoughts, but each time I got frustrated and tossed the paper into the corner trash can. It was not until I was sitting up front with the driver and we were passing fields of corn that appeared to be ready for harvesting that an idea struck me as if it had been planted in my brain.

Tom arranged for our Thanksgiving show and the following week's show to be pre-recorded for broadcast. This gave me some time to relax and head toward Townsend to spend time at the bed and breakfast and have a Thanksgiving meal with Tammy and her guests. This was always an exciting time for Tammy, a time she cherished because of the memory of Cliff and his love for the fall of the year. Since Millie and I also loved this season, being in my home town and celebrating Thanksgiving there would be enjoyable. I called Tammy and told her of my plans. She laughed and said, "Ricky that is great. I will bake another turkey. The house is full with guests and even more scheduled for the Thanksgiving lunch. Don't worry, I have reserved you a room."

My time with Tammy and the guests at the bed and breakfast for Thanksgiving was relaxing as well as fun just to mingle with the guests, many who recognized me and wanted autographs. After eating a fat-filling meal, I actually played the piano that was in the dining room area and everyone joined in singing some old traditional Thanksgiving songs. This was a lot of fun and had no stress to it because I was doing something I thoroughly enjoyed. After the guests had departed and the clean-up was finished, Tammy and I sat at a table drinking coffee and reminiscing about past Thanksgivings with her Cliff and my Millie. We also talked about times with our parents when we were young and at home and digging into pieces of pumpkin pies and stuffing our mouths with juicy turkey and dressing. We laughed about some of the shenanigans we pulled as kids during the holidays and just enjoyed talking. It was my third Thanksgiving without Millie and Tammy's fifth. It was evident with both of us that we missed our spouses, but evident also that we also enjoyed each other's company.

That evening Tammy and I shared leftovers from the lunch and adjourned afterwards to the front parlor to enjoy more chatting and glasses of wine. Most of the guests had checked out leaving only four rooms occupied, including mine. It was a quiet evening with only the staying guests leaving for dinner and returning. Around nine o'clock, I was tired, but refreshed. I helped Tammy prepare the house for the night and then bid her a good night. We hugged but just a brotherly-sisterly hug with both saying, almost at the same time, that we enjoyed the day.

Morning came too early and as I peeped out the window, wearing just my underwear, I discovered it had snowed, dropping almost three inches over night. That would definitely prevent me from travelling back to Nashville. I decided to do my morning ritual and dressed to go help Tammy prepare breakfast since I doubted her help would make it there with the certain road conditions. As I expected, Tammy was in the kitchen by herself, so I pitched in and followed her direction to help get everything prepared for the guests and for us to enjoy breakfast while gazing out at the snow covered grounds.

I called Tom to let him know I was snowed in, but he only laughed and informed me that I was not alone. Nashville had received over four inches of snow and the roads were almost impassable, even with trucks out sanding. Since the television performance had been pre-recorded for the week, I advised him that I would be back in time for preparing for the next show. I settled in to help Tammy check out the guests who had to leave, advising them to be careful. One couple decided to stay another day until road conditions were better. We watched the news discovering lots of accidents. I was relieved that I really did not have to go anywhere.

∞

The view from the front of the bus had enlightened me with thoughts regarding creating lyrics that Millie and I could use for the duet Pastor

Thomas requested. I sat there starring until I was brought back to reality by Odell Rinehart, our bus driver who had been with us from the time we purchased the buses. O, as we sometimes called him, said, "The sky is getting darker. Looks as if we might run into some bad weather soon. Cheyenne could have some rough going this time of year."

"O, yeah. You could be right. Hey, I am going back to my room to jot down some thoughts. You and Tom may want to check the weather forecast and call the coliseum for information."

I made my way to my room and settled in jotting down some words, trying hard to create what I had in mind. After a few minutes, it came to me and I was almost finished when Tom knocked on the door, opening it, and telling me it was snowing. He doubted that we would make Cheyenne by our projected arrival time. He had contacted the coliseum office and was advised that there was four inches of snow on the ground with a prediction of at least two more before midnight. The temperature was dropping and by ten o'clock the next morning, the manager there would make a decision as to whether to try and continue our performance or to cancel.

"Gee, Tom. This would definitely be a wasted trip. What is the deal?"

"Well, from what I understand from the person I was speaking with, is that if the show is canceled, we will still be compensated, and the ticket holders will be given one year to use the tickets for another performance of equal or greater value on available comparable seats. I guess we need to find accommodations for tonight and verify our status for performing after ten in the morning. It will still take us time to get there, depending on road conditions. My recommendation is to agree to the cancelation and then check on our next point of performance."

"Not much choice, is there?"

"Nope. What are you working on?"

"Pastor Thomas wants Millie and me to do a duet. Millie wants me to create a special song for us. I think I have the lyrics I want now. It is a crazy idea, but I want to monologue these lyrics with an old hymn. My thought is that while Millie plays and sings the hymn, I will intersperse the monologue with each verse. I think it will be unique combining the two. What do you think?"

"Well, most of what you create is good. Let me see the lyrics and maybe we should get some thoughts from Vic."

Arriving back in Nashville after the weather improved, and after bidding Tammy not a "good-bye", but an "I'll see you soon", I had left Townsend to meet with Tom and at my house to discuss future plans. Our CMT contract for one year would soon be expiring and we needed to decide what our next steps would be. Our ratings continued to be above average with special guests and wonderful entertainment. Our CMT producers were definitely interested in the show continuing for another season, and our sponsors had great success advertising during the shows. No problem with any of those issues.

What Tom and I decided was that we would commit to four more weeks of live shows and four weeks of pre-recorded shows to provide ample time for CMT and our producers to find a replacement for our time slot. However, Tom and I knew that this had to be agreed to by everyone involved. Not ready to share this information with the others in our group, but Tom and I decided that our next big venture would be something that could be our last efforts and then maybe fully retire. We would plan a final world tour for at least twelve to fifteen months before calling it finished. Presenting this to everyone would cause some disbelief and some excitement, but there might be members would elect to quit the group.

Vic pondered over the words that I had scribbled and then asked what hymn would be used. When I told him, he said, "That is a unique idea. The words you wrote definitely go along with the verses, but isn't there only three verses in the song and you have four here?"

"Yes, I am aware of that. I will start the recitation with the music intro before Millie starts to sing the words to the song. I will end just after she sings the last verse and conclude with my singing at least one line of the chorus."

"Sounds like a plan to me."

Being on the road for over six months and with plans for several other performances, both television and one live radio interview, I advised Millie of my thoughts, showed her the lyrics and we discussed the song. However, it would be around the following Thanksgiving before we could do the duet. Breaking this to Pastor Thomas would have to fall on Millie's part since I doubted I would be able to attend church services for the next several months. Being on the road is a hard life, and separation from Millie, even though we talked every day, was very difficult for me. I am certain it was even more difficult for Millie.

As it planned out, Pastor Thomas was elated with the arrangement of my lyrics and the background song. Also, as it worked out, Tom did not schedule any performances around Thanksgiving in order that Millie and I would have an opportunity to be in church together and to perform the arrangement. Millie and I practiced at home with the songs before I had to hit the road again for scheduled performances. I promised Millie that we would have some time to practice before we actually performed for the church congregation, after I got back home from tours.

Time just flies, or so it seems, and I was back home as promised. Millie and I did at least a half-dozen run through sessions at home and several Saturday nights at the church before our Sunday debut. I don't know why I was nervous, but Millie tried to reassure me that we would be great and that everyone was looking forward to hearing what we created for them. Pastor Thomas listened to us Saturday night and expressed to us that it would be a huge success. As many times as I had performed before thousands of people, mostly fans and others who came for the first time, I had stage fright thinking about doing this at church.

Sunday morning came, and as usual, Millie had to teach her Sunday school class and I attended the men's class with everyone there asking questions about my tours until the teacher said he needed to get on with the lesson. After Sunday school, I joined Millie at the piano as she softly played while people entered and were getting seated. Pastor Thomas did his usual routine with one of the deacons providing updates on up and coming church events. After the responsive reading and prayer, Pastor Thomas said, "I know everyone enjoys Millie's music and hearing her sing solos as well as singing with the choir. But today we have a special reward for you. Ricky Snyder is here with his wonderful wife Millie and together they are going to perform a duet, one that I asked them to do, and Ricky wrote the words for a recitation along with Millie singing a background hymn. I know you will enjoy this performance. Ricky, Millie."

I thought it best to explain what Millie and I were going to do before we started. "Thank you Pastor Thomas. Thank you to everyone here today. I am so happy to be able to do this with Millie. Her voice is so refined next to mine, so I know at least half of this performance will be enjoyable. The words I will be reciting were written while I was on the road between performances. Millie and I have practiced some, so I really hope you enjoy it. Millie will be playing and singing the verses to *Bringing In The Sheaves* and I will be reciting a monologue appropriate to each verse of the song. I call the words, *The Harvest*. Millie, if you are ready."

Millie started playing as I started the first verse of the recitation, then she began singing the first verse of the hymn. I joined Millie after my recitation of the words and sang the chorus with her. The congregation was quiet, but seemed to be attentive to our music.

> *Lord, you know how many times I've walked these furrowed fields,*
> *And Lord, you know the times they've been too hard to till,*
> *And Lord, you know my plantings haven't always brought a yield,*
> *Yes Lord, you know exactly, exactly how I feel.*
>
> *Lord, you know there's a weariness in my bones,*
> *And my old mule's tired from pulling against the stones,*
> *And Lord, at day's end, I'm ready to go on home;*
> *Lord, I'm waiting for the day this grain will be full-grown.*
>
> *Lord, sometimes a dry spell just kills the whole crop,*
> *And Lord, sometimes the rain just beats it till it drops;*
> *And Lord, I worry until I see that grain top,*
> *But, you know Lord your overseeing just doesn't stop.*
>
> *But Lord, as I walk now, the grain up to my knees,*
> *The sun and rain just right, the grain blowing in the breeze,*
> *I see the caring that you show, especially for me,*
> *And Lord, I know you've done it all, every bit for free.* [12]
>
> *Bringing in the sheaves.…..Lord, bringing in the sheaves.……*

---

[12] Written by Donald Arlo Jennings around 1999 and revised January 2015.

After we finished, a silence seemed to hover over the congregation. I looked at Millie and she shrugged her shoulders as if to say she was surprised. But then, a thunderous applause exited from within the church and people started rising to their feet. Pastor Thomas came to my side with one hand on my shoulder and the other on Millie's. He waited for some quiet, but finally waved his hand to the congregation for them to be seated. He praised Millie and me for our performance and me for the outstanding words that blended so well with the hymn. All I could say was, "Thank you!"

CMT, our producers and our sponsors agreed to our plan to have only six more weeks of the show. I planned with our next performance to tell our viewing audience that in six weeks the show would end a very great season and super guests for the last performance so we would end the season with excellent ratings. I wanted to thank them for all the support and praises for the show.

Tom scheduled the start of the world tour beyond the time of year of Millie's death but insisted I needed to be more involved with me versus just grieving. I was still suffering her loss and planning how I would cope with my future. I told Tom that it seemed just like yesterday when I was at the hospital with her and hearing her doctors describe what would be her final days. Pastor Thomas was there, and he was with me through the whole process. I canceled everything to be with her, as I should. Now, I seem to continually deal mentally with that time, long ago in reality, but present in my memory.

I don't know how I will deal with being on the road, around the world for almost two years, but time will tell. Tom, Vic, and Darren and a number of the troop elected to make the "adventure" as we called it. That was very pleasing to hear, and since most of us had been together for almost thirty years, this would be a great climax to a stupendous career. I just did not know what I might do after this was over.

Millie's health over the years seemed to play hardball with her. The hysterectomy caused other internal problems, but she dealt with them even though I knew she had a lot of pain. The benign tumor in her breast meant a constant monitoring of her conditions. Through all the years we were married, we consoled each other in many ways. I was on the road so much, but we always talked every day, and when Millie had health issues, I canceled performances and stayed with her. It seemed that in the later years of our marriage that the times this occurred were most often.

We had been married for twenty-three years when Millie told me that she was having chest pains. We both thought this might be her heart, even though she had no family history, however limited, and no real reason to suspect such a condition. We scheduled an appointment with her primary care physician who, after running some tests, decided she needed to see a heart specialist. That was a good approach, but the specialist found nothing wrong with her heart. The next step was a MRI of the chest. This was scheduled at the hospital. The results were not good. The MRI showed several spots on her right lung and a larger spot on her left lung. Since she was having some difficulty breathing, a pulmonologist was called in for a deeper examination.

Millie was scared, but I think I was frantic. I could not bear the thought that Millie could have a serious problem. But, this dealt a huge blow to both Millie and me when an oncologist was called in. The diagnosis was clear that Millie had stage two lung cancer. While this was treatable, the outcome was obviously disturbing as the type cancer was quickly spreading. We were advised that medications would not be effective and that our only hope was both radiation and chemotherapy. I shuddered at the thought of both these treatments.

The oncologist advised that treatments needed to be started immediately. We agreed, but Millie wanted to know how all this would affect her. He told us that she would most probably be sick from the radiation treatments, but she would still be able to lead an almost normal routine. However, he was very open that once chemotherapy was started, she would possibly lose her hair and be very sick. This to me did not feel like a great approach to recovery. On the outside, Millie was advised that she may have to have part of both lungs removed if the treatments did not produce the results desired. I was worried sick. Millie was taking this in strides, but I knew she was stressed to the limit. I advised her to take a sabbatical from teaching, but she wanted to go as long as she could before just giving up something she dearly loved to do.

The radiation treatments started and I had to take Millie to the cancer center at least four days a week. This proved to be somewhat painless and the treatments were scheduled later in the days in order that Millie could teach. However some mornings she was sick, couldn't eat, and was exhausted. This required her substitute teaching her class on those days. The treatments continued for over three months, and while some of the smaller spots on her lungs showed a decrease in size, the larger ones did not appear to shrink to the degree the oncologist desired. This was discouraging. Before starting chemotherapy, the oncologist wanted at least two months between the radiation treatments before starting chemo. During this time, now almost eight months from the time she was diagnosed, Millie was becoming weaker. If she did not get some strength back soon, it would mean delaying further treatments. I was not dealing with this very well. I think I was more worried than Millie.

Time was both with us and against us. Millie did not gain a lot of strength and lost a great deal of weight. While she really could not afford to lose much weight, her oncologist was concerned that unless she did gain some weight this could also delay further treatments. My cooking was not acceptable to this situation, but I did hire a great cook and housekeeper. I also hired a full-time nurse to essentially live with us to provide Millie with around the clock monitoring. This did improve the situation and Millie did start improving both in her health status and putting on some weight. Regardless, her breathing became labored and resulted on her being on oxygen full-time. Now I really insisted that she take the sabbatical in order to fully recuperate. Another MRI showed some improvement in her condition, but there seemed to be continued growth of the larger tumor. Surgery was recommended before chemotherapy could commence.

I found myself slipping outside where Millie could not see me and I would cry until I had to go in and wash my eyes to rid them of the redness before approaching her. She was becoming more confined to being seated or lying down. This concerned me since she really needed a lot of strength to undergo surgery. We would hold each other and just talk about everything we had shared. We remembered the good ole days, but we were cherishing each moment we had together.

Millie did not want me to grieve, but she knew her days were limited. I was beside myself. What would I do without her? I would hold her hands and we would cuddle with our heads touching. I wanted so much to comfort her, but the pain she was experiencing was probably much greater than she admitted. My pain was in my heart for her. I wanted the best outcome, that she would fully recover and we would grow old together. Millie seemed to understand that time was running out for her, and she expressed more concern for me. I told her the surgery and other treatments would definitely restore her to perfect health. She would squeeze my hand and just smile. She knew better.

COMPANIONS
Remembering

I found it somewhat difficult to call Tammy regarding the world tour and telling her about being out of the country for almost two years. Difficult not in the sense of missing someone, but difficult in the sense that I always spoke to Millie every day while on the road, and while I did not call Tammy every day, she was someone that I could count on to listen to events about my day and for me to hear about hers. I enjoyed her companionship, both just talking on the telephone and whenever I took the opportunity to spend time in Townsend at her bed and breakfast. We had become good friends and we both understood that nothing more would ever develop beyond that point. She had a host of friends and many more who where no more than strangers but who stayed with her from time to time as guests. That was me, to a degree a guest, but I was not a stranger to her or her to me. We were friends.

She was curious as to why I would give up a promising television show to travel the world. To me it was my final exit, my final debut, my way of ending a career in person that I knew would go on for many years through records and albums. Tom and I had discussed cameo appearances and I would continue to write songs that would probably be recorded by other artists and I knew that Alvin would continue with my songs, recording them with his producers and singing them on his tours. I knew Tom would eventually retire or continue to help Alvin with his career. This was something we both spoke about at times. He was over sixty and I was approaching my mid-to-late-fifties. I knew Vic would probably become a church music director, what we talked about many times at Juilliard.

Darren would find another group to join helping with the technical side of the performances. He not only was a great technical guy, but smart and everyone just loved him. Darren would also finally retire and spend time with his grandchildren. I knew some of the members of my band would find other bands to join. Maybe one or two would actually retire or just do minimal work with other groups. Some would continue to be backup players at the studio for other groups. Maybe some would tag along with Alvin. What would I do, I could not explain that to Tammy much less to myself. But continuing to write and enjoy music seemed reasonable at the given moment.

Tammy and I talked on the telephone for over an hour. It was good. I needed the uplifting that she always brought to me during our conversations. I promised to come to Townsend and spend some time at the bed and breakfast after returning home from the tour. I probably promised her more profoundly than I promised myself. I just did not know. I wanted the tour, but I think I wanted peace of mind more. This would be one of my last chances to perform featuring all the songs I had written and recorded along with old hymns, and older songs from major performers. Tom and I knew it would be good. Tammy knew also. My only regret, the ache deep in my heart was that Millie would not be with me. I also regretted retiring without her by my side. After a long conversation, I bid Tammy a good night leaving her with, "I'll see you soon."

After the call I just sat back in the recliner in the den, sipped some wine and half dreamed and half remembered my life with Millie, just as if it happened yesterday. I think sometime between my remembering and dreaming the morning came.

The surgeon who operated on Millie was not only a great surgeon, but a wonderful Christian with an outstanding personality that made you appreciate him in all aspects of his profession. He prayed with Millie and me before she was prepped for surgery. I stayed with her as long as they would let me. Pastor Thomas was there with me as well as Tom, Vic and Darren. Church members dropped in and would stay a while, but the surgery was taking much longer than the surgeon had told me. I was worried sick, but Pastor Thomas stayed the duration and insisted that we all go to the cafeteria for some food. I wasn't hungry, but he said I needed to maintain my strength. I needed to be there for Millie when she came out of surgery.

After about six hours, the surgeon came out of the operating room and approached us. Pastor Thomas stood up with me as the surgeon said, "Ricky, good news and bad news. Millie's surgery went well and she has been moved to the recovery room. You can see her once she is awake and able to see visitors. The bad news is that once I was in her chest, I discovered that the tumor was much larger than we really were seeing on the pictures. I thought at first that I would just be able to do a segmentectomy or just removal the cancerous tissue from her left lung. It then looked as if a lobectomy would be required. That is removing an entire lobe from the lung. However, under more examination, I knew we had a bad situation. Ricky, I had to do a pneumonectomy, removing her entire left lung. This will definitely extend her recovery time. My main concern is that the right lung will be healthy enough to maintain her life."

I was in total shock. I sat down. Pastor Thomas sat with me and held onto my shoulder. I really did not know what questions to ask, but I finally said, "Doctor, what are her chances?"

"She is a fighter, but it will take some time before we can make any type determination about the right lung. With the amount of radiation and chemo she has had, that has helped, but could limit her time. We can only pray for a miracle at this time."

"And if we don't get a miracle?"

"Seriously, maybe four months, six at the most, but I have seen patients live a year or more. It is in God's hands now. You will have to be her main support and ensure she is careful with her activities, that she never overdoes anything that would challenge her breathing or over task her health. It will be a slow recovery and, if I might add, a challenge to you to maintain a positive attitude."

I just sat there and stared into the open space in front of me. I was devastated beyond what I thought I could ever be. Pastor Thomas was very consoling, but neither he nor my closest friends could understand the thoughts going through my head. I never in my life thought that I could lose Millie in any way, much less to cancer. I always thought that I would go first and I worried about how she would survive. Now I wonder just how I will survive if Millie doesn't make it.

After many days in recovery, Millie was moved to inpatient status. I was there with her every day and stayed many nights in her room. After she was able to sit up and actually eat some solid food, she constantly smiled and told me she was doing okay, but that her chest felt as if something was missing. She was still on oxygen and had so many tubes running into her that I told her she looked like a string puppet. She threatened my life if I tried to dangle her with the tubes. It was so good to hear her laugh, even though it strained every ounce of her strength. I would sit and hold her hand and we watched some horrible reruns on the television, or should I say I did because she kept dozing on. I would read to her, and make up words that were not part of the story. She would slap out at me and tell me to behave, read it right, or she would not listen. We actually had a good time.

Her hospital stay was much longer than expected. Many doctors came to her room. She had wonderful care, and joked with all the nurses, especially the one who kept telling me I should sing to Millie. I laughed and told her that I wanted Millie to get well not to relapse. Millie would strain to laugh, and told the nurse that if I did sing, too many people would come to the room and she would be suffocated by the number of people packed in the small space. It was so good to see Millie maintaining her sense of laughter.

Finally I was able to take her home. With our in-resident nurse, we ordered a hospital-type bed in case it would be easier to manage both taking care of Millie and for Millie to get in and out more comfortably. Pastor Thomas was at the hospital for the discharge as were some of the ladies from the church. Tom and Vic were with me, but did not follow us home out of respect for Millie and me to get settled. Millie told me she was okay, but I could tell that sitting was uncomfortable for her. She looked like skin and bones having lost so much weight. I threatened to feed her bananas until she got fat, and she threatened to cut my hands off if I did. We both laughed.

At home, getting her settled was a chore, but her nurse made it seem so easy and handled Millie as if she were a precious ornament. Our cook prepared a very light meal for Millie and actually sat with her to help feed her while Millie kept insisting she was capable of feeding herself. But, as her nurse explained, Millie would doze off for a few minutes between bites. She needed rest, lots of rest. As the doctors said, keep her comfortable and as soon as she feels up to it, get her up and walking every few hours to build her strength and help rebuild some of the blood vessels in her chest. She needed to continue with the breathing apparatus and to continue on oxygen. Millie hated those tubes in her nose and would try to take them out every time her nurse turned her back. Finally I told Millie if she pulled them out one more time that I would duct tape them to her nose. We laughed about that for days. Millie was a champion, a really good patient, and still, even with all the problems, she was a delight to be around. Many of the teachers from Millie's school dropped by from time to time to bring flowers, books or some other gifts for Millie, and to just to pay their respects to me.

For Millie and our twenty-fourth anniversary, I had our favorite restaurant cater Millie's favorite dinner, had the florist bring in lots of roses, and I actually moved her to the music room, sat there with her, holding her hand, and singing to her and playing some of the hymns she loved on the piano. She wanted to sing along, but it just took too much of her strength.

Regardless, with all the care she received, and getting her up and about, making her walk every day, making certain she ate at least twice a day, Millie gained limited strength and actually put on several pounds. She was breathing easier to the point she didn't need to have her oxygen around the clock. I would gently pick her up, and with her nurse, we took her every other week to see her doctors. All her appointments were arranged in order that she only had to make one outing, but by the end of the day she was exhausted and would sleep for hours after we got her back home.

My producers and agent, along with Tom, were getting concerned that I was not able to be at the recording studio or to make any commitments for shows of any type. I missed the routine, but it was far more important to be with Millie. She would tell me to go away, go to the studio, be on a television show, but my mind and heart just could not leave her. I couldn't write songs, but would play the piano for her. She told me a couple of times that she wished she had the energy to play the piano, but just sitting there listening to me play zapped her strength.

Throughout the first couple of months of Millie being home, so many people came by to visit. It seemed a lot of people from the church would come by, bringing food, bringing gifts of flowers, books, magazines, cards, and just well-wishes and also prayers. Many of my troop members would drop by paying their respects. Even some of the professional musicians would drop by when they were in town, some to console me, others to hang out with Millie for a few minutes. All of this got to be too much for Millie, and I had to curtail the traffic to her bedside by keeping the visitors in the living room or den by insisting Millie was sleeping or just too exhausted to have guests at that time. Everyone understood, and no one left feeling they were either wrong for coming by or that I had ushered them out.

Millie did continue to gain more strength and was breathing so much easier even with just one lung. The oncologist did not push more chemotherapy or radiation, but prescribed some pills to take that had a small effect of chemo; however, not the strength that would impose an element of risk to her recovery. Within seven months, Millie was getting around the house under her own abilities, but was careful to rest adequately. She thought that it was time for me to get out and have a change of scenery. I told her the scenery looking at her was the most beautiful that could be found. She tossed a pillow at me. I did go to the studio for a while and met with the troops. Everyone was anxious to get back to work regularly, but no one was skipping out or looking for other opportunities.

I guess time had a way of creeping up on us. Millie seemed to be doing great and we were able to go out to a movie and have dinner without her being totally exhausted by the end of the day. However, she was never able to go back to teaching, but every once in while she would study hard and help teach her Sunday school class. It was so good to see her up and about and able to do limited things. Her doctors felt that her attitude about her health was a prime factor in her recovery.

Millie wanted to get away from, as she put it, the maddening crowd and she wanted to take a drive to Townsend and see "home" as she felt it would be her last time. I was indifferent to this, more than willing to take her, but very concerned if she could endure the trip. As usual, Millie won out. However, that did not stop me from calling her doctor inquiring if he thought she was able. He only assured me that what Millie thought she could do would be good for her, but not to let her drive. I consented and took the big Mercedes to provide a more comfortable ride for her.

We stopped at one of our favorite cafes and had a delightful time at breakfast that morning before heading out to Townsend. It was going to be her first really long car ride and I continued to push her as I drove to tell me if she felt okay or if this was being too much, but she insisted in doing the trip. We had fun driving, laughing and just being us. It was a long drive, just the two of us even though I wanted her nurse to travel with us, but Millie only laughed and said that this was our time and we really did not need a chaperone. How could I not laugh?

We actually stopped in Knoxville and spent the night at a great hotel, had a great dinner, and I insisted that Millie just rest before we continued driving the next morning. She actually said she felt great, but I could tell the hours just being up without bed rest were paying a toll on her strength. I made certain she took her medications. She called me a mother-hen, but I just kissed her and said I enjoyed being her mother-hen because I loved her. She just took my hand and we held each other close.

Townsend was great, but by the time we got there, Millie seemed exhausted. Instead of visiting friends, she just wanted to go to the church cemetery and pay respect to our parents, both sets being buried there. I stopped and bought bouquets of flowers for each grave. Millie was actually too weak to walk to the grave sites, but the fact that she was so frail, made it easy for me to carry her. She laughed and said that maybe I could carry her piggy-back. It was so great to hear her laugh. I sat her down on the ground between her parents' graves and we prayed for the love they shared and passed on to Millie. Next I carried her to my parents' grave site and we prayed there as well. Then I insisted that Millie should get back to Nashville. I put her in the car, reclined the front passenger's seat, putting a pillow behind her head, I told her to sleep and I would get us back home as quickly as possible. She did sleep most of the way.

Back in Nashville, I called Pastor Thomas and asked if we could meet for lunch. He was agreeable. I knew it was time to start some preparations regardless of how sad it made me. I was lost and needed a shoulder. Tom, Vic and Darren were always available, but I needed some personal counseling in how to cope with the situation. Pastor Thomas was a Knight in shining armor, a fresh breeze; he just knew the right words to say. I felt better.

Millie awoke one beautiful May morning and wanted to sit on the patio and enjoy the fresh air, hear the birds sing, and smell the aroma of all the flowers and blooming trees. We sat there for at least two hours both sipping coffee and just chatting about everything in general. We talked about when we were kids and she caught me peeing in the stream. How we laughed. She remembered the times she baby-sit for me and bathed me, sometimes drying certain boy parts very carefully. I told her she could bathe me anytime now. I remembered when we sat on the piano bench when she was teaching me to play. I teased her about rubbing my leg so far up that she caused me to have an accident. She remembered and told me that she did it on purpose. I believed her.

After a while, I said, "Millie, you know next month is June and it will be our silver wedding anniversary. What do you feel up to doing? I want it to be special for you."

As usual she touched my cheek and said, "Ricky, nothing would mean more to me than just being with you, alone, just the two of us. Get that nurse and cook out of my house, and let's do our own cooking, have a glass of wine, play the piano, and come out here and smell the flowers."

"Millie, you always were a cheap date."

"Well, I was dating a fellow who had no money."

"Well, if you hadn't taught me to play the piano and encouraged me along the way, I probably would still have no money, and you, you probably would have married some rich guy who swept you off your feet at college and took you away to California."

"No way, Jose. No way. You were mine from the start and now until the end."

"Don't put it that way. I want to keep you forever."

"You will in your heart."

Our twenty-fifth anniversary approached in June with me excusing our cook and her nurse for the day. I had four dozen roses delivered, four different colors. She loved yellow roses, but I want red and white as well as a soft pink and white rose that she always would stop and smell whenever we saw them. We both dressed up, and I decided to grill some steaks. Millie threatened me to the edge of my life if I cremated them as I had in the past. Me, I am not a cook. I have no specialty of any type in the kitchen, but I can do grilling without being a total failure. I did open a special bottle of vintage wine. In as much as she was able, with my help getting directions from her, we did the potatoes, salad, and she fixed peas and carrots while sitting down in the kitchen. I helped as much as she was willing to let me. I lit some candles for the table on the patio, and we sat side by side, kissing occasionally and I cut her steak, feeding her now and then. She teased me that she had reverted to infant status. I said never.

We laughed and she remembered our first meal as a married couple. She was a good cook then, not a great cook and no chef by any standards, but she had attempted meat loaf. She forgot to add an egg and the meat loaf just crumbled. It was more like loose hamburger than anything else. I teased her that she was just nervous about cooking for me. She told me that I made her nervous. So much to remember, so many good times. I really could not recall any time during our marriage that we had a fight. She said we could start now. I lightly punched her on the jaw. She kissed me. I said, "Happy twenty-fifth anniversary. I pray we have twenty-five more."

She kissed me again saying, "If only that could happen."

During July Millie seemed to relapse, losing strength, and finding it hard to breathe again. I called her doctor and he told me to take her to the emergency room and he would meet me there. Instead of using what strength she had to get into a car, I called an ambulance. I thought this would be easier and safer; definitely should she have problems during the trip to the hospital. Not only did her doctor meet us there, but he had both her oncologists and a pulmonologist with him. Millie was rushed to a room in the emergency department. The doctors asked me to stay close but not in the room at that time. I squeezed Millie's hand assuring her she would be okay. Personally, I did not believe that she would.

After several hours, her doctor told me that numerous tests had been run on Millie, including another MRI. I was standing and he recommended we go to the cafeteria and get some coffee. I looked at him and his face told me any news he had was not going to be good. We sat at the far end of the cafeteria where no one else was seated. "Ricky, I don't know how to say this other than just come right out with it."

"I understand. Your voice and face tell me it is bad."

"Yes. Ricky, the tumors have spread and not only in her lung, but we now see traces of damage to her liver. She is far too weak for more chemotherapy and I am afraid if we even tried that approach it would kill her. The best we can do is to make her comfortable."

Tears were running down my face. He reached over and grasped my arm. We were both silent for a few minutes. He was giving me time to come to grip with the situation. I was going to lose Millie. I asked him how long.

"Ricky, if you remember I gave you some odds when we first diagnosed Millie. She has lived beyond what both her oncologist and I thought she would. We think, the oncologist and me, that the upper limit is no more than two months. But, Ricky, she could go tomorrow. Have you two discussed her last wishes?"

"We have. Pastor Thomas has been shared with her wishes also. I just can't see going on without her. She has been in my life since I was born. We grew up together and I so wanted us to grow old together."

"It was not in God's plan for that to happen. Spend all the time you can with her. She has been transferred to a private room. Ricky, I doubt that she will be able to ever go home."

I spent many days and nights by her side. I saw her get weaker every day. We talked; or rather I talked for it was becoming difficult for her to speak because her breathing was so shallow. She started sleeping more and more until I doubted she even knew I was there. Here was such a vibrant woman, the love of my life, now confined to a bed, not realizing who was with her or maybe not even realizing where she was. Visitors were many, but I came to the rationalization that they were there more for me than for Millie. Millie never knew how many came by.

Pastor Thomas was there as many days as he could be supporting me and together we prayed over Millie. He and I talked about final arrangement for Millie. We slipped away one day and went to the funeral home. I picked out the type coffin Millie and I had discussed. She did not want anything elaborate, but I spared no expense. I wanted her to be comfortable even though I knew in my heart and my mind that she would not be in the coffin, only her body. I also knew that angels were preparing a place for her and making certain she had a piano in her mansion. Oh, the tears I shed. I cried.

Millie woke several times and wanted to go home, but she was far too weak to move and had so many tubes running in her body that trying to move her would probably just shorten her time. The doctors and nurses advised against taking her away from the hospital. I sat there with Millie just watching her sleep. She was still beautiful to me. I remembered our time together as the best part of my life, now changing forever.

Day after day I constantly stayed at her bedside. She would open her eyes and smile at me, and then drift off. The nurses kept a vigil eye definitely through the night and there was a constant flow of doctors and other care providers during the day. Many visitors came by wanting to just be respectful of both Millie and me. Pastor Thomas was there many times when people from the church visited. Many of my troops visited regularly.

July stretched her hospital stay into early September. She grew weaker and thinner, but was still beautiful to me. She slept more and the doctors told me that time was nearing since the only thing they could do was to keep her comfortable. I doubted that Millie was really comfortable, but the nurses assured me that with the medication she was not feeling a lot of pain.

I still remember the day, the time that I was sitting by her bed, holding her hand even though I realized she could not feel my touch. I was talking to her about our times together, just chatting, and not expecting a response. I looked at her and she just glowed, her eyes opened for a minute as if looking up at something. A smile came on her face. I stared at her. This seemed like a long time, but probably just a minute or two. She closed her eyes, still smiling, and I saw the line flatten on the monitor. I knew Millie had gone to Heaven.

There was a flurry of immediate activity by so many nurses and the crash team, but Millie was gone. They could not bring her back. She would not have wanted them to do so. I was crying as they pushed me aside. Her doctor came in and looked at Millie. He took me out of the room, more so to comfort me than anything else. Shortly they moved Millie out not wanting me to watch the process, but it was so hard for me not to want to walk along with them. I don't know who called Pastor Thomas, but he just seemed to appear out of nowhere. His comforting way with me did ease some of my pain, but nothing, nothing could take away the hurt that I was experiencing. I sensed a void in my life, part of me taken away. Pastor Thomas sat with me and we prayed together.

The funeral home director and other personnel were absolutely wonderful. So caring. I always thought that they took some advantage of people since grieving can make a person more open and receptive to doing the best for their loved ones. However, that was not the case. Most of the final arrangements had been made while Millie was still able. We did this together, and actually many of my final arrangement were made at the same time. I had to realize that if Millie went first, who would be there for me. Neither of us had any family even though Millie had an estranged nephew, I had no one. So it was important to handle some future initiatives however somewhat morbid.

Millie's coffin was more than she actually wanted, but no expense was spared. She wanted to be buried in her favorite dress and insisted that her Bible be put in her hand. All her wishes were honored. She was so thin, but she wanted an open coffin, as she said, so she could look at the people one last time before being closed up. Still nearing the end, she had a great sense of humor. I always teased her that I wanted to have my funeral first, and then die later just to see who would show up. She would smack me lightly and tell me that if I did that she would ensure me that no one would be invited. How I loved her.

Still sitting in my den sipping a glass of wine, I remember when Millie and I talked about where we should be buried. That was right after she had the mammogram that showed some tumors, but were benign. While we both loved our home town and grew up in the church there and our parents were buried in the church cemetery, we had spent most of our adult lives in Nashville. Millie was a pillar of the community; all her friends were in Nashville. She wanted to be buried in Nashville, in the church cemetery where she attended for almost thirty years, including the time she was in school. For me, she could have buried me in the woods somewhere, but wherever she was buried I wanted to be buried next to her. We made pre-arrangements and bought two lots in the church cemetery that overlooked the church. Now, thinking about it again, three years after her death, I wonder, just wonder when I will join her.

Finality is always dreadful. The preparation for the funeral went smoothly with many thanks and appreciations to the funeral home, Pastor Thomas, numerous church members, and many, many friends. Tom was by my side constantly. Vic and Darren were not far away. Receiving of friends would be before the service. Millie wanted two songs especially sung at the service and she had asked two very special ladies if they each would sing one of the songs. Pastor Thomas wanted me to say some special words, but my emotions were too strained to do so. He would do the eulogy and ask if people wanted to share some special moments or special remembrance of Millie's life. Songs would be sung, some music only played, the service would be about forty-five minutes, and then adjourn to the cemetery before a final reception. I was not only depressed, but felt so alone even with all the people around me.

We picked a Sunday afternoon for the service. Millie would have wanted it that way. I could hear her saying, "why have people dress up twice when they are already dressed for church?" That was Millie. I attended church services the morning before the funeral and it was as if the services for Millie had already begun. A mournful silence filled the church, and only a spray of flowers was placed on the piano where Millie had played for so many years and too many services to count. Another lady from the church played the pipe organ. I was tearful. Seeing the piano was hard, but hearing organ music made it sound to me so depressing, but I said nothing to Pastor Thomas.

After the service, several of us, including Pastor Thomas met in the church kitchen and family hall for a light lunch prepared by some of Millie's closest lady friends. I ate some, but it was so difficult to concentrate on food. I was shaking and Pastor Thomas got up, stood behind me, and put his hands on my shoulders. It was an act of comforting. He said, *"Millie is okay now. She is in a far better place."* I only responded that I knew.

As the receiving of friends started at one o'clock, the funeral home had placed her coffin at the front of the church. The spray I had purchased covered the entire top of the coffin. More and more flowers were brought in. A huge picture of Millie was beside the coffin. Other memorabilia and pictures were placed in the entrance alcove with more flowers. As friends started arriving, the line for receiving extended outside the main church entrance. Since I was the only family other than her nephew who could not travel to be there, Tom and his wife stood with me in the receiving line. Vic was there also, we were as close as two could be without being brothers.

The actual service was to begin at two o'clock, but the line was still long. Many of my musician friends were there, those who were not on road tours or unavailable to attend. However, they sent flowers and many had called in the days before expressing their condolence, well wishes and prayers. Pastor Thomas approached me and told me that he was extending the reception until three o'clock but that the service really needed to start at that time. I understood. I probably had never in my life received so many hugs and handshakes. Millie was well liked and with me being a famous musician, many fans came to express condolences. However, there were policeman outside to ensure no problems and to maintain a semblance of order.

I was getting so tired. About ten minutes before three o'clock, Pastor Thomas announced that he regretted so many people had not been able to get through the receiving line, but if everyone could be seated, the service would begin in ten minutes. By that time my feet hurt, my hands were shaking, and I had a headache. Fortunately Tom's wife had some Advil in her purse and I had a bottle of water, so some relief was possible.

As people continued to file in and be seated, music was playing through the speaker system. However, at three fifteen, that music stopped and Betty Fletcher who substituted as the piano player when Millie was not available started playing hymns on the piano. Pastor Thomas approached the podium behind Millie's coffin, raising his hand he said, *"Let us pray."*

His prayer was so sincere and reflected the words that I knew Millie would appreciate. As he stepped down, Betty started playing one of the songs that Millie definitely wanted sung. Millie had asked Martha Naisbitt to sing *Light One Candle,* an old Peter, Paul and Mary song. The words are so beautiful reflecting the pain, strength, and memory for the suffering. Martha's voice is so sweet and the way she sang the song brought tears to my eyes.

Following Martha, Deana Jones, Millie's dear and closest friend, with a voice that is so wonderful and one for which Deana could crack crystal reaching some high notes, sang *It Is Finished.* Her rendition of this song was so powerful I actually started crying. I was not alone. Many people in the congregation had tears in the eyes or were actually crying. What an incredible song. Pastor Thomas, with tears in his eyes, asked everyone to join with the Lord's Prayer.

Millie's Sunday school class of children sang *Awesome God* as a closure to the music before Pastor Thomas approached for the eulogy. *"I want everyone to know and to understand that it is a personal honor to speak about Millie Pendergrass Snyder today. If I could sum up her life in one word, it would be the word 'amazing.' Millie was a God-send to not only Ricky, but* to everyone's life she touched. Her dedication to family, friends, church, her school, her students, and even strangers was not only unique, but sincere. She was beautiful outside, but that was a beauty that was throughout her entire body. She had a heart of gold. She was accomplished on the piano, and not to shun Ricky in any way, but I really thought she was a better piano player than him." This brought laughter from the people there. I just smiled because I knew that to be the truth.

Pastor Thomas continued, "Millie had the voice of an angel. Her smile could only make you smile, even if you were somewhat depressed. She had a way of making everyone comfortable. We will all miss her. Millie was an only child, as is Ricky. Millie and Ricky grew up together from childhood as friends. Yes, she was a little older than Ricky, and she baby-sit for him when he was a lad, but they grew to love each other immensely. They married after Ricky graduated from Juilliard and as he put it, when he could afford to have a wife.

"Millie taught school, almost until the day she could no long stand under her own strength. The last two years of her life were painful. But we all know that today Millie has a new body, a new life, and is enjoying walking the streets of gold in Heaven and talking with old friends, her mother and father, and Ricky's mother and farther. She is probably telling them tales about Ricky, but bragging on his successes. Millie loved Ricky with all her heart.

"Millie and Ricky wanted children, but that was not to be. Millie sought comfort in being around children all her life, including baby-sitting for Ricky when he was a young boy. Children were her life, her career. She was a marvelous teacher and a mentor to every child. So many children have crossed her path during their lives and remember the joy she brought them and the lessons she taught them. This world is a better place because of Millie's presence on this earth.

"How many of you can actually say that you touched so many lives and made better people of those you touched? How many can say their music was a major element in sharing precious moments with students and this church's congregation? How many of us can be what Millie was, what she was every day of her life? Yes, her life was cut short by cancer. She suffered, but never complained. She held on to the last minute, drawing strength from Ricky and her God.

"Today we celebrate not the end of her life, but a new beginning. Yes, without a doubt we will all miss her. Ricky will be without the love of his life, his constant companion. Yes, they were companions.

"Don't think of this as a time of sorrow, don't thank of this as the end, don't think about what was, but of reflections of the wonderful times, the friendships, the love, the devotion, and the accomplishments of this wonderful person. Think of this as a new beginning..."

I have never seen so many flowers.

CPSIA information can be obtained at www.ICGtesting.com
Printed in the USA
BVOW08*1229211215

429451BV00011B/2/P

9 781489 705594